Also by

Bachelors of Battle Creek
Texas Mail Order Bride
Twice a Texas Bride
Forever His Texas Bride

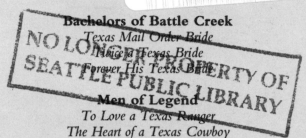

Men of Legend
To Love a Texas Ranger
The Heart of a Texas Cowboy
To Marry a Texas Outlaw

Texas Heroes
Knight on the Texas Plains
The Cowboy Who Came Calling
To Catch a Texas Star

Outlaw Mail Order Brides
The Outlaw's Mail Order Bride

Texas Redemption
Christmas in a Cowboy's Arms anthology

The OUTLAW'S MAIL ORDER Bride

LINDA BRODAY

sourcebooks
casablanca

Published by Sourcebooks Casablanca, an imprint of Sourcebooks,
Inc.
P.O. Box 4410, Naperville, Illinois 60567-4410
(630) 961-3900
Fax: (630) 961-2168
sourcebooks.com

Printed and bound in the United States of America.
OPM 10 9 8 7 6 5 4 3 2 1

To my critique partners—Dee, Bruce, Taylor, and Jodi. You make me a much better writer than I am. I couldn't do this without your suggestions, ideas, and gentle nudges. You inspire and lift me up every day. We celebrate the good times and you offer me a shoulder when things don't go right. Thank you for all you do.

Dear Reader,

In this brand new series, I write about an entire town of outlaws who are trying to make better lives for themselves, to satisfy their longing for families. Except finding wives is a bit difficult, because the panhandle of Texas is still largely raw land. They hit upon a plan of mail order brides and begin penning letters to prospective women, speaking of things they've never told another living soul.

Hope's Crossing springs from an outlaw hideout and is well-protected, which is crucial at first. One by one, these hunted men begin to emerge from the shadows they've lived in for most of their lives.

I hope you like this book and the others that follow. Maybe you'll step outside some dark night and listen for their voices whispering in the wind.

Linda Broday

One

MONDAY—WHY WAS IT EVEN A DAY OF THE WEEK? CLAY Colby thought about shooting whoever had the bright idea to make it one.

He'd always hated Mondays. They brought bad luck, and for a man living one step ahead of the law, he didn't need more. He'd gladly scratch each Monday off the calendar if he could. Let Tuesday or Wednesday take that space. Now there was a notion.

The giant orange ball of the afternoon sun hung midway on the horizon and his herd of goats bleated nearby. The temperature remained one degree shy of hell, and somewhere, a board banged in the incessant wind.

"Damn Mondays," he muttered.

On this particular day, his bride was arriving. In fact, she was overdue. His stomach was in a hangman's knot. Would he like her? Or she him? What if they hated each other? How was he going to make this work when it never had before?

Still, he had a dream and he needed the right wife to make it possible.

He'd already given up on trying to make her welcome perfect. If he just made it passable, that would have to suit. He'd cleaned and straightened the dugout as best he could, but it was a sorry-looking sight. Nothing much you could do with a home that was made of dirt. Except he had built his bride a plank floor. That helped the rough appearance a tad.

Maybe some flowers would spruce the place up a bit more. If he hurried, he could go pick some. Ladies seemed to like colorful blooms.

The tin box on a shelf above the cookstove drew his gaze. Four months ago, he'd opened a bag of Arbuckles and found a ring nestled among the dark coffee beans.

It had appeared to be a sign.

But maybe he'd gone loco and had ridden the outlaw trail far too long to ever be civilized. He was crazy to think of taking a wife.

He'd tried the same thing twice before and the women always backed out.

Would Tally Shannon do the same? As a betting man, he didn't quite like the odds. After all, he'd never heard of a mail order bride service for men like himself who couldn't advertise.

Shouts outside jarred him from his thoughts, and gunshots erupted before he reached the door. His dog's fit of barking made the hair raise on his arm. With reflexes as natural as breathing, he slid his long-barreled Remington from its holster and raced toward the chaos.

A raging inferno greeted him when he opened the door, heat from the fire blistering his face. *What the hell?* The odor of kerosene reached him, and Clay knew exactly how the ball of fire had formed so fast. Black smoke filled his lungs and he bent double, coughing.

Bullet raced back and forth in a frenzy, his barks becoming lost in the bedlam.

A hungry, belching fire was gobbling up the new buildings. They were the first two Clay had completed and sat opposite the row of dugouts and tents.

A hoarse cry sprang from him. "No! No! No!"

The town—his town—that he'd spent every waking moment working on for the last four months, was engulfed in searing orange flames. The fire licked toward the sky, a hungry beast devouring the lumber he'd spent every cent he had to get. Soon, the two buildings would be nothing but ash.

It was too late to save them. Everything was too damn late, just like before.

Clay stood frozen, staring out at the ruins of his town, fighting the memory of when he was fourteen and the devastating mistake that still haunted his dreams to this day. Rivers of blood. Bodies ripped apart. Horrible screams of the dying. The women and children he'd tried to lead to safety, caught with him in the midst of a bombardment as his best friend lay mangled—the light gone from his eyes.

A bullet whizzed over his head, and he dragged himself from the unforgettable horror, sprinting to take cover next to a wagon. Other men in the camp scattered to wherever they could find a place to shield themselves.

Montana Black stood in the middle of the chaos with a torch in one hand and his pistol in the other. His long, graying hair hung to his shoulders. "I warned you not to build a town and bring the law down on us, Colby. This is *my* hideout and *my* life you're messing with."

"Put down the gun, Montana, or I'll shoot you where you stand!" Clay yelled.

Clay's friend Jack Bowdre arrived at a gallop and took cover with Clay. Ridge Steele raced from his tent to join them a moment later.

"The damn fool." Jack let out a curse. "We should've taken care of him before we raised the first wall."

"Jack's right," growled Ridge. "Montana's been a thorn in our side since he got here. We should've known this would happen when he refused to stay gone after we ran him off. We should've fixed him permanently."

Montana yelled from behind a tall mound of dirt, "You can all go to hell, you bastards! Devil's Crossing is mine!"

Two of Montana's followers ran from the tent saloon, yelling and releasing a barrage of bullets. They ducked behind a stack of large crates, where one hollered, "Burn it down, Montana! We've got your back."

Clay returned fire and hit one of Montana's men. Jack winged another.

"I'm going to handle him once and for all. Cover me."

"I hope you know what you're doing, Clay" Jack muttered.

"Makes two of us. Say a prayer, Ridge." Clay met the preacher-turned-outlaw's gaze.

"Gave that up a long time ago. Not sure God listens to me anymore. My gun, on the other hand…" Saying that, Ridge rose, took aim, and fired.

Taking a calming breath, Clay stood and zigzagged his way across the open space to the opposite end of the dirt pile. His dog raced at his side, barking. Bullets struck the ground around him, but none found the mark. Montana's fist connected with Clay's jaw in welcome, and guns went flying.

Clay grabbed a fistful of Montana's shirt and delivered a blow to the face and one to the belly that doubled the outlaw over. Pouncing quickly, Clay brought his elbow down on the back of Montana's neck. The dog jumped and snapped and tried to tear into the old outlaw.

But the fight was far from over. Montana whirled and caught Clay's throat, choking the life from him. It took everything he had to thrust his arms up and break the hold.

"Get that dog away from me!" Montana kicked at the animal, who scampered back.

Clay and Montana went at each other like two snarling grizzlies: punching, wrestling, trying to get the upper hand. A roar inside Clay's head blocked out all sound. He had to win. He couldn't ask his bride to make her home amid killers and scum of the earth. Nor would he ask her to. And Tally Shannon might well refuse to live here unless he got rid of Black and his followers once and for all.

Clay had run off the bad seeds before, but they always came back, usually with a few more men than they'd left with.

Gasping for breath, Clay got Black in a choke hold. "Give up. Devil's Crossing doesn't belong to you. I *will* make this a thriving place."

Montana snarled, "I'll burn everything you build to the ground."

In a sudden move, Montana broke free and slammed a fist into Clay's jaw, knocking him backward. Pain shot through him. But as he landed, he spotted his Remington lying on the ground only a few feet away. Breathing hard and fighting to keep standing, Clay scrambled toward his gun while Montana ran toward a horse tied in front of the makeshift saloon.

For once, Clay would make his life count for something. This was his final chance to change. There would be no others. He'd used them all up. Clay stood and fired, the bullet striking the older man in the shoulder, spinning him around. Another bullet struck Montana's side as he pulled himself into the saddle. Bleeding heavily, he galloped away from the outlaw town with Bullet furiously racing along after him.

Clay took three long strides toward Jack's horse grazing beside Clay's dugout, intent on giving chase before common sense kicked in. He was needed more in the town.

While Clay and the others brought bucket after bucket of water from the windmill tank to throw on the fire, Ridge and half a dozen of the others rounded up Montana's wounded followers, taking their weapons. Jack walked behind, sure-footed despite the slight limp from a gunshot to the leg five years ago. Yet, make no mistake, the former lawman still had the toughness this life took. He'd never said what had changed him into an outlaw. Men like him didn't talk about their past. They lived with the motto—talk low, talk slow, with few words.

The short, bow-legged bartender, Harvey Drake, came from the tent. "I had no part in that."

"We didn't think you did," Jack replied. "But you had to have overheard them."

"I was busy unpacking the load of rotgut I just got back with and not paying them a bit of mind." Harvey shoved a hank of hair from his huge, owlish eyes. "You know me. I'm not a troublemaker. I keep my nose clean."

Jack snorted. "People change."

Harvey beat a silent retreat into his saloon. Good, or he'd find himself nursing a bullet wound.

Clay holstered his sidearm as he watched the beginnings of his town—his dream—turn to ash and rubble. Maybe this was a sign?

A slice of memory sent him back again to the end of the war. Despite being fourteen at the time, he'd probably seen

more than an eighty-year-old. Everything had lain in rubble—
death everywhere. He'd walked all the way home, finally
making it, only to find his parents had been killed and strangers
occupied their land. Every bit of his family gone.

Damn Mondays.

A hand on Clay's shoulder jarred him from the past. "You
all right?" Jack asked.

"I'm fine." Clay spoke of his body, not his heart.

"What are we going to do with those two over there?"

Clay glanced at Ridge, still holding a gun on Montana's
men. "How bad are they hurt?"

"We'll have to dig a bullet out of one." Jack brushed dirt
from his black shirt and trousers. "The bullet went through
the other one. But both are able to ride. I'm just not sure we
should let them go. They'll only join up with Montana again."

"I'm against letting them ride out, but we have no jail
unless we build one." Clay scanned the half a dozen dugouts
and crude shelters, his gaze landing on one that resembled a
cave in the wall of the canyon. "Put them in Montana's. He's
a dead man anyway if he comes back."

"Sounds good. I'll go patch those two up, then get them
put away. When is your bride arriving?"

"I expected her before now, but I'm glad she's behind
schedule."

The day passed slowly as they worked, until Clay dragged
his gaze from the smoldering ruins and squinted at the sky. It
would be full dark in a few more hours.

Clay's breath caught. Tally Shannon would see his failure
the minute she arrived. What woman would want to be married to someone who couldn't even carve out a decent place
for her? How could he ask her to share nothing but rubble?

Even if she agreed to stay, what kind of bargain would she
get with a broken man who'd dared to think he could rise
above his past? He snorted.

Jack rested a hand on Clay's back. "We can rebuild, Clay.
It'll just take a little longer for our dream to materialize, that's
all. If she's the right woman for you, she won't mind helping."

Clay watched Jack limp toward the men guarding Montana's followers. Maybe Tally would help. Or maybe she'd take one glance and hightail it back where she came from. Most likely the latter. What woman wouldn't run?

"I wanted everything to be right for her," Clay whispered. So she could see what he might become, given half a chance. His heart thudded painfully against his ribs. He had nothing more to show for all his years than that boy in rags coming home from war.

Letting out a deep sigh of frustration, Clay strode to a sparse patch of wildflowers and yanked the colorful blooms out, roots and all.

You could dress up a pig, but it'd still be a damn pig. One day he'd change all that, but for now he had to get ready to welcome his bride all over again. He wondered what she'd look like.

Not that it made a nickel's worth of difference. What was on the inside of a woman meant far more than outward appearance. What he yearned most for was a soft touch, a heartbeat next to his in the dead of night, someone to hold when he was finally still enough for the memories to catch him. His soul was weary of living on the run, always listening for the sound that would put him in a grave.

Luke Legend—an ex-outlaw himself, who operated the underground mail order bride service with his wife, Josie—said Tally was the toughest lady he knew.

She'd have to be to make her home here.

For a minute, Clay wondered what the minuses might be. Everyone alive had minuses, but none deeper or more lasting than his own.

Movement at the canyon entrance drew him. Apparently giving up the chase after Montana, Bullet trotted into what was left of the town and up to Clay for a pat on his large head, his tongue lolling out. Bullet's pedigree had been diluted so many times the large, stocky breed was anyone's guess. Clearly he had some wolf markings. The dog was a friendly sort—unless someone messed with Clay. Then, Bullet could put the fear of God in a man before he could blink.

"We're a sorry pair, you know that, Bullet?"

The dog whined in sympathy and lay down at his feet. They stood listening for the jangle of harnesses until well after dark, when it became painfully apparent that Monday's curse had taken one more toll.

She wasn't coming.

Part of him wanted to believe her party had started a day late. But the loudest part drowned out that hope, saying the lady had changed her mind.

Clay finally turned and went inside the earthen house to empty silence and let the wildflowers he'd picked fall from numb fingers onto the rough plank floor.

Two

DAWN CREPT THROUGH THE WINDOW THE NEXT MORNING, jarring Clay awake. Bullet's long, wet tongue snaked out to lick his face. "Go away." He turned over to go back to sleep only to have the hound clamp down on his shirt and pull. Clay pretended to resist for another minute or two before releasing a sigh and letting himself be tugged out of bed. "All right. I get it. I'm up."

After the coffee boiled, he took his cup and went out, hoping the fire had been nothing but a nightmare. It wasn't. The thick smell of smoke lingered in the air, his town a pile of ash.

Hell!

Things looked even worse in the bright light. Bullet ambled to the rubble and sniffed at the ground. Jack and Ridge came from their tents to poke around in the ruins, salvaging what they could. A dull throb in his chest, Clay joined them, his low spirits saying it was useless.

Jack met his gaze. "We found a few things beneath the rubble."

Ridge rubbed Bullet between the ears. "A few, but not enough. What do you think happened with your bride?"

Clay took a sip of coffee and kept his voice even. "Maybe she got smart."

"That's crazy thinking. A dozen things could've kept Luke Legend from arriving with her yesterday, so stop with the gloom and doom." Jack pulled a hammer from the ash.

"I know. I'm just afraid to hope anymore. How many times have I been down this road?" Clay set his empty cup down and closed his hand around a rake, determined to make the day worth something.

❧

Afternoon came and went, then suddenly, Luke's owl hoot and the jangle of traces filled the air, announcing their arrival.

She came.

Bullet barked and raced toward the wagon. Clay returned the call and hurried into his dugout to stuff the limp flowers he'd pulled yesterday into a mason jar. Nerves made his hands tremble. Clay gave the dugout one last glance, wishing it were made of wood, not dirt.

But if wishes were golden nuggets, everyone would be rich. If Tally was marrying him for his house, she'd figure out soon enough he wasn't the man for her. One day, he'd be able to give her better, but until then, the dugout would have to do. Assuming she stayed, that is.

His pulse racing, Clay went to meet his new bride.

He tugged the brim of his hat low and waited for the approaching wagon, recognizing one of the women as Luke's blond wife, Josie—which made the other one Tally. Her flame-colored hair glistening in the sunlight was breathtaking. Funny that she'd never mentioned the shade of her hair, only describing herself as tall and homely. He kept his eyes on her as the wagon slowly made its way to him.

Homely his hind leg!

But what drew him most was the defiance on her face and the determined glint in her eyes. Hard eyes that had seen too much pain and disappointment. She wouldn't back down easily—from anything. The gun belt and Colt strapped around her waist bore witness to that.

Her simple, yellow print dress matched the daisies he'd picked. He deduced from her appearance that she didn't cotton much to frills and such. He added that to the mental notes he kept of things she'd revealed in their correspondence, such as her love for watching sunrises and the beauty of sunsets. The clean smell of rain and her fondness for storms.

And how she hated men who kept women under their thumbs, unworthy of having an opinion of their own.

Tally had also revealed the fact that she was hunted and that there was five hundred dollars offered for her capture. She'd made no secret about it, as early as the first letter. He had a duty to see that no one claimed it. In those same letters, she'd spoken of a longing to walk free one day, to find a deep peace. He would try his best to see that she got that.

The wagon came to a stop. Clay couldn't take his gaze from the two women sitting on the high seat. "Ladies," he murmured in welcome. "Luke."

Luke Legend took in the rubble, his face hardening as he set the brake and swung down. "What happened?"

Clay forced himself to look away from Tally. "Montana Black took exception to a town here and burned it to the ground."

"Do you think Black is close?"

"Anyone's guess. We had a bit of a skirmish. He rode out on a spotted gray, bleeding like a stuck pig after I shot him, vowing to burn down the town every time we rebuild." Clay's glance strayed to Tally, her gaze on the burned buildings, the dugouts and tents. He winced and prepared himself, but she stayed silent.

Clay struggled to keep his voice even but didn't feel very successful, hoping Tally didn't notice. "I won't lie, Luke. I'm tempted to walk away, but I have others to consider now." He let out a loud sigh. "If Tally's willing, I'll rebuild one more time."

"Good." Luke squeezed Clay's shoulder. "Come meet your bride while I see to Josie's needs."

Jack and Ridge stepped from the makeshift jail to holler and wave at the company. Both had said they'd stay out of the way and let Clay have this time with Tally. But right now, he wished for his friends to join them and help with the awkward meeting. A deep breath of air bolstered him.

Everyone else faded into the background as he strode forward. He took Tally's hand, helping her from the wagon. "Welcome to Devil's Crossing."

Her eyes met his, and he found them the pale blue of a

winter sky. She didn't smile, but she didn't frown either, so he took that as a positive sign. "Thank you, Mr. Colby."

The next thing that drew his attention was a small, diamond-shaped tattoo on her cheek, like the brand ranchers used to mark their property. A small letter *C* was in the center.

Clay fought down rising anger. A woman, especially Tally Shannon, was no one's property. If he got a chance, he'd find pleasure in making sure whoever left that mark knew it.

"We're informal here. Just call me Clay."

"Clay, then. Come, Violet." She turned to lift a little girl from the wagon. Clay wondered if Luke and Josie had taken in a stray. The whole Legend family opened their hearts to unwanted children, so it stood to reason.

He turned to the matchmaking couple. "Miz Josie, you're looking like a rose in bloom."

Josie laughed. "More like a swollen watermelon." She laid her hands on her large belly. "I only have a little further to go before I can get my girlish figure back, thank goodness. I'm tired and I'm grouchy."

Luke put his arm around his wife's girth. "We can't wait to welcome our first."

"Looks like you've already started with the girl."

"She's mine," Tally declared, her voice holding a challenge. "If you want me, you'll take her too."

Three

Tally's eyes narrowed as she watched surprise ripple across Clay's tanned face. He scrubbed the back of his neck, and if she could hazard a guess, he was probably cussing a silent blue streak. Cuts from a recent scuffle lined his face, and bruises had begun to form along his jaw. Was this what she'd bargained for? Was he a man always spoiling for a fight? Still… he'd spoken with a gentle voice despite his hard, dark eyes. She recognized the longing buried beneath the words. Not like the men she despised, who cared for no one but themselves.

The man before her appeared different from the one she'd seen in the letters they'd exchanged—compassionate, seemingly able to read her mind, offering her a home. She'd read those notes over and over, hardly daring to believe he was real.

She was unsure he could deliver on his promises to provide a safe home—not sure she could deliver on her own promise to give him time either.

Part of her wanted to turn and run—except her feet were already firmly planted on this soil.

She'd thrown him for a loop, but it couldn't be helped. "I didn't have time to warn you that Violet was coming. The child needs me. If you want to back out, I understand. No hard feelings."

Clay Colby's eyes shifted, and he glanced down at the eight-year-old. Tally felt him size up the situation. Violet was clinging to Tally's dress with one hand and clutching a rag doll with the other. The large black dog had stopped barking and seemed friendly enough. It wandered over to Violet and licked her arm. She whimpered and jerked back in alarm.

"The dog's friendly, sweet girl," Clay said quietly.

"His tail is wagging to beat all and I think I see a silly, little smile on his face," Tally said, reassuring Violet. "What's his name, Clay?"

"Bullet."

Violet fumbled to locate the dog's head and petted it. Tally studied Clay's face and spotted the moment he figured out that Violet was blind. A pained look crossed his chiseled features.

"I welcome you both." Clay met Tally's eyes. "I hesitated only because this complicates things a bit. You see, I don't have a bed for her. If I'd known—"

"The apology is mine to make. I'm sorry for springing this on you." Tally placed a palm on the girl's shoulder. "I didn't know myself until I was about to leave and saw how devastated Violet would be if we were separated. She doesn't trust easily and we've formed a deep bond."

Clay shifted, widening his stance. "Anyone can see she's a special child."

He seemed to speak with conviction that came from a place deep inside, and from his letters, he didn't appear to be a man who said things he didn't mean. Their lives depended on her being right about his character.

A word in the right ear would put her and the others behind bars. She'd been taking care of the Creedmore escapees from the beginning—she was everyone's protector. Now she longed to be the one taken care of, to not have to lie awake listening for trouble.

Just once, she wanted to know what being protected felt like.

Clay Colby appeared more than capable. But what sort of husband would he be? Gentle? Domineering? Would he treat her as an equal? His voice was kind, but what of the physical part? Would that be a different story? He was so much larger. She could probably fit both of her hands into one of his. Tall and lean, he loomed over her, wearing some kind of invisible shield that said he'd suffered disappointment and despair.

The man who'd burned his town had probably struck a severe blow. In his letters, he'd spoken of his dream of building something lasting that would stand long after he was gone. Now, it lay in ash. Such a disaster battered a man's pride.

That kind of pain lived inside her as well, so she knew some of the frustration and anger he must feel. She wanted to reach out and comfort, yet she kept her hands on Violet.

Despite his recent loss with the town, she could see strength in his determined jaw and that appealed to her. Weak men didn't interest her. The muscles in his tanned forearms stood out and his torn shirt stretched tight across his broad chest and back. Tingles danced up her spine. Soon she'd lie beside this husband-to-be of hers. He already seemed too rugged, too…powerful.

Too able to read her thoughts.

The urge to take a step back came over her, but instead, she tilted her chin and met his brown stare, letting him know she would stand her ground. Luke strode from the wagon, his arm around Josie, silver conchos that ran the length of his black pant legs glinting in the sun. He still looked every bit the elusive outlaw he'd once been. For years, he'd been far more than a friend to Tally—he was the family she'd lost. The creak of the windmill drew her gaze. She closed her eyes for a second, soaking up the scrape and grind of the rod as it pumped water from the earth. When she was young, she'd often fallen asleep lulled by the music of a windmill. She hadn't realized how much she'd missed that until now. Standing before her future husband, in the wake of so much devastation, that sound grounded her and gave her hope.

Josie pulled away from Luke's side as they neared and hugged Clay. "I'm sorry about the fire. So devastating. When you first came to the Lone Star seeking our help, I knew you were a good, strong, decent man. The destruction here just makes me want to cry." She directed her next words at Tally. "You'll get no better husband than Clay. If you don't take him, why I'll…I'll divorce Luke and marry him myself."

"You'll have a fight on your hands, *querida*. No one can sing your bawdy saloon songs quite like you," Luke growled.

Tally didn't know what Luke was referring to, but Josie's

face colored and she gazed up at Luke in adoration. Tally loved watching them together. They hadn't been married very long, but even so, Tally wanted what they had.

Could she find it with an outlaw like Clay Colby? The question pressed on her mind.

If he discovered how damaged she was, he'd likely run far and fast, and she wouldn't blame him. Her chest pains that came and went, swollen ankles, aching feet—the nightmares— all would test his commitment. Guilt rose at keeping silent.

He was surely getting a pig in a poke.

Luke glanced at the wagon. "Before I unload, you two go somewhere and talk. Clay, if either of you want to call off this wedding, I'll take Tally and Violet back home."

"I'll do as you ask, but I don't need to think about it," Clay answered. "I want both of them."

Tally left Violet with Josie and followed Clay into his dugout. She liked the strong set of his jaw and broad shoulders. He gave the impression that he wouldn't give under a heavy load. The two-inch scar down his face and the revolver swinging from his lean hip suggested he'd seen trouble too many times to count. His dark hair sported a few silver stands at the temples and curled possessively over his collarless shirt like a gunslinger's hand around his gun.

She scanned the dim interior of the dugout, not caring that it was part of the hillside. She loved the scent of the earth and the safety Devil's Crossing represented. A stack of uncut leather lay in a corner, and the pink and yellow flowers on the table added an unexpected homey feel, even if they were a bit limp.

Tally eyed them closer and found roots hanging from a few. Well, the thought counted. This outlaw was already surprising her in a lot of ways.

"How old is the child?" he asked.

"Eight. She's small for her age."

"Have you tried teaching her to get around by herself some?"

"A bit but not enough. And all those lessons are no good here, where everything is new."

"It's important. I want to make sure she knows the layout, because here, you never know when she might need the information. I'd like to work with her, unless you object."

"Violet has this strong distrust of men, but with time, it'll get better." Tally motioned to the leather. "What do you make?"

"Saddles, harnesses, boots, you name it." Clay flicked her a nervous smile. "I know this doesn't look like much, but it's only temporary. As soon as I can, you'll have a real house."

Her mouth tried to turn up in a return smile but her nerves wouldn't let it. She sat at the table in the chair Clay pulled out for her and folded her hands in her lap. "Don't say anything you don't mean. I've been lied to enough."

He stood at the window, the sunlight casting his shadow across the plank floor. "Look, Tally Shannon, I never waste words, and what I say, you can count on. I want something better for you and already have the land picked out."

That statement dispelled some of her fear and put her more at ease. "What do you expect of me, Clay?"

"I dream of building a town here—proper, with establishments and a stage line. True, the men here are outlaws, but they're as determined as I am to mend their ways. Tally, I want far more than a six-shooter and notoriety. I want to thrive instead of only existing. I want…you." He paused as though fearing he'd revealed too much too soon. "But I can't do it alone. You can help turn this dream into reality. I'll protect you and Violet. If anyone gets past me, it'll only be because I'm dead. I expect you to sleep beside me, to share whatever comes our way, raise our children."

His sincerity rattled something deep inside her. She could *almost* imagine a life with him. Something told her he was probably as scared of the whole deal as she was.

"What are you wanted for, Clay?" she asked quietly.

With a heavy sigh, he pulled out the other chair and sat down. "Murder. Get one thing clear—I didn't choose this life. It chose me. I dispense justice when there's none to be had and I'm not sorry for it. Even so, I yearn for the day when there is no need for guns."

"This land continues to be too dangerous. I'll wear mine until it's safe to remove it." She wouldn't be caught unaware when trouble came.

"You might as well know that twice now I've tried to settle down and marry. But once the women found out what being married to me entailed, they changed their minds and I was left nursing hurt pride. All I'm asking for is one chance to show you the man I can become."

Tally was silent, watching his eyes. Eyes didn't lie. They showed a man's true heart. Clay spoke quietly, his voice breaking when talking about his struggle. This was the kind of man who'd still be standing when all others were lying on the ground.

"I have a strong back and two willing hands." He made a fist. "I don't shirk from hard work. But if this marriage to you doesn't happen, I won't try again."

His sincerity touched her. Lord knew she was no prize. A little over two years ago, she'd escaped an insane asylum along with a handful of other women like her, women whose families had had them committed for various reasons, but mostly to get them out of the way. Stuck them in there to die without getting their hands dirty.

The cuts and bruises on Clay's face drew her. He must've been caught without his gun. Or maybe he liked fistfights.

"Do you drink, and are you prone to fighting?" she asked.

Clay rubbed his jaw with his long, slender fingers. He had a gunslinger's hand. "I know how this looks, but I don't fight unless provoked and I only drink occasionally. You have nothing to fear from me. I'll never lay a hand to you or Violet."

"It's your word on that?"

Another heavy sigh left him. "I wish I could provide proof, but you'll just have to believe me. I don't beat women or kids. I give you my word and my solemn vow. I hope that's enough."

His gaze slid to the worn shoes peeking from under her skirt. He had to be noticing the bad shape they were in—the hole in the leather near the toe, the heel half off of one, and the scuffs that badly needed polish. Hoping he couldn't see her misshapen feet, she pulled them under her hem. Although he didn't stand in judgment, she couldn't bear him to see her looking this shabby.

Sharp pain shot into her chest and she focused on her breathing until it passed. He shouldn't see her secret this soon or he might send her packing.

With the windmill singing its own song outside, Tally glanced around the dwelling, her gaze landing on the print curtains on the window. Something told her that they were new. To make the home better for her? "Is there anything else I should know?"

He reached for her hand. "No. There's nothing else."

"But you still have a price on your head. What happens when the lawmen eventually find this place? They will. They always do."

Would he make her a widow, thrust back out on her own again? Clay frowned and turned her palm over, studying it. She didn't want to be alone, fighting for survival without him. For the first time, she'd had the promise of being able to relax her vigil. She was bone weary from being strong all the time, never able to let down her guard.

"I hope to get a pardon from the governor. I mean to apply at the first chance. If he refuses, I don't know." He met her eyes and she saw the worry that must surely keep him awake at night. "I guess I'll cross that bridge when I come to it. We might leave Texas and go farther west if you wouldn't mind being uprooted."

"I wouldn't object." Tally cleared her throat. "Now I have some things to ask of you. Refusal of any will be a deal breaker."

"Sounds fair enough."

"I'll help build your town, share your bed, and raise our children." She narrowed her gaze. "In return, you promise never to put me back in the asylum, and that you'll fight anyone who tries. Also extend that promise to Violet." She inhaled a shaky breath. "If anything should happen to me, you'll raise the child. You'll never collect the reward that's offered for me and I'll never collect yours." She paused before adding, "One last thing—you'll let me leave come spring if this marriage doesn't work."

Surprise shifted in his brown eyes. He clearly hadn't expected that last part. "You have my word on every stipulation." His attention went to the gun on her hip and she thought she saw a flash of admiration. "I only have one simple request. You have to promise never to shoot me, no matter how mad you get."

"That depends on what you do." She leaned close, putting her lips next to his ear. "Hurt Violet and I'll kill you in a heartbeat."

Clay chuckled softly. "Trust me, I'll never be fool enough to cross you. Nor will I ever cause that little girl grief. That's a vow I'll never break."

"Then we're clear." She straightened in her chair.

Clay leaned forward, propping his elbow on the table. "Are you crazy, Tally?"

She allowed a smile. "Some would say so. At times, I wonder. Back in Deliverance Canyon, I'd often wake in the dead of night and stand in the moonlight, letting the breeze brush my face. I needed the reassurance that I wasn't back in that hellhole."

"Do you mind if I ask why you were put there?"

"Dear Stepmother told them that I was a sexual deviant and preyed on children." She hated her strained voice.

"I can tell you're not. I assume she had a motive."

Tally's voice turned cold and hard. "My father was a wealthy man. He had quite a large estate that included land, money, and other possessions. When he died, she wanted me out of the way. I'd seen too much, had too many suspicions about mysterious happenings on the ranch. She put something in my food that made me deathly ill and unable to fight her or speak. Some men loaded me into a wagon, and Lucinda drove me to the Creedmore Lunatic Asylum."

"I've heard of the place. Most never escape—except in a coffin. You were lucky, Tally."

"Determination helps. I was there a year and suffered—"

Her voice broke. She forced herself to calm and continued. "Suffered crimes you couldn't imagine. But it only strengthened my resolve. I watched and waited for the right opportunity, and when it came, I took it. Five of us broke out that night. I've been back several times, once recently, for others like me."

"Why do they want to imprison perfectly healthy women? What do they gain?"

"Money. Families pay a good deal to get rid of women—and children—they don't want. Men at Creedmore are getting rich off them, and it's become a big, rotten business." She watched his eyes darken, his anger build.

"Why was Violet there?" His voice was tight, raspy.

"Her parents thought raising a blind child was too much trouble."

"Dear God! Such fools." Clay got to his feet so suddenly the chair toppled over. He picked it up and stood at the window, looking out the wavy glass.

She didn't know what the tall, broad-shouldered outlaw was staring at, but the muscles of his jaw worked and he clenched his fists hanging at his sides. Every tendon had stretched tight, like a wild beast ready to spring.

Could such a man love her? He had his town to occupy him, his thirst for amnesty, his need to dispense justice burning like a bright flame inside.

An ache filled Tally. Could he make a little room in his heart for her?

She bit back a sob that tried to escape. Would she ever find someone who loved her fully and completely? Or would she have to settle for less, as she'd done most of her life? She was tired of settling. She wanted to be *all* of someone's world, not just a small part. She yearned to fill a man's heart so full that his love for her spilled out all over the place.

A glance at the bed—hardly wide enough for one person, the ropes taut beneath the mattress—created a bead of moisture that trickled down her spine. It bore resemblance to the one in her cell at Creedmore. Unable to breathe, she jerked to her feet.

"This will not work, Clay Colby."

Four

Tally hurried from the dugout to where Luke and Josie Legend stood with Violet. "Luke, you have to take me back."

Clay raced out after her, hollering, "Now hold on. What did I do?"

Luke straightened, the silver conchos on his pants catching the light. "*Un momento, por favor.* Give Clay some time. I know you can work it out."

"Tell me what the damn problem is." Clay reached to touch her shoulder before letting his hand fall. "Maybe I wasn't clear enough. I said I want you and Violet. I'll make things better."

"That bed won't work and there's no place for Violet. I want to get my own before we wed. That's all." Tally watched deep relief wash over the hard angles of Clay's scarred face and guilt tugged at her heart.

She softened her voice. "It's just the bed—not you, Clay. A woman has to have certain things."

"Well, I certainly understand that." Josie set her long, blond hair in motion with a vehement nod. "A bed is important." Her eyes softened when she glanced at Luke and added, "But not always the *most* important."

Tally had no trouble reading her meaning. When you were with the person who loved you, nothing else mattered. But Tally didn't love Clay. She didn't even know him yet. Right now, this was nothing more than an arrangement.

Either with or without Clay's help, she meant to free all the women in Creedmore and find new lives for those in Deliverance Canyon. That was what haunted her, drove her every waking moment, and all she'd thought about for over two years.

Luke paced back and forth, scowling, muttering rapid-fire

words in Spanish. Then he paused and switched to English. "Josie and I can go back for it. There's no reason why you can't stay here and get acquainted. Besides, it's too dangerous with the men looking for you."

Of all people, she knew the trouble stalking her. Not for the first time, she regretted asking Luke to take even greater risks on her behalf. They'd been forced to take a roundabout route coming here to lose the two riders trailing them. Could she really ask more of him? Of Josie, while she was so swollen with child?

The answer was no.

Clay turned her to face him. "I'll build you a suitable bed and one for Violet. I guess I never gave a lot of thought to that and I'm kicking myself. I'll have one to your liking by tomorrow's end. Trust me, pretty lady."

Tally met Clay's eyes. They reminded her of the first turn of dark, rich soil after a winter's sleep. Trust? She trusted no one. "I'm just nervous. You've worked so hard, and here I am complaining."

Clay's hard body loomed over her, making her feel so small. The scent of him couldn't rise over the smoke that still lingered in the air, but she thought he'd probably smell like sagebrush and leather. He had callouses on his hands from trying to make the town into something, and she read hope on his face.

"We'll work this out. Just don't give up on me. On us." His words came out raspy.

"I promise."

Luke smiled. "See? *Magnífico*. Give me a list and I'll bring everything next time I come. For tonight, Tally and Violet can sleep in the dugout. When would you like to be married?"

"I just love weddings. I can sing." Josie sighed and laid her head against Luke's chest.

"Oh no you won't, *princesa*." Luke smoothed her hair. "You don't sing for anyone but me. Those bawdy songs aren't for weddings."

Josie picked some lint from her husband's dark shirtsleeve

and raised her eyes innocently. "The next time we get married, I hope you're awake for it, sweetheart, or I'll just have to sing."

Tally loved watching the two, who were still pretty much newlyweds. Over the months, she'd picked up some tips from them on how to make a marriage work. Mostly it seemed to be mutual respect that made a partnership work. Her gaze moved to Clay, who hid a grin.

He cleared his throat. "We've sort of gotten off the subject. Tally, when would you like to be married?"

"Sunrise has always been my favorite time of the day. Sunrises are new and fresh and full of promise." She smiled up at Clay. "It'll be perfect."

The deep worry in his eyes left Tally shaken. He seemed afraid that she'd bolt like all the others, but she couldn't blame him. That would scar anyone. She'd surprise him.

"Your wish is my command," he said softly.

"Then sunrise it is." Luke scanned the fledgling town. "Where's Ridge Steele? I don't care what he says, he's still a preacher and I need to talk to him about the service."

"He's with Jack and the two prisoners." Clay glanced toward Montana's former living quarters. "I need to see about them."

"I'll go with you." Luke kissed Josie's cheek, saying he wouldn't be long.

"While you men do that, me and Josie will fix supper." Tally glanced around for Violet and found the eight-year-old sitting with Bullet, petting his soft fur. That Violet had strayed from Tally's side was a good sign.

Under a deep cinnamon sky, Tally took in the tall walls of the canyon, the narrow entrance that could keep out the curious, listened to the creak of the windmill that soothed her ragged nerves. It was peaceful here, and trouble seemed far away.

But would it stay like this or would her past come after her? And would she be ready?

≈∽

The campfire burned low and the women had long gone to bed. Clay sat smoking and talking with Luke about rebuilding the town. "I'll get busy making more saddles and halters to trade you for more lumber," Clay said. "And I finished those new boots you wanted."

"No one is a better saddler than you. I can't wait to see them." Luke pitched a stick into the fire. "Looking at this rubble—it would've been easy for you to ride out and not look back."

Clay took a drag of his hand-rolled cigarette and stared at the glowing end. "I couldn't. Others depend on me."

He'd make Tally Shannon proud to be married to him if it took the rest of his life—and he'd pray she didn't leave come spring.

Why the hell had he agreed to that anyway? It was as good as accepting their marriage had an expiration date.

One by one, Ridge, Jack, and three other men joined them. Ridge passed around a bottle. Bullet moseyed along and flopped down at Clay's feet for some petting.

"I need to put that bed together for Tally. Is any of that extra lumber still stashed next to the saloon?" Clay asked.

Jack leaned back against a stump and stretched his legs out in front of him. "Yeah, it's still there, and Skeet hauled in a fresh load of hay yesterday."

"Thanks, Malloy." The man had proven invaluable at keeping the horses shod and cared for. Clay stared into the blue-and-orange flames. "I hope you're all coming to the wedding. She wants it tomorrow at sunrise."

Jack rubbed his leg around the spot where he'd caught a posse's bullet a while back. He took a swig from the bottle and passed it. "Ridge and I won't miss seeing you tie the knot, brother."

"That Tally Shannon is sure a looker," Malloy said. "I think I'll start writing to some of those women. Sometimes in the dead of night, I wake up with loneliness gnawing on me like a starving coyote. This is no kind of life."

Ridge reached into his pocket and drew out a letter,

handing it to Luke. "Deliver this to Savannah when you're back in Deliverance Canyon. I hope one day she'll marry me. Just not sure she's brave enough yet."

Jack and a man named Dallas Hawk also handed letters over. Like Ridge, Jack was corresponding with one of Tally's friends living in Deliverance Canyon. Hawk was writing to a woman in prison with a year left on her sentence. Hawk seemed to feel a kinship with her. There'd been a rumor that the big outlaw had a fondness for stage holdups, but Dallas never did talk much.

Luke and Josie didn't know what their bride service meant to men like them, lonely men who yearned for a bit of softness to balance this hard, unforgiving land.

Clay glanced at his dugout, where Tally lay sleeping. His lady had haunted eyes that spoke of unbearable suffering and pain. He'd caught winces when she walked. The diamond-shaped tattoo on her cheek said the rest. A mist blurred his vision. He wished he could remove that from her, save all the women like her. He itched to ride down to Stephenville and burn the Creedmore Lunatic Asylum to the ground.

For Tally, he'd do anything.

"How did you get rid of the bounty hanging over your head, Luke?" Ridge asked. "Last I saw, it was two thousand dollars. I'd appreciate any tips."

The firelight flickered across Luke's tight, grim features, and Clay was glad the half-white, half-Spanish man was a friend.

"Wasn't easy." Luke scowled into the night. "I paid back every bit of money I stole. And I finally found the man who'd framed me for that federal judge's murder. I chased him for two years—I'd just about given up catching him. In the end, he's the one who shot and almost killed me."

"I'm glad you survived. You're doing a lot of good now." Ridge's voice held a tinge of sadness. "My case is different from yours. I can't bring those men back to life. Me, Jack, and Clay are going to try writing the governor for a pardon."

"That's a great start." Luke glanced toward the wagon where Josie lay. "Having a family is worth doing anything for.

Do you ever get any troublemakers from Mobeetie, what with it being only a day and a half's ride?"

Clay had always called that haven for raw, ruthless men Hidetown and probably always would, no matter what name others bestowed on it. "They aren't welcome. They come, we run them out." He stared into the flames. "Luke, do you mind taking those two men of Montana's with you when you leave? I don't know what to do with them. Can't turn them loose and can't let them stay."

"Sure." Luke chuckled. "I'll drop them off with my brother Sam in Lost Point. Sometimes it sure helps having a lawman in the family. I'd be surprised if those men don't have a bounty on their heads. If they do, I'll bring you the reward, Clay."

"It'll sure come in handy. With enough money, we might be able to afford to buy all the building supplies we need." Clay had never even considered a reward. "To be honest, Ridge and Jack probably shot those two. I was busy with Montana."

"It was a group effort," Jack growled. "Besides, in this town, what belongs to one belongs to all."

Clay was quick to set them all straight. "Except for my soon-to-be wife. I'm not sharing her. You'll have to get your own."

Chuckles erupted with some ribbing, and the lighthearted moment eased some of Clay's nervous jitters.

❧

After telling Violet a bedtime story, Tally lay in the dark dugout, listening to the rhythm of the windmill and the men's voices outside. Hoots of laughter occasionally reached her ears. She wondered what they talked about. She liked how these men were so easy with one another. It never occurred to her that hardened outlaws might crave companionship as much as women. But watching Clay earlier, she'd seen his desperate need for someone to share his life with. And she'd glimpsed instant panic on his face when he thought she'd leave.

She grimaced, wishing she'd handled the bed situation

better. She should've explained, but the less she said about Creedmore the better.

Throwing back the worn quilt, she rose, tucking the covers around Violet, who softly snored, and went to stand at the window. Clay was easy to spot in the middle of the group of outlaws. The proud set of his broad shoulders drew her gaze.

This man with a bounty on his head had claimed her for a wife.

Tally allowed a smile. For the first time since her father had died, someone wanted her. Clay had promised to fight for her. And Violet, too, even though he'd never seen her before.

He hadn't spoken of love in his letters to her, and neither had she. It was far too early to know if that was possible. What he *had* talked about, however, had touched a chord in her. Things like his desire to better himself, the way he needed to matter to someone, and about his dream of one day being able to travel freely, and not once glance over his shoulder or wonder who lay in wait in the darkness.

Tally touched the mark on her cheek, wishing for the very things Clay's heart yearned for. But even if she were to achieve her goals, she could never get away from the tattoo. That had been done on purpose, placed for everyone to see.

For her, there would be no chance of a life beyond the safety of Devil's Crossing. Even if by some miracle the men from Creedmore stopped looking for her, she'd never fit in with regular society. She'd seen and done too much to truly be civilized. But here, at least, she'd have a place. Anticipation built inside her for the coming dawn. She would marry this dreamer and stand by his side through everything that came.

Twinges of pain raced down her neck, then it felt as though someone had a fist around her heart, squeezing. Tally stiffened, trying to ready for the shooting pain that pierced her. She clutched her chest, holding back a cry, until it passed. How long could she hide this?

Clay's laughter drifted through the door. Tally let the

curtain fall back into place and returned to bed. She stared up in the darkness, imagining lying with Clay beside her, until her eyes grew heavy.

And she dreamed.

༒

She was bouncing around in the bed of a wagon. Her head pounded and she tried to touch it, only to find her hands tied. What was going on?

"We're here," Lucinda ground out. "Your new home."

Where was "here"? A door opened and some men came out. Lucinda told them to get Tally inside and handed the tallest man a wad of money.

Panic raced through her and she tried to cry out, but her mouth refused to work. Strong hands gripped her and dragged her into a stone room that smelled of vomit—and death. Her teeth chattered from the cold. Where was she? What was happening? Tally couldn't get her tongue to move, words to come from her mouth. Her eyes didn't want to focus.

Shadows swathed the man standing over the table where they'd laid her. "Now, let's see what we've got." He turned to the woman beside him. "You said you just want her gone and don't care what happens to her in here?"

"Make her life as miserable as you can before she dies," Lucinda Shannon snarled. "I never want to see her again." Although shadows hid her stepmother's face, Tally knew Lucinda's lips would be set in a thin, straight line. Like always.

"A pleasure doing business with you. I trust you can see yourself out."

Footsteps moved away and the door shut, sealing Tally's doom. His hands moved over her body, squeezing, pinching, taking what he wanted. She tried to fight, to yell and scream, but still couldn't move her tongue or her arms. In her drugged state, she could put up little resistance.

She was at the mercy of an evil man. And no one knew where she was.

Her scream came no louder than a whimper as they

removed her clothes and replaced them with a shapeless, scratchy gown.

So cold. So scared. So alone.

Her situation became clear. The woman she'd been no longer existed. In just a few short minutes, she'd become a nobody—just a thing for others to do with whatever they wished. Tears slipped from the corners of her eyes. Her hell had begun.

Tally jolted awake, her heart racing. She wiped her tears and forced herself to take deep breaths, assuring herself over and over that she wasn't in Creedmore.

Still gasping, she went to the door and threw it open to gulp the fragrant air so different from the stale rooms of her prison. A cool breeze caressed her face, calming her. Someone touched her arm, and she was startled to find Clay in the darkness, only inches away. Had he been standing guard?

"What's wrong, Tally?" Concern laced his deep voice.

She started to reach for him, wanting his touch, but drew back a little. Trust had to start from someplace. She couldn't continue this way. Hesitant and unsure, she laid a trembling hand on his arm.

"Please hold me, Clay. Just for a little while," she whispered. "I need…"

Without a word, he wrapped his arms around her and she found safety and blessed security in his heartbeat so close.

Five

THE TEXAS PANHANDLE WAS NEVER STINGY WITH ITS BREATH-taking sunrises, but the one that greeted Clay the next morning was likely the grandest he'd ever seen. Sweeping brushstrokes colored the magnificent sky with vivid golden hues, like nuggets glistening in a pool of clear water. As he stood in awe, slashes of rose, purple, and turquoise appeared, blending and swirling into a portrait too beautiful for words to capture.

He and Tally stood on the rim of the bluff overlooking Devil's Crossing. The outlaw town was invisible down below, cloaked by the rocks and brush. He turned to face the friends gathered around.

And the woman he would vow to care for and protect with his life.

Tall and graceful, Tally wore the sunny, lemon-colored dress she'd arrived in the day before. And Clay had nothing fancy either—just plain, everyday clothes, which were good enough. They weren't trying to impress anyone.

Eyeing her dress, Clay could see a place where she'd mended it. There were probably others as well. He made a silent vow to buy her the prettiest dresses he could find the next time he went to a town of any size. And he'd make her a new pair of boots to replace the shabby ones she wore. Although she tried to hide it, he could tell by her limp that her feet killed her.

Something had happened. While his lady was in Creedmore? Maybe.

His lady. The words didn't seem real yet. He reached for her hand and found it a chunk of ice. A glance at her smooth complexion, marred only by the mark on her cheek, revealed the effects of little sleep. But the scared angel he'd held last night had vanished. In her place stood the bold, self-assured woman he'd first met. She didn't smile.

He studied her proud profile, facial bones delicately carved. A full, lush mouth. And her hair—wind-whipped strands of fire. Something stirred inside him and awakened a deep yearning.

"Are you sure about this, Tally? You can still back out."

"This is my path to follow, and follow it I will."

"So will I." Maybe this once, the bride wouldn't walk away and leave him before the ceremony. But they had yet to speak their vows. At least she'd left off her gun and holster, although he suspected she was rarely without the hardware.

She hadn't said what had sent her running to the door the night before, and he hadn't asked. He'd learn soon enough. Just like he hadn't told her that he'd planted himself outside the door to make sure she and Violet came to no harm.

He'd guard those two with his life. They'd given him a reason to keep breathing.

Bullet scampered to Violet, who stood on the other side of Tally, begging for some attention. She shifted her doll to her left hand and petted him, talking softly. Girl and dog appeared to have become inseparable in less than a day, and Clay was happy to see it.

Ridge Steele, tall and somber in his black frock coat, stood before them with his tattered Bible, his gun hanging from his hip. He hated to be pressed into service—a reminder that he still couldn't reconcile his past deeds with his teaching. Like them all, he struggled to find his way.

"We're gathered here on this fine morn to join Clay and Tally together as one mind, one heart, one purpose," Ridge began.

Violet, wearing a crown of braided daisies, removed her hand from Bullet and clutched Tally's dress. Clay glanced down at her upturned face and winked before he remembered she lived in darkness. He ached for the pretty little golden-haired girl. He couldn't imagine such a life, with peril at every turn that she couldn't even run from.

He swung his attention back to Ridge and repeated his vows. His eyes misted as he realized all a marriage entailed. From now on, he had to put Tally and Violet before his own needs. That was the true mark of a man.

"Do you have a ring, Clay?" Ridge asked.

"Of sorts." Clay fumbled in his pocket for the ring he'd found in the sack of coffee beans. He took Tally's right hand and looked deep into her eyes. "This isn't much, but it's all I have right now. I'll buy a better one later to match my pretty bride."

He slipped the silver band on her finger. The small, sparkly stone glittered in the sun, but he had to stifle a curse when he realized that it was too large. "Sorry about the fit."

"It's perfect." Tally gave his hand a reassuring squeeze but still didn't smile. "I'll wrap string around the band and it'll be fine."

"Just until I can do something better." She was clearly used to settling for less, but Clay would get her a ring that fit one day or die trying.

Ridge concluded the ceremony. "You may now kiss the bride, Clay."

Swelling with emotion, Clay pulled his beautiful Tally close and lowered his mouth. At the touch of her lips, warmth swept the length of his body.

He slid an arm around her and splayed a hand on the curve of her back. Happiness surged, making him tremble.

He was no longer alone and he asked for nothing more.

This marriage might not be perfect, but they'd try to find a way to make it work.

Whether intentional or not, Ridge had left out the obeying part from Tally's vows. Thank goodness. Already this early in their marriage, Clay knew that the words *obey* and *Tally* were never to be uttered together. She was a free, independent spirit and he wouldn't have her any other way.

The kiss ended and Tally raised her eyes. "Mr. Colby, we'd best get out of these clothes and get busy. The day's wasting."

"Yes, ma'am." Clay doubted ten sticks of dynamite could wipe the grin off his face. He took Violet's hand. "Let's go, pretty girl. I'll walk you to the wagon."

She raised her panicked face. "No, I want Mama Tally."

"Okay, honey." He and Tally hadn't talked about the girl and her adapting to him. It was all going to take getting used to. And maybe even longer for someone who couldn't see his face. Maybe she would grow more comfortable after he spent some time with her.

Violet took hold of Tally's hand, whispering loudly, "I don't know him."

"Give her some space, Clay." Tally solemnly met his glance. "She doesn't trust men, but she'll come around."

"I have all the patience in the world for her—and you."

Her quiet optimism about Violet offered hope. Tally made him believe that he could have everything his heart desired.

Yes, maybe even love over time. If he played his cards right.

Clay watched how careful Luke was with Josie, helping her to the wagon. His wife carried the dream for their future. Clay's gaze swung to Tally and found her expression guarded. Probably trying to figure out what she'd gotten herself into. The early rays of sunlight fired the red of her hair, making it flame, and his breath caught in his chest. With luck, maybe one day she'd grow fat with his baby.

Still a bit hesitant and unsure of her reaction to his touch, he slipped his arm around her waist and leaned close, inhaling her fragrance. "How did you like the sunrise, Tally? I ordered it specially for my beautiful bride."

"The sky, the ceremony was everything I'd hoped. I never thought you'd have a ring though. It's lovely." And then she smiled for the first time since he'd met her, and he'd never seen anything so dazzling.

It felt as though he'd just emptied a full bottle of whiskey in one gulp.

It was a beautiful day in which to begin the rest of his life.

Tally stood with Clay, waving goodbye to Luke and Josie. She'd thought she might dread this moment, but looking deep inside, she found no twinges of regret. It had been time to listen to Luke and Josie and her heart, although it had taken courage to leave the safety of Deliverance Canyon. This marriage could be a big mistake, but she realized she wanted to be here. Surprise accompanied that admission. How could she feel so at peace about a place this soon? Could it be possible that it might not be the place at all?

It could be the feel of Clay's nearness and his strong arm around her. She liked this man, her husband, wanted outlaw or not. He carried the scent of this wild Texas land and power in his touch. Yet, the look in his eyes spoke of doubts. He didn't fully believe yet that dreams really could come true.

But hopefully he would.

She let her arm slip around his waist and wondered at her boldness. She glanced up into his honest brown eyes that seemed to promise things he couldn't find words for. She couldn't imagine why any woman would turn him down. Didn't they see what lay buried under all the loneliness and isolation?

Tally smiled at her new husband, and he brushed her cheek with his calloused finger. She did belong here. With Clay Colby. At least until spring. Who knew beyond that?

A conversation she'd had with Hester Mason came to mind. She'd met Hester while inside the asylum—things would've been a lot worse if not for the woman. She'd come to take over the care of the women in Deliverance Canyon, but even knowing Hester was now in charge, Tally had balked at leaving.

"You've worked tirelessly toward the survival of the escapees, Tally," Hester had said. "But it's your turn to find a better life, to find the man who'll love and cherish you. You've earned some happiness."

"What about you, Hester? You deserve it, too. We all do."

"I'm old and long past matters of the heart. All I want is to live out my days here in this place. There's beautiful peace here." Hester had patted Tally's shoulder. "You go and try this marriage thing out. If it works, then maybe some of others can get out of here, too, and walk in the sunlight."

Hester knew Tally wouldn't abandon them and meant to carry on her work of freeing the women of Creedmore. She'd also gather supplies for them, and if those escapees wished to move farther west, Tally would take them. Clay was another matter, and she saw no reason at present to have to choose between them. This was her pledge to those women, her vow to herself.

A niggling in her brain said that maybe one day she might be forced to split her loyalties—her husband or the women of Deliverance. She wouldn't relish that decision.

Clay pressed a hesitant kiss to Tally's forehead, jarring her from her musings.

"You look a million miles away," Clay remarked. "Having second thoughts already?"

"Not yet." Her gaze found Violet nearby with the dog. "Devil's Crossing might be good for Violet—and me."

"Music to my ears." He released her. "I guess I'd best get back to work on that bed, Mrs. Colby. It'll be dark before we know it."

His nearness made her heady and Tally had trouble keeping her thoughts straight. "While you're doing that, I'll start clearing away the charred mess here. Luke will be back in two or three weeks with the new lumber. We want to be ready. What do you have in mind when you get those two buildings back up?"

Clay ran his fingers through his dark brown hair. "A mercantile for one, and a small hotel for the other. A place for Luke and Josie as well as folks passing by. Traders come pretty frequently. And maybe one day a stage line will add us to their route."

"We should think about a jail soon. We're going to need one. I'm glad Luke took those other two away—I didn't like the looks of them." Luke had bound and gagged them before throwing them in the back of the wagon, but their surly attitudes had revealed the depth of their hate for Clay. If they happened to escape, this would be the first place they'd come.

"You're right about the jail. For now, I'll rig up some sort of temporary cells. Many towns hold their prisoners in iron cages right out in the open. I reckon that'll work until we can build something better."

Ridge strode toward them, leading a half-dozen men. They were loaded down with the makings for a new bed. Jack limped behind them, pulling a few bales of hay on a sled for the temporary mattress.

"Guess I'll get to work." Clay paused, then kissed her cheek. "Tally, thank you for taking a chance on me. I promise never to make you regret it."

But he surely would. Tally shifted her gaze away from him. "A wagon rolls much smoother if both of the team pull equally."

"I like that. We *are* a team in this marriage." Clay grinned. "Equals."

Through half-lowered lids, Tally admired his backside as he went to meet his friends. He sure could fill out those trousers, and his stride was loose jointed and easy, like a wild, beautiful mustang.

What would he become after darkness fell?

Nervous jitters rattled her. She stood, inhaling the fresh air until she'd calmed, reminding herself that she was no longer imprisoned in Creedmore. Clay appeared to be patient and kind. A man with such a gentle touch wouldn't hurt her.

And if she was wrong about Clay and he ever did hurt her…she'd shoot him without blinking an eye. From now on, no one would ever touch her without permission. She'd rather make herself a widow.

Six

DUE TO THE HEAT, THEY ATE OUTDOORS THAT EVENING AT THE tables and chairs Harvey Drake brought out from the saloon. Afterward, Clay took Tally's hand. "I want to show you something. I've asked Jack to stay with Violet until we get back. This won't take long."

Violet glanced up in panic. "Don't leave me. Where are you?" In her haste, she stumbled over a chair and sprawled.

Clay picked her up but felt her stiffen and handed her to Tally.

"It's all right, honey," Tally soothed. "You can come." She threw a shawl around her shoulders. "We're all yours, Clay."

That they were, and Clay counted himself a very lucky man. He put Violet between them, each taking a hand. Maybe this would help his relationship with the child. "It's only a short distance. We'll be back long before dark."

"Do we ride?"

"Nope, we walk."

They passed the burned buildings that had begun to look better. Even though Tally had worked like a little soldier, cleaning up the rubble, a lot more remained to be done. He liked how she'd taken the men in the camp in hand and organized their efforts. Her philosophy seemed to be that if you lived here, you shared the work. It meshed with his own beliefs.

Bullet trotted from the shadow of some mesquites, his tongue lolling out, eyes lighting up to see his new friend. He came right to the girl and nudged her hand. Of course, that prompted a stop before continuing on.

Clay glanced at Tally's profile. She smelled of some kind of flowery soap. After she'd stopped work for the day, he'd taken her to an outdoor bathing room he'd rigged. He was proud of it, a small eight-foot-high wooden enclosure with five buckets of water perched on a shelf up top. Small ropes were attached to each bucket for the bather to pull when time to rinse. She'd lost no time in trying it out with Violet.

When they got back from this trip, he'd take his turn. He wouldn't crawl into bed with Tally without washing.

Thoughts of sleeping beside his new wife brought jittery nerves. What if he grunted or talked in his sleep? Worse yet, what if he didn't remember she was there and rolled on top of her or kicked her? He doubted he'd make a very good bedfellow. He'd probably scare her half to death.

He pushed aside some brush and let her through to the ground he'd cleared. The layout of their future house was pegged into the ground with string. "This will be our home."

Tally's eyes glistened. "I love it, Clay. Show me the rooms."

He pretended to open the nonexistent front door and bowed. "Your Majesties." Then he led her and Violet into the pretend parlor, the kitchen, and the bedroom, stepping over the thin, white twine. "I'll just need to make a slight adjustment for Violet. She'll need her own bedroom. But that won't be a problem."

Nothing was too difficult when it came to his two ladies.

"For me?" Violet asked.

"Yes, baby girl." Clay knelt and took her hand. "Do you know that I'd do anything for you? If it's fine with your mama, I'd like to spend some time with you tomorrow. We can get to know each other. Would that be all right?"

"I don't know. Will Mama be there?"

"We'll have to see about that." Clay stood and gave Tally a questioning glance. But all he got was a shrug.

Clearly, they had some work ahead in figuring out things.

Tally smoothed the top of Violet's hair. "Honey, why don't you sit here in the beautiful sunset with Bullet while we finish?"

The girl jerked in panic and grabbed Tally's skirt. "You won't leave me?"

"No, honey." Tally moved to stand where one wall would go. "Clay, the rooms are quite spacious, and the view here where the canyon opens up into a valley is breathtaking. We can watch the sky in the evenings."

Clay scowled. That had never occurred to him. "I completely overlooked that. I'll add a wide window here for the winter months. And I'll build a porch for the summer, so we can sit out here."

Only, would she be there for the summer? His stomach twisted. Although he didn't know how he'd find strength if she wanted to leave, he wouldn't stop her.

"That would be lovely." Tally turned and the fading sunlight tangled in her copper-colored hair, shooting golden fire through the long strands.

The sight of her was heart-stopping. His mouth dried and he reached for her. Something akin to fear instantly filled her eyes.

"I only want to hold you, Tally. A harmless kiss."

"Sorry."

"Nothing at all to be sorry for. I never want to force you to do anything you don't want." He gently tugged her against him and placed tentative lips on hers. He gave her a moment to relax, then settled his mouth firmly on hers. The kiss was raw and jarred Clay to the bottom of his boots. An overwhelming tenderness rose for this woman who'd taken a chance on him.

Their breath mingled as passion deepened. It didn't surprise him that she tasted of the sweet peaches they'd had with supper. But Clay also tasted something else. Yearning?

Deepening the kiss, he explored the soft lines of her back, her waist, and the gentle flare of her hips. Tally leaned into him, clutching his vest, returning all that he gave.

Ripples of wonder went through him. He was surprised at the depth of her passion. Of his too.

For a moment, time stood still and he savored this new life. Some women were like diamonds, with many facets that revealed different colors and depths depending how you turned it. While he couldn't yet know for sure, Tally seemed to have that inner fire. Already she'd amazed him at the ease in which she'd taken charge of the men, both at the burn site and in rearranging the dugout for the new bed he'd built for them and moving their old one into a cubicle for Violet. Each man seemed enamored of her.

He just prayed he wouldn't mess this up, and he vowed to show her the man he could be.

Tally pushed away from him, her breath ragged. "I should get back."

Clay captured her palm. "I didn't mean for that to happen. It was just the beauty of this place, the fresh air, the waning sunlight…"

"I wasn't offended, but don't expect too much of me."

"If I'm moving too fast, just tell me. We're not running any race." He raised her chin to study her blue eyes. "You must be worried about sleeping with me. I vow to you right here, right now, that I'll not do anything you don't want. I'll never force myself on you. I never have—on any woman."

Tally lightly touched the scar on his cheek. "If I thought you would, we wouldn't be having this conversation. But we both have things in our past to overcome. I still have night-mares about being at Creedmore, so don't be alarmed if I sit up in the dead of night, struggling to breathe."

So that was why she'd come running outside. Whatever she'd experienced there, it must've been horrific.

"Does it happen regularly?"

"They're becoming less frequent, but when those memories do take hold, I'm helpless under their power."

Clay tucked a wayward curl behind her ear and kissed her cheek. "If I could take every bad memory from you, I would in a heartbeat. I can't imagine what you've endured. If you ever want to talk about it, I'm here. Otherwise, I won't ask you for details."

Tally stepped away from him. "Talking serves no purpose. It changes nothing."

Her hard tone told him more than her words ever would.

The monsters at Creedmore must've tried to break her. Only it sure looked like they hadn't succeeded, and that was a testament to her immense strength.

"We'd better get back. Are you ready?" At her nod, they went to Violet, curled up sound asleep, using Bullet for a pillow. Clay forced a chuckle. "I think she's tired."

Tally's gaze held love for the child. "Can you carry her?"

He nodded and lifted the girl in his arms. On the way back, he and Tally discussed how best to handle the child's fear of Clay. "I want to spend some time with her tomorrow. I'll show her the goats and how to navigate around a little, and things to avoid."

"That's a good idea if she'll let you." Tally let out a sigh. "She's been through a lot."

"Tell me a little about her background."

"I only know her family was mean and ugly to her because she was different and required more care." Tally glanced up at him with her winter-blue gaze. "I don't think she's ever had a speck of love or even kindness."

Emotion filled Clay's voice. He hated the gruffness. "Well, she'll get plenty here. We're her family now." You didn't have to be born to someone to be family. The one you chose was often much better. Clay had lost his at a tender age and had never found a replacement.

Until now.

&

Violet woke up the minute they stepped into the dugout, freezing in Clay's arms. "Mama Tally?"

A flash of pain crossed his eyes, and he quickly put her down. "You're all right." Tally quickly soothed the girl and got her in a soft nightgown. "Are you happy, sweet girl?"

"As long as you're here too. I like Bullet. You'll never go away and leave me, will you?"

"No, definitely not. Please try not to be afraid. These men aren't like the others."

"Do you promise?"

"I promise. Mr. Colby and his friends will never hurt you." Tally kissed Violet's cheek and wrapped her in a hug. Her heart broke for the child. She, too, had seen the darkness in men's hearts. But Violet was only a child and unable to use logic. To her, all men posed danger.

"Mama Tally, what does Mr. Clay look like?"

What an odd question. But Violet had to be curious. "Well, let's see. He has very kind brown eyes and his dark hair curls around his collar. His smile makes me feel warm and cared for. Someone hurt him bad though."

"How do you know?"

"He wears a scar on his face."

"Did it make him cry?"

"I don't know, honey." Somehow, she couldn't see Clay crying, no matter how wounded.

"But he's not mean?"

He could turn out to be, but no matter how wary life had taught her to be, something inside of her doubted Clay could ever be mean. "No, honey. I don't think so. Want me to tell you a bedtime story?"

"Yes. The one about the three piggies."

They settled on the bed and Tally spun the yarn that never was the same way twice. The child loved variation. When she finished, Tally asked, "Do you want to say your prayers?"

Violet knelt beside her small bed with her hands clasped together. "Thank you, God, for watching over us. And tie all the mean men up so they can't hurt us. Amen."

Tally tucked her in, kissed her forehead, and stepped around the blanket that separated Violet's little cubbyhole from the rest of the dugout. She went to sit with Clay at the table. "I suppose you heard that?"

He took her hand, drawing little circles in her palm before meeting her eyes. Her stomach flipped upside down, as it had earlier when they'd kissed. She stroked the fine hair on his arm.

He cleared his voice. "She's terrified of not only me, but of losing you. I see why you had to bring her."

"I hope she gets better and doesn't cling as much. But I make no promises."

"Not asking you to." Clay leaned and kissed her behind the ear, the day's stubble brushing her skin. "You smell very nice. Humor me—what kind of soap do you use?"

"It's lavender. Josie gave me three bars for a wedding present. Until now, I've always used just plain soap, whatever I could make from lye. Why?"

"I want to make sure you never run out." He stood and pulled her up against him. "Dance with me."

She sent a startled glance around the small room. "Where?"

"Right here. It's small, but we might manage." His hold was light, his arm trembling. "This brings back memories of my mother and father. They were so much in love, and as a boy, I watched them dance in the yard in the moonlight, always imagining that's what married life should be like. I want our marriage to be spontaneous and fun, Tally. To whip off your apron and twirl you around the yard."

His admission jolted her and his voice dripped with longing.

"It's been so long I probably don't remember how." She let herself relax and began to softly hum a waltz. Their first steps were hesitant, but soon they fell in step with each other perfectly as they moved around the plank floor. Unable to avoid the cookstove and table and chairs, they bumped into them and tried again. They finally ended up standing still and swaying in the center of the room. That was fine with Tally's aching feet.

"Who taught you to dance, Clay?"

"A lady in a saloon in Cimarron, New Mexico Territory. Lord, could she dance. She moved like rippling water. Dancing is one of my favorite things to do, only the number of lady partners around here has been a mite slim." He flashed a smile and her heart fluttered. "You're very good at this."

"My father taught me. And my brother, Brady."

"Your brother?" Clay stopped, surprise on his face. "You didn't mention him in any of your letters."

"I thought some things best to wait until I was here. Brady died in an accident only a week after my father passed." Tally recalled the horrible nightmare, made so much worse by not knowing the exact cause and fearing Lucinda's wrathful nature. She struggled with tightness in her throat, the words barely squeezing out. "Brady was working alone in one of our pastures, rounding up some strays. We found him bleeding, his spine broken."

Clay drew her close and she welcomed the comfort. "That must've devastated you."

"Best we could figure, his horse had trampled him." Tally wrapped her arms around Clay's waist and rested her head on his chest. "After the lengths that Lucinda went to in getting rid of me, I can't help but wonder if she had a hand in Brady's death too. She was determined to get her hands on everything, and his accident was far too convenient."

"Do you think she might've killed your father?"

"I have no proof, but yes, I do think she did." She stepped back and winced at the sudden movement that sent a wave of pain through her foot.

Lesson learned. Clay's eyes darkened. She would never be able to hide anything from him. He seemed to notice every detail, but then, maybe that's what had kept him alive.

"Tally, I've seen how you walk. Are your feet hurting you?"

She stilled, her voice low when she spoke. "You promised not to ask details of my time in Creedmore. I should get ready for bed."

"Sit." Clay held out a chair. When she dropped onto the seat, he removed her shoes and pulled her stockings off. A gasp left him that he tried to cover with a too-bright smile. He lifted each red and painfully swollen foot and gently massaged the twisted toes and misshapen bones. He turned his head and coughed, trying to hide the glisten of tears.

"Please, don't." But he wouldn't let her pull her feet back.

"Don't deny me this pleasure. Picture your favorite place and let me take you there."

Tally closed her eyes and let his tender touch carry her to the place where she'd grown up and a time when she'd known no pain. She ran laughing through lush fields of hay and across the wide meadow, into welcoming arms, and had never felt so cared for.

When he finished, Clay kissed each foot and stood. "I'll make myself scarce while you get ready for bed. Need to check on the goats anyway." He started toward the door and paused, his back to her. "Tally, I can't do any asking around myself, me being wanted, but the Legends have considerable influence. We'll try to find out about your brother and father."

"Thank you, Clay."

The door shut, leaving Tally alone with her jitters. Although Clay had promised not to do anything that she didn't want, she was nervous about sleeping next to him. She went to the new bed.

There on her pillow lay a pretty purple wildflower.

Clay amazed her. The notorious outlaw danced up a storm *and* he had the soul of a romantic. She picked up the bloom and sniffed the sweet fragrance. Clay surprised her at every turn. He'd learned a lot about how to please a woman. Dancing, rubbing her feet, and now this.

No doubt the handsome man had seen no shortage of willing teachers.

The thought soured her stomach. She didn't want to think about anyone he'd been with before her. Still, she did owe those women a debt of gratitude. The way he moved suggested that he'd probably be a very accomplished lover. Her stomach clenched as dark memories swarmed, choking her.

Would he be disappointed in her? She knew nothing of gentleness.

She pulled her nightgown from a small trunk and shook out the wrinkles. In short order, she exchanged it with her dress, then brushed out her hair and braided it. She'd just crawled beneath the light covers and tucked her pistol under her pillow when Clay entered with wet hair, bringing the fresh night air and scent of soap with him.

"Everything's fine outside." Clay sat on the side of the bed and removed his boots. "A few of the men are keeping watch for

Montana Black in case he decides to come back. I don't expect to see him for a while, mind you. He's too hurt right now."

"But you do think he will return someday."

"Hope I'm wrong, but yes, I think he'll have to come, if only to defy me."

Clay unbuckled his gun belt and laid it aside, then removed his shirt. Tally longed to run her hand across his broad back where the muscles rippled. He was taller than her brother's six feet, but Clay struck a better figure. She tried to turn away yet found herself watching him undress. He certainly didn't appear to mind.

She'd felt his lean, hard body when he'd held her in his arms. The barely restrained power emanating from him said he would deliver swift punishment to those who wronged him.

Wearing only the bottoms of his long johns, he crawled next to her and blew out the lamp. What she'd thought would be plenty of room in the new bed for them both was suddenly gone. His large presence swallowed up the space—both in the bed and in her thoughts.

Their legs and arms touched, and she had to steel herself to keep from jerking away.

For a moment, she struggled to breathe, fighting to force air into her lungs. But when Clay didn't reach for her, she relaxed.

"Tally, you can trust me." Clay turned on his side to face her. "From now until you decide differently, all we'll do when we go to bed is sleep."

"I just have to get used to this is all. I vowed to be a wife to you and I will." She couldn't see him in the pitch black, but she could feel his eyes on her.

She yearned to reach out and touch him but thought maybe that would invite problems.

"There's no hurry." His voice rumbled in his chest and throat like the words were fighting to get out. "Like I said earlier, we're not running any race. But I'm going to reach for your hand now, Tally. I need to hold it because you already ground me in a way nothing else does." Then he added, "Don't pull that gun from under your pillow. I know it's there."

"I promise. You're a strange man, Clay Colby."

He chuckled softly and took her hand. "I won't deny that. Too much time spent alone, I expect. Tell me about a happier time. Something from when your mother was alive."

"In the summer, I used to sneak off and go swimming at this pretty little creek that runs through our land. My brother tied a rope to a tree limb that stretched over the water and we'd swing out and let loose. I loved that. We'd laugh and tease each other until the sun started going down. Then we'd hurry home." Tally's voice softened. "Wonderful smells would come from the kitchen, and Mama would have a peach pie baked."

She squeezed his hand. "Peach is my favorite. What's yours?"

"My mother used wild blackberries because they were prevalent in East Texas. Lord, that was a long time ago. I'd forgotten how good it tasted. But you won't find me backing up from any kind of pie. I've been known to make a glutton out of myself." He chuckled again and the sound seemed to vibrate inside Tally. Then his voice turned dark. "It all ended at fourteen-years-old and I went off to fight in the war."

"Why when you were so young?" She couldn't imagine. Had they let boys fight?

"They needed me. My father was a cripple, and it ate him alive that he couldn't join the fight. I figured I'd do my part and his too. More than anything in the world, I wanted to make him proud that I stood tall for what our family believed in."

Pain filled Clay's voice and Tally wanted to cry. Damn the war!

"My brother went at the same time I did—he was eighteen. I never saw John again. I guess he got killed. Who knows? Things were in such chaos it was hard to find anyone." Clay let out a deep sigh. "I like to think he's alive and happy somewhere."

"I'm truly sorry. Maybe he'll turn up sometime. Stranger things have happened." Tally wiggled and her leg pressed against Clay's. She didn't move it back. She'd been so frightened before, but now the contact made her feel safe and connected to life again in a way she hadn't since her mother had passed.

"But didn't you go home at war's end to see your mother?"

"It was the first place I went, but my parents had died and strangers lived in our home, farming our land." His voice came thick, tight.

"Clay, I'm so sorry—what it must've done to you."

"I got over it—or so I lie to myself." He brought her hand to his mouth and kissed it.

"You have a most gentle touch." She closed her eyes to soak in the closeness she'd longed for in her dreams. She could almost forget that she'd vowed to trust no one.

Except that would be dangerous.

"For you, always, pretty lady." He brushed her cheek with a finger and she could feel his warm breath floating against her face.

The declaration washed over Tally like warm honey. Lying in the darkness, it was easy to talk about things, to be with him. Against her better judgment, she inched a little closer. "That brings me to something. I notice how Josie calls Luke 'sweetheart,' and it fits. I don't know what to call you."

"Your heart has to decide that. When it does, you'll know." Clay brought her hand to his lips and kissed her fingers. "I think we're good for each other, Tally. I'm going to tell you something I've been thinking a lot about."

"What's that?" She was curious what her new husband had found to while away the time.

"I know neither of us *feel* love for each other yet—it's too soon for that. But love can take all sorts of forms. You can love someone without being *in* love with them. Like a mother for her baby or siblings for each other. Love without the physical part." He laid her hand on his chest and Tally could feel his strong heartbeat. "Do you understand what I'm saying in my bumbling way?"

"I'm not really sure."

"What I'm trying to say is that I've made a conscious decision in my head to love you until it can seep into my heart." The bed shifted when he raised on one elbow and let a finger drift down her throat. "I love you, Tally Shannon."

Seven

TALLY STIFFENED, PONDERING CLAY'S WORDS. FINALLY, SHE realized they were true, and maybe she could choose to love him back.

Only she didn't dare. One chink in the armor would let hurt inside.

"Don't expect too much this soon." She paused, her breath hitching and unsteady as fear of the darkness rose. "Sometimes the night presses against me. Would you hold me until I fall asleep?"

"I thought you'd never ask." He slid his arm around her and drew her close.

She laid her head on his shoulder, her palm on his chest. She wasn't afraid of this man who'd chosen to love her as easily as he'd chosen to look up at the stars. She'd seen his gentleness with Violet and the pain in his eyes at her fear of him. "Tell me about your goats."

Clay's soft laughter filled the space. "My goats? Your curious mind can think of nothing else?"

"Stop laughing. I don't know anything about goats," she said defensively. "My family dealt in cattle. Now, as the wife of a goat herder, I should probably learn about them."

"First of all, Mrs. Goat Lady, we have to milk them every day just like bovines. The milk Violet drank this morning came from the goats. She must have loved it, since she asked for another cup. Milking the animals works about the same as cows, only everything's smaller. We can make cheese and butter from it, and the milk makes great soap. Violet will have nothing to fear from them. They're harmless."

"Do you pen them up at night?"

"Nope. Doesn't do any good. They're notorious for finding ways to get out. I gave up trying and just let them roam."

His voice rumbled in Tally's ear. She loved the warm sound that sent delicious prickles through her.

Clay continued, "Another good thing is that they're very loud, and they let me know when trouble is about."

Tally drew tiny circles on Clay's chest. "That's all the good stuff. What's the bad?"

"They eat everything," he answered without hesitation. "They're very destructive. And don't bend over when they're near or they'll butt you."

"Sounds like some people I know." She smiled in the darkness. "I think I might like being a goat herder's wife."

They lapsed into silence. Tally lay listening to Clay's heartbeat and feeling the strength of his chest beneath her palm.

Tomorrow she would write a letter to Hester Mason and all her friends in Deliverance Canyon and pass it to the woman who would come to give Tally a report. This endeavor was better than she'd ever let herself imagine.

Clay already loved her inside his head.

She mentally shook herself and prayed she wasn't seeing only what she wanted to.

Clay dove into work the next morning with a vengeance. After demonstrating the goat milking to Tally, he left her to that chore and tackled the burned buildings. He'd meant to try to spend time with Violet, but when she refused to take his hand, he'd dropped the matter. There'd be other days. He wouldn't force her. He stopped every so often, his gaze drifting to his lady as she walked the perimeter with Violet, looking at everything. They'd made great strides in their relationship last night as they talked in bed. Tally had wanted his touch and that made him a happy man. He knew he'd never grow tired of holding her.

While she hadn't spoken of her time in Creedmore, he'd gotten enough from Luke and Josie to know it was a miracle she had emerged sane.

His heart swelled with pride. Tally's freshly washed hair

shone in the light and her lively blue eyes glistened. This wife he'd gotten was as tough as a piece of shoe leather. He was happy to have eased the pain in her misshapen feet for a little while last night.

Jack Bowdre followed his gaze. "She's a good one, Clay. I hope Darcy has the same steel in her spine. Darcy won't say what happened to her in that asylum, but anger comes through loud and clear in her letters."

"Don't give up on her, Jack." Clay laid a hand on his friend's back. "It's only been two days and Tally has already changed my life. Darcy may be just what you need." His gaze swept to Tally, who'd plopped down to let Violet play with one of the baby goats. Bullet lay beside the girl, looking none too happy to share her attention with smelly animals that bleated.

Although they still had work to do on their marriage, Clay was happier than he'd ever been.

～

The days passed, and two weeks had gone by before Clay knew it. He loved having Tally next to him every night, although they'd yet to do more than kiss and touch. He knew he had to go slow and give Tally time to adjust, but he prayed they'd see a break-through soon. He'd also made some progress with Violet, and the girl didn't panic when he touched her now. She even talked to him some. Those were mighty big steps and heartened him.

Clay was helping Jack and Ridge with chores around the town when suddenly the goats panicked, bleating and bound-ing for cover. Bullet sprang to his feet, barking furiously. The dog raced toward riders coming through the secret path in the rock wall of the canyon. The fact that they used the back way, not the main entrance, shot a warning through Clay.

The hair rose on the back of his neck. He threw down the charred lumber and hurried to Tally. "Get Violet inside and stay there."

"Be careful, Clay." Tally didn't have to say a word to Violet. The child appeared to have sensed danger and clung to her dress, her face colorless. "Did they see us?" Tally asked.

"I don't think so. They're not close enough." He gave her a quick kiss and went to intercept the three riders.

The riders halted in front of him. Clay's arms hung loosely at his sides, and he stared at them through narrowed eyes. "You must be lost, gentlemen. This is private property. State your business."

Thank goodness they were about two hundred yards from the house and Tally wouldn't be able to hear. However, she would see what was happening, and he hated that.

Jack, Ridge, and a dozen outlaws formed a formidable line on either side of Clay. The strangers' stares were as hard as their faces. The older rider had a neatly trimmed beard that matched his red hair. Clay put him in the vicinity of forty or so. Another was stocky and around Clay's age. One word—hostile—described the set of his face and body.

But the third rider—he brought a layer of ice snaking up Clay's spine. A gold tooth flashed in what appeared to be a permanent sneer. His hooded eyes were sullen and filled with contempt. The way he sat in the saddle, gazing at Clay with superiority, said he was the leader of this trio.

Bullet stopped barking and bared his teeth, ready to tear into them. Clay ordered him to quiet down. The dog obeyed but kept a wary gaze on the strangers.

"We're looking for a dangerous woman." The red-haired speaker started to thrust a hand into his vest.

"I wouldn't do that, mister." Clay pulled his gun from the oiled holster before the older rider could swallow.

"I was getting the reward poster. May I?"

"Nice and slow," Jack drawled. "Or you won't get a second chance."

"My name is Pollard Finch. We're looking for some dangerous escapees from the Creedmore Lunatic Asylum." The man held out a hand bill with Tally's picture front and center. "I know that woman's in the area. She might have a child with her."

Clay's eyes never left Finch's. "Haven't seen her."

"Look again," Finch insisted.

"Mister, this Remington says demands will be a mite unhealthy for you." Clay wanted to strangle this trio with his bare hands and feed them to the buzzards. His gut said at least one of them had hurt Tally. His bet was on Gold Tooth. The man had that smug look Clay hated. He ached to drag him from his horse and let Bullet have some fun.

"Get off this land!" Clay's sharp order burst forth hard and unyielding.

Finch backed his horse up. "We didn't come looking for trouble."

"Even so, you found it," Jack Bowdre ground out. "If you value your hide, I'd heed the warning and turn around. Go back where you came from."

"Tally Shannon is as crazy as an owl-hoot, and she'd as soon shoot you as look at you," snapped Gold Tooth. "Though God Almighty, she's a wild tiger when it comes to pleasuring a man. I especially enjoyed taming that one."

Rage blinded Clay. An uncontrollable need for justice for Tally exploded inside him. He yanked the surprised man from his horse and jammed the seven-and-a-half-inch barrel of his Remington into the space between the bastard's hooded eyes.

Eight

TALLY'S HEART POUNDED AGAINST HER RIBS. HAD THE MEN outside tracked her here? They were too far away for her to make out, but the horses were another matter.

"They're here," Violet whispered, rocking back and forth.

"No, I'm sure it's just men who got lost." She desperately tried to loosen the iron fist of fear that gripped her chest. She hurried Violet to her enclosed bed, to safety behind the curtain. "We have to hide, honey. Be very quiet." She placed the girl's doll in her hand.

"Don't let them take me back." Violet's fingernails dug into her arm.

"I won't, honey. I'll shoot the first one who tries and any others who follow." Tally needed to comfort the child, but she also had to see what was happening, to see if the men had started moving their way. "I have to go look now. You stay right here and don't make a sound."

Tally gave Violet a kiss and closed the curtain, then moved to the side of the window to peek out. From there, she watched the scene unfold between Clay and the men from Creedmore. Her cold hands shook, but a calm had begun to erase her panic—until she noticed the big grullo. The horse was unusual, and she knew only one man to ride one: Slade Tarver. Just then, sunlight glinted off the gold tooth of the man she hated with every fiber of her being. She feared and abhorred all three of the Creedmore men, but she reserved the most for Slade Tarver. He'd gotten a thrill out of causing her pain and had devised many, many methods of torture.

Clay yanked Slade from his horse without warning and stuck his gun to the man's head. She didn't know what Slade had said, but she could hazard a guess or two.

She muttered a silent prayer that the other two men, which

had to be Pollard Finch and Jacob Abram, wouldn't shoot Clay. Only a fool would try. But if they did, both men would be dead in an instant. The outlaws had formed an impenetrable line of defense.

Still, Finch and Abram had followed Tarver, and that didn't say much for their judgment.

In the midst of it all, she found herself praying that Clay wouldn't send Slade to hell. Never mind how much the man deserved it—killing a person scarred your soul.

Tally knew firsthand. During her desperate escape, she'd stabbed a guard in the heart when he'd tried to stop her and the other women from fleeing. She'd never forget the feel of the knife sliding into his chest, the way the light went out of his eyes as life ebbed from him. He hadn't been the only one to feel the sharp blade.

Furthermore, if it came to her life or theirs…she'd do it again in a heartbeat.

A painful memory flashed. Slade had locked Agatha into one of the cells they'd built under Creedmore. Her crime was not moving fast enough to suit him when he'd given an order. He wouldn't give Agatha water or food. A week had passed before Tally found out where her friend was—she'd pocketed her ration and snuck down while everyone slept.

Slade had found crumbs on the cell floor and was furious. He took Agatha out onto the grounds and made everyone watch while he shot the woman in the head.

The flashback brought bile into Tally's throat. She'd failed Agatha. But she wouldn't fail anyone else. She set her jaw. She'd save those she loved and find justice for those who died.

Tally turned back to the scene playing out two hundred yards away. The anger in Clay's movements, his explosive reaction toward Tarver and his minions, charged through the walls and penetrated her as surely as a knife blade.

Clay had admitted he was wanted for murder. She didn't know how many men he'd killed, but something told her that if Slade so much as blinked, another name would be added to the total.

"Please don't scar your soul any worse, Clay." Tally moved back from the window before the riders happened to catch movement. "Not for me."

∼∾

The darkness Clay fought to keep at bay burst from its locked cage. His finger tightened on the trigger. He only had one thought—to wipe the sneer off Gold Tooth's miserable face. Behind Clay, the line of outlaws stood with weapons drawn on the two still on their mounts.

"You told me exactly what I wanted to know—Tally Shannon is here," the man spat.

Clay leaned forward until his nose almost touched the bastard's. "I wouldn't be so sure of that," he said in silky, quiet voice. "I'd as soon blow your head off as not for what you said about any woman."

The leather creaked when Jack shifted in his saddle. "He always reacts this way when men speak ill of a lady. Don't mean one thing except he holds womenfolk in high regard."

Clay moved the gun from Gold Tooth's forehead and shoved the barrel in the man's mouth, loosening a few teeth. "Unless you want to eat some lead right now, you'd best apologize for your indecent remarks."

Pollard Finch yelled, "For God's sake, Slade, do it! Or we won't get out of here alive."

"Two seconds, or you'll sit at the devil's table," Clay growled. "What'll it be?"

Slade tried to speak around the gun barrel. Clay moved it a little so his tongue could work.

"I'm sorry." Slade spit blood along with his words, but his eyes were still defiant.

"Louder!" Clay yelled. "And say exactly what you're sorry for."

"Do it!" Pollard yelled again.

"For God's sake, apologize and let's get the hell out of here!" the stocky rider cried, his hostile expression long gone and replaced by panic.

The immediate rage Clay had felt intensified. He wouldn't be able to hold himself back much longer. The horrible mistake he'd made at fourteen would not be repeated here—or ever again. No innocent people would die because he messed up. He would protect Tally and Violet to the last drop of blood.

Deadly calm filled him. "What'll it be?"

"I'm sorry for disrespecting a woman!" Slade screamed.

Satisfied, Clay yanked the man from the dirt and pushed him toward his horse. "Ride. If we ever see any of you here again, there'll be no talking. You'll be dead before you can blink. Consider this your only warning."

Without a word, the trio turned their horses and galloped from Devil's Crossing as though a pack of flaming hounds of hell were chasing them.

Clay kept his gun cocked and ready to fire until they'd vanished from sight, then he holstered his weapon and strode to the dugout. Tally stood near the window, her gun in her hand, eyes blank, expression unreadable.

"They're gone." He stepped closer. "I doubt they'll be back—at least not for a while."

"I couldn't see the men, but I recognized their horses. Slade Tarver rides the grullo, and his friends own a pinto and dapple gray." Tally holstered her gun. "The one you put in the dirt is the worst. I was afraid he'd kill you. Slade Tarver is as mean as they come. He always carries a knife in each boot and looks for reasons to use them."

Clay allowed a tight grin. "I kept him a little too busy to get to them."

Following the sound of their voices, Violet stole from her cubbyhole and launched herself at Tally, clinging to her waist. Clay wanted to reach for her but knew that would frighten her more. The child was shaking, and despite Tally's calm exterior, he imagined she was a mess of nerves inside as well.

"Come here, Tally." He stretched out a hand to her. "You can relax."

"I can never let my guard down." Ice coated her crisp words, but she was clearly shaken. "The other two men were

Pollard Finch and Jacob Abram. They're sheep, for the most part. Tarver has no trouble getting them to do what he wants."

"I have bullets for sheep as well as their leader." Clay reached for her again, but she seemed frozen, as though afraid to abandon her post at the window.

"Is he hurt, Mama?" Violet whispered.

Tally met Clay's gaze. "No, honey. Would you like to see for yourself?"

Silence filled the space between them like fragile spun glass as Clay waited for Violet's answer. He was afraid to take a deep breath for fear the glass would shatter.

Finally, Violet whispered, "I'm scared."

The air left Clay's lungs. If those bastards did this... He shook with a need to make someone pay. "That's all right, baby girl. You can go at your own speed."

And if she never took him into her heart? He'd find some way to accept it.

Tally must've sensed his great disappointment. She laid a hand on Violet's shoulder. "Want to come help me check on the goats to see if the babies are with their mamas?"

"They must be real scared." Violet took Tally's hand.

"Don't wander too far," Clay warned. He sat in the emptiness after the door closed behind them, feeling like pounding something. He had to saddle up and take a ride. He wouldn't rest until he knew for sure Pollard, Slade, and Abram were far away from here.

Tally's and Violet's lives depended on him now, and he took the job very seriously. As he climbed on Sundown's back, he recalled Tally's question last night about pet names. Angelique Pascale, the hot-blooded Frenchwoman in Cimarron who had taught him to dance, had used many whispered endearments. She'd told him women adore men who spoke pretty words to them. He'd gotten quite an education from her. One phrase stuck in his mind.

"*Ma ange guerrier*," he whispered, even though he knew he butchered the French.

Tally was his warrior angel.

Wild and untamed, like the raw Texas land, ready to battle evil forces.

She was all that and more. And he wanted her. Oh Lord, how he longed to make her his. But she wasn't ready. She still fought too many demons.

Until she purged Creedmore and those memories, he'd wait.

However long it took.

Nine

THAT NIGHT, WITH VIOLET ASLEEP, TALLY DANCED WITH CLAY again. Each time he held her in his arms, she forgot about the pain in her feet. She'd suffer anything to feel his heartbeat next to hers. He held her, gentle, as though she was fine china. Lord knew she hadn't been that in a long, long while.

Damn her inability to trust what her heart saw! She wanted to so badly.

Despite his large body, he was very light on his feet. But then he loved to move and had confessed as much. Would that carry forward into making love? One day, on her terms, she'd find out, but she couldn't put him off forever.

She smiled up at him and got lost in his shadowed brown gaze. Tonight, his eyes weren't laughing. Instead, they were somber and deadly serious. "Is the scene with Tarver and his men still on your mind, Clay?"

"You don't know how much I wanted to kill them and feed their carcasses to the coyotes. Only one thing kept me from it—your face when I closed my eyes. But it was a mistake letting them live. We haven't seen the last of them and that worries me."

It did a sight more than worry her—it terrified. They would return. Oh God, she needed a plan. Where to go, what to do.

He twirled Tally around, and they bumped first into the table and then into a chair.

"I know." She swallowed her panic. "But as I watched from the window, I prayed you'd fight the urge." Tally tried to smile, but her mouth wouldn't curve. "Shooting them would only have added more scars to your soul. I know what it's like."

Clay stiffened in surprise and stopped. "I should've guessed you had taken a life, since you wear that gun. I assume you're quite an expert shot."

"It's nothing I like to talk about. I only killed to protect myself and the other escapees." Tally traced the two-inch scar on his cheek. "How did you get this?"

"A saloon fight in Cimarron. A customer lit into one of the working women with his fists. I slung him across the floor. He came up with a broken whiskey bottle." He gave her a wry smile. "My reflexes were dulled by alcohol that night."

It appeared her cowboy was a defender of women, but then, she'd half-suspected that already. Her wedding ring caught the light and winked on her finger. A tiny grin curved her lips. "Let's go to bed."

He brushed her cheek with a knuckle, his eyes darkening. His fresh scent swam around her, intoxicating and exciting. "Only if you wear your hair loose, my angel warrior."

The unfamiliar term jolted her. "What did you just say?"

"My angel warrior, and that describes you perfectly." He lightly brushed a fingertip across her lips. "You're far more than anything I ever could've dreamed up."

His words touched her. Would it be so wrong to let down her guard? She'd thought men with compassion and honor had died with her father and brother. Either Clay was skilled at hiding his true nature, or he was exactly as he appeared. Still, she couldn't help but wonder if he'd turn on her in anger one day when she least expected it.

While it didn't seem possible at this moment, she knew men often changed over time.

"I'm undeserving of admiration, Clay," she said quietly. She had such ugliness inside.

He pushed her hair aside and kissed her neck. "The first time I laid eyes on you, my mouth got all dry and my poor heart about jumped out of my chest. You have a kind of beauty I've never seen before, that comes from the inside and spreads out. Now, I'll check on things while you get ready for bed," he murmured and turned toward the door.

Her gaze followed his lean form. The door closed softly, taking the air with him.

As she changed and brushed her hair, she thought of the

different stages of her life so far. With her parents, she'd been a child, learning about the world. In Creedmore, she'd discovered cruelty far beyond what the mind could comprehend. To survive, she'd had to quit living in dreams and face harsh reality.

Then there was life in Deliverance Canyon with the women like her. She'd been forced to keep watch every second because their lives and safety depended on her.

Now, she was married, with yet another facet of life to learn. This one wasn't so simple. So far, she loved sharing Clay's world with him, but who knew when it would evaporate like smoke through a keyhole? She couldn't let down her guard. Not for a moment. Still, his soft endearment had touched her.

"My angel warrior," she murmured, putting a finger to her lips where a tiny smile formed.

She couldn't wait to lie next to her dreamer's hard body, to feel his gentle breath fanning her face, his hands touching her. For a few precious hours, she could pretend that this world didn't include men like Slade Tarver.

She hadn't always been so distrustful. But then there had been Rowena. A fellow patient, Rowena had befriended Tally, winning her trust by caring for her after a beating. During a weak moment, Tally shared her plans to escape. Only, when she'd put her plans in motion and crawled from a bottom-floor window, Slade Tarver was waiting—along with Pollard Finch.

They'd dragged her away, laughing about how quickly Rowena had spilled the plan.

They'd strapped her to a table and struck the bottoms of her feet with a board until she lost consciousness. When they finally released her, she was weak and in agony, unable to walk. It had taken months to recover.

Lesson learned. Never, ever trust anyone.

Now, Tally wondered why she'd let her need for a gentle touch override everything she knew.

One hard fact hit her—if Slade and his followers got her again, she wouldn't survive.

Her hands shook. Evil had invaded the supposed safety of Devil's Crossing. Although Clay had promised to protect her and Violet with his life, he couldn't. He didn't know what he was up against.

Now that Tarver had found her, she stood at a crossroads. Stay? Or leave?

Sweat formed on her palms. The truth was, there had only been one safe place since Creedmore.

She really hated to leave the new life she'd found with Clay, but she had to see things as they really were instead of how she wished them to be. She quickly re-braided her hair.

Needles of pain suddenly pierced her chest, and for a long moment, her breath hung suspended. She pressed her hands over her heart and willed the episode to pass before Clay came back inside. Cold sweat trickled down her spine. She focused on her breathing, and minutes crept by before she calmed her racing heartbeat and the pain left. Would whatever this was one day take her life? That seemed something she ought to consider.

But later. She had far too much work to do first. She had to get Violet to safety.

When Clay returned, she lay in bed, facing the wall, pretending to be asleep. But instead of relief that he didn't bother her, she found her heart crying for his strong arms around her. Craving for his tender touch, his lips on her skin, kept her awake.

Tally lay stiffly, praying for the morn. She knew what she had to do, but that fact didn't make the decision welcome.

At the soft whisper of dawn, Tally rose with Clay and started breakfast. While the bacon cooked, she dressed Violet and combed the girl's hair. They spoke quietly as a plan formed in Tally's mind. But first, she had to pretend it was a normal day full of work.

Guilt gripped her as the small stone in her ring sparkled in the light. She tried to push it away, but the knowledge of her coming betrayal persisted. She should leave the ring behind. But she couldn't bear to remove it. The silver circle was a symbol of hope, and where she was going, little of that existed.

Tally opened the door and called to Clay. He came in and kissed her cheek as he did each time he entered or left. Immense guilt flooded over her.

Clay sat at the table and reached for a piece of bacon, putting two on Violet's plate. "I put bacon on your plate. Eat up, sweet girl."

"Thank you, Mr. Clay." Violet almost smiled. "One day when I get real brave, I'm gonna see what you look like."

Clay's eyes swung to Tally, and she could tell how Violet's attempt at conversation moved him. The question in his gaze prompted her to explain. "Her fingertips are her eyes, and she sees by running them across things she's curious about."

"Baby girl, you're already one of the bravest people I know. Let me know when you want to see me." He cleared his throat. "Tally, what are your plans today?"

His question caught her off guard and she swallowed guilt. "I think Violet and I will go look for berries. I'd like to make a pie." She glanced up with innocent eyes. "That is, if I can borrow a horse."

"Sure." He shoveled a bite of eggs into his mouth. "I'll need mine, but we have a few extras. I'll rustle one up. I don't want you going far, though—we don't know who might be lurking about. You should find some wild plums a short distance from here. I saw them the other day. But I doubt you'll find any berries. Those will be up near the Canadian River and it's too near Hidetown, which is full of dangerous men."

"It appears plums will have to do." Tally rose to get the coffeepot and refilled Clay's cup. "We have lots to do here to get ready for the new lumber." She thought of her furniture, the mattress Luke was supposed to bring, and hoped he wouldn't be upset to find all his efforts wasted. "And you?"

"I've got to ride out to check on a friend in a camp nearby. He was sick last time I passed by." Worry crossed his brown eyes. Clay would be the kind of man who cared about everyone. "Out here, it's easy to die with no one the wiser."

"When you get this town built, filled with businesses and people, it'll be much better. You're doing a good thing here."

He covered her hand with his and she found the gentle touch almost more than she could bear. She was the biggest traitor. "Tally, I'll make this a good, safe place to live in. I swear it." His deep voice sent warmth through her but couldn't melt the layer of ice inside.

Warrior angel? She scoffed. Warriors didn't run. They stayed and fought, giving their all.

But she also had Violet to consider.

"I know you will." She wished she could stay to help him. A voice whispered in her ear, urging her to tell him. He trusted her. She'd said solemn vows, given her word to stay and make this marriage work. But that was before Tarver. He'd be back, only a matter of time. She knew the bastard inside and out.

She opened her mouth to speak, but he rose and kissed her cheek, then lightly touched the top of Violet's head and went out the door whistling.

The sound meant he was happy.

A hard lump sat in Tally's throat. Leaving would devastate him.

A sudden stillness froze everything inside her. By coming to Devil's Crossing, she'd drawn trouble to his door. Because of her, he was now in Tarver's crosshairs. She couldn't let Clay lose everything he yearned for—possibly even his life.

Dear God! She clapped her hand over her mouth to block a rising sob. She had to leave—for everyone's sake.

Swallowing past the blockage in her throat, she hurried with the dishes and straightened up the dugout. Then she stuffed a bag with their belongings and took Violet's hand. "Let's go, honey."

"I want to play with the goats and Bullet," Violet complained.

"I'd like you to come with me." Tally pulled the girl close for a hug, mindful that she was ruining all their lives. Violet seemed to feel safe here, only she wasn't—and never could be again. Damn Slade Tarver! Why couldn't he let them be?

"It'll be nice feeling the breeze blowing through our hair as we ride," she told Violet.

"Can Bullet come?"

"No, honey. He needs to stay here."

One last glance at the bed where Clay had placed a purple flower on her pillow brought tears stinging the back of her eyes. She'd do anything to stay—except risk being caught and returned to Creedmore. She never should've agreed to marry. Not just Clay, but anyone. She'd never rid herself of the stains on her soul, the blood on her hands, or the men chasing her.

She touched her cheek and the tattoo that had been put there as a mark of ownership. No one would ever own her. The weight of the gun hanging from her hip was reassuring.

The blacksmith, Skeet Malloy, was waiting outside. He tipped his hat. "Mornin', ma'am. It's a mighty beautiful morning for a ride. Clay asked me to bring Sugar over. She's a good horse and not one to leave you stranded." He handed her the reins of a white mare.

"Thank you, Mr. Malloy. I'm sure she'll do real fine." Tally patted Sugar's neck.

The balding, jovial man wiped away the sweat that rolled down one side of his face. She liked his gentle eyes and slow way of talking. Some might say he chewed his words before letting them escape. She couldn't imagine him ever getting mad enough to kill anyone, but apparently he had. Or done something equally bad to be on the run.

Violet threw her arm around Bullet and buried her face in his fur. Her crying ripped Tally's heart out. How could she separate Violet from the dog she already loved so much?

"Don't ride too far now," Malloy warned. "That riffraff over at Mobeetie are a bad bunch. If you have trouble, fire your pistol in the air and we'll come running."

"A good plan." Tally smiled, determined not to lie again. She'd told far too many already.

"What's wrong with the little one?" Skeet asked.

Tally forced a smile. "She wants Bullet to come with us. You know how children are."

"Not exactly, ma'am. It would be a good idea to take him."

Fine. She saw no way around it. She might as well steal Clay's dog and make it complete.

"Guess you're right." She got on Sugar, and Skeet Malloy handed Violet up in front of her.

The jovial blacksmith waved as they rode off with Bullet happily trotting beside them. Tally didn't let herself look back at the place that harbored this ragged group of outlaws. Like her, each man was simply trying to survive as best he could. In the end, though, they were nothing but shadows living on the fringe of society. Their deep yearning to live respectable lives and have families brought tightness to her chest. She prayed they wouldn't give up in the face of the slim odds and her betrayal.

"Where are we going?" Violet clutched her rag doll tightly.

"Back to Deliverance, honey."

Riding in front of Tally, Violet sniffled. "No! I don't want to leave Bullet and the baby goats. Mr. Clay will protect us. He did yesterday. We need his guns."

"Believe me, I don't want to go either."

"Then why?" Violet demanded.

"Those men will be back, and when they come, maybe Mr. Clay won't be near. Deliverance is the only safe place." Tally took a settling breath. In over two years, no one had found them there. She shouldn't have left, shouldn't have allowed the burning need for a proper life influence her thinking.

She had to think with her head, not her heart.

"Please stop." Tears bubbled in Violet's sightless eyes. "Mr. Clay needs us."

Surprise jarred Tally. "Why are you concerned about his welfare? I thought you were afraid of him."

"I am a little. But I heard tears in his voice. He's real sad. I think he might be nice. You said so."

It was also the tears in Clay's voice when they were alone that had shaken Tally, but he was strong. She chewed her lip. For all Brady's strength, too, her brother had died.

Everything was getting jumbled in her head, and it was hard to sort it out. She would when she reached safety.

"You'll have to trust me to know what's best." Tally gently rubbed the girl's small shoulders, wishing things hadn't gotten so complicated.

Maybe they were better off living with no hope at all than in sight of a little. Glimpsing a life of possibilities made going back to nothing twenty times emptier. The farther she got from Devil's Crossing, the more life seemed to ebb from her. She swallowed a rising sob.

All she had to do was turn back. Everything she yearned for waited for her to claim it.

Each moment alone with her husband flashed before her. His kindness. The purple flower on her pillow. His respect of her space and recognizing the fact that she needed time. His body next to hers when they danced. How he'd thrown Tarver into the dirt and showed the piece of dung how small and insignificant he was when confronted with true power in the right hands.

Tally snorted. Some warrior angel. She'd tucked tail and run.

Turn around and go back, a voice said. *Clay can protect you. Tarver has no chance against someone with strength and honor like him. You made promises that were supposed to have meant something.*

Violet rode silent and still, facing the stark landscape in front of them. Bullet followed loyally at their side.

She realized then that she couldn't do it—she couldn't take *everything* from Clay. She had to send the dog back. Tally stopped the mare and dismounted. "Go back, Bullet. You can't come."

The dog stared at her, his tongue lolling out the side of his mouth. He started toward her. Tally picked up a stick and shook it at him. "No. Go home!"

"No, Mama. No!" Violet cried. "Please let him come."

Confusion crossed Bullet's dark eyes. He cocked his head to the side and whined.

"Get out of here!" Tally hollered, a tear trickling down her face.

Bullet lay down and stretched his forelegs out in front of

him and began to crawl. Between his barking and Violet's sobs, she could barely think.

Finally, she got back on the mare. Holding Violet securely, she took off at a gallop, and though the dog tried his best to keep up, they soon left him behind.

Feeling like she'd killed the faithful companion, Tally kept a sharp eye out for other riders, her gun within reach. An hour down the little-used trail Luke had taken when they came, she stopped at a stream rising from some rocks where she could water the horse. Off to the side was a deep ravine.

Always conscious of their safety, she dismounted, pulled her gun, and strode to the drop-off. It plunged a good twenty feet, and a tangle of brush grew down into the gully. She scanned every inch but saw no one lurking and slid the gun back into her holster.

Violet was still sobbing, somewhere the dog hated her, and the pretty little horse was giving her the evil eye.

She'd been stupid to think running was best. She'd get some water and think.

The decision made, she returned to Violet, still waiting on the white mare. "It's a hot day. Would you like a drink of water, honey?" She swung the girl from the saddle.

"No." Violet dragged her arm across her nose.

"All right." Tally led her to some big rocks all jumbled on top of each other as though toys, carelessly tossed. "You can rest here."

Violet sat with a long face. Tally led the horse to the water and lay down beside the stream to scoop some into her own mouth. A bird squawked at her from a clump of broomweed, and overhead, the blue sky seemed to stretch forever. She removed the bandana from around her neck and wet it to wash her face. The day was a scorcher and it wasn't even noon.

She rose and let her gaze sweep the miles of open country. Violet had never had any pets in Deliverance because noisy animals would attract hunters. Now, she'd given the lonely child what she most wanted—a dog and goats to play with—only to snatch them away. She was a failure at motherhood.

Apparently at marriage as well.

But she was finished jerking back and forth, wanting to run and yet longing to return. She made her decision—she *would* go back, and she'd fight hard to be the warrior angel Clay thought she was.

"Okay, honey, let's go home." Her excited announcement was met with silence. Tally turned, alarm crawling up her spine.

Violet was gone.

"Where are you, Violet? This isn't funny. It's too dangerous away from here, sweet girl." Tally's heart pounded and her breath came in panicked gasps. She climbed the rocks, getting a long scrape on her arm, desperate to see better. But there was no sign of a little, lost darling.

What had happened to her? Tally hadn't heard other riders or the crunch of footsteps. She glanced at the way they'd come. Had Violet decided to try to walk back? Very possible, the state the girl had been in. Back down on the ground, she walked along the ravine, checking for anything to indicate Violet had tumbled down. She saw nothing—no loose dirt, no torn fabric, no doll. Finally, she returned to the area where Violet had sat, but the jumble of footprints made it difficult to tell much of anything. Finally, she climbed onto the mare and rode toward large clumps of juniper, mesquite, and scrub oak in hopes Violet might've wandered into them.

"Violet!" Tally rode through the brush and between scrawny trees that barely offered any shade. She called the girl's name over and over with no response. Fear knotted in her stomach. Poisonous snakes, tarantulas, scorpions, and sharp-toothed animals thrived in this environment. Slade Tarver could've taken her. Anything could've happened.

Her breath caught in the tightness of her throat. Even angry and upset, Violet would answer—if she could.

A dark silence spread inside and around, choking her.

Clay's words sounded in her head. *Out here, it's easy to die with no one the wiser.*

Tally had to face one very hard, very terrifying fact—Violet might not answer because she was dead.

Ten

INDECISION TWISTED INSIDE TALLY. SHOULD SHE STAY, GO back, or keep moving forward?

Violet wouldn't know which direction to strike out for Devil's Crossing—if that was where she'd headed. But she could've gone anywhere. To check all directions would take too much time.

Waiting for some sign to tell her which way to go, she swung toward the thunder of pounding hooves. One rider coming fast. Tally drew her Colt and took cover behind a mesquite.

She inhaled some panicked breaths and waited. She recognized Clay's brown-and-white paint, Sundown, first. Then she recognized him by the set of his broad shoulders. Weak with relief, she stepped from her hiding place.

Clay reined up. Grim lines cut into his face, accentuating the scar. His dark eyes revealed confusion and hurt. The sharp edge in his voice cut through her like a knife. "This isn't the short ride you described. Thank God Malloy watched the direction you came and hurried to find me. Mind telling me why you left?"

"I will, but right now I have to find Violet." Now that help had arrived, she couldn't stop her mouth from quivering.

"What do you mean?" Clay dismounted and reached for her, searching her face. His arms were the one place she wanted to be. "Where is she? Did someone take her?"

"I don't know." She straightened her spine and told him everything. "I didn't hear any horses or footsteps or anything." She rested her forehead against Clay's shoulder. "Violet was really upset at leaving Bullet and the goats. I've never seen her that way. Honestly, I really think she struck out on her own, walking back. Only—"

"Only she can't see which direction to go," he finished for her. "It's hard telling where she is."

"And she doesn't know the dangers of this land. She could've been snakebit or anything. What do we do? How will we find her?"

Clay shaded his eyes and glanced up at the sun, possibly to check the location in the sky. "How long has it been?"

"I don't know. Maybe twenty minutes."

"Afoot, she couldn't have gone far. That's a good thing. I can cover more ground, since I know the terrain." He folded his arms around her. "I'm glad you're safe. You can't imagine my worry. We're going to find her. I won't stop looking until we do." He paused and the anger was back. "But after that— you promised to give me until spring."

Tally cringed at the hard tone of his voice. She'd deeply hurt him and eroded his trust. She'd walked out on him just like those other women in his past. Did the same damn thing.

"I deserve everything you're itching to say." She stepped back and dropped her shield back into place. "But Violet first. Tell me what you want me to do."

Clay rubbed the back of his neck. "I'll look around the creek, see if I can spot her footprints. Since I didn't see her coming, we have to assume she probably went either north or east, toward Deliverance."

"South of the creek is a deep ravine. What if she stepped off the edge and tumbled down? I looked from up here but didn't go down there." She glanced up. "Clay, what have I done?"

His stricken eyes shot pain through her. "Don't borrow trouble. Mount up."

They returned to the creek, and Clay searched every inch of ground, looking for any clues. Tally stood silent, listening to the sound of the creek, the wind, the birds, the rustle of the brush. But there were no cries from a lost little girl.

Clay straightened and moved slowly around the boulders, reading the prints. Tally held the reins of both horses and followed. Finally, he spoke. "She went this way."

Relief spread through her. At least they had a starting place.

Only, ahead of them lay a series of gullies and drop-offs with a single narrow trail winding through them. They had to find her before she got hurt.

Tally froze with that thought. Danger lay everywhere.

She hurried to catch up to Clay. His face was set, his eyes glued to the ground. He seemed locked deep in his own thoughts and she doubted he would even hear her speak, so she stayed silent and searched both sides of the trail for clues, listening to every sound.

"Violet!" Clay hollered. "Violet, I'm here. Come out, baby girl. Let's go home."

There was no answer. They went a little farther and Tally spied her rag doll next to a bush. "There, Clay."

He picked the doll up and dusted it off. His haunted, desperate eyes darkened, but he said nothing, just stuffed the doll in his saddlebag.

They stopped to call her name again and again.

"I can make out faint footprints that must belong to her. I'll find her soon." But Clay directed his hopeful, yet tight, words into the distance, not at her.

Tally swallowed bitter regret. She deserved his anger. Her betrayal had cost her a friend, a husband. "I hope you're right." She yearned to beg his forgiveness but now was not the time. He wasn't of a mind to do anything except find the little girl who needed him.

Suddenly, Clay came to a dead stop and raised his head.

"What do you hear?" she asked.

"A faint cry." He cupped his hands around his mouth. "Violet! Where are you?"

"Here," came Violet's weak reply. "I'm here."

Clay plunged down the right side of the trail and into a thicket. Tally followed, ignoring the sting of the thorns pricking her arms and penetrating her dress to the soft flesh beneath. Nothing mattered except Violet's safety.

"Help me!" The girl sounded near.

They rounded a small incline and there sat Violet, holding her leg, tears leaving trails through the dirt on her face.

Clay rushed forward and scooped her up. "I've got you, baby girl. You're safe."

"I waited and waited for you. Where is Mama?" Violet asked.

"I'm here, honey." Tally kissed her cheek. "I was so worried."

Violet gave a shuddering sigh. "I don't want to leave you. I don't want to leave my dog."

Tally met Clay's angry stare. "You don't have to, honey," she said. "We're going home."

"I'm glad. I fell and rolled a long way. My leg hurts."

"I'm sorry." Tally wiped away Violet's tears. "We'll fix you up as good as new."

"You bet, baby girl." Clay's voice was hoarse. He carried Violet up the incline, held her while Tally mounted up, then handed her over.

Clay's cold features told Tally all she needed. Now for their talk and facing his feelings of betrayal.

She prayed he'd understand why she'd left. But if he didn't?

She refused to think about that.

❧

Winding their way back home, Clay glanced over at Violet, asleep in Tally's arms, lulled by the rocking of the mare. His heart melted at the teardrops lingering on the child's lashes. They'd almost lost her. The experience seemed to have changed the girl and lessened her fear of him, letting him carry her up the steep incline, not shrinking from his touch. She'd wanted to come home—to him.

He glanced at Tally's stone face. She hadn't spoken since finding Violet. The beautiful eyes of the woman he'd married were somber, sad, and lonely.

"Why did you run?" The question squeezed through his stiff lips. "Why did you break your promise to wait until spring? I thought your word meant something."

Her winter-blue eyes lifted. "I panicked. All I could think was that Slade Tarver had found me. In Deliverance Canyon, no one had ever found me. I felt exposed here."

"I vowed to protect you." His quiet words had the effect of a rifle shot. "Don't you trust me to keep *my* word?"

Tally kept her eyes averted, her voice lowered. "I can't trust anyone, but I'm really trying with you, Clay. I've suffered the sting of betrayal before, and a lesson was hammered into my brain. Tarver, Finch, and Abram knew a million ways to make you wish you were dead." Tally chewed her bottom lip. She swung to face him, and he couldn't bear her hard gaze that cut like bits of glass. "They caught me once"—she struggled to speak—"and I paid dearly for trying to escape. That's why even to this day, I walk with pain. You've seen my misshapen feet."

"I think it's time to talk about it." Unimaginable horrors flashed into mind, squeezing the narrow passage of his throat, and his words came out bruised. "What did they do?"

"Maybe it will help you understand my reasoning."

"I'm listening. I want to know what made you so distrustful."

"A woman I thought was a friend betrayed me."

Clay's heart ached as he listened to her speak about Rowena and the foiled escape plan that led to Tarver beating Tally's feet with a board, breaking the bones. With each new revelation, he wondered again at her will to survive. There was surely a lot more that had happened deep inside Creedmore. The darkness inside him roared, fighting to get out, to find some balm to soothe her wounded spirit. He moved his large paint closer and took her icy hand.

Her eyes met his and he saw the depth of her suffering. "I meant my marriage vows with all my heart." Her voice broke. "Leaving was foolish and I realize that." She paused and was silent so long he didn't think she'd continue. Finally, she spoke, anguish in each word. "If they catch me again, they'll kill me. I know that as sure as I'm breathing. That's what drove me to saddle up."

The fear and anger in her voice shot an ache deep inside him that no tonic, medicine, or ointment could fix. Her blue gaze had darkened to almost black and all the makings of a frightening summer storm roiled in their depths. But she still held that jutting chin raised. Tarver and his group might've put the fear of God in her, but they hadn't destroyed her will.

"I've found men who prey on women turn to worms when up against someone who's not afraid to call them out." He leaned to brush a tendril of hair back. "Darlin', I'm not afraid of the devil. I've faced him many times. They won't get near you again. I'll make sure of it." Clay would do whatever it took to guarantee her safety. He understood a lot better now, and all the hurt and bitterness he'd held toward her for leaving vanished. He'd made a lot of headway into figuring her out, but even so, he knew he'd only scratched the surface.

What else was buried so deeply that maybe she could never share?

And there was more, that much he knew.

"I know you're not afraid." She moved her hand from his to steady the reins. "It's me. I have trouble believing that good will triumph over evil because I've seen too much bad." Her brittle laugh appeared to mimic her state of mind. "You got a rotten deal when you married me, Clay Colby."

The set of her mouth, her words, her stiff posture seemed to brace her against a raging storm.

"Let me be the judge of that. Tally, I have to make sure… Do you want to return to Deliverance Canyon? If so, I'll take you and make sure you get there safe. But, if you stay with me, I need to know you'll never sneak out again. Make up your mind now, so I'll know what to expect."

"I won't make promises I can't keep."

Her words sent hurt barreling bone deep into him. He blew out a breath. "Fair enough."

"I only know that I want to live in Devil's Crossing. With you. I'm just not sure Slade Tarver will let me and that makes me fighting mad."

The silence between them was broken only by the scolding of nearby birds in a scrub oak and a rabbit hopping across the trail.

At last, Tally spoke. "Clay, you're a good man and don't deserve someone like me. I don't know how to be a wife, how to let anyone into my heart. All I know is how to be me—a woman who's had to be a caretaker and protector.

I don't have a clue how to turn that job over to someone else, even though I yearn to. I can only depend on myself with certainty."

Her chin quivered. He wanted to pull her into his arms and tell her everything would be all right. But he didn't deal in falsehoods.

"Tally, we both have things to overcome. We'll never be perfect. I won't give up on you." He glanced at her, wishing he could read her mind. "But don't you give up on me either."

His words were met with stony silence.

"Can you at least tell me the next time you take a notion to leave? That's all I'll ask."

She swung her cool winter gaze to him. "I can do that."

He had to try to fix this situation—give her some room to decide what she truly wanted.

"To ease your fears, I'm going to implement a few changes." He maneuvered his paint around a patch of cactus. "I'm moving out of the dugout. You and baby girl will have it to yourselves. I won't come back until I can earn your trust and I know for sure you want me."

"Clay, that's your home. I can't ask that of you."

"It's not anything but dirt without you there in body, mind, and spirit." His voice became raspy. "When you get ready, we'll try again."

Although he understood why she had trouble trusting, disappointment flared at having a wife he couldn't hold, couldn't lie next to. But clearly things had been moving too fast. Besides, he had to protect himself. The lesson he took from this was that Tally had the power to destroy him. If she left for good, he feared the deep, dark pit he'd fall into. Only this time, he wouldn't have the strength to crawl out.

The best thing he could do was protect her and Violet, no matter what.

"I'm blocking the back entrance to Devil's Crossing, and we'll post guards at the front day and night," he continued. "I'm going to do everything within my power to make you safe. I won't betray your confidence, but I'll stress to the others how critical this is and that we have to keep strangers out. Given what happened, they won't argue."

"Your town won't survive if you bar everyone from coming in."

"We can close the way in until we get the town built. By then, I *will* have taken care of the threat." He glanced at Violet, asleep in Tally's arms. "I haven't seen this vision of what life can be like only to have it slip through my fingers."

Tally sucked in a quick breath. "What are you going to do?"

"Whatever I have to. Might be best to take the fight to them." Already, a plan was forming. He needed to make a trip to Creedmore and settle this once and for all.

"No! Please." She clutched his arm, color drained from her face. "You could be caught, Clay. They'll kill you. Don't do this because of me."

A glance at her poor foot in the nearest stirrup set his blood boiling. He'd kill the torturing bastards as soon as he got the chance.

His eyes locked with hers. "If not for you—who?"

He'd vowed to protect and care for her for the rest of his days, and no one and nothing would stop him. Tally had given his life meaning and brought peace to his soul.

Now it was time to give the same to her.

Eleven

TALLY STOOD SILENTLY, LOOKING OUT THE WINDOW OF THE dugout at the men working on clearing the last of the burned-out buildings. It was just past the noon hour and the sun created shimmering waves on the rock walls of the hideout.

Jack Bowdre, who had a little medical training, had just checked Violet's leg and said that to his untrained eye it appeared to be just a sprain and scrapes. After treating the scratches with salve and wrapping her knee, the former lawman had limped out.

Tally realized she was twisting her wedding ring and glanced down. Light from the window glinted on the silver band, bringing out the sparkle from the small stone. The day she'd arrived, she'd stood in this same spot and worried about having to settle, and just once wanted to be all of someone's world. She had gotten that only to ruin it. Now she had to settle for what she could get. She wondered at Clay's real reason for moving out. He'd claimed it was for her sake, but was it? He'd been so angry. Not that she blamed him. He had every right. And he'd never believe she'd changed her mind and had decided to come back before Violet disappeared.

Maybe he'd already had a gut-full of trying to live with someone haunted by dark memories she couldn't shake.

Behind her, Clay quietly stuffed some of his things into a burlap sack. Her heart was breaking. Violet was on her bed, playing with Bullet, even though she kept turning toward Tally. Whining, the dog laid his muzzle on her hip.

Strange how the girl had the ability to sense trouble in her world of blackness. Violet seemed to know she and Clay were having difficulties. The back of Tally's eyes burned.

Why couldn't she find the right words to say, to tell Clay to stay? Who would hold her when the night terrors came?

Clay put his sack by the door and stared at the pile of raw leather in the corner. "Do you mind if I leave that? I have no other place that will protect the leather from the elements."

"Yes, of course." Tally would welcome things that reminded her of him.

"Are you mad at us?" Violet whispered.

He glanced at Tally. "No, I'm not mad, honey. When you grow up, you'll understand."

Violet frowned. "Where are you gonna sleep?"

"I have a place all picked out in the house I'm building for you and your pretty mama."

Tally moved to Clay, yearning to lay her head on his shoulder. She needed him to ground her, but she didn't dare be so familiar. Instead, she rested her hand on his arm. Violet's questions were ones Tally wanted to ask him. He was solid beneath her touch. Only, would he vanish like smoke if they couldn't reconcile?

Violet let out a deep sigh. "Someday when I get real big, I'm going to find all the bad people and shoot 'em."

How the child related Clay's leaving to bad people, Tally didn't know. Maybe she thought Clay was going to look for them. She swallowed a rising sob. Watching him pack up was tearing her heart out. This was his home. If anyone was going to leave, it should be her.

"Tally, can I have a word outside?" Clay asked.

"Sure." She kissed Violet's cheek and put her doll in her arms. "I'll be right back, honey."

Violet raised her head and whispered loudly, "Tell him you're sorry so he'll stay. Please?"

"I will." Though it probably wouldn't do a lick of good. Tally picked up the sack Clay had dropped by the door and followed him out. Why did it feel like he was moving to the other side of the world? She already felt so alone, so sad, the house an empty shell. Nothing more than a place to sleep—and pray that daylight would come.

Since her arrival, she'd thought the windmill sang a song. Now it seemed to be crying.

Several of the men shot curious glances their way when they stepped into the sunlight, then went right back to work.

"Clay, what will you tell the men?"

"That I need to guard, that you and Violet don't feel safe, and that I need to work on our house." He held his hat in one hand and tucked a strand of hair behind her ear with the other, his hand moving to her jaw as if desperate for some connecting touch. Sorrow in his brown gaze pierced her. "Don't worry. I'll protect your confidence." He inhaled deeply, the two-inch scar on his face white against his tanned skin. "I've never been much good at sorry-saying, but I do apologize for failing to see how deep your fears go. I should've known."

"No, the apology is mine to make. I betrayed you and I'm so sorry." She nuzzled her face against his hand. "I don't want to lose what we've found. Will you hold me in your arms and dance with me each night before bed until we can live together again?"

Surprise rippled across his features. "I'll do anything you want."

His sudden smile sent her heart into a frenzy. His white teeth dazzled against his tanned face. The breeze blew a lock of hair onto his forehead and she yearned to brush it back. To press her lips to his. But she stood there like a smitten schoolgirl.

"Dallas Hawk can play the heck out of a fiddle. I'll ask him to play for us tonight." Clay put on his worn hat and adjusted it. The shadow of the brim made it difficult to see his eyes.

"I'd like that." Tally took in his lean form and her heart raced.

"I've been meaning to talk to you about something. We still need to teach Violet how to get around. Blind folk usually walk with a long cane that lets them manage quite well to avoid obstacles and alert them to danger. The men and I will build trails for her to follow around the town, and stretch ropes to guide her."

"You're right, Clay. I've been remiss in teaching her here, but I did work with her some at our home in Deliverance

Canyon—like counting steps to chairs and the door, feeling her way around the house—but I wasn't able to build her anything special."

"Glad we're in agreement. I'll make her a walking stick." Clay lowered his mouth to her ear. "Meet me by the campfire tonight and we'll have our waltz."

"Tonight then."

He pushed back his hat just a bit and winked, sending flurries slow-dancing up her spine. This outlaw seemed an expert in knowing how to flirt. Heat swept the length of her body.

Before she could think of anything to say, the moment passed and Clay straightened. "Right now, I need to block off that entrance and post a guard."

"I'll take Violet to see the goats. I'm truly sorry. About everything." Tally glanced down, unable to bear the sadness in his face.

Why couldn't she could be a true wife to Clay, trusting him with all her heart and soul?

Clay put a hand under her chin and gently brought her face around. "I'll gladly work my fingers to the bone every second of every day if it means taking worry from you. I chose to care for you from the start, and that hasn't changed. This is what a true husband does for his wife. Never feel guilty for anything where I'm concerned."

But I do, and pretty words can't change that.

He turned to walk off.

"Clay?"

"Yeah?" He swung around.

"Despite how it appears, I'm no quitter. Please understand. I didn't want to leave but I thought I had to protect Violet." She was going to fight to keep her marriage.

"Glad to hear it, Tally. I hope you find what you need to give us a chance." Without saying more, he picked up the bags and his bedroll and went to join the others at the burned buildings. Loneliness seemed to ooze from his tall, powerful figure.

Tally bit her trembling lip. Why couldn't she forget and live her life? Why hold on to her pain?

Violet groped her way through the door, accompanied by Bullet, and slipped her hand in Tally's. "It'll be okay, Mama."

Tally closed her eyes for just a moment and took a calming breath. An empty feeling sat in the pit of her stomach. "Let's go see the goats."

"Can I sleep with one of the babies?"

"No, honey. They have to stay with their mamas. If not, their mamas will be sad and cry. They need their babies with them just like I need you with me."

Violet let out a long-suffering sigh. "Okay, but I really want to."

"I know." Tally helped Violet navigate up the incline where the goats usually stayed. A sudden thought hit her and she wondered if the root cellar, small though it was, had something in it to make a pie with. That would help dispel this heavy gloom. She sat Violet on a rock and gathered two goat kids for her to play with. Bullet lay at her feet, his eyes sharp, always on guard.

The men were also only a few steps away. Violet would be all right.

"Sit right here for a moment." Tally kissed the top of the girl's head.

"Okay, Mama."

Tally hurried to the root cellar next to the house that Clay must've dug when he made his home here. She brushed aside the spiderwebs and stepped inside. The shelves were only partially filled. Nothing was put up, because of course they didn't have a garden. A few non-spoilage items from a mercantile sat there. She blew off the dust and rotated each can, finding three large containers of peaches. Those would work. Instead of a pie, she'd make a cobbler for everyone. With the fiddle music and dancing, it would seem like a party.

They might just find a moment of fleeting happiness—even if it vanished with dawn.

≈

That night, Clay sat with the men around the campfire. Darkness spread over them like a wool blanket. His heart was heavy that everything he'd yearned for seemed to be slipping away, and he kept losing track of the conversation. A few hours ago, he'd sent two of the men out with instructions to find Slade Tarver and the others and make sure they weren't doubling back. Now, he regretted not telling the men to kill them. Every fiber of his being wanted them dead and in the ground. His family wouldn't be safe until they were.

He drew his attention back to the men around him. They'd feasted on rabbit and quail for supper but Tally hadn't come out. Maybe she'd forgotten her promise to dance with him. Or maybe she hadn't meant to at all.

Maybe his wife was a person who couldn't keep her word. He'd met folks like that, who had good intentions but never followed through.

Had she made the request out of guilt? Who knew?

His fellow outlaws kept glancing at him. Sure, they wondered what had happened. He saw the questions in their eyes, but no one asked. Instead, they talked of plans for the town and whose turn it was to relieve the guard at the entrance.

Jack nudged the preacher. "I think it's your turn, Ridge."

"Hey, I had the afternoon shift." Ridge glanced at Skeet Malloy and drawled, "If memory serves, you haven't taken a shift today."

Clay tossed a stick into the fire. "I don't care who does it," he snapped. "I just want someone up there. I'm guarding from midnight to dawn. No one had better get through unless it's someone we know. We're keeping Tally and baby girl safe."

His exploding anger brought mute stares from the group but Clay was past caring. Misery wound through him. He stared toward the lit dugout. Everything he cared about was in there. What were Tally and Violet doing? If Tally wasn't coming, why wouldn't she let baby girl come and sit by the fire? He'd just begun to make headway with her.

For two cents, he'd knock on the door and ask why.

Just then, Tally and Violet stepped out. Tally was struggling to carry something and had no hands to guide Violet. He noticed the wince she tried to hide as she walked. Clay jerked to his feet and rushed to help as unexpected happiness over a kept promise surged inside him.

"Here, let me either have that pan or take baby girl."

"Hi, Mr. Clay," Violet said, angling her head toward the sound of his voice, clutching Bullet, slowly feeling her way across the uneven ground. She stumbled and went down on one knee. Clay picked her up.

"Hi, yourself, sweetheart."

Tally chewed her bottom lip. "I should've called for you to come help, but I thought I could manage." She glanced up. "I made a surprise. I hope you like it."

She didn't smile but that was all right. She was here and Clay was up for the challenge. The men jumped to their feet and one offered her his seat.

The firelight brought out golden strands woven through the red and made Tally's hair a dazzling shimmer in the glow. "Thank you, Mr. Hawk, but I'm not ready to sit just yet. I have more to bring out."

Again, he noticed pain crossing her face and wished she'd take Hawk up on the chair.

Regardless, she went around the circle and said hello to each, touching a shoulder here, an arm there. Clay watched the men's happy smiles at being treated so politely. He knew they treasured each word and noticed how the mood had suddenly shifted from somber to happy.

He carefully took the cast-iron pan that was wrapped in flour-sack dish towels. Setting it on a small table they'd brought out from the saloon, he took Violet's hand. "I'll keep her with me while you finish. Or tell me what you want and I'll go get it."

"No, that's fine. There isn't much else. You stay here," she insisted, and told Violet the same.

His gaze followed her trim figure as she strode back to the abode. The soft sway of her hips with each stride set his heart thudding. Tally was one fine-looking woman. And she belonged to him—as long as he could earn her trust before spring.

Twelve

THE PEACH COBBLER WAS THE BEST CLAY HAD EVER TASTED. OF course, the fact that Tally sat beside him and baby girl seemed to have shed a lot of fear of him might've had something to do with it. A warm feeling wrapped around him like a honeysuckle vine in summer.

Dallas Hawk set his empty bowl on the table and reached for his fiddle. He drew his bow slowly across the strings, and the makeshift town was soon filled with sweet music.

Clay stood and held out his hand to Tally. "May I have this dance, pretty lady?"

Her eyes darkened in the shadows. "Yes, indeed, Mr. Colby."

Despite the formality, Tally was light in his arms. He could hardly breathe with her so near. He buried his face in her hair and inhaled her sweet fragrance. Her curves molded against his hard body as though she'd been created just for him. The night was just about perfect. A full moon came out and shone down, blessing them with silvery rays of light.

Clay held her close, and they glided effortlessly across what remained of the grass burned by the heat of the summer sun. The open space allowed them to make sweeping circles for once.

He placed his mouth on her temple, breathing deeply and counting his blessings. "Thank you for this."

"I know how you set such store by dancing. And I like it too. I had forgotten how happy it makes me."

"I think the moon is jealous of your beauty. You don't know the picture you make. I'm glad you wore your hair down." The ends of it brushed across his arm. He inhaled the lavender fragrance, pleased that she enjoyed using the outdoor bathing closet.

He twirled her around with one hand and she laughed. The

sound made him feel like letting out a whoop. He brought her back into his arms and she melted against him, so warm and tantalizing, with just a hint of danger lurking underneath. Strange how a change of scenery made such a difference in her mood. He closed his eyes and imagined running his hand over her silky body.

A sudden thought struck him. He stopped. "I just remembered your feet. You should sit down."

Tally shook her head. "No. When you're holding me, I don't feel my feet. It's like I'm dancing on a fluffy cloud. They'll be fine for a little while."

Her admission sent happiness cartwheeling through him. "Good."

A hunger rose inside, more powerful than any he'd ever known. He longed to make her his in every way. Maybe this was a start. His self-imposed exile might not last too long, not if he had his way.

They danced to another tune and Clay relished every second with her in his arms, her heart beating next to his.

Tally glanced up. "I forgot to ask. How was the friend you went to check on earlier?"

"He's up and around. I was glad to see it." Clay twirled her around and brought her back against him. "I apologize for my anger. If I'd known what Tarver had done to you, I'd have put a bullet in his head when I had the chance."

The breeze lifted a tendril of hair and dropped it across her face. Clay smoothed it back, watching her expression darken as it seemed to do each time mention was made of the man.

"He'll be back to even the score, Clay." Her voice was flat. Resigned.

"Let's not ruin tonight. We came to dance." Clay swung her back into time to the music.

If and when the bunch did come, they'd find his Remington cocked and loaded.

But for now, he soaked up the moonlight, the fragrance of the land, and his warrior angel pressed against him. *Ahhh*. He could get real spoiled.

After his dance with Tally ended, each of the men clamored for a turn. That they treated her with respect, like a treasure, made Clay happy. They all dreamed of homes and family just like he did.

He sat next to Violet and watched the rapture on her face. Maybe she hadn't heard music in a while—or ever.

"Want to dance, baby girl?" he asked.

"I want to, but…I'm scared."

"Of me?"

"Will you hurt me?" she asked in a small voice.

The air left him as though someone had driven a fist into his gut. He took her hands. "I will never, ever cause you any hurt. You know why?"

She shook her head.

"Because you're my little girl now and I love you."

"Nobody ever loved me before except Mama Tally. My real daddy said I was the devil's child. Are you sure you love me?"

"I'm sure. How about a dance?"

"Maybe for a minute. Can my mama see me?"

"Yes, she's very close and she's smiling."

"Okay." The child waited for his touch with a slow smile stretching across her face.

Clay set her on his boots and held her secure. As he moved to the music, he watched the joy in the child's face. Though she never complained, her dark world had to be terrifying at times. He could take a lesson in courage from her.

Violet raised her face. "Music makes me feel like Cinderella."

"Cinderella?"

"Mama tells me stories, and one of them is about a girl named Cinderella."

"Oh, I see." The corners of Clay's mouth twitched. "Does this story have anything to do with cinders?"

"No. It's about a girl who meets a handsome prince, but he won't look at her because she's very poor. Her fairy godmother gives her some glass shoes except she loses one. Then the handsome prince finds the shoe and they get married. Kinda like you, Mr. Clay. When I was lost, you came and found me."

"I sure did." A lump blocked his throat.

What had come over the child to be so talkative? Not that he would complain. This was the start he'd hoped for. Maybe it would get easier with the ice broken.

Violet didn't dance long before she wanted to find Tally. Clay took her to where her mama was sitting, giving her feet a rest.

Tally kissed her cheek. "Did you have a good time, honey?"

"Uh-huh, I liked it."

Happiness burst inside Clay's chest. He was making headway.

The moon rose higher and higher in the sky until at last the party ended. Dallas Hawk put away his fiddle and the men adjourned to the makeshift saloon.

Clay carried a sleepy Violet and walked Tally home. At the door, he set the girl on her feet just inside the dugout.

"Good night, Mr. Clay." Violet yawned. "Thank you for the music."

"You're welcome, baby girl."

"Honey, I'll be along in a minute. Just sit at the table. It's six steps to the right." Tally propped the empty cobbler pan on her hip and pulled the door shut, leaving herself and Clay alone. "Thank you, Clay. I had a wonderful time. It was almost as if I was a girl again, at home on my daddy's ranch. I've never had anyone court me."

"Then get used to it, because this wasn't a one-time thing."

He brushed a knuckle across her tattooed cheek, wishing like hell he could remove the constant reminder of the hellish place. He wondered if there was a way to take it off. If so, that would free not only Tally, but the other women who had been branded the same way. But there was no doctor around to ask.

"You don't know how you've changed my life already, Tally. You and Violet have given me a reason to get up in the mornings and double my efforts on this town."

The moonlight scampered through her hair as she met his gaze. "I'm glad we help."

"A sight more than that. Loneliness and death walked in

my shadow each moment of every day. I used to curl up with a bottle of whiskey at night and escape into oblivion." He allowed a grin. "I've lost my taste for liquor. Now, I crave the scent of lavender and your beautiful face."

Tally laid a light palm against his jaw. "You don't have to flatter me with pretty words. I'm glad you found what you need, but I can't take any credit. Thank you for tonight. I loved it."

"This is only the beginning." He moved closer and lowered his head to press his lips lightly to hers. The kiss rekindled sleeping embers, and sudden heat flared through his body.

Oh, for one night with his warrior angel, skin touching skin.

Feeling the wild beating of her heart and knowing he'd caused it.

To make love until dawn.

He explored the smooth lines of her back, the ridges of her spine, his breath mingling with hers. The sweet taste of peaches met his tongue, adding to the special, unexpected moment.

Tally gripped his vest with her free hand, a promise whispering in the gentle breeze.

Ending the kiss, Clay pushed back disappointment that things could go no further tonight. He couldn't live the rest of his days with hunger constantly gnawing on him. Still, he wouldn't regret giving Tally space, and time, to trust him. She needed room to discover who he was and learn that she could believe in him.

He knew the cobbler, the dancing, the kissing had done wonders for him. With luck, it had for her too. Maybe, just maybe, he would be back in her bed before too much longer.

❧

Clay kept watch all night, listening for trouble and ready to take action if it called. To while away the hours, he found a hefty branch of a mesquite tree. After stripping away the bark and smoothing it out by the light of the moon, he adjusted the length to fit Violet. It would do quite well and he'd start teaching her how to use it in the morning.

Not that he really knew much about the teaching part, since he'd only known one blind man. He'd have to rely on logic and pray it would be enough. Somehow, he'd teach the girl to be independent. That was important.

Just as the sky began to lighten and the town stirred, he heard the jangle of traces. Minutes later, he noticed a heavily laden wagon approaching. He made out two women and an old man, and they appeared harmless enough. He grabbed Violet's walking stick and scrambled down from his perch to plant himself in front of the barriers. The obstructions amounted to wagons loaded with hay that could be easily rolled aside.

"Morning," he said. "Can I help you?"

The old man removed his hat and scratched his slick, bald head. It appeared his snow-white hair had slid off and his mouth and his chin had caught it. "Morning, sir. Would this be Devil's Crossing?"

Surprise jolted Clay. No one but outlaws knew of this place, and these people definitely weren't the lawless sort. Clay glanced at the towering load of belongings. If one thing shifted, it was all coming down. "You've found it. Do you have business here?"

"We're coming to settle," said the old woman sitting next to the man. "We heard what you're trying to do here, and we want to help."

The old man patted her hand. "I'm Tobias January and this is my wife, Belle."

A younger woman sitting next to Belle lowered her head covering. "Hi, Clay."

Clay moved closer to get a better look. "Rebel? Rebel Avery?"

"For a moment, I thought you might've forgotten me." Rebel laughed and leaned forward, her green eyes sparkling. "I've missed you. Cimarron wasn't the same after you left."

"You mean quieter?" Clay had done his share of hell-raising and had kept the undertaker in business.

"That too, but I meant to say boring. You livened that town up. When Tobias and Belle said they were coming, I asked to ride along." Rebel's black hair slid over her shoulder and spilled over her large bosom. "We have to make up for lost time, cowboy."

Rebel had worked in the Wildcat Saloon in Cimarron and they'd shared good times and bad. But now his thoughts were on how Tally was going to take a brash woman like Rebel.

One who'd staked her claim on him five years previous.

He had to make it plain that things had changed. "I'm married, Rebel." Clay's statement was met with uncomfortable silence.

Finally, Rebel forced a laugh. "You always were a kidder."

"Not joking. I tied the knot a few days ago. I can't wait for you to meet her." Clay just hoped Tally didn't shoot her on the spot. He turned to Tobias January. "Drive on in. We'll have breakfast soon. I'll introduce you to my wife and the others, then you can pick out a spot to camp until we can get you a more permanent home."

Tobias cackled. "We weren't expecting a hotel. Just a spot of ground where we can lay our heads."

"Before you throw in with us, you ought to know that an outlaw set fire to the buildings we'd already completed. We have to start from scratch. Also, the outlaws are still a threat. They've vowed to return."

"I'm a fair shot with a rifle," Tobias replied. "I'll help fight 'em."

Bullet bounded up to Clay and nudged his hand, begging for attention. He ran his hand over the soft fur. "One more gun might make all the difference. A friend will arrive with more lumber in a few days and we'll be ready to build again."

"Good. That will give us time to settle in." Tobias met Belle's eyes as he patted her wrinkled hand. "We're home, precious."

The old couple's love shone like a beacon in the night. No telling the storms they'd weathered during their married life, but they were still going forward with optimism and courage.

Clay noticed that Dallas Hawk had come to take his turn to guard. Clay spoke to him, then led the town's first outside residents inside.

Although Rebel might soon find her way back out once Tally got through with her.

He groaned. This was going to be anything but a picnic.

Thirteen

BY THE TIME SHIMMERING ROSE AND PURPLE HUES BROKE through the gray dawn, Devil's Crossing was beginning to stir and Tally almost had breakfast ready for Clay. He'd be hungry and tired after keeping watch all night. She'd already completed her chores and had fresh goat's milk on the table. Violet sat outside the door, soaking up the dawn's rays.

The child had been scared, so Tally had finally relented and let her into bed with her, after which they'd both slept better.

Still, the yearning for Clay's arms had never left her, and she found herself listening for the sound of his breathing. Tally had never expected this emptiness. She shouldn't miss something that was still so new. But tell that to her heart.

She reached into the oven for a large pan of biscuits. On the way to the table with them, she saw movement through the window.

Violet turned her head, listening. "Mr. Clay."

Tally moved to get a clear view, and anger rose inside her. Clay was heading toward the dugout carrying a long walking stick. Pressed close to his side in a red dress was a woman, her arm wrapped through his. She appeared about Tally's age, as best she could tell. The woman's midnight hair ruffled in the breeze as she laughed and glanced up at him. Clay threw back his head and roared, laughing fit to beat all. Tally scowled, her stomach tightening.

Who was that woman, and why was she with her husband?

Furthermore, why did *he* look so happy when she was totally miserable?

Just then, the woman's eyes locked with Tally's through the window. The bold creature gave her a smirk that seemed to say Clay was all hers.

Anger rushed over Tally like muddy floodwaters of the

Brazos. Of all the nerve! Her gaze shifted to the elderly couple walking behind Clay. Though she appeared far too young, maybe this dark-haired husband-stealer was their daughter?

Hmph! Tally leaned forward until her nose was almost pressed against the windowpane. Realizing she must look like an urchin staring at food inside a café, she backed up. She couldn't let anyone see the chaos twisting and turning inside her.

Still, she hadn't exactly given Clay much incentive for staying faithful. Clay pulled free from the woman, shifted the walking stick, and took Violet's hand. Satisfaction swept through Tally that the woman had to relinquish her hold on him.

Tally plunked the biscuits on the table and scurried back to the kitchen before they came inside. She glanced in Clay's shaving mirror, the one still hanging on the wall that he'd forgotten to take when he'd moved out.

Her tattooed cheek! She'd never given any thought of what to say to new people. She swung around in a panic, looking for anything that might help conceal it but saw nothing. Finally, she raised her chin in defiance. She'd done nothing wrong. Still, fear gripped her that someone might turn her in for the five-hundred-dollar reward. What could she say? Nothing unless they asked. And if they did…heaven help her.

She shifted her gaze away from the hideous mark. Light from the lamps revealed she should've taken more care with her appearance that morning. She hastily unpinned her hair and let the loose strands fall across her cheek. Hopefully, the tattoo wouldn't be that noticeable.

Clay carried Violet inside and spoke without glancing at her. "Tally, come and meet our first new residents." He took the walking stick from the old man and propped it beside the door.

With one last look in the mirror, she pasted on a smile and gave herself a stern warning to be polite. "How wonderful. And just in time for breakfast." Thank goodness she'd made extra, just in case some of the men stopped in to eat.

She offered her hand to the elderly gentleman. "I'm Tally Shannon…" She shifted her gaze to the pretty young woman before adding pointedly, "Colby."

"Tobias January, and this is my wife, Belle." Although the old man had to be way past his prime, his eyes twinkled like stars. He had one of the snowiest and longest beards she'd ever seen, hanging almost to his waist.

Tally kissed the old lady's wrinkled cheek and welcomed her. She already felt drawn to Belle January, who reminded her of her grandmother long ago. Her face was timeworn, her eyes milky, but her knotty, misshapen fingers closed around Tally's with a firm grip. A thousand memories hid behind those pale blue eyes. Already she seemed like a dear friend.

"I'm so happy to meet you," Tally said. "I look forward to getting acquainted." Only then did she acknowledge the woman whose presence she likened to a hissing snake. There was no ignoring her. "You can call me Mrs. Colby. Are you related to Belle?"

"Just a friend," the newcomer said, giving her a thin smile that failed to hide her resentment. "I'm Rebel—Rebel Avery. Clay and I are"—she beamed up at him—"dear friends."

Fury climbed up Tally's neck at the woman's implication that there was much more to their relationship. Clay refused to look at Tally, and that said far too much.

"I'm sure you'll have a lot to talk about," Tally managed past her clenched teeth.

"I met Rebel when she worked at the Wildcat Saloon." Clay helped Violet into a chair at the table and pulled out one for Rebel. "She was always ready when I was looking for a dance partner. Or a glass of whiskey."

I'll just bet.

Rebel appeared ready for most anything, especially when it came to Clay. She could barely take her eyes off him now and stared as if she was picturing him without clothes.

Thankfully, Tally remembered her manners before she buried her hands in Rebel's hair and yanked it out. "Breakfast is ready. If Clay will bring in some extra chairs from the saloon, we'll eat."

"I'll help," Rebel was quick to volunteer. Of course.

The two went outside and came back carrying three more

chairs. Rebel placed hers next to Clay's, so close she was near in his lap. He finally glanced across the table at Tally and helplessly shrugged his shoulders.

She quirked an eyebrow at him and stabbed a fork into the sausage patty so hard it dented the tin plate, the sound loud in the room, then smiled sweetly at Clay. "Eggs, dear?"

"Clay always eats three eggs every morning," Rebel answered for him. "He has a healthy appetite." The woman glanced at the plate of eggs. "Those yolks are a little too runny."

Steam came from the top of Tally's head. For two cents, the woman would wear the eggs.

"They're fine," Clay insisted, his frustrated gaze locking with Tally's. "Just the way I like them now."

Rebel snorted but kept silent, her hand covering his.

"In most cultures, a man being married means he's taken," Tally said silkily. She gave the woman a cold smile. "In less civilized places, when a woman latches on to someone else's husband, the wife just whacks off the woman's hand and is done with it. But it's entirely up to you, Miss Avery. Personally, I prefer things simple and fast."

Clay choked on his biscuit and Rebel quickly put her hand in her own lap.

"What did she say, dear?" Tobias asked his wife.

"Tally said she's going to whack off Rebel's hand if she doesn't watch what she's touching." Belle glanced at Tally and winked.

"Violet, honey, you're not eating much. Are you sick?" Tally felt the child's forehead.

"No, Mama." Violet pulled Tally down close and whispered in her ear, "I'm scared. Can I sit in your lap?"

Without a word, Tally transferred her. Soon, the remainder of the meal was taken up with the "Remember When" game Rebel played with Clay.

Tally turned her back on them and focused her attention on the Januarys. "I'm curious. How did you hear that we're building a town here?"

"An old outlaw I used to know came through Cimarron

and told us." Tobias took a drink of coffee. "I gathered up my tools—I'm a carpenter and coffin maker by trade—and my Belle packed the wagon. Here we are. There's nothing much I can't build."

"That's very true. My Tobias is also a gunsmith on the side." Belle wiped a crumb from Tobias's beard with a napkin. "We know the problems with building a town. Tobias and I started two others in years past, only to see them fail. We're bound and determined to help you make this one work. And…our youngest son took to the outlaw trail." The old woman's voice broke. "He died before he could set things straight."

Tally's heart ached for the old couple. "I'm so sorry."

Tobias cleared his voice. "If we can help some of the men here, it will feel like we did something for our boy."

"Well, we're mighty glad you came." Tally put Violet's milk glass in her hand. "It's a monumental undertaking."

"My hands aren't much to look at, but they still fit plows and hoes, and I can sew and cook." Belle reached for a piece of sausage. "There's not much I can't do."

Tobias laid his fork down. "Towns are the only way to tame this land. They attract good, solid people with skills, and that runs out the bad seeds like Montana Black. Your man told me how the outlaw burned down what they'd built. Just a shame."

Her man? Tally wasn't too sure of that. She glanced at Clay, who appeared to have lost sight of the fact that other people sat at the table. Right at the moment, she wasn't at all sure what he was to her.

"Maybe we'll get a sheriff soon." Belle turned to speak to Violet. "You have such lovely hair, child. Tobias and I have three granddaughters and five grandsons. Course, they're all grown now. When they were small, they used to follow us around like little puppy dogs. They could ask more questions than a squirrel has nuts. How old are you, sweetheart?"

"Eight," Violet answered. "Did you have any little girls like me?"

"Yes, I sure did. You have a pretty name, you know.

I've always adored purple violets. I named my two girls after stones—Pearl and Jade." Belle chuckled. "They were such tomboys. Always trailing after their six strapping brothers."

"My goodness, you had a brood." Tally couldn't imagine having that many children—or siblings. She and her brother, Brady, had been each other's best friend. Older by two years, Brady had watched out for her. They were enough.

"Violet, do you like magic?" Tobias took out a coin and rolled it between his fingers.

The girl scrunched up her face in thought. "What is that?"

"It's making things disappear," Tobias explained. "I can make this coin vanish."

Tally smiled and said low, "Violet can't see, Tobias. Your magic won't work on her."

"I'm sorry." The man's face reddened. "I didn't know."

Violet leaned toward the sound of his voice and whispered, "Can you make that woman disappear?"

Tobias chuckled and whispered back, "I've been trying."

"We have to be nice, honey." Tally wiped milk from Violet's mouth.

The girl sulked. "I don't think she's very nice."

No need to worry that Rebel overheard. She was too busy laughing and carrying on with Clay to pay attention to anything else. Tally narrowed her eyes. She was going to have a talk with Clay.

Very soon.

Belle patted her hand. "Don't worry, dear. I know how to fix that. At least for a while."

The minute the meal was over, Clay stood. "Tobias, let's go find you a spot to claim and meet the others."

The two men went outside. Belle caught Rebel's arm before she reached the door. "Rebel, dear, we need help here. There are dishes to wash, floors to sweep, and whatnot. I'm sure Tally has a list. And we have to unpack the wagon when Tobias finds us a good place to camp."

"But—" Rebel sputtered. "I don't do that kind of work."

Tally eyed the red satin dress that, if she could hazard a

guess, was probably one of the woman's more conventional ones. The neckline dipped far too low, but at least the dress hem met her ankles.

This was going to be fun. She gave the women a much happier smile. "We don't have the luxury here of picking and choosing chores. Belle, I was thinking of making a garden. I'm not sure what has time to grow this late in the planting season. I brought a few seeds with me."

"No worries about that," Belle said. "I toted a lot of fast-growing kinds. Beans and peas only take sixty days or thereabouts to make, and beets are shorter than that. All we have to do is decide on a plot of ground. Later on, we can plant winter squash and turnips." At the commotion outside, a smile curved Belle's mouth. "I hear bleating. How many goats do you have?"

"A whole, whole bunch," Violet said. "They have little babies, too."

"I hate the smelly animals," Rebel said, wrinkling her nose. "They're good to eat though."

Panic crossed Violet's face. "No!"

"She won't, Violet." Or Tally would have a say and Rebel wouldn't like that one bit.

"There ain't nothing sweeter than goat kids," Belle said, kissing Violet's cheek. "We'll have to visit them." She swung around to Tally. "Have you tried making cheese from the milk yet? You'll find none any tastier."

"That's what Clay said. We'll have to make some." Tally glanced at Rebel, whose expression now matched her name. The woman was seething, her arms crossed over her rounded bosom. The chore list was growing longer by the second, and Tally's determination grew stronger along with it.

If she could only get Clay alone, she'd get a few things straight, but by the time she finished the dishes, he was nowhere to be seen. Jack and Tobias said he was getting some sleep, so she had nothing left to do but focus on her chores and keep an eagle eye on Rebel. Tally wouldn't put it past her to curl up with Clay when he caught some shut-eye.

But what about tonight, when everyone went to sleep? Would Rebel go to him?

And more importantly, would Clay turn her away? He was a lonely man.

Tally found herself in a quagmire. There was no doubt in her mind that Rebel would gladly take advantage of Clay's new living arrangement.

The safety of Devil's Crossing that had first brought Tally peace of mind might very well end her living here. If things began to look hopeless, she'd have no choice but to pack up and leave.

Her stomach twisted. Clay would find a willing bed partner if he was looking for one.

The more she learned of Rebel, the less she liked. The saloon girl was lazy and either trying to slip away from Tally and Belle, or standing at the door gazing out at the men while Tally and Belle did all the work.

Once, Tally caught the woman marching purposefully toward the tent saloon, Harvey Drake, the short, bow-legged bartender, standing in the open flap. They talked and laughed for a bit, then Rebel returned.

Tally paused in tilling the garden. "One thing you need to know about us and this town, Rebel."

The woman turned. Her face had reddened from the heat but resentment burned in her eyes. "What's that, Tally?"

"If you stay here, you work. Everyone has to pull their share of the load." Tally wiped her forehead. "If you have no intention of helping, then it's best you move on."

"If you think you can kick me out, you better not try. You're not the one in charge here."

Hot fury climbed up Tally's neck. She kept her voice low. "I'm the one you should worry about. You don't know the things I'm capable of."

Rebel's eyes widened in challenge. "Is that a threat?"

"Take it however you see fit, but I'd watch the shadows." Tally moved over to Violet, who had attached herself to Belle. The old woman's gentle ways had drawn the child. Bullet lay in the turned earth, Violet's guardian always.

"Let's stop and rest," Tally suggested to Belle. "We need to cool off and get some water before we have a heat stroke."

"I agree." Belle leaned heavily on Tally as they made their way to the shade of the windmill and the refreshing water in the tank. Violet followed, clutching Tally's dress with one hand and holding to Bullet with the other. The dog was extremely patient with her, as though sensing Violet's blindness.

Rebel shot a longing glance toward the saloon and sighed before joining them.

While they drank their fill, Tally stared at the shambles left of the town that so resembled the ugly mess inside her, and deep sadness washed over her. She sensed her marriage slowly slipping away and didn't know how to stop it. Even if she begged Clay to move back in, he might refuse. The thought of his rejection stilled everything inside her.

Should she let Clay go? Or fight like hell for the man she wanted?

Tally clenched her jaw. She'd do whatever she must to save her life here. Clay Colby was hers and no two-bit husband-stealer was going to take him.

Fourteen

THAT AFTERNOON, AFTER CLAY SLEPT FOR A FEW HOURS IN THE new house he was building, he went to Violet and knelt down in front of her. "I think it's time you see what I look like. All right?"

"Okay. I'm not very scared of you now."

"Good." He took her hands and placed them on his face. *Please let Violet trust me.*

"I want you to see what I look like so you won't be afraid of us spending time together. I'm going to teach you how to get around so you won't have to have someone hold your hand. Do you want that?"

Wordlessly, Violet nodded and slowly ran her fingertips across every inch of his face. Clay didn't move, barely breathed.

"What is this rough place?" she asked. "Was someone mean to you and hurt you?"

Clay wasn't sure what to say. He was feeling his way the same as Violet.

At last he said, "It's a scar where a knife cut me."

"Does it hurt?"

"Not anymore."

"Did a mean person do it?"

"Yes."

"A bad man hurt me too. I asked God to tie up all the mean men before I went to sleep last night. Sometimes they get loose. I'll pray again tonight and ask Him to tie them real good and tight—with a better rope this time, so they can't hurt us."

"Thank you." Clay kissed her cheek. "I'm not ever going to let anyone hurt you. All right?"

She burrowed against his chest. "I think you must be an awful brave man, Mr. Clay."

"I don't know about that, but I do know that you and your

mama are the most precious things in my life and I'll fight to the last drop of blood to keep you both safe."

Violet patted his face. "I'm glad, so we can stay here."

Thickness filled his throat. Why he'd been given all this now, after so many years alone, he didn't know. He swallowed hard to clear his voice. "You're everything I ever wanted, Violet." He took her small hand and laid it on his chest. "I have you tucked deep in my heart. Do you feel it?"

She nodded. "I wish I could see you for real. I know you must look like a handsome prince. Mama says those are the best kind. But I can see inside you and it's beautiful."

Clay let out a small cry. This child had such a way of putting things. Tally watched from nearby. He gave her a wink to let her know things were fine, remembering her words the first day and a promise to kill him if he ever mistreated Violet. She hadn't known he'd never cause the girl any harm.

"Let's get to your lessons, baby girl." He took Violet's hand and showed her how to use the walking stick he'd made, always speaking to the girl with a gentle voice and light touch.

While his men dove into making trails and stringing up rope to guide her around the town, he taught her where it was safe to go. An area of danger where the saloon sat. "Stay away from over here. When you hear the windmill get loud, you know you've gone too far."

She finally took the walking stick alone. Clay held Bullet and stood poised to dive in if she ran into trouble. The first five or six steps were shaky and she fell twice. Each time, Clay waved Tally back from rushing to the rescue. He picked the child up, dusted her off, and set her again on her feet.

"You're doing real good, honey. It's going to take practice. Are you scared?"

Violet shook her head. "I like being able to go places by myself. It's fun."

"That's my girl."

After many more falls, by the time they quit for the day, Violet had become more self-assured. And Clay was happy to spend time with her at last. She was still hesitant when her old fears seeped in, and sometimes when he reached for her too quickly, her eyes grew round and her heart raced as though she feared his touch. Soft words and a light hand soothed her.

They seemed to take two steps forward and one back, but all in all, he was pleased and so was Tally, who hovered near like a nervous mother hen.

Once Violet was playing with Bullet, Tally strode to him, her long legs closing the space between them. "Thank you, Clay. You don't know what this meant to her. And to me."

He wanted to take her in his arms and kiss the worry from her eyes. Instead, he casually draped an arm around her neck and let his hand dangle. Her nearness made his heart stampede. "We still have more work to do, but I think this was a good start. She's beginning to trust me."

"That's a huge step. Clay, I wish…"

"I know." He, too, wished that she could trust him. "It'll come."

Her gaze moved to Rebel, who'd joined the men and was laughing at something they said. "Watch out for her. Rebel wants you back and doesn't care how she does it."

It appeared the warrior woman was coming out. Clay put his mouth to her ear. "You have nothing to fear, darlin'. I know all about the Rebels of this world."

If only he was half as knowledgeable about warrior angels.

Clay's reassurance did little to calm Tally. Rebel posed a huge threat, not only to her marriage but to her security. One thing the woman was not—slow-witted. She could sneak out some night and turn Tally in for the big reward.

On the other hand, Belle was such a delight and Tally knew she'd found a fast friend. She had only to pull away the mask of age to glimpse the young girl inside.

"I'm a wanted woman, Belle," Tally confided, speaking

low, while they drew fresh water for the men. "I'm sure you wondered about this mark on my cheek."

"I learned a long time ago to stay out of other people's business." Belle picked at the hem of her apron with her misshapen hands. "I figured you'd talk in your own good time."

Tally told her a little about Creedmore and her escape.

"I'm glad you're out of there." Belle's voice lowered. "Tobias rescued me from a mean group when I was a young girl. He was an outlaw and a hell-raiser back then, but he saved me from a fate worse than death." Suddenly, Belle grinned. "I straightened him out."

"He's a wonderful, caring man. You did a good job, Belle."

The old woman patted Tally's hand. "Clay Colby's worth saving too. Don't give up on him. I see what you're wrestling with, but he's one of the good ones. After Tobias rescued me, my grandmother saw how I struggled to reconcile the past. She said that tragedy spares no one. We have to battle it as we would an intruder and keep pushing it out." Belle leaned closer. "There are threads of meaning, even in the darkest moments, when we can't see past our fear."

Thick emotion closed Tally's throat as she hugged her new friend. "You are a very wise woman, Belle January, and I'm so glad you came."

"Me, too. Just be still and listen to your heart. Be willing to risk everything for love." Belle motioned to Clay. "He's yours if you want him."

Was it that simple? Was she willing to risk everything in the hope that what she felt was love? Hadn't she already risked enough coming here? The promise she'd made Clay weighed heavily on her.

"You've borne much sorrow. You can have happiness though. Just reach out and grab it." Belle threw out her arm, snatching the air.

Thinking over all that Belle had said, Tally turned back to the task at hand. She and Belle, mostly by themselves, unpacked the wagon and stretched tents before finishing the garden. Rebel, meanwhile, stood back and told them what they were doing wrong. Once Tobias marched up to the woman and laid down the law, things went much smoother.

After the camps were set up, they helped the men. Clay's idea of making trails and stringing guide rope was going to make a huge difference in Violet's life. At that point, of course, Rebel never once complained, just flying in and making herself useful. But then, that might've been because she was in close proximity to the outlaws. The woman just seemed to thrive in their company, and Tally envied how easily she talked to them. They spent much of the afternoon in laughter, which made the work go faster.

Belle moved closer to Tally, her eyes twinkling through the milky film. "I think we've discovered a secret. If we want Rebel to do any work at all, have the men come help us."

"That does appear the case, Belle." Tally grinned. At least Clay was too busy to spend time with the hussy.

But what would happen come nightfall? Worry again crawled up Tally's spine. She didn't trust this siren in red any farther than she could sling a snake.

Like any man alive and breathing, Clay would probably welcome a warm body curled next to him. One who hadn't wounded him.

Hell and tarnation! She'd created a bad situation and didn't know how to fix it.

This thing between Clay and Rebel was deep. They shared far too much. Tally had overheard them reminiscing about close calls with death and nights spent together. In fact, Rebel had treated Clay's wounds on more than one occasion and kept him from dying.

What had Tally done? She swallowed past the lump.

Ran out on him, lied, betrayed his trust, just like all the other faithless women he'd tried to marry. That's the history they shared.

She couldn't compete with Rebel. So how could she fight her?

Shooting her automatically sprang to mind. But that would only make everything worse. If Rebel didn't die, Clay would probably take over her care and nurse her back to health, after which he'd never speak to Tally again. No, she had to think of something else.

If only one of the other men would take an interest in Rebel. Yes, that was it! They were all hungry for a wife.

Travis Lassiter caught her attention. He could turn any woman's head with his ready grin and blond good looks. And Rebel had already let her hands stray to his broad chest.

Besides, they had a lot in common. Travis had once owned a saloon, after all. At least until one night he killed two men who'd hurt and abducted one of his working girls. The story was that Travis tracked them down single-handedly and killed them in cold blood.

When Travis went to the water bucket for a drink, Tally followed.

"Hot day, ma'am." Travis offered her the cup.

"Go ahead and drink, Travis. I'll wait." She watched him guzzle his fill. "What do you think of Rebel Avery?"

Travis grinned. "She's real pretty. I wonder if she'd dance with me tonight."

Tally moved closer. "She likes you. I can tell. Ask her to come and then look at the stars afterward. I'll bet she'll snap you up."

"Do you really think so?" Travis wiped the sweat from his brow. "I'd sure like to kiss her."

"You won't know until you ask, but I'm sure she'll say yes. She's a very lonely woman." Tally glanced at the brazen hussy. "I think you're exactly what she needs—a strong man."

"All right, you've convinced me. Thank you, Miss Tally." Travis went back, whistling a happy tune.

She watched him sweet-talking Rebel and oh how the Jezebel loved it. She threw back her head and laughed, then kissed Travis on the cheek. The first part of Tally's plan seemed to be working.

But night was falling fast, and along with it came jitters.

A heavy mist enveloped the town that night. They shared an evening meal outdoors, laughing and talking. Tally sat with Belle and Tobias. Clay ate with Jack and Ridge. It didn't take long for Rebel to pick up her plate and join them. Clay seemed cold and remote, his features hard.

A hard ache settled in Tally's chest as she tried to ignore them. Try as she might, she couldn't keep from glancing over at them. She hated this gnawing jealousy. If only she knew magic and a spell to change Rebel into an ugly, warty toad. But magic was not going to fix this.

Dallas Hawk finished eating and picked up his fiddle. Soon every nook and cranny of Devil's Crossing was filled with music and laughter.

Clay came to Tally and Violet and held out his hand. "Let's dance, baby girl."

Violet's face lit up and she nodded. Clay whisked her away and she clung to him tightly, as though afraid he'd vanish.

Tally watched for a moment, glad to see Violet smiling.

Belle nudged her. "Those two look beautiful together."

"Yes, they do."

Tobias shook his head. "There's nothing worse than being unwanted."

And that's exactly how Tally was beginning to feel. Violet returned from her dance as night drifted over them like a black fog. She sat next to Tobias, her head leaning against him, and was soon fast asleep. Clay had worked her hard, teaching her some independence.

Even Violet would not need her soon. Then Tally would truly be alone. Her thoughts sank lower when Clay asked Rebel to waltz. With an aching heart, Tally rose, unable to watch him spin Rebel around the makeshift dance floor.

Tally would put Violet to bed and dance alone in the dugout, dreaming of Clay's strong arms around her.

"Tobias, let me take Violet."

"I'll carry her," the man insisted. "Me and Belle can put her to bed. You stay."

As she stood, trying to think of an excuse—a headache maybe—she felt a tap on her shoulder.

"Dance with me, Tally." Clay's voice washed over her like gentle waves on a shore. She spun around to tell him to go jump into a big pile of fresh manure. But the loneliness in his dark eyes sent her resentful words fleeing.

"Go on," Belle whispered in her ear. "It'll do you a world of good. You can talk."

"In that case, I'd love to," Tally said at last. She put her hand on Clay's shoulder and he whisked her away into a waltz in the warm Texas night.

Clay's hold was firm on her back, the buckle of his gun belt pressing against her stomach, his breath fanning the tendrils of hair at her temple. "I've missed you."

"It certainly didn't look like it a minute ago. You can't take one step without bumping into Rebel. Or dancing."

Clay let out a long sigh. "Tally, I told her I was married and things are different now."

"Apparently not firm enough."

Frustration tinged with anger filled his voice. "What do you suggest? She has nowhere else to go, and she's on the run from a man in Cimarron who claims she stole a good bit of money from him. She's asked for protection, and I won't turn her away."

He raised his arm and Tally turned under it. As compatible as they were in gliding effortlessly in a series of turns, they were not so in working out their marriage. In fact, they seemed to be pulling in opposite directions. She tried to block the feel of him against her, the longing in his voice, the fresh scent of him drifting around her, but his nearness overwhelmed her senses.

Yet, somehow, she had to stand her ground. "She's in love with you, Clay."

"Hell, she's in love with every man." He pressed his lips to her cheek and murmured in her ear. "It's you I want—you I need."

His declaration caught her off guard. Once, she would've believed him, but after giving her what had seemed a cold shoulder all day, it would take much more than words to rebuild what little trust she had to give.

"You could've fooled me." An awkward pause filled the space between them as they moved to the music. Finally, Tally whispered, "What happened to us, Clay? You feel a million miles away."

"If I'm not mistaken, this is what you wanted. You couldn't have someone near that you can't trust."

Guilt sat thick in the back of her throat. He was right. "I didn't want…this. I thought we'd continue to work on our marriage. But it seems you've already given up." Tally stepped out of his arms and turned back to the group.

Clay caught her hand. "I don't give up, Tally." He released a sigh. "She's an old friend, nothing more. How many times do I have to say it?" His dark eyes searched her face as he brought her closer. They moved fluidly across the clearing in wide circles, stopping in the shadows at the edge where lantern light couldn't reach. "Rebel and I once had a"—he paused— "fling, during one of the darkest times in my life. I owe her for saving my life." His warm breath caressed her face. "But it's over. Those feelings are gone."

Yeah, well, tell that to the Jezebel.

Tally tensed. "Are you trying to convince yourself of that—or me?"

The breeze toyed with his dark hair and he gave her a smile that dripped with sadness. "I never would've known my wife was the jealous sort."

"I won't have her thrown in my face."

Clay's face hardened. "That's not what I'm doing. Sure, I got carried away at breakfast and let her dominate the conversation with our reminiscing. I admit it and I owe you an apology. I'm sorry."

At least he seemed remorseful, if his somber expression gave any indication. And to cling rigidly to her suspicions would make her look like some frumpy old biddy. Wouldn't it? "Maybe I had everything all wrong. I want to believe you, Clay. I really do."

A voice in her head whispered, *Ask him to move back into the dugout. That would solve the problem. You told him you wouldn't quit on him or your marriage.*

The whole thing came back to trust. Did she or not?

What if he refused to move back? She'd have no hope left. If only she knew where she stood.

"What do you want, Tally? I've done everything you asked."

She played with the ends of his hair that curled around his collarless shirt. "I want to go back to the way things were on our wedding day, when we were happy."

The music and gaiety intensified behind them, and she knew if she looked, she would see Rebel dancing away in the middle of it all. A few of the outlaws danced with each other, as men were sometimes prone to do when women were in short supply.

"Maybe this will convince you." Clay lowered his lips to hers in a searing kiss that was raw and full of need.

A new hunger sped through her like a thousand stampeding buffalos. Her knees buckled and she clung to him, cursing her weakness for this tall outlaw who gave her a good life where was once a lonely existence.

His hands slid down her back to her bottom and anchored her tightly against him. Tally parted her mouth slightly, and he slid his tongue inside to dance with hers.

As the kiss deepened, she became aware of his hard thighs pressed to hers, his jutting need. Her breath hitched and the length of her body quivered. She'd never known this hot achiness before. Desire mounted, and if they'd been naked, she wouldn't have had the strength to deny him.

When the kiss ended, it left an empty, aching void inside her.

"Clay." She pulled him closer.

His touch, his lips, his scent were again everywhere, leaving a scorched path.

Her stomach fluttered and dipped and she clung to him to keep from falling.

Another hot, tongue-thrusting kiss left her head reeling.

He was tender and hard and passionate. A man who could

draw a gun and aim in the blink of an eye, yet help a little blind girl learn to be self-sufficient. A man who could make a woman feel the most cherished in the world. His steady heartbeat pounded through his shirt.

Clay's ragged breath came loudly. "Tally," he murmured against her lips. "You're all the woman I'll ever need. Anymore and I'd lose what's left of my damn mind. I can face off against the meanest gunman at ten paces with no problem, but, lady, you scare the pants off me."

Tally slid her hands around his waist, pressed her face against his shoulder. She inhaled the fragrant night air and knew deep regret. "I wish I could go back and change some things. I wouldn't have run from you, from this place. We've both made our share of mistakes."

He moved her hair aside and kissed the sensitive skin behind her ear. "We have to forget about those and move forward. Someday, I'm going to make mad, passionate love to you and wipe your memory of everything, everyone, before you came here."

Again, the voice came in her head. *Tell him he can move back.*

But before she could get the words past her tongue, Clay dropped his shield back in place and the closeness was gone. "I have guard duty in a few hours and you should probably relieve Tobias and Belle."

"Yes, of course."

They made wide, sweeping circles across the sparse grass in silence to rejoin the group as the last note from the fiddle faded.

Clay released her. "This is going to get better."

"I hope. Thank you for the dance." She felt so cold without his arms. "I should go to Violet. She loves the walking stick and trails you made."

"Each day will give her more confidence. I'll walk you to the door." Clay draped an arm around Tally's shoulders.

She searched for something to say that might change their relationship back to the way it had been before she'd messed up and Rebel had come. Conflicting emotions raced through her. She wanted to believe Clay that Rebel meant nothing. He didn't know how devious women could be.

Rebel knew exactly how to get what she wanted. If he chose her, Tally would pack her things.

At the door, Clay glanced back at the group around the campfire. The woman in red satin was the life of the party, it seemed, and Clay appeared anxious to get back. She wanted to ask him not to dance with Rebel, but to do so would make her seem petty and insecure.

Clay swung back to her and brushed a kiss across her lips. "Nothing's changed. We're still the same two people we were."

"Are we?" Tally ached to lay her palm against his face, to smooth away the lines. But he seemed distracted.

His eyes were bathed in dark shadows. "Sleep well, Tally. I'll keep watch over you."

"That means more than you know." Struggling to hold back the tears, she kissed her fingers, laid them to his lips, then slipped inside the door.

⚬₰⚬

Long after Belle and Tobias had left, Tally stood at the window, gazing out at the boisterous group by the fire. She'd never felt lonelier and more cut off.

The plaintive notes coming from the fiddle drifted through the wall as Dallas set his bow in motion. The old couple ambled into the clearing to dance. It quickly became apparent that they were more than novices, their steps sure, their hold on each other unbreakable. She could hear them laughing, see devotion in every touch, and such a yearning rose inside her for the same.

Harvey Drake stepped into the lantern light. He turned in a circle, kicking up his bow legs and his heels and whooping to beat all.

Tears stung the back of her eyes. One thoughtless blunder had cost her everything.

Yes, Clay had kissed her with such passion. But had he been thinking of Rebel?

Tally gripped the curtain and watched the woman in red dance with Travis Lassiter. Rebel threw back her head in laughter, then yanked Travis so close that not one bit of space shone between them. She found his mouth and delivered a hot kiss.

"Maybe she'll leave Clay alone," Tally muttered to herself.

Yet when the music ended and Dallas launched into another tune, Rebel pulled Clay up from the circle of men. Tally closed her eyes, her hand over her mouth to stop the cry.

What if Clay had sold her a bill of goods? What if his words—the kiss—had been meant to placate the unhappy little wife?

Her stomach churned, whipping up a froth.

Tally opened her eyes and could just make out Clay, standing at the edge of the light, arms folded over his chest. Jack Bowdre said something to him and they got in a scuffle. Tally pressed against the windowpane, wishing she could hear. Both men were obviously angry, but Ridge Steele broke them apart before they threw a punch, and Jack limped off to the makeshift saloon.

What was that about?

Everyone sat back down and someone brought out a bottle. Clay tipped it up and practically drained it. An ache pierced Tally, taking her breath. That he'd turned to whiskey to drown his pain meant that he was wrestling with something.

Her? Rebel? His loneliness? Any one of them could easily be to blame.

Belle had said that Clay was one of the good ones and worth saving. Her advice sounded in Tally's ears. *Be still and listen to your heart. Be willing to risk everything for love.*

Was she willing to trust the voice deep inside her? Willing to risk it all?

Damn Rebel Avery!

Listen to your heart, Tally.

Fifteen

A SOFT TAP AT THE DOOR ALERTED TALLY. CLAY? SHE HURRIED to open it, but the face staring back startled her. "Alice! What are you doing here?" She kept her voice low so as not to wake Violet.

The fifteen-year-old wrung her hands. "Hester Mason cut her leg bad. I didn't know what else to do but come to you for help. I followed the map you left so I wouldn't get lost."

Her mind whirling, Tally quickly pulled her inside and smoothed Alice's wild brown hair. Hester's wound must be serious to have sent Alice.

"Honey, tell me more. Is it oozing puss?"

"Yes, and the skin around it is hot to the touch. Hester thinks infection might've set in."

It sure sounded like it. Those young women didn't have the knowledge needed for healing such a wound. She'd have to go. Tally stilled, recalling her conversation with Clay when he'd brought her back the day she'd run for Deliverance Canyon. He'd been hurt deep down. She wouldn't do that to him again. The thought of giving Rebel a chance at him...

Still, Hester's life was in danger and she could die. Tally chewed her lip and paced.

Alice's stomach growled.

"I'm sorry, honey. I didn't ask if you'd eaten. You must be starving." Tally led her to a chair at the table. "When did you last eat a meal?"

"Two days ago." Alice gave her a wan smile. "I don't need much. Just a bite or two of anything if you have extra. I won't put you out."

Tally pulled out a skillet and scrambled the girl two eggs, adding a piece of toast, and set it in front of her. Alice's eyes grew round and she dove in. She and the other women in

Deliverance Canyon deserved to live in the open, not huddling in fear like a bunch of rats. They must need supplies.

"Alice, don't you have any medicines to treat Hester's wound?"

The girl laid down her fork. "We ran out. Had to treat a bunch of accidents after you left."

"You'll stay the night and I'll decide what to do come morning." She'd confide in Clay and tell him she was leaving. It was the decent thing to do.

But already, her heart ached to leave him.

Clay pushed away the bottle of rotgut Rebel tried to hand him, noticing that everyone else had vanished, leaving them alone together.. "No more," he growled. He had to keep his head clear for guard duty, and the outlaws around them were already in various stages of inebriation. Absently, he shuffled a deck of cards, his mind on Tally. His gaze swept to the dugout where he wanted to be.

"More for me then." Rebel turned the bottle up and drank in long swallows, then burped, wiping her mouth on the back of her hand.

"Where's Travis?"

"He went to fix up his place." Rebel cast Clay a pouty scowl. "You know I never like sleeping alone, and since you're not offering…" She let the sentence trail.

Clay let her hint slide. "Treat Travis nice. He's a good man."

"But he's not you," she reminded him softly. "I saw you first. You care for me, Clay. I know you do."

"As a friend, nothing more. How many times do I have to tell you that I'm married now, and Tally has my heart? What you and I had is over." Although the words were firm, his voice was gentle. He didn't want to hurt her and prayed it wouldn't come to that.

Hopefully, she'd turn her attention elsewhere.

Yes, loneliness ate at him—loneliness he'd thought his

marriage would cure. But the ache that rose inside was for Tally, not Rebel. He glanced again toward the dugout. How he'd love to be curled up next to her, his leg touching hers, soothing her worry.

Kissing her.

Memory of their earlier kiss sharpened the yearning to a finely honed edge. Her lips had carried a taste of desire and smoldering passion.

Hell! Whoever told him he was good husband material must've had their brains scrambled.

Jack Bowdre had called him a jackass. "Can't you see what you're doing to Tally?" he'd hollered. "She's a damn fine woman and deserves much better than you."

The finger jabbing into his chest had made Clay boil. "Stay out of this." He'd angrily shoved his best friend.

"You're a fool," the ex-lawman had flung at him, shaking his head sadly. "To be clear—if I have to choose between you and Tally, I'm on her side."

The fire crackled and popped as Clay now stared sourly into the flames. Again, he swung his gaze toward the dugout, thinking he'd heard the door opening. But he saw nothing in the darkness. Must've been wishful thinking.

"You loved me once. You can again." Rebel rested a hand on his thigh. "I know your secrets. I know the things you speak of in the dead of night. I know your body as well as my own."

Clay lifted her hand off him and stood. His words came out hard. "There are plenty of men in this camp happy to while away the hours with you. You're skilled at making men care for you, and you've had more lonely cowboys in your bed than I can count." He whirled to face her. "So don't tell me I'm the only one."

Snatching up his things, he went to relieve the guard. He was early, but at least he'd have plenty of time to think in solitude.

He'd try to talk with Tally again tomorrow, try harder to lay her fears to rest. But he had a sinking feeling that Rebel would do everything she could to make sure his efforts were wasted.

Tom Smith, the guard on duty, glanced up at Clay. "Sounds like I missed the fun tonight. I sure would like to have danced with Rebel."

"You'll get your chance. I'll make sure of it tomorrow night," Clay said, assuring him. In fact, he'd pawn Rebel off on just about anyone who'd keep her attention.

"Looks like rain." Tom put his rifle over his shoulder.

"Yeah, smells like it too. We can use some."

Tom glanced down at the town. "I let a young girl through a little bit ago. She said she needed to talk to Miss Tally. I hope that was all right."

"I'm sure it was. Thanks for telling me." Clay made himself comfortable against a boulder and wondered what the girl could've wanted with Tally. He hoped nothing had happened to the women in Deliverance.

But if Tally left, would she tell him as she'd vowed to do?

He wished he'd brought his leather goods to make the lonely hours go faster. The saddle, reins, and harnesses he'd been working on were only half done. The wedding and everything that followed had taken his concentration and time, but he had to get back to his job. He'd owe Luke Legend for the lumber that should arrive any day.

The harnesses would just take a few hours to complete. At least those would be done. Luke had asked for ten sets, and he had five.

But what he really itched to make was a new pair of boots for Tally. She needed some badly. He would choose his softest leather and put a cushion of lamb's wool inside so she would hopefully be able to walk without too much pain. His admiration for her had grown even more after learning what Slade Tarver had done to her feet. The bastard! Anger shook him and he longed for the day when he could take Tarver from this world.

But for all Tally had endured, she never complained. Just went about the business of living as best she could.

A loose rock rolling down the steep bluff alerted him. He jumped to his feet, his gun drawn. "Whoever's there had better speak up," he barked.

"Don't shoot. It's me, Tally."

Surprise rolled over him. Had she come to tell him she was leaving? Or did she plan on bashing his head in? From what little she'd revealed, she knew ways to kill a man.

And this distance between them that Rebel caused only confused the issue.

He reached for her hand and pulled her up onto the rocky outcropping, the spot offering a clear view in all directions. "To what do I owe the pleasure, Mrs. Colby?"

"We need to talk." Tally stepped away from him, her arms folded.

The blunt statement got right to the point. Good. He liked things simple, with no beating around the bush. Except her eyes were flashing in the darkness like streaks of lightning. Hell!

"Make yourself comfortable." The granite lines of her face told him all he needed to know—he was in hot water. And from the anger in her face, this talk might take all night. He spread out his bedroll for her to sit on. She dropped onto it and he sat next to her—on her gun side, where it would be harder for her to draw and shoot him.

"First though, a young friend from Deliverance came to me tonight asking for my help."

"Tom told me he let her through. What does she want from you?"

"Clay, I need to leave. Hester Mason, the woman I left in charge, cut her leg, and from Alice's description, it's infected. Untreated, she could lose it."

"Don't they have medicines and herbs for things like this?"

Tally sighed. "They ran out. Also out of food. They need supplies and we have a little extra here I can take."

"Sure, we'll help all we can. I'm glad you came to me. We're much stronger working together. Darlin', let me help. You don't have to shoulder responsibility for them alone. We'll think of something so you don't have to leave."

"What else can we do if I don't go?"

"Let's send Jack with Alice. Of all of us, he has some medical knowledge from the war. We'll load him down with everything your friends need." Clay took her hand. "It makes more sense than uprooting Violet again. You saw how distraught she got when you tried to leave before."

"I know. Do you think Jack will go? You haven't even asked him."

At least she hadn't discarded the idea, and that was something. "He'll go."

"I really feel like I should be there with Hester. It's hard to turn their care over to someone else after all these months." She faced him. "I led them out of Creedmore, protected and fed them. I'm not sure I can let anyone take over, but I'm trying."

"If Jack can't or doesn't want to go, I'm taking you."

"Fine." Her reply came through stiff lips. She watched the approaching storm. "I saw you and Rebel tonight. Can't you see she's trying to drive a wedge between us?"

"No one can do anything unless we let them. Trust me, Tally. It's over between me and her, just like I told you." He put a finger on her chin and turned her face to him, softening his voice. "You said you wouldn't give up on us."

"Maybe it's you who has." Anger hardened her beautiful features. "Your actions are what I see, and they're not matching your words."

"She's only a friend," he shot back.

Tally gave an unladylike snort. "I wrestled with temptation tonight. I wanted to come out there and confront you both, except my good sense won out."

Surprise rippled through him. "If you had, you'd have heard me tell Rebel I have no plans to change my marital status and I'm very happy you're my wife."

"Are you? Happy, I mean."

Clay turned her hand over and kissed her palm. "You have so much more to offer than Rebel. You're fine china, and she's pottery. Not that I'm criticizing her for being who she is. The hard truth is that she thrives on the rough atmosphere of saloons, on the flirting and the chaos, and loves that life."

In a moment's silence, the howl of a coyote sounded in the distance and a chorus of crickets chirped nearby. He met Tally's dark gaze and touched her cheek. "Rebel is my past. But you…darlin', you're my future. We have a good life ahead of us—if you stay. I can't shake the feeling that you still have one foot out the door."

"I made a huge mistake in leaving before and I regret letting my fear win." Tally huffed out an angry sigh and glanced up at the cloudy, dark sky. "In truth, I'm madder at myself than you." She glanced away. "I don't blame you for moving out. That's the only choice I left you. You didn't deserve getting me for a wife." Her voice hardened. "Maybe I really am as crazy as they say."

Clay yearned to press his lips against the long column of her throat, yearned to touch her, to hold her in his arms and talk of everything and nothing, the way they had in bed the first nights.

Only she wouldn't welcome that in her state of mind.

"You're not crazy, and I don't want to hear you talk like that. This is only temporary," he said softly. "I moved out because I can't live with you until I stop seeing distrust in your eyes."

Tally shifted and he watched her chin quiver.

"It seems to me the best way to gain trust and straighten out our marriage is lying next to each other." Her voice broke. "Not this distance that I hate."

"Do you want me to move back in? Is that what you're saying?" Clay searched her eyes in the stillness that followed, looking for clues to her thinking. The hard lines of her features showed no sign of softening. Still, she hadn't shot him yet, so that had to count for something.

She whispered at last. "Yes."

Happiness surged through him. Yet, he had to find out something first.

"Can you look at me and believe with all your heart that I can keep you safe?"

He was met with stony silence. "Did you come up here because you trust me less with Rebel than with you? Do you fear that I'll wind up in bed with her if I'm not in bed with you? Is that the whole sum of it, Tally?"

Sixteen

THE QUESTION HIT HOME. IT WAS TRUE. BUT MOSTLY IT WAS Rebel and her ability to charm men that Tally didn't trust. She chewed her bottom lip and glanced up at the sky again in time to see a blinding flash of lightning. The smell of rain was thick on the bluff overlooking Devil's Crossing. Those jagged flashes seemed to be inside her as well, playing havoc with her nerves.

Misery wound through her and she was so confused. Everything had gotten all wadded up in a tight ball. Yet he wanted honesty and that's what he'd get.

"I came up here tonight because I need to figure out where I'm going. When we married, my dream was nothing more than for a real home and family." Tally sought the courage to say what she must. "But after being here with you, I realize that it's not enough without love. I want to know what love is like between a husband and wife."

Clay put his arm around her and pulled her against him. She whimpered and laid her head on his shoulder. "If you're asking me to tell you where you're going, you've come to the wrong place. I'm only muddling through myself. I know little more than you, darlin'."

"But you've traveled and met so many women."

"That doesn't teach you much. I've never come across any as pretty and smart as you. And I never loved any, not even the ones I asked to marry me."

"I'm sure you learned a lot about women though. You had to."

"Some, I reckon. One thing I know is I haven't lived in saloons most my life to be taken in by a schemer like Rebel. I know who she is and what she has for sale—and I'm not buying." He moved Tally's hair aside and kissed her neck.

"She doesn't interest me. You do. When I'm with you, I feel like I have my finger in water that's being struck with ten thousand bolts of lightning. My whole body is alive. You excite and thrill me at the same time."

"Don't just say that to spare my feelings."

"I mean every word." The brush of his fingers along her arm brought tingles. "Now that I don't seem to be in your crosshairs anymore, I want to get something off my chest. You saw me dancing with Rebel tonight and I'm sorry about that." Clay winced. "Want to know why?"

"Enlighten me."

"She vowed to leave me alone if I waltzed with her just once more—for old times' sake. Only she kept trying to get her hands into places they shouldn't go."

Tally glanced up. "You could've pushed her away."

"You didn't see the times I removed her hand only to have it right back. Rebel thought she could wear me down." His voice tightened. "She learned different."

"But for how long? She seems to have a very short memory."

"Besides coming to tell me about your friend Alice, did you come up here to get me to move back into the dugout to save me from her?"

Tally made a wry face. It sounded so tawdry put that way. "Something like that." She paused a moment, listening to the rumble of distant thunder. "As long as we're confessing—I want to tell you something."

"Go ahead. Shoot."

"When I got scared and ran, I stood at that spring, thinking about what I'd done and feeling horrible for betraying you. I knew it wasn't fair to you. I had made the decision to come back, only when I swung around to tell Violet, she was gone."

"Why didn't you tell me at the time?" Clay asked.

Tally lowered her eyes. "I didn't think you'd believe me. You were too angry and hurt."

"You're right about that. I felt like I'd been kicked in the teeth by a mule." He let his fingers drift down the long column of her throat. "That's water under the bridge now."

"Hold me, Clay, just for a little while. Let's forget about everyone. Pretend everything is all right."

The instant their lips met, all the turmoil inside her settled. Tally clung to him and kissed him with searing passion, holding back nothing. Belle had been right. She just needed to listen to the truth in her heart. Right now, it was saying she could have everything she'd ever wanted…if she'd just trust and reach for it. Clay *was* worth saving. Together, she and Clay were going to build a wonderful town here and make a good life.

Aching hunger spread through her. He ground his mouth against hers, and Tally unbuttoned his shirt, laying her palm against the warmth of his skin. He was hers.

"I want you, Clay. Tonight. Right now," she murmured against his mouth.

He pulled back to study her. "Do you know what you're saying?"

Tally's eyes met his. "I want to be your wife in every way, and I don't want to wait another minute. It's time we consummated our marriage—assuming you still want me. From the very first, I haven't made any of this easy for you and I'm sorry."

She held her breath, waiting for him to spurn her.

"Of course I still want you. Good God, woman! I've waited for you to say these words ever since you rode in with Luke." He paused. "Only—are you positive?"

"I am." Tally tried to control her shuddering breath, but panic made it nearly impossible. All she knew of men she'd learned at Creedmore, and pain had been on the menu each day. She closed her eyes to block out the horror, only to have Slade Tarver's leer staring back from behind her lids. And next to him stood Pollard Finch, with his thick, groping hands. Even in sleep, attempts to escape them seemed useless. It was almost as though her fate was tangled with theirs, and they would always be waiting in the shadows.

Clay's hands engulfed hers. "You're shaking. What's wrong?"

"Bad memories. I try to forget, but then there they are. Please make them go away."

"I'll do my best."

Tally swiveled in his arms. She placed her hands on each side of his face and kissed him with a hunger that flared to life the instant their lips met. The anger and confusion she'd felt melted away.

Silently, he caressed her arms, her back, her throat. A rumble rose from his chest as he returned her kiss.

"Tell me how to do this, Clay," she mumbled against his mouth, ending the kiss.

"Lie back." He removed her shoes and slid his palms up the length of her legs. Then, one after the other, he massaged her feet, kissing her toes. The pain that plagued her began to ease, along with her panic. Clay wouldn't hurt her. He cared for her. To confirm it, his gentle touch whispered against her skin like the soft fuzz of a baby bird.

Little by little, she relaxed under his patient caresses. This was going to be all right.

He kissed her behind one ear and left a trail of kisses down her neck to the wild pulse beating in the hollow of her throat. Tally slid her hand into his hair and held him there while she tried to absorb the multitude of sensations playing havoc with her body. She'd never known gentleness like this. Touches that made her melt. Never had she known a man like Clay. Tingles waltzed up and down her spine to match the chaotic flutters in her stomach.

Clay placed her hand inside his open shirt. "I have scars inside—and out. I want you to touch them."

Without hesitation, she explored the hard muscles that formed his chest, wondering at her outlaw's lean build. Not one ounce of fat was anywhere on his body. She did, however, discover healed bullet wounds. Quite a few in fact.

Suddenly, she was grateful to Rebel for whatever part she'd played in treating some of these. If not for the woman, he might've died. She vowed to be kinder.

Tally threw back her head to allow him greater access to her throat. "You make me crazy with want. Make love to me."

He gave her a slow, sinful grin that showed his teeth. "You

don't know how much I've wanted to hear you say that. Relax and let yourself feel."

One button, then two, then all, he slowly undressed her, kissing the skin he bared as each item fell away. She lay back on the bedroll, jagged streaks of lightning flashing around them.

The storm grew fierce, wind buffeting them atop the bluff and whipping her hair.

"Tally Shannon, you're the woman I've always wanted." He let his fingertip drift across her skin. "You're so beautiful it hurts to breathe. Even down to the little mole near your collarbone."

He spoke of no one she knew. "I don't know how you can say I'm remotely pretty. You must be drunk, because I'm as plain as the day is long and I won't pretend otherwise."

"Silly woman. I walk around half crazy out of my head, needing to see you, to feel you, to know we have this life together. Lady, you make me dream of the future." He brushed her cheek with the back of a knuckle. "My warrior," he murmured, nibbling, teasing, kissing her lips until she was breathless.

Now that her initial panic had passed, she tried to pull him on top of her, desperate to feel every inch of him. She had to have this man, have more of his feather-like caresses. The air smelled fresh with wildflowers and rain, the storm intensifying. The gigantic crack of thunder seemed to come from inside her, breaking away long-formed barriers.

"Let me get out of my trousers at least," he protested.

"You're too slow." She propped herself on an elbow and watched him undress in the bright flashes that lit up the sky. The possibility of rain didn't bother her. She welcomed it, if only to banish the sultry summer heat for a few hours.

Clay had a beautiful body, perfectly formed from his broad chest and lean waist down to his long, muscular legs. He picked up their clothes and wrapped them in a slicker he'd brought, then stashed them in a crevice in the rocks.

When he was done, she took his hand and pulled him down beside her. "Make love to me, Clay. Take me to a serene place where trouble can't find us."

"Not yet. I want to satisfy my feel of you first. I've waited a long time for this and I'll not be rushed." He explored, kissing his way down her body—stroking, gliding, fondling.

The pleasure was almost more than she could bear. Her nipples rose to hard pearls, all of her clamoring for his attention. Each touch heightened the ache for more, and when Clay pressed his lips to the soft flesh inside her thighs, she arched her back and a low moan rolled from her throat. "More."

Her hands moved along the muscles of his back, then rose to plunge again deep into the softness of his hair. She clung to him, as if afraid he'd leave her in this ragged state. Something beautiful waited for her. She could feel it, almost touch it, but not quite.

The storm grew, both inside her and in the heavens, the rumble of thunder getting ever louder. Clay's fingers played upon her body as though she was a musical instrument, and a moist sheen covered her skin.

A caress here.

A light nip with his teeth there.

A flick of his tongue. Sucking. His breath hot upon her skin.

And she did the same to him, savoring the taste of his body. He lightly pulled her bottom lip into his mouth with his teeth. Everywhere he touched brought pleasure beyond belief.

"Clay."

"Open your eyes wide, keep them open, and look in my face." Clay stared deeply inside her, seeming to know where her fear lived, only a heartbeat away. "I'll never hurt you, darlin'."

He tasted, smoothed, and caressed her, explored the soft folds that protected the entrance to her core, placed a finger into her slick passageway. At first she stiffened, then relaxed and let currents of rapture race through her, thrusting her toward something mysterious and exciting.

Higher and higher she rose, reaching for whatever this was, consumed by an overwhelming hunger for completion.

The warm rain came down in sheets, the wind pushing it sideways, drenching their naked bodies.

A dam burst all of a sudden, wave upon wave washing over her body, bringing her to a place of perfect beauty and calm.

Her heartbeat thundered like the heavens above her. Tears spilled down her cheeks. She felt cherished, her soul more contented than she could ever recall.

In the space of a heartbeat, Clay was poised above her. "If you want me to stop, say the word."

"No, please. I want all that you have to give." She'd truly go insane without all of him.

He kissed her lightly, then more urgently. He lowered himself until her swollen breasts pressed against his chest, his hips to hers. It seemed hot embers lined her body, making her yearn to feel every delicious inch of him on top her.

"Don't close your eyes," he murmured. "Let me put new, good memories in your head to replace the bad."

Clay plunged deep inside her and she'd never been so overcome with emotion. She stared into his eyes, lifted a hand to caress his rugged jaw. There was no pain or fear, and that surprised her. Tally relaxed totally, becoming a lump of melting hot desire. He moved with a slow in-and-out rhythm, the strokes driving her out of her mind. She wanted him. Now. She needed this fire inside quenched.

The wind kicked up in a fury around them, raindrops peppering her face and eyes. Not once did her gaze waver from Clay's. She kept her eyes locked on his beautiful brown ones.

The rain pelted them, drenching her hair, providing slick wetness for their bodies and drove the rhythm faster and faster to match the fury of the storm.

In the flashes of jagged, silver streaks, Clay's eyes revealed fevered passion and sweet misery.

Tally threw her arms around him and clung, moving until light and love and utter pleasure blended together into a ball and shot off into the dark sky. She jerked and trembled, straightening from head to toe in the whirling rush of release.

The storm washed away everything from the past—all the hurt and pain and darkness. When she came back down, she lay basking in the beauty and completeness of their love.

Clay collapsed on top of her, breathing heavily, his heart beating wildly against hers.

Tally kissed his shoulder, burying her face in the hollow of his throat. Water rolled off his back, cooling her, banking the embers of the raging fire that had encompassed her.

"I didn't know it could be like this," she murmured in wonder.

"How?" The word came out rough and hoarse.

"I didn't know that lovemaking could be free of pain, that it could bring this immense pleasure." Or that it would be something she didn't have to fear. Delicious heat curled inside her, and happiness wove through her like the golden threads of a beautiful cloth.

Clay raised on his elbow, brushing wet hair from her face. "You're something else, pretty wife. I've never known such peace, such contentment. If I die tonight, I'll die a happy man."

"I don't want you to die."

"I have no intention to."

His lips were warm on hers as his hands moved slowly down her body. Their tongues lazily swirled around each other's as their hands touched, stroked, savored every inch of warm, wet skin.

"I've always loved storms. Rain washes away all the dirt and filth, making things new again." Like their relationship. Tally kissed away the raindrops poised on the tips of his long, dark eyelashes. This outlaw had awakened her to so much delight. A world that had only joy.

Naked, he sat up, resting next to the boulder. He pulled her back flush against him and crossed his arms over her chest. She could hear a rumble of contentment in him as he moved her hair aside and nibbled on her neck and shoulders. They sat in silence, watching the heavenly light display, the rain falling gently now and cooling their fevered skin. His warm breath whispered at her temple.

Tally didn't know what love was, but the new stirrings inside her were forceful and strong. Maybe she could choose to love Clay as he did her until she figured out what her body was telling her. But from now on, he was hers and she belonged to him. Whatever came, they could handle it together—one body, one heart, and one fierce will to fight anything or anyone who tried to rip them apart.

Despite caution, she found her heart opening like the petals of a flower slowly unfurling, revealing beauty and wonder she'd never had.

She was truly home for the first time.

Seventeen

THANKFULLY, THE STORM PASSED ON, AND CLAY WALKED
Tally back to the dugout before Violet or Alice woke. He
paused at the door. "I'm glad you came to me last night. But I
won't move back yet. Not until you can come to terms with
your feelings." He kissed her cheek. "After last night, maybe
you can start to put those ghosts to rest."

"Thank you for awakening me. I'd never made love before
and you were so gentle."

That told him some of what she'd endured. Who knew
what they'd forced on her?

"Always. I'll never knowingly cause you pain." Hopefully,
now that she saw what he was like, she could ask him soon to
move back in.

Clay whistled while he milked the goats, his heart happier
than it had ever been.

Then, he found Jack and asked him to escort Alice back to
Deliverance Canyon and treat Hester Mason's leg. "Will you
do it?"

"Sure. I'll get some yarrow, comfrey, aloe vera, and a few
more things together for poultices, and get ready to ride out.
From what I've heard about those ladies, they're awful skittish.
Will they trust me?"

"They have to. Alice will help ease their fears." Clay laid a
hand on Jack's shoulder. "Thanks."

"Don't mention it. I'm glad to help, and there's nothing to
do here until Luke brings more lumber. Speaking of that, he's
way late."

"Yeah. I hope nothing's happened. Jack, take a packhorse
with you so you can replenish those ladies' supplies." Clay
paused for a second to find the words he owed his faithful

friend. "Sorry for being a jackass last night. We've ridden together far too long to squabble."

"Yeah, we have." Jack grinned. "I noticed quite a rosy glow on Tally's face this morning and I'm guessing you put it there."

"Tally is the only woman for me and has been from the first." Clay kept his gaze on Violet to make sure the kid didn't wander from sight.

"Glad you found some sense. Thought I was going to have to knock some into your thick skull." Jack turned his gaze toward a group of men outside the saloon. "When Luke gets here, they won't have time to lounge around like this."

"Nope. I'll make sure of it." Clay grinned. "This trip will give you a chance to meet Darcy Howard. You've been writing her for a few months now."

"Think she'll like my boyish charm?"

Clay chuckled. Nothing about the hardened outlaw looked boyish. They parted ways with Jack going to make ready for the trip.

Jack rode out with Alice immediately after breakfast and Clay went to work on the new house, getting everything ready for the lumber when it did arrive. After making love to Tally, he felt reenergized. Hope surged in his heart.

A short time after he started readjusting the pegs and enlarging the house to include a room for Violet, Rebel appeared.

At first, he didn't mind, but when she seemed to have settled at his side for the day, he'd had enough. "Rebel, I'm sure there are other jobs you need to be doing—clothes to wash, garden to tend, any number of things. I suggest you go see to them."

Rebel pouted. "You don't want my company?"

"Not at the moment. I think you're just doing this to get under Tally's skin."

"So what if I am? She doesn't know what she's got."

"That's not your place to decide. We're making headway."

"And that's why you're sleeping here and she's in the dugout."

Clay laid down the stake and ball of string. "That is our business. Now go."

She pouted and huffed but left him to work.

A few hours later, he went for water and stopped dead in his tracks. Rebel had hung a sign in front of her tent that said *Doctor*. Men were lined up, waiting. Bullet began to whine and limp like he was about to lose a leg and slowly made his way to the end of the line.

Aw hell! Clay called to Tally nearby working in the garden.

"What is it?" She crowded beside him.

"That." He pointed to the tent. "Looks like Rebel's opened a medical practice."

Tally let out a gasp of surprise. "Well, she needs attention and I guess this will get it. Those men don't have one thing wrong with them, but they'll make up anything to have soft hands touching them." She leaned forward, squinting. "Is that Bullet?"

"Yep. The crazy dog's holding up his leg like it's about to fall right off."

"Don't begrudge him, Clay. Even dogs need attention too."

As they watched, two more outlaws stumbled to the line and got into place behind Bullet. "It's a good thing we don't have any lumber yet or we'd get no work done."

"Then she's not hurting anything." Tally's voice was soft as she tucked her hand around Clay's elbow. "I can afford to be understanding."

Clay met her gaze, drowning in the depths of her blue eyes. "Where did the real Tally Shannon Colby go?"

She slapped his arm. "That's not nice. I can be understanding."

Yeah, but not with Rebel.

Belle January emerged from her soggy tent and waved as Clay tried to avoid the biggest of the mud puddles left by the storm. The place was a mess, and the ground would take days to dry out. He strode in the direction of a patch of flowers. Or maybe they were weeds. He didn't know the difference, but they were pretty and his lady loved yellow.

Halfway there, he turned and looked back. The sunlight

sparkled in Tally's auburn hair, stealing his breath. Plain his hind leg! Nothing was further from the truth. He pursed his lips and whistled a jaunty tune. From where she played nearby, Violet tried her best to mimic him. Each day, he saw her sweetness more.

He had a family.

The memory of last night filled his head, and he wanted to shout to the world that Tally was his woman. So much happiness spread through his heart it threatened to spill over the sides.

Clay gazed at the muddy, fledgling town. The need to start rebuilding rose up stronger than ever. He had some mighty big dreams, and time was wasting.

❧

The stifling afternoon heat was bearing down on the town when two gunshots rang out. Clay threw down his awl and leatherwork, leaving them in the shade of the windmill, and ran in the direction of the sound. He yanked out his Remington, trying to figure out where the gunman was.

Tally gave a cry of alarm and ran to meet him. "Violet's gone!"

"When did you miss her?"

She grabbed his arm, fear frozen in her eyes. "I just went inside to stir the beans and add some salt pork. I wasn't gone more than fifteen minutes at the most."

"I'll find her, you can bet on that."

"Violet was having a good time exploring her new independence with her walking stick and Bullet, and I let her leave my sight. What have I done, Clay?"

"You haven't done anything. I'll be back." Clay gave her a quick kiss and joined Ridge, Dallas Hawk, and several others who'd heard the gunshots.

"Best I could tell, the shots came from outside the compound." Ridge swung around, scanning the rocks in all directions.

"Violet's missing." Clay took a ragged breath. "We've got to spread out and find her. I hope she's not with the shooter. Whoever it is better not have hurt that child."

Ridge Steele flipped open the cylinder of his gun to make sure it was fully loaded. "If he has, I wouldn't give you a plug nickel for his chances of living."

"Amen to that," came a mumbled agreement from the men.

They ran down the muddy path through town that separated the burned buildings from the living quarters. The charred odor of the rain-soaked ashes invaded his mouth and nose. Clay sprinted past the tent saloon, now collapsed on one end from the storm. He was aware of others behind, but he didn't turn to check that they were following. He raced past Skeet Malloy's blacksmith shop and skirted the corral. The horses were skittish, their eyes wild.

The man keeping watch hollered down from his post atop the bluff. "The shots came from near that old tree just outside. Didn't see anyone though."

"Thanks. You saved us some time." Clay hurried through the opening and cautiously made his way forward, scouring the brush and rocks.

He raised a hand to signal for quiet and heard a loud sniffle. Violet? Sounded like her. Then a dog barked, and he knew he must've found the girl. He rushed forward, scanning the tangle of brush. "Violet!"

"Hurry," Violet sniffled.

"Be careful, Clay," Jack warned. "You don't know what you're getting into."

"Don't worry, baby girl. I'm coming." Gripping his gun tightly, Clay waded into a stand of mesquite, thorns poking through his clothes. He pushed aside the branches, hoping a bullet didn't find him in his hurry.

Fear gripped his heart and climbed up his spine, his breath uneven and catching in his chest until his lungs hurt. She was out there alone and unable to see. He was afraid to move, to breathe, to consider how this was going to turn out. He couldn't take Violet's lifeless body back to Tally. He couldn't.

The brush rustled and Bullet bounded out. Clay knelt to check for any wounds but found none, not even the pretend limp the dog had developed that morning. Bullet whined and bit down on Clay's pant leg, trying to pull him forward. Violet was close, he could feel it.

Bullet let go of his trousers and barked before turning into the brush. Clay followed, thousands of little warnings inching up the short hairs on the back of his neck. He pushed aside one more mesquite branch. He saw the girl and froze.

Violet was muddy from the knees down and Montana Black had his arm around her.

Clay lunged, sticking his long-barreled Remington to the man's head. "Blink and I'll kill you. Just give me one good reason not to blow you into hell."

Montana's eyes widened and his mouth hung slack. "I didn't harm the kid. I saved her." Breathing hard, Montana held up a deadly rattlesnake that must've measured eight feet long. Longer at one point, since the head was gone. "Missed my first shot. Damn, my blurry vision." His knees appeared to buckle, and he suddenly collapsed to the ground.

Violet sat down beside him, laying her head on Montana's chest. "My friend's hurt. Can you fix him?"

"I don't know, baby girl." Clay knelt over Montana and pushed away his shirt to expose the festering bullet wound in his shoulder. The smell of decaying flesh swam up Clay's nose. The outlaw was in a bad way—not only his shoulder but his leg wound also. He'd tied a bandana around the hole in his thigh and everything was stiff with blood and leaking pus.

Montana grimaced. "I hurt like pure hell. Why weren't you a better shot, Colby? I wish I was dead."

Clay yanked Montana's gun from his hand and stuck it in his waistband. "Yeah? Well, that makes two of us."

Just then, Hawk and Ridge crashed through the brush. "Thank God he didn't hurt Violet," Ridge said.

"He's my friend." Violet hugged Montana. "He killed the snake and saved us."

Ridge snarled, "It's the first time he's ever done a lick of good in his sorry life."

"Says you." Montana glared. "I'm not all bad. I could tell right off that this sweet little girl couldn't see. She was walking with that long stick over there and that old snake came slithering out of the tall grass. It was within striking distance when I fired the first shot."

"Make him well," Violet begged. "Please."

"We'll do our best, honey." Dallas picked her up. "Clay, I'll carry her back to her mama while you tote Montana."

"Don't forget my stick, Mr. Hawk."

"Right." Hawk took it from Ridge, and they moved out of view.

Clay glanced at Ridge. "Which end do you want to carry?"

Ridge shook his head. "I don't know which smells worse, so guess it don't matter."

"Hey, I'm not dead. I can hear you," Montana protested weakly.

"Good." Clay bent over him and clutched his shirt. "Listen to me and listen good. Give me one good reason why we should take you back to Devil's Crossing and patch you up. And, understand this, even if you can come up with one, there's got to be some changes."

Montana stared silently up at them.

Clay let go of his shirt and nudged his bad leg with his boot. "Well?"

"You're a bastard, you know that?" Montana spat sourly.

"Ridge, I reckon he wants to die right here. We might as well oblige him." Clay took several steps.

"Wait just a goddamn minute!" Montana called.

Clay turned. "What? I don't have all day to waste."

"I have some information in return for fixing me up." Montana lay back, gasping.

Clay and Ridge exchanged glances. Was this just another ploy to get what he wanted?

"Talk," Clay snapped.

"Make a deal first." Montana reached into a pocket and pulled out a folded poster. "This proves what I'm about to say."

Clay spread it out and pain shot through his chest as he stared at Tally's face. It offered five hundred dollars for her capture. A fortune. "Where did you get this?"

"Before I say a word, promise that you'll fix me up." Montana wiped his mouth with the back of his hand.

Ridge knelt beside him. "We'll do our best to save your miserable hide. What do you know?"

"After you shot me, I could barely cling to the reins. My horse eventually wandered to the water hole. I met up with some bounty hunters who were looking for Tally Shannon."

Clay frowned, trying to piece the timeline together. Did this happen before or after Tarver and his boys had come to town? "Montana, did you send them to Devil's Crossing? You knew I was marrying Tally."

"They already knew it." Montana's voice was getting weaker. "They talked about the things they were going to do to her, horrible things no one—man or woman—should endure. Like skinning. You're a bunch of tough hombres here, but Tarver and those other two are twenty times worse than you."

The pieces were beginning to fit. Montana had met up with Tarver and company *before* they arrived in Devil's Crossing.

"How did you get here and where is your horse?" Clay scanned the area but didn't see the animal.

"Once I got away from them, I found a place to hole up, but then I started getting worse. I knew the only help was here, so I started back. I fell off and my damn horse galloped off." Montana licked his lips. "I could sure use a drink of water."

"Even your horse left you to die." Clay squatted on his heels. "You haven't told us anything we don't already know. Tarver and his followers came, and I got rid of them. They weren't so tough after all. Were you thinking to turn Tally in for the reward?"

"No. I need the money bad, but I wouldn't do that to a woman."

It seemed there was a first time for everything.

"I got skills you can use. I can help get this town going." Montana clutched at Clay's shirtsleeve. "Just give me a chance."

Ridge snorted. "What can you possibly know how to do other than fight, cuss, and kill?"

"I used to be a freighter. I can haul things and you won't

have to see me often." Montana fell back and let out a loud moan. The man peeked at them from one half-closed eye, checking to see if they were softening. "I promise not to burn down anything again. All right?" Montana's dirty hand clutched at Clay's trousers. "That pretty little girl liked me."

"She's blind." Ridge got to his feet. "If Violet could see how ugly and mean you are, she'd have nightmares for sure."

The old outlaw was going to die unless they did something. But Clay had to press for more while they had him over a barrel. "Promise also not to tear the town down by any other means."

Ridge grinned. "I think we might ought to get it in writing too."

"Damn, I didn't bring any paper." Clay grinned back. "I wonder how close Montana is to passing out. He's lost a lot of blood. He could die before we get back with paper and pencil. But then again, that would save patching him up."

"I'll sign whatever you want in my own damn blood!" Montana yelled.

"As rank as he smells, I'm surprised he hasn't attracted the coyotes." Ridge wiped the sweat from his forehead. "Tonight for sure. Here come a string of ants. They'll eat him alive. It sure looks like he could use that drink of water."

"I didn't bring nary a drop." Clay shrugged. "Well, it's not really our problem. Let's go."

"All right, dammit." Montana tried to pull himself up but was too weak. "You win. I won't do anything to mess up your *prissy* little town."

Clay slapped Ridge's shoulder. "Hell, I didn't know Devil's Crossing prissed."

"The things we learn." Ridge picked up Montana's legs and Clay got the man's shoulders. "Clay, I know the real reason his horse ran off."

"Yeah. Couldn't stomach the smell." It appeared Rebel was going to get her first real patient. Clay grinned. It didn't pay to ask for things or you'd get them in spades.

"Well…I… You can't put him in here," Rebel sputtered. "He's far too sick for me. And stinky." The lady in red held her nose. "Besides, he owes me money for"—she paused with downcast eyes—"services rendered…last time he came through Cimarron."

Clay bit back a grin before pointing to her sign. "That there says that you're the town's doctor. You can't turn Montana away. You're all we have. His wounds are infected and he'll die without treatment."

"I'll help." Tally's voice rang out from the dugout doorway. She strode toward them. "I'll help you bathe him, and together, we'll pull him through. Unless you don't want my help, that is."

Rebel stared for a long heartbeat before finally taking her hands from her hips. She turned to the line outside her tent opening. "Sorry, boys, you'll have to be patient until I can get to you."

Clay and the preacher outlaw carried Montana inside the *doctor's* office. Tom Smith, the guard from the previous night, sat on the only cot with his shoe off and pant leg rolled up.

"Tom, honey, you'll have to get up," Rebel said sweetly. "I'll trim your toenails after I make Montana comfortable. Don't you worry none though. You're next on my list."

"Just don't forget. I got real pain here." Tom reached for his boot and limped out.

Clay laid Montana on the cot. His feet hung off the end a good foot. He met Tally's glance and smiled. It appeared their explosive lovemaking of the previous night had dramatically altered her feelings toward Rebel. Strange how a rivalry could end once a threat was laid to rest. He watched Tally's quiet and capable movements as she calmly assessed the man's injuries. He helped her strip Montana down and drew a sheet over the man's hips.

Memories of last night swirled in his head. Tally and that storm combined were almost more than he could handle.

She'd given as much love as she was capable of, and the taste of her still lingered on his tongue. He reached for her hand and squeezed her fingers, wishing they had nothing more pressing to do than climbing the bluff again.

Rebel returned with a pail of water and some cloths. "It's cold, but I don't think we can wait for water to heat. Good Lord, I don't think he's taken a bath in six months! It'll serve him right to get one with cold water."

Tally turned to Clay. "Can you keep an eye on Violet until I finish here? That girl has taken to her newfound independence like a bird that's learned to fly."

"Sure, darlin'. I'll try to keep her out of trouble, but I may have to clip baby girl's wings a tad." He grinned, pushing back Tally's hair. He cupped her cheek and captured her enticing mouth with a kiss that stole every thought from his head.

Behind them, Rebel was throwing things. He ended the kiss and turned to find her staring a hole in him, clearly fuming about the change of events. Good. Maybe she'd gotten the message.

"Tally, holler if you need me. I won't go far." Clay gave Rebel a smile. "Don't kill Montana. He's made promises."

Before Rebel could reply, Clay held the tent flap for Belle, on her way in.

For a moment, Clay watched Violet explore. Her excitement in discovering the smallest things about her dark world was something to see. She picked up a rock, examined it, and smiled. He'd give anything to know what she was seeing with her fingers.

Tobias fell into step with him. "You're in a much happier mood, Colby. Glad to see it."

Clay glanced toward the bluff where his world had shifted amid thunder and lightning. "That was some gully washer last night. I guess all I needed was a good old thunderstorm." And his wife's satiny body beneath him.

Two riders came through the town's opening and he recognized Pete and Otis, the men he'd sent to track Tarver, Finch, and Abrams. He hurried toward them.

They dismounted and Clay had never seen two more weary riders. Both were covered with mud.

Pete attempted a smile but seemed to settle for a quick quirk of his mouth. "We found 'em all right. After we finished with 'em, they're limping back to Creedmore. I don't think you have to worry too much right now."

"Good." The news gave Clay satisfaction. "You and Otis get some rest and eat."

He watched them make their way toward the watering trough for their mounts and went to give Tally the good news. She needed all she could get.

If he could save her and those women in Deliverance Canyon, maybe it would atone for his mistake so long ago that continued to haunt him.

Eighteen

FOUR DAYS PASSED WITH MONTANA'S LEG CONTINUING TO worse. If he didn't get a doctor soon, he would die. However, Tally and Belle continued to do everything they knew to save him.

On the fifth morning, Tally woke up with Clay on her mind. He'd spent as much time with her as he could. He'd picked flowers for her, toted water to her garden, and helped with Violet. But they hadn't made love since the night of the storm, much to her regret.

"This is ending today, one way or another," she muttered to herself. "I can't live like this."

She'd made a commitment to Clay and she meant to honor it. They were married and they needed to act married. If she didn't grab this, the only thing left for her would be a life of loneliness, listening to the sound of her own heartbeat in the dark, praying dawn would come soon. She'd die a shriveled, old woman.

This wasn't about Rebel. It was about her, and a change was coming.

After cleaning up the breakfast dishes and getting Violet out into the sunshine, she grabbed her shawl. She met Clay and Rebel coming from the new house. Rebel gave her a knowing stare and the lift of an eyebrow. The urge rose in Tally to claw her eyes out.

Clay removed her hand from his arm. "You need to see about Montana, Rebel."

"Just a minute, Rebel." Tally gave her a wide smile and took her aside. She put her mouth to the woman's ear. "I don't know when you're going to give up and realize that Clay does not want you. His days *and* nights are about to get very full, if you know what I mean. So keep your grubby hands to yourself, honey."

Behind her, Clay cleared his throat and Tally caught his smile before he could hide it. Rebel gave her a look that could kill and flounced away.

"There, I'm glad I could have that conversation with her. God bless poor, misguided people." Tally's smile faded and doubt set in. She took a deep breath. "Clay, can you talk?"

"What's on your mind?"

"Clarity. It seems to me that marriage problems might be easier to work through if the couple is living in the same house. We made commitments to each other, and it's time to honor those. We promised certain things and I want to be a real wife. It's time you moved back into our house." She hesitated a moment. "Will you?"

"Can you give up some of that fierce independence and trust me a little?"

"That's a work in progress, but I'll keep trying until I get there." Tally moistened her dry lips. "I told you I'd sleep beside you and weather the storms. I need you, Clay."

"Are you sure?" His voice thickened. "Once I move back, I'll be there for the duration."

"I'm sure." She laid a hand on the side of his jaw. "My bed is very lonely."

"Then I reckon I need to fix that." His voice roughened as he put a finger under her chin and pressed his lips to hers.

For the next half hour, he moved back into the dugout. Violet couldn't stop grinning and getting in the way. You'd think he'd been gone a month the way the child carried on.

"And you won't ever leave us." She jostled his arm when she felt for his hand.

"Nope, this is for good." He glanced at Tally. God, she was beautiful! Sunlight streamed through the window, picking up the vibrant russet and gold of her hair with a radiance that stole his ability to think. The worry and hard glints had vanished from her blue eyes. They'd grown softer, reminding him of a winter sky—pale, pristine, the color so pure it make him ache.

The lazy contentment rippling under his skin reminded him of the night they'd watched the storm, wearing nothing but satisfied smiles. Violet's small hand curling in his drew attention back to his daughter.

The word lodged in his brain. But that's who she was—his daughter.

Violet's grin stretched. "We all got someplace to belong, and this is where you're supposed to be."

"That's very true." Clay picked her up and slung her over his shoulder. Bullet barked and jumped up on his leg.

Violet giggled. "Where are you taking me?"

He strode to the door. "I'm going to find a patch of yellow and purple wildflowers and let you pick some for your mama."

"I like to smell flowers. They must look awful pretty, sorta like God smiling."

It suddenly felt as if a fist had knocked the air out of him. His voice was raspy. "How did you know, baby girl?"

Violet shrugged. "I just did. God smiles at me all the time."

Clay put an arm around Tally. They were a family, the ones who gave his life added meaning. But how long would this last? A black storm loomed on the horizon, and only one question remained: How bad would it be?

∞

A plum-and-indigo twilight colored the rugged Texas landscape when Luke and Josie Legend finally returned. They led a caravan of wagons, six to be exact, each piled high with more lumber than Clay had ever seen at one time.

He whooped and rode out to meet them. "You don't know what a welcome sight you are. I never thought you'd bring all this at once."

A grin broke across Luke's dark features, and the ex-outlaw rested his arms on his knees. "Sorry we're so late. It took time to put all this together and bring enough manpower too. We're going to stay and help you put this town together, board by board."

His brother, Houston, hollered from the second wagon. "Colby, you're going to get your dream one way or another. Might damn well harelip the governor, though!"

Thickness clogged Clay's throat. He didn't know what to say to these men who'd become like family to him. It took him a moment to find the words. At last, he spoke. "I'm sure your father had plenty to say about you taking these Lone Star men from the ranch."

"Nope." Luke pushed back his hat and wiped his forehead with a shirtsleeve. "This was Stoker's idea. An early Christmas present."

A dozen extra men and all that lumber was some gift, and Christmas was a long way off. On the other hand, Clay was relieved not to find Luke and Houston's brother, Sam, among the bunch. Having a sheriff invade their hiding place was not something any outlaw wanted to see. Sam would've made them all more than a little skittish.

Clay tipped his hat to Luke's pretty blond wife. "Miss Josie, how are you faring? I figured with all the jostling in the wagon on these trips back and forth, you'd have had that baby by now."

She chuckled. "Nope. I think the little squirt is afraid to come out. He thinks we'll put him right to work."

"Smart kid." Clay laughed.

"We still have plenty of time before the big event." Josie sighed contentedly and wrapped her arm around her husband.

Houston hollered out, "Hey, Clay! Lara gave birth to our son, Crockett, a few days ago!"

"You don't say! A celebration is in order." Clay had forged a lasting friendship with the oldest Legend brother the previous year when he'd helped drive two thousand longhorns up the trail to Dodge City and ran into more trouble than they bargained for. "What does Gracie say about her baby brother?"

Houston's smile couldn't get any wider at mention of his daughter. "The little general has gotten even bossier than usual, if you can picture that."

"I can only imagine." The child sure liked to shake her finger and give everyone what for.

"How's Tally?" Josie asked.

"She's just fine." The leather creaked as Clay shifted in the saddle. "I'm sure you ladies will have plenty to talk about. Better get moving. We'll sit down to supper soon."

The most god-awful sound reached his ears. It began as a horse whinny, then changed to the loudest braying he'd ever heard. He swung around to see another wagon coming alongside, this one pulled by a pair of braying mules. The woman driver wore a large, floppy hat and was smoking a cigar. What in God's name?

Houston grinned. "Oh, I almost forgot. Meet Dr. Marguerite Cuvier, or Dr. Mary as we call her. She's recently moved from Indian Territory. She finally got her wish and made it to Texas."

Dr. Mary shifted her cigar and reached for Clay's hand. "Nice to meet you. I hear you're in need of a doctor in this new town. I'd like to settle here."

Uh-oh! Rebel's new position hadn't lasted long. Clay didn't think she'd take this lying down. Still, treating Montana definitely hadn't been to Rebel's taste, and Dr. Mary appeared quite capable of holding her own. She appeared to have plenty of grit and didn't look like she'd back down from anyone. A necklace made of bullets hung around her neck. Houston had described that string of spent ammunition to him last year on that cattle drive, and Clay was happy to see it at last. It was pretty unusual. The piece of jewelry would make a person think twice before tangling with her.

"Drive on in and make yourselves at home," Clay called. He galloped ahead to tell Tally they needed lots more food.

And he wanted to be there to intervene when Rebel found out she'd been replaced—again.

⤳

Tally leaned against Clay, his breath fluttering the hair at her temple, as she watched the approaching caravan. He held Violet's hand and Bullet sat at the girl's feet. The wagons rolled to a stop and everyone climbed down. As soon as Luke helped Josie to the ground, she waddled over to hug Tally.

Her condition made Tally a little nervous, her size making her look ready to pop any minute.

"Luke tried to talk me into staying home, but I insisted on coming. I couldn't wait to see you." Josie turned to study Violet. "You've changed, girl. What's happened?"

"My…Mr. Clay taught me how to see with a long stick." Violet beamed full of pride. "And I can walk holding on to the rope on the trails." She pulled Josie down. "I found Montana and he's hurt real bad. He's my friend."

Tally draped an arm around Violet's small shoulders, wondering what she'd been about to call Clay. Was she thinking of him as more than someone she lived with?

Josie glanced at Tally, confusion on her face. "Isn't Montana the outlaw who set the town on fire?"

"Uh-huh, but he didn't mean it." Violet firmly took her stick with one hand, the other grasped Bullet's fur, and she went off to explore the world that still held much mystery.

Tally's gaze followed the girl to the tent where Montana lay. "It's a long story, Josie. That girl adores Montana. He saved her from getting snake bit."

"She doesn't even resemble the same frightened child. It's amazing." Josie linked her arm through Tally's. "We have some catching up to do. How are things between you and Clay?"

"They're good—now. I'll tell you later. First, I need to round up more supper." Tally had swung toward the supper that was cooking when Rebel raised her voice.

"Lady, I don't know who you think you are, but I'm the doctor here." Fire shot from Rebel's eyes as she blocked the entrance to the tent, barring Dr. Mary.

The cigar-smoking doctor calmly studied Rebel. "I didn't intend to take your place, miss. I hear the man inside is pretty bad off and you may have to amputate his leg." Dr. Mary shrugged. "It takes a powerful arm to saw through a thick leg bone, but if you can handle it, then I'll help Josie and Tally with supper." She turned toward the bubbling pots at the campfire.

Tally grinned, and her liking for the bullet-wearing doctor grew right then and there.

"Wait. Don't be so hasty." Rebel ran after the doctor and yanked on her arm. "I was only filling in until you got here. I'm more than happy to turn the job over to you. I'll just find something else to do that's less…messy. Like trimming toenails and barbering. I can cut hair real good. These men are a shaggy lot. Why, it might take me a few months to whip them into shape, and by then, it'll be time to start over."

This was getting more entertaining than a peephole in an outhouse. Rebel sure knew when to hold 'em *and* fold 'em. Tally needed to help Belle with supper, but she couldn't tear herself away from the drama unfolding. Josie appeared to be just as riveted.

Rebel clutched the doctor's arm tightly. "I'll even let you use the tent until you can get your own set up. No charge. Montana Black is all yours. I'd be obliged if you'd take him off my hands."

Tally hid her grin. Rebel was quick to get rid of anything that spelled real work. True, Dr. Mary had exaggerated some, but Montana was still a very sick man, requiring a lot of care.

"Only if you're sure." Dr. Mary pried Rebel's fingers loose. "I wouldn't want to put you out and you've already gotten started."

"No, please." Rebel's wild eyes darted, pleading. "I barely got set up. It stinks bad enough in my tent to gag a maggot. I've already thrown up twice this afternoon. I'm just not cut out for this doctoring business. There's no blood or amputations in cutting nails and hair. That's got to be my calling."

"Put that way, I guess the only thing for me to do is take care of this poor, sick man." Dr. Mary patted Rebel's hand. "If you need something to settle that stomach, come see me."

"I will. Oh, I will." Rebel headed for the group of men at a fast trot.

Tally turned to Josie. "I wish we'd had Dr. Mary when Rebel first rode in. Come, let me introduce you to Tobias and Belle January. They're already like family, and I love them dearly."

Belle glanced up from stirring one of the pots and laid down her big wooden spoon. "You ladies are two peas in a pod. I can see how happy you are just being together."

Tally introduced Josie. "I met this woman last year and knew I'd found a lasting friend. Josie went through quite an experience with Luke, and now they're about to have a new addition to their family."

"Do you mind if I lay my hand on your belly?" Belle asked.

Josie smiled. "Not at all. He's sure squirming today. Not sure why he's so restless."

Belle rested a gnarled hand on Josie's stomach and worry crossed the old woman's face. Tally wondered what she thought, but she wouldn't ask in front of Josie. Belle composed herself quickly and winked, giving Josie a smile. "I think he'll be here very soon."

"Oh no, ma'am." Josie's eyes widened as she sat down. "He can't come until I get back to the Lone Star. Luke's father, Stoker, will kill me. Besides, I have my heart set on Dr. Jenkins to help me."

Tally met Belle's worried glance and gently warned, "Josie, have you ever considered that your plans could change? Babies have a way of coming whenever they choose."

She hoped not, though. Whatever would they do if things took a turn? How would they keep a babe alive that had been born too soon? Tally had complete faith in Belle's sense about these things though. The woman had lived way too long not to know what she was talking about.

"Nope, this one is going to follow the schedule, and my calendar says he's not coming for another two months." Josie's glance slid to Luke and softened. He'd hunkered down on his heels with Clay, Jack, and Ridge, drawing in the dirt. Houston strode toward them.

Tally supposed the men were discussing the buildings soon to go up. The happiness on Luke's face made her heart swell. Like Clay, he'd gone through things no man should have to and cheated death more times than he had a right. The look of peace her old friend now wore had come very slowly. Just this once, she prayed, please let Belle be wrong. Don't let anything ruin the perfect life he and Josie had found.

Best to keep busy. Tally turned to the blissful blond woman

who'd stolen Luke's heart. "Josie, we'd best see to supper. Our men will be starving."

Before they took a step, Violet came from the doctor tent, holding her stick in front of her, feeling her way. Bullet rose from his spot near the opening and nudged the girl's hand. A smile formed on her face and she gave the dog a hug. Love burst in Tally's chest as she watched her sightless daughter make her way toward the men, using the sound of their voices to guide her. Violet had bravery and spunk—and Clay had helped her find it.

Their life was pretty darn good, too. But for how long?

The secrets she kept could ruin what they'd found. Clay would have to know sooner or later. She rubbed her eyes to rid them of the haunting images of what she'd done. Dear God!

This unforgiving Texas land either made a person stronger or crippled their spirit. There were no half-measures or promises. Somehow, someway, Tally would find strength to fight. Having Clay back in the dugout strengthened her sagging resolve. She was his wife and it didn't hurt to remind him of his vows. Herself too. She'd lost sight of what she'd promised.

What they had wasn't perfect, but neither was life. Like the town, her marriage still appeared a work in progress.

Nineteen

IN THE WEEK THAT FOLLOWED, EVERYONE WORKED FROM SUNUP to sundown—sawing, hammering, and nailing. The new buildings were making Clay's dream of a town a reality again and that thrilled Tally. She yearned for her husband to succeed. He'd struggled too hard for too long.

They'd made love every night since their talk, and Tally had never felt so complete. She was slowly losing some of her independence and letting Clay make the decisions. He had her best interests at heart, and she knew he would not do anything to cause her grief. This morning, he made her close her eyes and brought her into the dugout. She opened them to see two new dresses on the bed. She turned to him. "What's this?"

"I asked Josie to pick you up some new dresses, but when she got here and compared them to one of your old ones, she decided to alter them to fit. She just finished."

Tears hovered behind Tally's eyes. "Oh, Clay. I haven't had anything new in a very long time. They're beautiful. Thank you."

Clay kissed the back of her neck, his touch warm against her. "I want to give you nice things. You work so hard and never complain. I can't wait to see them on you."

"Is it okay if I wait until after I bathe tonight? I'm all sweaty."

"I understand, and of course it's all right. I have to get back to work anyway."

Tally kissed him and he went out, leaving her with her pretty dresses. She sat on the bed and fingered the texture of the fine lawn muslin of one—a sea green—and lifted it to her face. Clay's thoughtfulness and caring brought tears. She couldn't help feeling treasured. The other dress was a simple calico that she could work in. The print of small white flowers against a blue background was very pretty. She'd needed a few new clothes but had hesitated asking Clay.

She wiped her eyes and thought of this man she'd married. He was a mixture of contrasts. He could explode in rage when faced with evil yet make love to her with such gentleness. And he paid attention to her needs, like these dresses.

How she'd gotten so lucky, she didn't know.

⁓

Over the last few days, Josie Legend amazed Tally. The woman appeared to have gotten a new head of steam, and despite her big stomach, had taken over most of the cooking. So far, she showed no sign of slowing.

Rebel had hung out her barbering shingle, so after the men stopped work for the day, they lined up for a haircut and shave, nail trimming on the side, and whatever else the woman could think of. She had a booming business, and not a big surprise, nighttime appeared to be her prime hours. Tally wondered what else she was offering in that tent but didn't really want to find out. Since Clay had assured her he was giving the woman a wide berth, she saw no need to poke her nose into Rebel's affairs.

The saloon was another lively place once the end had been rebuilt, and Rebel's laughter often drifted through the canvas walls, yet Clay never spared it a glance.

One evening, as the shadows grew long, Tally was happy to see Jack riding in, covered in trail dust. He dismounted and went to her. "Infection is gone from Hester Mason's wound and I left plenty of herbs and supplies to last awhile."

She hugged him. "Thank you, Jack. I was so worried. If anything happened to Hester, those women would be at a great loss. And you saved me from going."

Clay walked up and slid his arm around her waist. "Everything goes better when we work together."

Jack slapped his hat against his trousers and dirt flew. "Tally, why didn't you tell me how bad things are for those escapees? Those women are barely surviving."

"I know, but no one would believe unless they saw it."

"Well, we've got to do something quick."

Tally felt the urgency as well. The sand in the hourglass was down to a few grains. She and Clay had to put together a plan and soon.

As though Clay read her mind, he rasped, "We'll get them out." He swung to Jack. "Did you talk to Darcy?"

Jack's face darkened. "We talked."

"And?"

"I don't know. I just don't know. She's torn." Jack limped toward the trough with his horse.

Tally's heart ached for the tall outlaw and the life that appeared beyond reach.

Clay draped an arm around her neck. "We can't fix everything, darlin'."

❧

That night, after putting Violet to bed, she pulled back the covers and slid in next to Clay's warm body. She rested her head on his chest, the soft beating of his heart beneath her ear. Each joining of their bodies had become even more special. One by one, his gentle caresses and words of comfort slowly filled in all the holes that riddled her heart.

He drew her close, one hand resting on her stomach. "I don't know what you see in me, but I'm glad you're my wife."

"Clay, Rebel really is a thing of the past, isn't she?"

He nuzzled behind her ear. "Absolutely."

"I keep seeing her coming from where you are." She drew lazy circles on his chest. "I don't think you understand how devious some women can be." And he definitely couldn't see the knowing smirks Rebel kept giving her.

"There is one thing you ought to know about me. I'm a one-woman man. My heart only has room for one and that's you." Clay kissed her as his palm slid across her flat stomach—and lower.

"You have the softest skin I've ever felt. You're so beautiful. Sometimes I think this is just a dream. If it is, I never want to wake up." His raspy voice was thick with emotion.

Tally put Rebel out of her mind once and for all and relished Clay's gentle touch that awakened every sense, made her dream of a forever.

Heated passion raced through Tally, making talk a tad difficult.

"I aim to make you beg for mercy, pretty wife."

"Oh, you are, are you?" Tally grinned into the dimness surrounding them.

The next moment, she gave a little cry as he fondled her breast, raking a thumbnail lightly across the swollen nipple that greedily raised, begging for more. His lips found hers and she was lost in a haze of heated desire for this man who'd first seen something worthwhile in her letters to him.

A curl of fire slid lazily along her spine and made her breath hitch in anticipation. This husband of hers had quickly learned what she liked, and he took every chance to make sure she got the most pleasure from their lovemaking.

He tweaked, nibbled, licked, and kissed his way down her body until she throbbed with overpowering hunger. This level of heat wouldn't be satisfied until Clay climbed on top of her. Though he seemed in no hurry, and therein lay a problem. She was ready for him now. This raging need inside her cried for fulfillment.

His hand slid down the length of her, his fingers dawdling at every hill and valley until she was ready to scream. Clay Colby's slow hand drove her insane. But she did her own share of stoking the fire. She slid her hand between them and stroked his swollen need. Ragged moans escaped from his throat.

Finally, he raised himself over her and she welcomed him.

They did their best to keep quiet, for fear of waking Violet behind the curtained wall. Pleasure washed over Tally in waves, building with each stroke. Gasping, she reached the pinnacle and fell over the other side, into a beautiful, tranquil place where there was no pain, no heartache, no worry.

She lay limp, her bones fluid, drifting, savoring her happiness.

When her heartbeat slowed enough and she could speak, Tally kissed the hard planes of his chest. "I'm glad we have enough men to guard at night so you don't have to take all the shifts."

"That makes two of us. It's been nice having the extra willing people."

His deep voice rumbled against her ear. She loved that sound that reminded her of the wheels of a train—always pulling a load, always moving forward, always strong as steel.

"I can't believe how fast the buildings are going up." She drew lazy circles on his arm. They'd already framed two and would start putting on the walls and roofs soon, and that was in addition to the work Clay had started on their house. "I'm happy you're building us a new place to live, but I wonder if you aren't rushing things. Maybe we should focus on the stores and businesses first."

"Nope." He lifted her hand and kissed the back. "With each board we nail, it's one more plank in the foundation of our marriage. We're building both, one board at a time."

Tally glanced up at his profile in the darkness and traced the scar from someone's angry knife that ran along his cheek. "I never thought of it that way. Both are going to be sturdy."

"Yes, ma'am. For a fact." He rolled a lock of her hair between his thumb and forefinger. "You have the most beautiful hair this side of glory. I never get tired of looking at you. Who would've thought this old, scarred-up outlaw would find a woman like you?"

"Scarred-up maybe, but you're not old. You have your best years ahead of you."

Clay sighed. "Sometimes I feel as old and worn-out as this land. And then I look at you and think I'm twenty again. You were worth every bit of the wait." With a light palm on her throat, he hungrily kissed her upturned mouth.

Outside, goats bleated, and inside, Bullet moved through the dugout, a silent guard. They were safe, happy. Secure.

Clay's soft breath ruffled at her temple, his hand lightly resting on her stomach.

Tally drifted off with a smile on her face. She'd never known such peace.

A woman's sudden scream cut through her languid dream.

For a moment, she was back in the dark gloom of Creedmore Lunatic Asylum.

Tally covered her ears to block out a woman's screams. She made herself as small as she could in a corner of her small, dirty room. The screams continued and Tally curled tightly into a ball. If Tarver came to her room, maybe he wouldn't see her. Guilt rushed through her that someone else was suffering in her place. Where was the knife she'd stolen from the kitchen?

Clay's voice penetrated the nightmare. "Wake up, Tally. Something's wrong."

Finally, the dream released its hold. She wasn't in Creedmore.

Another scream ripped into her, sounding like something from a wild animal.

"Josie!" Her heart thudding against her ribs, Tally leaped from bed. She and Clay frantically dressed and bolted from the dugout, leaving Violet asleep.

Luke ran from the wagon where he and Josie had made their bed. "Dr. Mary! Come quick!"

The doctor hurried from her tent, clutching her black bag tightly. Houston raced past Tally, his face haggard, eyes grim. He joined his brother, who stood with Clay, surrounded by the chaos of the night.

Tally didn't break stride, arriving at Josie's side with the doctor.

Sweat drenched Josie's face. "He's coming! He's not supposed to come now. Oh God, he's not supposed to come yet. Please save him. Luke needs his son. Don't let this babe die."

"Lie back, Mrs. Legend, and try to relax." Dr. Mary's voice was calm, her touch comforting. "I'm going to see what's happening. It could be nothing." But when Dr. Mary lifted the sheet, Tally could only stare in horror at the soaked blankets Josie lay on. No one had to tell her what this meant.

She inhaled sharply. Reaching for Josie's hand, she gave it a comforting squeeze. "Hold on, Josie. Don't panic. Take some deep breaths. We're going to get you through this."

"I'm scared. The babe is too early. Oh!" Josie moaned and gripped her stomach.

Dr. Mary laid her hand over Josie's. "Now, honey, don't fight the contractions. Just relax and let it happen the way it's supposed to. Women give birth every day."

The doctor's tender ways with Josie and the calm that oozed from her voice bolstered Tally. "Josie, I'm going to get Luke to carry you to the dugout. Our bed will be much more comfortable. And I'll get some water heating, Doctor."

"All good ideas." Dr. Mary drew a light blanket over her patient.

Tally met Belle as she climbed from the wagon and laid a hand on the old woman's shoulder. "It's as you feared."

"I didn't want it to be true." Large tears rolled down Belle's wrinkled cheeks. "I knew by how the little thing was twisting and turning that something didn't seem right."

"The doctor will do her best." Tally tenderly smoothed back a strand of silver hair from the old woman's face. "Can Violet sleep in your tent?"

Belle managed a wan smile. "Absolutely. Let's move her now."

With a nod, Tally hurried to the men, and in no time, they had both Josie and Violet moved and settled.

Inside the dugout with Josie on the comfortable bed, Dr. Mary took Tally aside and spoke low. "The babe is breach. This will be difficult at best."

She didn't need to be told what the worst would be. "Have you told Luke?" Tally glanced at her old friend.

He sat beside the bed, his large hand clutching his wife's. Tally blinked hard, overcome by the lines of worry etched on his face. Tally'd once brought Luke back from death's door after he'd been shot up, and he'd never once abandoned her and the other women hiding in Deliverance Canyon. The man who'd kept them in food and supplies now faced the possible loss of his child—and maybe his wife as well.

A breach birth…she'd heard how often they'd had to bury the child. And sometimes the mother too.

"Yes, he knows." Dr. Mary's gaze followed Tally's. "I'm told that man has seen his share of trouble, but he appears strong. I can't get him to leave his wife's side."

"He loves Josie so much." Tears stung the back of Tally's eyes as she gathered every soft cloth she could find, then hurried to the well. She drew a pail of water and placed it amid the glowing coals of the campfire to heat.

As though sensing she needed him, Clay moved beside her and put his arms around her. She leaned into his warmth, borrowing from his strength, thankful he wasn't the kind to run from trouble.

Clay held her tightly to him. "How bad?"

"She may lose the baby. It's breach." Tally rested her head on his shoulder and took comfort in his hand rubbing her spine. "If this babe dies, I don't know that Josie can take it. Or Luke either. They've pinned so many hopes on this child. Oh, Clay, my heart breaks for them. Do you think it was from all the jostling in the wagon, making those trips here?"

"I suppose it's possible, but I sure hope I'm not to blame."

"Whatever happens, it's not your fault. Josie is too headstrong for her own good. Luke tried to get her to stay behind this time, only she refused."

Giving her one last kiss, Clay released her. "You need to go. Don't worry about baby girl. I'll see to her."

Tally nodded, unable to speak any more past the lump in her throat. Before she took a step, she heard Clay mumble, "Damn Mondays."

Dr. Mary worked tirelessly through the night with Tally and Belle helping at her side. Luke refused to leave, holding Josie's hand, love and dark worry clouding his eyes. Several times, he turned his head into the shadows, to hide his tears, she suspected.

Would their marriage withstand it if the baby didn't survive—or worse? Tally tried to brace herself against the possibility of Luke not only losing the infant but Josie as well. The woman was so weak and fading in and out of consciousness. If Luke lost both...

Outlaws like Luke and Clay needed very little reason to let anger and despair take over and return to their old ways. That was often easier than learning to live with loss.

Tally glanced out the window where Clay stood smoking, waiting with the nervous men. She admired the strong set of his shoulders and lean form. Would they face this same situation one day? It was a distinct possibility that she could be with child right now. She placed her hand on her stomach. But that would be a miracle after everything that had happened to her at the horror that was Creedmore.

Behind her came the whisper of desperation as Dr. Mary worked to turn the baby in Josie's womb.

The minutes ticked slowly by.

With each passing breath, Tally's heart pounded harder.

She clenched her hands together and prayed.

After what seemed an eternity, she heard the doctor's relieved sigh. "I got the babe turned, Luke."

"My child's going to be all right?"

"Not saying that. There are no guarantees in this life. From what I've heard about you, Luke, you should know that. Your wife is unable to push and that compounds the situation." Dr. Mary washed her hands, then turned her attention to Josie, checking her breathing.

Josie lay with her eyes closed, her face ashen in the lamplight.

Worry darkened Dr. Mary's eyes and fear again swept up Tally's spine. If the doctor, with all her knowledge and ability, had doubts about Josie's and the baby's chances, then Tally had little hope left to cling to.

Luke leaned over his wife and brushed damp tendrils of hair from her face. "Fight, *corazón*. That's what you told me as I lay dying. Fight with everything you have—for me and our unborn babe. We're a family and, *Dios mío*, we're going to stay one. Do you hear me?"

Although his words appeared harsh, Luke wrapped them in velvet. His agony was hard for Tally to bear.

Josie's mouth moved and her eyes opened. Her voice was

weak. "Luke, I never thought I'd love anyone the way I love you. Promise to raise our child yourself, not give him to someone else to care for. A son needs his father."

"Don't talk like that." Luke sobbed brokenly. "You're going to come through this."

The lump in Tally's throat blocked the air. Even though she knew it was a real probability, she couldn't face the thought of having to bury her friend.

"Promise me." Josie tried to grip Luke's vest, but her hand dropped limply. "Promise."

"I will so long as you don't give up fighting." Luke kissed her forehead. "*Princesa*, I'll never stop loving you."

Josie's breath burst from her, she stiffened, and fear widened her eyes. "Oh!" With a little whimper, Josie went limp and lost consciousness.

Dr. Mary pushed Luke aside and raised Josie's eyelids to check the pupils. "She's slipped into unconsciousness again. We've got to get this babe out. Luke, it's best if you wait outside."

Luke released Josie's hand and ran his fingers through his dark hair. "Can I do anything, anything at all?"

"You can pray."

White-faced, Luke grabbed Tally's shoulders. "Let me know what's happening or by God I'll bust in here."

"I will." Only, if things took a turn, how could she tell him he'd lost everything again?

Houston emerged with Clay from the shadows and took his brother's arm. "I think we can use a stiff drink."

Clay gave Tally a kiss. "If you need me, I'll be here." Then he followed the men into the endless night.

The coming hours held the answers to everything. How often she'd huddled in a cold corner in the black inkiness of Creedmore, filled with uncertainty and dread. She already missed Clay's touch, his strength, his quiet confidence.

The doctor reached for her black bag and pulled out a strange-looking apparatus.

Tobias January is a coffin maker. Tally didn't know why the thought popped into her head. Her heart would break into a million pieces to hear the sound of his hammer.

She swallowed a sob. Would the coming morn bring life? Or death?

Twenty

THE FIRST RAYS OF DAYLIGHT BROKE THROUGH HEAVY clouds that hung like a shroud over the tiny town, and Clay rubbed his weary eyes. The endless night had taken such a toll on everyone, huddled together in worry. Everything stood silent and still, every creature and blade of grass. Even the windmill blades seemed frozen in place.

Waiting.

Hoping.

Willing the sound of an infant's cry to fall on the hushed breeze. But all the world had stopped, time ceasing to exist.

Luke glanced up with hollow eyes as Clay handed him a cup of coffee. Luke rose, took three strides toward the dwelling, then halted.

"We should know something soon." Clay poured himself a cup of coffee, then sat down to roll a cigarette. The bag of Bull Durham was almost empty, but smoking was the only thing that settled the jagged edges inside him. Strange that Luke didn't smoke. Most outlaws did. Maybe he'd ask him about that one day.

Houston strode from the corral where he'd been silently watching the horses. "Any news?"

"Nope." Clay's thoughts turned to Tally and how the agony must be killing her. He yearned to take her in his arms and tell her everything would be all right. But would that be a lie?

He dragged his attention back to Houston and followed his gaze to Luke's bent form. If Luke lost Josie or his child, it would likely send him spiraling into a dark place from which escape might be impossible. Clay knew too much about dark, hopeless places like that.

A sound alerted him. Clay swung to the door of the

dugout to see Tally. He pushed to his feet, broken by the anguish on her face.

She went directly to Luke. "You have a daughter, but she's struggling to live. She desperately needed two more months in the womb, but if we can keep her warm and fed, she has a chance."

Luke blinked and swallowed hard. "I want to see her."

"Of course. We…" Her voice broke. "Josie is very bad."

A wounded cry sprang from Luke's throat as he stumbled toward the dwelling.

Clay broke away from his friends and went to Tally. Her heart hammered wildly. He'd sworn to protect her, but how could he protect her from this? She buried her face in his shoulder, trembling, trying not to give in to her fear. He suspected once she let the dam break, she might not be able to stop it.

"I curse this land, Clay. It takes and takes and takes until our souls are bare. That babe didn't ask for any of this. She's innocent. Why does she have to pay?"

The torment in her voice cut into him. "I wish I knew. It seems like we've had nothing except trouble, but this land gave me you, and for that I'm deeply indebted." He tucked a flaming curl behind her ear, pressing a light kiss to her lips.

For a moment, they held each other, drawing comfort and strength to face whatever the coming day brought.

"Sometimes, if we're lucky, there's a crack in the darkness and light seeps in. You're my light, Tally. My hope, my salvation, my future."

She wrapped her arms around him and stared up with shimmering eyes. "Strange, but that's exactly how I feel about you."

His touch gentle, he ran his hand up and down the curve of her back and waist. No words were necessary. The pall of death covered the town, holding them in its grip, and the only way to cope was in each other's arms, as one against overwhelming odds.

Slowly, he became aware of the stirring town and the people drifting around them.

With great reluctance, Clay released her. "You should eat

something, darlin'. It's going to be a long day, and maybe you can spend a few moments with Violet to let our daughter know you're all right. She cried out for you in the night and I held her in my lap until she fell back asleep. She senses things and is very worried that you'll disappear."

Tally ran a weary hand over her eyes. "I'll have a talk with her and maybe take her to see the goats."

"Excellent idea. Speaking of those critters, I need to milk them." Before Clay could move, Luke came from the dugout.

"I have a daughter." Luke gave Houston a half smile, as though fear held him back, and shoved his hand through his black hair. "A little girl and she's beautiful, like her mother."

"We'll have to think of a good name for her." Houston gave him a rough, brotherly hug. "Pa needed another granddaughter."

The two brothers had a deep bond between them and Clay envied their closeness. He wished for his own brother, John Colby. To see him once more. But chances were high that he lay on some battlefield, his bones bleaching under the sun, forgotten, alone. Hopefully, someone had buried him. Clay prayed they had.

Yeah, he'd like to tell John how much he loved and missed him.

Violet emerged from the January's tent with Tobias. Tally gave a cry and hurried toward them. The old man was a huge help with the girl—always so patient and loving. Violet called him "Grandpa," and that's exactly what he was to her.

Clay walked beside Tally, finding a great need to keep his family close. He'd learned the hard way how fast it could all end.

"I've got a need for some kisses, sweet girl." Tally wrapped her arms around Violet and kissed her cheeks.

The girl's smile stretched as she snuggled into her mama's softness. "I missed you, Mama. How's Miss Josie?"

"She's real sick, sweetheart."

"Will you get sick too?"

Clay picked Violet up. Bullet barked and danced around his

legs, begging for attention too. "No, baby girl. Mama won't get sick. Don't fret about that. Okay?"

"Did Miss Josie have her baby?"

Tally ruffled the dog's ears and tossed a stick. "Yes, and do you know what she had?"

"A girl like me?"

"You guessed it. A sweet little girl, and she's a pretty thing, with lots of dark hair like her daddy."

A wistful look crossed the girl's face. "I wish I could see her."

Tally pulled back Violet's light-golden hair, her heart aching. "I'd give anything if you could, sweetheart." Tally cleared her throat and went on. "When she gets stronger, you can hold her and trace her face with your fingers."

"I can't wait."

"We can't either, baby girl." Clay set her on her feet. "Want to come and help me milk the goats?"

"Okay, but I need to ask you something."

"What's that?"

"Will you please be my daddy?"

Thick emotion rendered Clay unable to speak for a long moment. At last, he managed, "I can be whoever you want, baby girl."

She slipped her small palm inside Clay's hand. "Okay, Daddy, let's go."

Clay met Tally's teary gaze and she smiled. He cleared his throat. "Yep. I can sure use you. Those ornery goats settle right down when you're with them." Clay turned to Tally. "Eat something to keep *your* strength up, darlin'."

He let his free hand slide down the curve of her tattooed cheek before giving his daughter his undivided attention.

❧

Tally watched as they headed up to the noisy goat clan, and she laughed to see the frisky animals scamper around Violet. The girl's squeal of delight was music to her ears. She was slowly figuring out her world and putting people in it who made it brighter. She'd given Clay such a huge gift just now. With a sigh, she turned, aware of a delicious aroma teasing her nose.

Dressed in his usual black shirt and trousers, Jack Bowdre bent over the Dutch oven while Houston held out a plate. "Come eat, Tally."

She crossed the space with her long strides and accepted the food, touched by his caring. "This smells great, Houston."

He winked. "Jack and I know our way around a campfire."

The fragrance wafting from the eggs, peppers, and bacon made her mouth water. She put a forkful in her mouth and groaned. "This is so good."

A smile curved Jack's mouth. "Glad you like it."

Houston's gaze swept to the dugout and pain filled his brown eyes. "Cooking is the only way I know to help."

She didn't know this Legend brother as well as she knew Luke and Sam, but she was just as much at ease around him. All the brothers were tall, but this one was big like his father, Stoker. Clay had told her about Houston and how close the two of them had become.

"Hey, you can't take all the credit." Jack Bowdre hooked his thumbs in his gun belt. "I did my share with this meal."

Houston snorted. "Yeah, you added the salt and pepper and stirred the pot." For a second, everything appeared normal and death was forgotten.

Tally took another bite. "You're both godsends, and that's all I can say."

She turned away, but an argument between Jack, Ridge, Dallas, and Travis drew her back. It appeared to have something to do with drawing straws to see who would help Belle take care of Montana.

"I'm not going to wash his nasty butt, and that's all I'm saying about it," Dallas said hotly.

Ridge patted his Schofield hanging at his side. "I have a bullet that needs someplace to go. Wouldn't much matter if it went into Montana, as mean and bad-tempered as he's been."

"I agree." Jack stared toward the doctor's tent. "I'd let the bastard die if it wouldn't make extra work for Belle January.

That old woman's a saint in my book, but she's no spring chicken. We've got to lighten her load."

Dallas let out a long breath. "Oh, all right. I'll fetch and carry whatever she needs this morning, then one of you can take the afternoon. But I draw the line at being sociable to Montana Black. He can kiss my rear—so long as he washes his face first."

Skeet Malloy doubled over laughing. When the blacksmith sobered, he said, "I'd pay to see that."

Footsteps crunched behind her. Tally turned to see Rebel approaching. Something had shaken the good-time girl. She carried a bundle of lamb's wool, and her face was drawn. "Can we talk, Tally?"

"Sure, if you don't mind doing it while I eat. I need to get back soon and help Dr. Mary. How about if we sit by the windmill? Its music soothes my soul, and I can use that right now."

They moved to the cool shade at the base of the wooden tower and sat on the edge of the tank. Tally closed her eyes for a moment and listened to the creak of the rod going up and down.

"I heard about Josie's babe coming so early." Rebel brushed her fingers across the soft lamb's wool in her arms. "I want her to have this. It might keep the infant alive."

"That's real kind of you. The tiny girl might stand a chance if we can keep her warm and fed." Tally set the plate beside her and reached for her former rival's hand. She'd never seen Rebel so disturbed. "Thank you for this. Even though we keep a heated rock under the child at all times, this will be a tremendous help."

Rebel's chin *quivered*, of all things, and she bit her lip. "I had a babe once." Rebel's voice came low, almost a whisper. A tear slid down her cheek, followed by another. "A little boy. He only lived a month, but I loved him with every bit of my heart."

"Oh, honey, I know you must've." Tally put her arm around the trembling woman, their differences forgotten. "I'm really sorry you didn't get to keep him. Each loss steals a piece of our souls, but to bury a child is the worst kind of pain imaginable." She paused before quickly adding, "Or so I'm told."

"I never knew who the father was. I was real wild back then."

Tally couldn't imagine Rebel being any wilder than she was now. "Life has a way of stomping us into the ground sometimes."

Rebel angrily swiped her tears away and collected herself. "It was probably for the best, you know? I couldn't have given him a good life. But there's something about holding a fragile being in your arms and knowing he's a part of you. I hope Josie's babe survives. Do you think…do you suppose I could help care for the child?"

"I'm sure of it. We can use you." Tally removed her arm from around the woman. "In fact, let's go right now. The doctor needs that lamb's wool, and you can take the next feeding shift." Since the infant was so tiny, Dr. Mary had shown Tally how to use an eyedropper. They painstakingly gave her three droppers full of warm goat's milk every hour around the clock.

They headed to the campfire, where Tally gave Houston her plate and thanked him for the food. "Can you fix a plate for the doctor and bring it to the door?"

"Sure, Tally. Anything to help." He glanced at Rebel curiously but said nothing.

The dugout was dim when Tally and Rebel entered. Luke, his gun belt low around his hips, was cradling his bundled daughter against his chest, humming to her. Tally was struck by the contrast between his size and how tenderly he held the babe—small enough that she could fit in one of his big hands.

Dr. Mary bent over Josie. Tally moved to the end of the bed. "I'm sorry to be gone so long. How is she?"

"Hemorrhaging bad. I've got to get the blood stopped or we'll lose her." Dr. Mary gave her a weary smile. "Can you make another thick poultice? I've got to get more healing herbs inside her and we have no time to waste. While you do that, I'm going to try something I observed in medical school."

"What's that, Doctor?"

"They pressed on the big arteries on each side of the abdomen. Sometimes that works in stopping blood flow. At least it did that once."

At least they had something else to try. Dr. Mary moved into position and began pressing. Tally took the jar of ground herbal powder down with trembling hands, mixed a good portion with yarrow leaves and water until she had a thick, brown goo. She dropped a large bit onto a clean cloth and handed it to Dr. Mary.

"This has to work. It just has to."

If not, Josie's would be the first grave in the new town.

"Goldenseal is the best there is to stop bleeding." The doctor bent to place the poultice inside Josie. "And with the yarrow added and pressure on the arteries, it should work well."

While Dr. Mary applied pressure on the arteries, she asked for a thick cloth, then some water to bathe Josie's face, then asked her to check on the baby. After Tally did all that, the doctor put her on the left side of Josie to press down hard on the other artery. She followed the doctor's every movement, praying that their efforts would save Josie. She was vaguely aware that Rebel stood silent, watching.

After what seemed like hours, Dr. Mary glanced up and Tally unclenched muscles she didn't know she held rigid and breathed deeply. "Doctor, Rebel brought some thick lamb's wool for the baby."

Rebel's satin dress rustled as she stepped forward. "It's the least I can do. I don't need it."

"Bless you. It's exactly what I was wishing for. Tally, lay that on the bed and swaddle the babe in it," Dr. Mary ordered, still pressing hard on Josie's abdomen.

"Thank you for giving this up, Rebel." Luke's deep voice made his tiny daughter stir. Tally watched how the infant turned toward the sound of her father. Even so small, the baby girl seemed to know him.

Perhaps the very young knew things on a deeper level than she thought.

He brought the infant over, carefully eased her into the warm cushion of lamb's wool, then tucked the soft fabric snug around the small body to hold in the heat. "There you go, sweetheart. Sleep and dream of being a princess, because that's what you are." When he glanced up, tears shimmered in his eyes.

A lump tightened in Tally's chest. She laid a hand on his arm. "Houston made breakfast. Go get yourself fed. And coffee. You look like you can use some."

With a nod, he crossed to the bed and pressed his lips to Josie's colorless ones. He stood for a long moment, gazing at his wife and daughter as though afraid of seeing them perhaps for the last time, then turned and went out the door.

Dr. Mary's quiet voice filled the room. "Tally, can you check the packing to see if the blood flow is slowing?"

"Sure." Saying a prayer, Tally lifted the light blanket. "It soaked the new packing but maybe it happened before you applied the pressure."

"Possible. I'll work a bit longer and change the packing, then we'll know more."

Rebel pushed back a loose tendril of hair and tugged up the low bodice of her red satin dress. "I came to help, Doctor. I can feed, warm a rock, or anything else you need."

"I can use every hand." Using her head, Dr. Mary motioned toward a crock on the table. "Rebel, ladle out a few spoonfuls of milk and warm it. It'll soon be time to feed the little one."

Tally moved to the bed and took Josie's lifeless hand. "Has she woken at all, Doctor?"

"No, but that's not unusual. Sleep might help her regain strength…if we can completely stem the hemorrhage. Come and apply pressure while I change the packing."

Tally moved to the doctor's side and did exactly as she said.

Jack appeared at the door with a plate of food. Dr. Mary thanked him and set it aside, then changed Josie's packing.

"The trick seems to be working," Dr. Mary announced. "The blood is slowing." She washed her hands and sat down at the table to eat.

Rebel removed some heated water off the stove and set a

small container of milk in it to warm. When the saloon girl allowed herself to think about someone else, Tally marveled at her competence. This painted a very different picture from the woman so full of laughter who'd been hell-bent on rekindling her romance with Clay. Tally found her heart going out to Rebel and kicked herself for judging too harshly.

No one spoke. Tally shivered. Even though Josie's skin was cool beneath her touch, death hovered much too close for comfort. Time appeared to be measured by the sound of the hammers outside as work on the town commenced.

Each nail driven in was another triumph for the living—as long as Tobias's hammer alone stayed idle.

The doctor stuffed the last bite in her mouth and came to relieve Tally.

Weak cries, no louder than a kitten's, came from the tiny babe. Tally picked up the fragile life from a box near the stove, then cradled the child against her. She hummed a soft lullaby she remembered from her childhood so long ago, before the world turned dark and ugly.

Despite the soft hum, the cries continued. Tally walked to the bed and laid the tiny bundle under the blanket, the baby touching Josie. Suddenly, a hush settled over the dwelling.

It seemed as though by some strange sense the child knew she was with her mother.

Tears bubbled in Tally's eyes. She leaned over. "Wake up, Josie. Your daughter needs her mama. Don't you want to see how beautiful she is? She needs a name."

But Josie slept on.

Tally went to the window and gazed out across the town. Luke stood apart from the outlaws around the fire, staring into the horizon, the plate of food in his hand untouched. Deep pain lined his face until it more resembled a cratered minefield. In this state, he seemed unable, or unwilling, to name the child. His little daughter needed what no one could give.

Tally didn't want to consider the possibility, but if the child gave up fighting, how would they word her marker? Nameless child of Luke and Josie?

Pain-riddled memories of Creedmore suddenly rose. Tally's lip trembled.

She knew she'd have to tell Clay her secret. But how?

And would he still want her?

Twenty-one

THE FOLLOWING GRAY MORNING HELD NO CHEER. THE SKY reflected the concern on each face. Clay rolled a cigarette and lit it, his gaze moving to Luke, sitting alone by the campfire, staring into the flames. His heart ached for his friend, and he knew no words to ease the pain reflected on his face. Luke could face down and kill a man at twenty paces, but he'd be entirely lost without the woman who'd weathered good times and bad by his side during their short marriage.

Movement at the window captured Clay's attention. He met Tally's stare through the thick pane of glass, worry lining her beautiful features. Never had he felt so helpless.

No gun or bullet could fix the enemy Josie and Luke fought.

Clay breathed deeply of the humid morning air and rose. His search for Violet found her with Belle and Tobias January. Satisfied she was looked after, he strode to the dugout. At least he might be of help to Tally.

A twist of the knob opened the door and he met Tally's eyes. "If the doctor can spare you, come and take a walk with me before I start work today. I need to know you're all right."

Tally managed a smile, such as was possible under the circumstances. "Dr. Mary, can you do without me for a bit?"

Muted light through the open doorway glinted off the doctor's bullet necklace. "Take a break. You've earned it. Besides, Rebel's here, and we'll feed the babe. I'll go check on Montana once you're back, but I hear Belle's taking good care of him."

"Okay." Tally reached for her shawl hanging on the back of a chair and threw it around her shoulders. "The fresh air will do wonders."

A light knock sounded on the door, and Tally opened it to find Tobias. The old man handed her a burlap sack. "I found a patch of yarrow. Sort of figured you might run low."

Dr. Mary appeared beside Tally. "Tobias January, you're a saint. I don't know how you knew, but I could kiss you."

The grizzled old man's face flushed. "Glad you can use it. Tell me if you need more." Tally added her thanks and Tobias left.

Clay put his arm around his wife, and they went out together. "Violet's with Belle, so don't worry. Let's go check on our house. I'd like to see what you think."

Tally snuggled against his side and Clay anchored her there, loving the feel of her body next to him. He cast her a sideways glance. "I'm glad I convinced you to come. I needed to be alone with you for a few moments. Just us."

"I'm sorry our routine got upended. I miss our private time too. And the dancing."

Something about the way their boots struck the rocky ground brought a sense of peace to Clay's soul. He hoped it did to Tally as well. She looked very pretty in that new calico dress. He didn't think she'd had many new clothes in the last few years, and he loved making her eyes light up.

"Though it's only been a short time, it seems forever since Josie screamed out in the night." He glanced down at her, marveling how the sun's rays coming through the clouds caught on her hair, bringing out the fiery glints mixed with gold. Tally reminded him of shifting, ever-changing smoke—elusive, impossible to contain, and at times hard to see through. Just when he thought he had her all figured out, she showed him how little he really knew.

Tired lines deepened around her eyes, but you'd never guess the depth of her exhaustion by the way she kept on taking care of everyone. He had no idea how she kept going, kept giving.

His voice trembled. "It's difficult to watch Luke. I've never seen anyone so broken." He tightened his arm around her a little more and buried his face in her hair. "But I would be too if it were you lying in that bed so near death."

Tally's voice was soft. "I think Luke's afraid to give the babe a name. Maybe afraid once he does, she'll die."

"I disagree. I think he's waiting for Josie to wake up so she can help with the chore. They only had a boy's name picked out."

"Just goes to show you can never tell about these things. I just pray Josie makes it."

"I'm worried what Luke will do if she doesn't." Clay didn't know how he'd keep living if anything happened to Tally. Strange that they'd only been married a month and yet he couldn't remember what life was like before her. He'd waited ten years for her to come along, and when she had, she'd filled every inch of the empty loneliness.

He placed a kiss at her temple. "Do you think Josie and that baby girl will make it?"

"Hard to say. Josie's lost so much blood." She leaned into him, laying her head on his shoulder. "Sometimes I catch the worry on Dr. Mary's face when she looks at the two of them. I know she's doing everything in her power to pull them through, though. If anyone can save them, it'll be her, no question about that. I've never met anyone like her."

"Me, either. She sure took care of Houston's daughter Gracie last year after Gracie ate some jimsonweed and almost died. Houston and Lara feared they'd have to bury the child beside the trail in Indian Territory."

"The doctor was out there in the middle of nowhere?"

"Nope, she was in the nearest town. Houston and Lara rode like the devil to get Gracie there in time to save her." Clay guided Tally around a pile of lumber and into their framed-in house. They had yet to put up walls and the roof.

Tally gave a pleased cry. "I didn't dream you'd gotten so far along. This is wonderful!"

"What do you think?"

"It's everything I dreamed of. I can see how much larger it'll be than the dugout. This house is everything I ever imagined it could be, and we'll be very happy here. You're a magician, Clay, the way you adjusted the plans you'd already made to give Violet a room to herself."

His words came out raspy as he moved behind her and

folded his arms across her chest. "I devote myself to things of importance. Baby girl needs her own space. And I made another small room next to ours, just in case we should have a child." Clay nibbled behind her ear, noticing a strange look on her face. She was probably thinking of Josie.

"Yesterday, Rebel confided in me that she once had baby, a boy. But he died not long after she gave birth." Tally turned, her eyes searched his face. "Did you know about that?"

"News to me. Must've been after I left Cimarron. What did she say?"

"Not a lot, but she gave Josie's babe some thick lamb's wool that she'd kept from that time." Tally laid her hand on Clay's stubble-rough jaw and he wished he'd taken the time to shave. "She was sobbing, simply heartbroken remembering her son. My heart went out to her."

For a long moment, he searched his mind, trying to remember Rebel back then, whether she'd said anything, but drew a blank. In that life in Cimarron, she'd been as carefree as she appeared to be now.

"Did she mention who the father was?"

"No. From what I gathered, it could've been one of any number of men."

Yeah, there was always someone in her bed. Damn this gray morning. He blew out a breath. "I'm sorry to hear about that. Rebel likes to pretend nothing bothers her, but it does."

"I'm learning there's more to her than I ever thought." Tally was silent a moment. When she spoke again, her voice was barely louder than a whisper. "I knew a woman like her at Creedmore. I didn't like her too much at first and thought she was selfish and a backstabber. But she saved my life one night."

The blood stilled inside him. This was important. "Tell me more."

"You've heard enough." Her face appeared made of stone.

He coiled a fiery lock of her hair around his finger and held it to his nose, breathing in her fragrance. "Talking might help put it to rest."

A tremble went through Tally and he held her closer.

"Maybe." After a long pause, she spoke. "I talked back to Slade one day, spat in his face. He exploded and went crazy. Said he'd break me one way or another. Full of rage, grabbed me by the throat, squeezing the life from me. I was gasping, couldn't breathe. His eyes held this strange glitter, and he kept ordering me to call him master."

"The bastard!" The words exploded before Clay could stop them. He'd kill the vermin the first chance he got, and that was a promise. The need to ride out and close Creedmore's doors once and for all rose up in overpowering waves, but so many things made it impossible to leave. He bit back a curse.

"I struggled with him, clawing at his hands. Blackness began to close over me. A woman named Felicia appeared, wearing very little. She tugged on him, saying she'd show him a real good time, until he finally released me and went with her." Tally gave a wounded cry and Clay watched shadows darken her blue eyes.

"What happened to Felicia?"

She pushed herself away from him. "They killed her." The sharp words could've sliced through steel.

"Dammit! Don't let the memories get to you, darlin'. That place and Tarver don't deserve a second thought. As soon as I can arrange to leave, they'll be nothing but dust."

A cry rose up and she covered her mouth with a hand.

"What is it?"

"Slade Tarver. He's not going to give up, Clay." She gripped his shirt. "Do you think they've come back?"

"No. Pete and Otis made sure they wouldn't. They have enough just trying to get back to Creedmore to give you a thought. And if they ever make their way here again, it'll be the last mistake they ever made." He'd empty his gun into them without one moment's hesitation. He planned to take care of them long before that though.

Little by little, the fear in her eyes left and the tension eased from her body.

Clay buried his hands in her hair. "Did I tell you how

beautiful you are today in that blue dress? I'm the luckiest man on earth to have you."

A tiny smile curved her lips as she slid her arms around his neck. "You have a silver tongue, my handsome husband."

He captured her lips in a kiss he prayed she'd remember for a long time, letting his hands drift down her curves to her luscious bottom. He lost all track of time. It was just Tally and him and their hunger for each other's touch. They kissed and caressed, whispering quiet words of hope. He yearned to see her naked and run his hands over her bare skin, but that wasn't an option in broad daylight with three dozen men milling about.

Footsteps dragged him from the sensuous haze surrounding him. A man cleared his deep voice. "Sorry to interrupt."

Irritation climbed up Clay's spine. Scowling, he swung around to see Jack grinning like a fool and snapped, "I've shot a man for less than this."

"So have I." Jack didn't budge.

"Do you mind if I spend a little time alone with my wife?"

"Dr. Mary needs Tally," Jack answered.

"She'll be along in a minute."

"Stop it, Clay." Tally punched his arm. "The doctor needs me." She gave the former lawman a smile. "Sorry, Jack, Clay's a bit cantankerous. Is there a problem with Josie?"

"I'm not exactly sure. Dr. Mary just sent me to fetch you." Jack shifted the weight from his hurt leg. Clay had tried to get him to see a doctor about it back when he got shot, but he'd refused. Fool man. "Something's wrong with Rebel though," Jack said. "She ran crying from the dugout."

"Oh dear. I was afraid of this."

Clay took her hand, and they followed Jack back to the compound. Rebel was nowhere to be seen. "Would you like me to help you find her?"

"No, Dr. Mary wants me. Thank you for the lovely, peaceful hour." She kissed him and hurried toward the dugout.

"Mama, Mama," Violet cried. "Wait."

The girl tripped over Bullet and sprawled in the dirt. The

dog was licking her face as though offering an apology. Clay and Tally reached her at the same time. Clay dusted her off while Tally wiped her tears.

"Are you hurt, honey?" Tally gently kissed her cheek.

"My knees," Violet sobbed. "I heard you coming and was afraid you wouldn't stop. You're always with the doctor."

Clay hugged her close. "Baby girl, your mama has to take care of Miss Josie and the baby right now. She still loves you just as much as ever."

Violet touched Tally's face. "Do you, Mama? Do you love me as much as Josie's new baby?"

Tally kissed Violet's tear-stained cheek and smoothed back her hair. "Of course I do. There's no contest. You're my daughter and I'll always carry you deep in my heart. Clay, bring her into the dugout so she can be near. Her being there for a little while won't hurt a thing."

"And I can hold the baby?" Violet asked hopefully.

"Honey, she's much too fragile right now." Tally gently rubbed the girl's back. The love passing between his wife and daughter brought a lump to Clay's throat.

He picked Violet up and carried her into the dugout, where he sat her on a chair. "You be a good girl and do as your mama says."

"I will, Daddy."

Clay kissed her cheek. "I love you, you know." He rose and squeezed Tally's hand. "I'll only be a step away if you need me."

The baby's weak cries filled the room. He'd never heard a more pitiful sound.

"You don't know what a comfort your presence is, Clay. Now go, so I can work." Tally shifted away from him to speak to Dr. Mary. "What's happened?"

Twenty-two

"JOSIE'S TAKEN ANOTHER BAD TURN." DR. MARY'S GRIM VOICE filled the dugout.

A knot formed in Tally's stomach. She pulled her gaze from Clay's disappearing form and got her thoughts back on the latest crisis. "What can I do?"

"The baby needs to be changed and fed. I have my hands full with Josie, so if you can tend the babe, I'd appreciate it."

"Sure thing, Doctor." Tally set to work, talking to Violet the whole time.

After putting a replacement rock in the oven to heat, she set a bit of milk warming, then changed the baby. In no time, the baby went back to sleep in her box beside the stove, tiny belly full and snug in the toasty lamb's wool.

Luke came in a little while later and sat with his daughter, staring at the life he and Josie had made. He glanced up at Tally and the corners of his mouth quirked in a fleeting smile. "I'm going to shoot any half-grown boy that looks at my daughter. I know that much right now."

"No, you won't. You'll want to, but you won't because you love her too much and her happiness will be the most important thing to you."

Dr. Mary swung to him. "Luke, you'd best come. I don't know how much longer Josie has."

Tally took the baby and watched him stumble to the bed, his holster catching on the back of the chair. Wearing gun belt, boots, and all, he lay on top of the covers and gently took Josie in his arms.

Violet looked up from the floor where she sat playing. "Mama, what's wrong?"

"Josie's just very sick. How about we go outside and see what your daddy's doing?" She took Violet's hand.

"Okay. And I want to visit my friend Montana too. I'll bet he misses me."

"Oh, honey, I know he does."

They stepped out into the bright sunshine and the bustle of the men working, trying to build something lasting. Only for what? Would people ever really want to live here, where death rode the wind?

They walked up to the garden. Violet loved touching the things that grew. Crushing pain hit, so severe it doubled Tally over. She let out a cry, gripping her chest. She couldn't breathe, couldn't think, couldn't see.

"What is it, Mama?" Violet patted her arm. "What's wrong?"

When Tally didn't answer, Violet called out, panic in her voice. "Mama?"

Still unable to speak, Tally sat down and pulled Violet onto her lap. They sat there until the shooting streaks subsided.

Violet had tears in her voice. "Mama?"

"I'm okay, sweetheart. I'm right here. It was just a pain. Nothing to worry about."

"It sounded real bad."

Tally forced a laugh and tickled Violet. "I'm fine."

After checking to see if there was a change in Josie, Tally spent part of the afternoon with her daughter, loving the sound of her laughter. While Violet explained to Montana all about Cinderella, the prince, and the wicked stepsisters, Tally went in search of Rebel. She found her tucked into a hollowed-out place in the canyon wall near the windmill. The woman stared into space with unseeing eyes.

"Rebel, are you all right?" Tally moved closer and crawled up beside her.

Rebel's eyes were red and swollen, but she wasn't crying. "Sorry. I just couldn't handle watching that sweet little darling clinging to life. You know?"

"Yeah, I know." Tally reached for Rebel's hand. "It's hard and she reminds you too much of what you lost. No one thinks ill of you."

"I'm sure they wouldn't waste one minute of sympathy."

"There's one thing you need to know about the people here. We've all seen hard times, and each one of us has had to do unspeakable, horrible things to survive. So we don't judge. As Ridge Steele says, that's not our job. Our job is staying alive."

The comforting creak of the windmill filled the silence that followed. Tally closed her eyes to soak up the peace its music brought.

"Sometimes I wish I was dead," Rebel whispered.

"Don't ever wish that, Rebel Avery." Tally grabbed her shoulders and gave them a good shake. "They'll lay each of us in the ground all too soon, so we need to keep living our hardest and making our time count. Don't you think Josie would love to have more days, weeks, months with Luke and that baby?"

Rebel jerked away. "What good is time? I have no one, nothing."

"Then just go and wallow in self-pity. You'll find yourself cold and alone." Without another word, Tally stalked back toward the dugout to check on Josie. The pounding of the hammers of men building the town accompanied her like a trained animal.

They continued with the poultices around the clock, desperately working to save Josie. At the close of the next day, Tally was spending some much needed hug time with Violet when she saw Dr. Mary standing outside the dugout, puffing away on a cigar. But the big smile on her face was what caught her attention.

"What are you happy about, Doctor? Tell me it's good news!"

"The miracle of life, Tally. Josie woke up and her bleeding is slowing. The herbs and pressure on the arteries worked."

It took a moment for the words to sink in but they finally reached Tally's brain. "Josie will live?"

"She has a fighting chance now." Dr. Mary shifted her

cigar. "I think she just needed Luke beside her. It's odd, the connection those two have. I see it in you and Clay, too."

"It's the power of love, Dr. Mary, but I don't know about me and Clay. You see, we married as strangers and we're still getting acquainted." Tally touched the diamond tattoo on her cheek. Maybe one day they would share that sort of love. After her wounds healed. "I hope in time we can come to love each other—for Violet's sake, if nothing else."

"I have only to look at you both to see what you cannot." Dr. Mary's gaze pierced her. "Do you mind if I take a closer look at that mark on your face?"

"I don't mind."

Dr. Mary put her cigar out and stuck the stub in her pocket. She touched the tattoo and peered at it intently for what seemed an eternity. Finally, she spoke. "Unless I miss my guess, this is a tracking mark."

"I'm wanted." Tally stepped back, holding her head at a defiant angle. "The overseer at the Creedmore Lunatic Asylum put it on here so I'd be easier to find. I escaped, and they have a reward out for me. But I'm not crazy, and I'm never going back there. They'll have to kill me."

"I can see you're as sane as I am." Sympathy shone in Dr. Mary's hazel eyes. "Would you like the mark to disappear?"

Would that be possible? If so, it would free all the women hiding in Deliverance Canyon. They could go wherever they wanted, without the tattoos to identify them.

Excitement washed over Tally but she tamped it down, not letting her features reveal the hope burgeoning inside. "Do you know of a way to take the tattoo off?"

"I'd have to do some reading first, but maybe. I saw a doctor at the hospital where I trained remove a small one about the same size of yours with some success." The doctor's strange necklace rattled when she reached into her pocket, drew out the cold cigar stub, and stuck it in her mouth. Fumbling for a match, she lit it. "Filthy habit. I've tried to stop but always end up going back." Smoke curled around Dr. Mary's head. "We've had a hard time of it with Josie."

"You've earned a smoke, Doctor. About the tattoo—what would we need, and will it be painful?"

"I won't lie—the pain will be severe. And there are no guarantees it will work. It could leave you with a scar."

"I'm no stranger to pain. Or scars. I want to try it, no matter the outcome. And if it works, I'll bring all the other women like me here, so you can remove theirs also." Tally wasn't sure if they would all welcome the procedure, mind. The agony would be a deciding factor, and a few of the women had already suffered every last ounce they could bear.

And if it didn't work? Tally didn't figure she'd lose anything.

"How many of you are there?" Dr. Mary's question was gentle.

"Fifteen." It broke Tally's heart that so many had never made it outside Creedmore's walls. She had a score to settle with Slade Tarver, Pollard Finch, and Jacob Abram. But mostly Slade. She itched to put a bullet between the eyes of the man who'd cost her the most.

One day…someway…she'd see him dead. And dear stepmother Lucinda too.

"I'll have to send for silver nitrate and tannic acid. The rest of what I need I can make here." The kindly doctor's skirt swished as she walked with Tally. "I don't know that I could've survived what you had to endure. You're very brave. Even the best of those places are pure hell."

"I didn't do anything—except refuse to die."

"That's just it. So many would've given up."

"You give me far too much credit. I simply lived one minute at a time."

The door opened and Luke emerged, a load visibly lifted from his broad shoulders. Although he didn't smile, the deep worry had vanished. "They're both resting peacefully. Thank you, Doctor. If I paid you all the money in all the banks, it would never be enough."

"I don't want your money, Luke. I'm glad my—our—efforts paid off. It took all of us." The bullets on Dr. Mary's necklace clinked together as she went inside, reminding Tally of the frailty of life.

In this untamed land, a body never knew what the next moment would bring. She glanced over at the working men. The sound of their hammers was a constant during the daylight, ceasing only when darkness stole over them. They built for a bright tomorrow, dreaming of a time when this would be a bustling town that brimmed with businesses and people.

"Move forward instead of back," she whispered. But how, when men wanted her dead?

Clay climbed from a ladder and strode toward her, his Remington in the holster tied to his leg by a narrow leather strip. At that sight, Tally realized she hadn't worn her gun in a number of days. Until lately, she'd never been without it. She was getting much too comfortable here. Her hand flew to her mouth.

Slade was out there somewhere, waiting for her to make a mistake. Waiting to grab her. She had to stay focused—not only for herself but for Violet as well.

"Hey there, pretty lady." Clay reached her and pulled her into the circle of his arms. "I saw the doctor taking a break and sense some news. How are the patients?"

Her gaze followed Luke as he reached for the coffee sitting in the coals of the fire. She pushed aside her worry and smiled. "Josie woke up. Not out of the woods yet, but on her way."

"And the babe?"

"Holding her own."

"Hallelujah!" Clay lifted her up and swung her around.

"Put me down. Everyone's looking."

"Let them." He slid her slowly down his long frame, his dark eyes smoldering.

Her heart raced and her breath hitched as she met the heat building in his stare. This tall, rugged outlaw, who'd taken a chance on her, sent warm tingles up her spine. His eyes were making downright sinful promises.

A sudden realization shook her. She loved him. She loved this man who'd given her so much.

His lips found hers, and the moment they touched, thoughts of everyone except him vanished. Her heart hammered against her ribs and heady need spiraled through her, spinning and tumbling.

But this was broad daylight, with everyone moving about.

"I want you, lady," he murmured against her mouth.

Tally quivered with desire as she leaned into the strength and safety of his arms, burying her face in the hollow of his throat. "All the men are staring."

"They're only jealous."

Finally, Tally stepped from the circle of warmth. "We can't do this now, and you know it. Whatever will Violet think of her mama and papa?"

"Violet can't see us, and besides, she'd be thrilled that we're not fighting."

"You're hopeless, Clay Colby." Tally slid her arms around him, relishing the rippling muscles of his back, his trim waist, the hope he put in her heart.

"Maybe so, but I know what I want and that's you." He tweaked her nose. "We can't have our bed back yet, but maybe we can sleep together tonight. Can we?"

"I'll find out, but I'm sure I won't be needed." Goose bumps prickled her skin at the thought of lying next to Clay, listening to his soft breathing, snuggling into the curves of his hard body. Her breath caught. "Where will we sleep?"

He nibbled her neck. "I have a good spot already picked out."

"Oh, you do?" Tally grinned.

"Yes, ma'am. For a fact." Clay nuzzled behind her ear. "I'm going to curl your toes, whisper sinful things in your ear, and make you beg for mercy."

"Goodness." Tally traced the line of his lips with a fingertip. "Then I suppose I just need to pray for nightfall." She hoped it hurried.

Her fingers tangled in his hair as the scent of sagebrush and leather drugged her senses.

With the moon shining high overhead, she'd show him tonight how much she loved being his wife.

Twenty-three

THAT NIGHT CLAY MADE THEM A BED OF HAY IN THEIR HALF-finished house and scattered wildflowers all around. With a dozen lit candles adding a soft touch, he went to find Tally. She'd just tucked Violet into bed in Tobias and Belle's tent.

He'd already given the men orders not to come near the framed-in house, or they'd find a loaded gun in their face. This was his and Tally's private time and the men had best respect it.

Tally gave a little cry the moment she saw what he'd prepared. "Clay, this is so romantic and sweet." She rested her palms on his leather vest. "You constantly surprise me."

"That's my plan." His voice became hoarse, raspy. "I don't want you to get tired of me, because I happen to like having you around. In case you haven't noticed, I like it a whole lot."

"Funny, I was thinking earlier how content I am being here." Tally glanced up. "The stars seem so close tonight. It's almost as though I can reach up and pluck one." She snuggled into the curve of his arm. "Do you know how rarely I felt this secure before I came here?"

Clay tightened his hold. Although he suspected the answer, he wanted to hear her to say it. "No, how often?"

"Not once. I used to live in constant fear, afraid to let deep sleep claim me, or I wouldn't hear trouble coming. I'd be up a dozen times a night, checking on the ladies, listening to every noise, sniffing the wind." She shifted and glanced up at him. "Now I don't have to. But I still worry about my friends and I wonder if Hester's leg is all right."

"If they weren't, I'm sure Alice or one of them would be back."

"It's just hard letting go of the need to protect them." She trailed a finger down his jaw. "Clay, Dr. Mary told me that she might know a way to remove these tattoos from our faces. How would you feel if I didn't have it anymore?"

A jolt of surprise swept through him. He didn't know it was even possible. The scent of wild sage, yucca, and the wildflowers that lined a path to their bed drifted on the breeze. The hoot of a nearby owl added serenity to the night.

"Honestly, I never see that mark. All I see is the dream and hope in your eyes. Will the removal hurt?"

"Yes, so I'm told."

"Then don't. I'm not sure I can stand to see you in pain, darlin'. You've been through far too much already." He inhaled, letting the fragrance of her hair engulf his senses. "On the other hand, without the tattoo to identify you, you'll have more freedom to come and go. That mark keeps you a prisoner here. If you want this, I'm right beside you." Clay's hand curved below the softness of her breast as he kissed her tilted mouth.

Suddenly, all talk of tattoos and escapees from Creedmore melted away, leaving only heated passion and a need that left him shaking.

Clay undressed her, lightly caressing each patch of exposed skin, watching goose bumps rise. When he'd bared her, he laid her on the bed of hay and quickly shed his gun belt, boots, and clothes.

The sight of her lying there, surrounded by flickering candles, the moon casting a pale glow on her—he sucked in a breath. His angel. He let his gaze slide lazily down her body, taking in each dip and curve.

"You don't know what you do to me."

She reached for his hand and tugged him onto the scented bed. "You talk too much."

Yeah, well, if she didn't look so much like an angel, he could hobble his tongue. However, he was in no mood to argue. Fire in his belly demanded he quench it. He lay on his side next to her and slid his fingers down the column of her throat. He was unworthy of someone like her. He'd killed too many men, had too much blood on his hands, buried too many mistakes.

Lived with demons he couldn't shake.

A tremble ran through him as he crushed her to him, his lips on hers, sealed in the kind of kiss that burned into his brain, a brand that only she could create.

Tasting the intensity of her need, he slid his palms down her body. Touching. Smoothing. Stroking. Worshipping this woman who'd thrown her lot in with his.

If he lived a thousand years with her, it would be too short.

The fragrance of the night seemed to hold them in a cocoon where they were safe. Somewhere off in the distance came the faint murmur of men's voices.

When they ran out of air, Clay broke the kiss. Their breaths mingled and he inhaled her soft freshness. "I need you, Tally," he murmured against her mouth. "Don't ever leave me."

Her promise to stay at least until spring popped into his head. If she left…

Oh God, he couldn't bear to think of that. She was part of him now. She was more than a wife—she was his very lifeblood.

He trembled as love for her washed over him. He'd chosen to love her the day they met, but now his heart was opening and taking her deep inside, where he'd never let anyone. She filled his life with hope and promise, and he'd never felt this way about any woman.

While he wasn't looking, the chosen love had become the real and lasting kind. The thought shook him. There were no half measures now.

He loved Tally with every ounce of his being. She was his fire, his flame. Forever.

"Clay," she whispered against his ear. "Don't hold back. Make me whole."

"Not yet." He ran his palm down each shapely leg, then massaged her feet and kissed them. Moving back up, he drew his palm across her flat stomach and took a breast in his hand, rolling the hard nipple between his fingers.

The hiss of her indrawn breath reached him. Tally gave a

low cry and arched her back. She thrust her hands in his hair and pulled his mouth to her. He flicked his tongue across the swollen peak and sucked it inside.

She twisted like a bucking bronc, her raspy breathing loud on the slight breeze. Clawing his back, she tried to pull him on top of her. "Now, Clay. Now."

He raised and covered her body, sliding into her moist heat. Her muscles contracted, gripping him tight. Relaxing. Tightening. Squeezing around him. She wrung every emotion from him.

Clay settled into a rhythm that Tally joined. He was on fire and Tally had the means to douse his flames before he burned up completely and turned to ash.

She begged him to go faster and harder, which relieved his worry that he was hurting her. With each stroke, the waves built higher until they towered. It would be a hell of a ride when he slammed back down to reality.

The heat in his belly grew, the flames spreading, licking higher and higher. As intense pleasure washed over him, he stared into Tally's face. Light from a nearby candle flickered in her winter-blue gaze, and the fire reflected there was the most beautiful he'd ever seen. She was the sun when he rose each morning. The moon when he slept at night.

As he shuddered and tumbled through time and space, he could feel her soul connecting with his, and they were joined so completely it brought tears to his eyes. This was the purest form of love he'd ever known.

His limbs shaking and quivering, his breath ragged, Clay collapsed beside her and pulled her close, resting a hand on the curve of her hip.

Tally pushed hair from her eyes. "What happened, Clay? Did you feel that?"

"I did." He stared at the stars dotting the dark expanse above. "I love you, Tally. I really, deep down love you. This is nothing like when I told you I was going to choose to love you. This is different and it makes me..." He paused and faced her. "A minute ago, I felt like I was dissolving into you.

I became you and you, me. We were truly one person, one heart. Does that make sense?"

"I felt it too." Tally tenderly cupped his jaw. "I think I first came to realize that I loved you when Josie almost died. But now, I have to tell you and not leave anything important unsaid, just in case…"

"Nothing is going to happen. Get that thought out of your head." Clay regretted his rough voice, but it hurt too much to even consider the possibility of life without her.

"But it might. You know Slade will come back with more men sooner or later. That's just a given. When he does, I won't have left anything unsaid. My love is solid and I'll never feel this way about another as long as I live."

Her vow created a tranquil glow around him. He finally had what he'd searched his whole life for. He blinked away the sudden mist in his eyes.

"Get some sleep." He tucked her head onto his shoulder, her heart beating in rhythm with his.

Hours before dawn came, Clay woke to find her gone. The candles around the bed had gone out. He sat up quickly, a knot forming in his stomach. Jerking to his feet, his gaze swept the half-finished house. "Tally, where are you?"

Movement in the shadows revealed her location and concern replaced his worry.

Naked, Clay moved closer and saw her sitting behind a beam, her knees drawn up to her chest. Naked also, she was staring into the blackness. He dropped down beside her. "What's wrong?"

"I couldn't sleep. Sorry to bother you."

"I didn't know where you went and it scared me a little." Well, a lot to be honest. "Why can't you sleep?"

Tally swung to face him, her eyes like pieces of glass. "A secret that I was going to take to my grave."

Everything inside him stilled. If it caused this much distress, it wasn't anything light. He yearned to put his arm around her but she didn't appear to welcome his touch. She seemed far from reach.

"Would you like to talk about it? I don't judge."

"You deserve to know this. I don't want secrets between us."

"Some need burying. Better that way." He laid his hand on her knee and felt the quivering inside her. He had his own secrets, and shame, he'd never speak of to anyone—not even Tally. "Come back and lie down."

"No. I need to get this over with. It'll affect your decision about our marriage."

"There is no deciding. I don't care what it is. You're mine and nothing will change it."

"Don't be so sure." She stared off into the inky night. "You've pretty well guessed from what you've heard about my life inside the walls of Creedmore. Horrible things were done to me, things you can't imagine. When dear Lucinda dropped me off, she told them to make me suffer unbearable pain. In fact, she gave her blessing to anything that made my life a living hell." She took a shuddering breath. "They tattooed my cheek." Her lip quivered but she held strong. "They tried daily to break me, never stopping. Beat my feet, took everything I had until I escaped."

Clay could only guess what that entailed. He reached for her. "You survived. There's no need to say more."

She pulled away and rubbed her hands on her knees as though they were stained. "I did survive, but I may have lasting effects. That's what I'm trying to tell you." Her voice dropped to a whisper. "I lost two…babies."

Good Lord! Clay clenched his fist. He leaped to his feet and stalked to the edge of the boundary of the house. He'd never wanted to hit anything so bad. Slade Tarver and whoever else would see justice—either at the end of a rope or by a bullet. Didn't make any difference to him, but he would see them dead just as soon as he could leave.

Behind him came a sniffle, reminding him that Tally needed gentle understanding, not anger. He'd deal with his own feelings later. He retraced his steps and sat back down, pulling her against him. "That was then. This is now. You're safe and they can't hurt you anymore."

"Stop." She took his face between her hands. "Listen to me. Slade gave me a horrible concoction—pennyroyal, blue cohosh, and Lord knows what else. But I drank it. Willingly." She put her knuckles in her mouth in an effort to stop the keening sound. Her hand shook. "I killed my babies. Me. Because I wanted nothing of those men inside me."

The horror of what had happened sank in. Clay buried his face in her hair, clutching her tightly. "It's all right. You had good reason."

Tally sobbed, her tears wetting his skin. "I killed them. What kind of person am I?"

"You're a woman who wanted to spare her children the torture you were in. If you'd somehow managed to hide your condition and given birth, they'd likely have killed the babies the second they were born. Or used them, made them suffer in order to keep you in line. What you did was merciful and showed the depth of your love."

"That's not all."

Dear God! What else could there possibly be?

Tally pulled back. "Those herbs were very powerful and there's a chance I may have damaged my body. I might even be unable to have children now. Clay, if I can't give you a child, I'll give you a divorce."

The words slammed into him with the force of a cannonball and sent him reeling.

"No. You promised to give me until spring." Panic and fear made it hard to get the words past his lips. He'd take her however damaged she was. "Talk to Dr. Mary. But the outcome doesn't matter. None of this changes who we are and the love we have for each other. Lady, I vowed to cherish and protect you until death do us part, and someone will have to put a damn bullet in me to stop me from doing that."

He smoothed back her hair. "Think about this. Children come in other ways—our daughter did."

Hoping she took heart, he gently pressed his lips to hers and rubbed her spine of steel, letting the silence of the night heal their spirits.

Tally had rescued him, and maybe he'd done the same for her if she could just let herself see it. He prayed for a chance to love her as she deserved. To dance in the rain. To make her life better with each sunrise. To erase all the bad from her memory.

Twenty-four

MIDMORNING OF THE FOLLOWING SUNSHINY DAY, DR. MARY caught Tally. "Now that Josie is on the road to recovery, would you like to start taking back ownership of yourself?"

The possibility made Tally's heart leap. "As soon as possible. But I thought you had to send for some things you needed."

"I asked Ridge Steele to make an extra stop for it when he rode over to Tascosa and he's already back."

The fragrance of newly cut lumber scented the air as Tally scanned the fast-rising town, finally spotting Ridge talking to Jack and Clay. The former preacher stood out as always, with his dark trousers and frock coat hugging his tall frame. He was never without that coat, even in the August heat. Or his guns—one on each hip. Clay had told her how quick he was to draw and let bullets fly, never missing his chosen targets. He'd be good to have near in a fight.

She dragged her attention back to Dr. Mary. "Then I think we should get started."

"Good. While Montana's sitting outside with Violet, let's go to my tent."

Moments later, they stepped inside. A brown bottle, a pan of water, and what appeared to be a tubular aloe vera stem sat on a small table. She inhaled a deep breath, calming her nerves. She'd faced much worse pain than whatever this could be. But she couldn't help but long for Clay's strong hand around hers.

Dr. Mary walked to the table. "As I told you before, this will hurt. The way this works is that I first make a solution of tannic acid and water and insert that under the first layer of skin the same way they made the tattoo the first time. After that, I'll wash with cold water, then apply juice from the aloe vera. This is the most painful part."

Tally pointed to a stick of silver nitrate. "What about that?"

"After we let the aloe vera penetrate, I'll rub the silver nitrate over the tattoo and cover it with a bandage. It'll take around two weeks, during which the skin on the site will turn black and hard, and that section will fall off, taking the tattoo with it." Dr. Mary laid a hand on Tally's shoulder. "I won't lie. This is very agonizing, and you might be left with a scar. Are you sure you're up to it?"

Only the pounding of hammers outside broke the silence in the tent as Tally considered everything. Finally, she raised her chin. "I'm positive." While she didn't welcome misery, she'd do anything to rid herself of the tattoo—and hopefully all the mark reminded her of.

Though she doubted that. The memories were embedded too deep.

"Then we'll get started. I think it would be best for you to lie down."

Tally made herself comfortable, praying that she would be able to take the searing pain. Using a needle, Dr. Mary began the task of puncturing her cheek and inserting the tannic acid solution underneath. The agony almost made Tally cry out. She tried to focus on happy things—like lovemaking with her husband. She still carried the taste of Clay's kisses on her lips from the previous night. It had thrilled her heart to hear him voice real love for her.

This man, who'd lived such a violent past, loved her. Their talk afterward had been necessary, and she was glad to have the burden of her confession off her shoulders. He knew all her secrets now.

"There." Dr. Mary laid down the needle. "I'll let you rest before I do more."

"No, I can handle this." Tally just wanted to get it over with.

"All in good time. My hand needs to rest. It's getting shaky and that will worsen the pain." Dr. Mary helped her to a sitting position. "I've known few people with your strength, Tally. But you have a will of iron. You fascinate me. Can I ask how you came to be here in Devil's Crossing?"

Tally found herself telling Dr. Mary, spilling her story, right from the day Lucinda had poisoned her. The doctor was easy to talk to, and Tally found herself confiding the details of how she'd arrived at Creedmore and some of her ordeal while there.

"Those places do little more than allow crime to flourish!" Dr. Mary spewed. "It's a sin and a disgrace how easy it is for people—whether back East or here—to hide someone away to die. I'm sure you suffered terribly. How long before you escaped?"

"I tried several times unsuccessfully but I didn't make good on it until I'd been there about a year."

Dr. Mary patted Tally's leg. "Like I said, you astound me. How did you meet Clay?"

"Through Luke and his underground mail order bride service. I took a chance and agreed to marry Clay sight unseen." Tally let a smile form. "It's the best decision I ever could've made. But…about Creedmore again. I have some more things to discuss with you, if you don't mind."

"I'll give you my expert opinion."

"I conceived twice while there. The men gave me a strong tea to drink." Tally's voice quivered and she had to take a deep breath before going on. "I…I killed…" A sob burst from her mouth. "I killed my babies."

Tears welled in Dr. Mary's eyes. She put her arms around Tally and held her tightly for several minutes, rubbing her back. "You did what you had to. I admire your enormous will to live."

Tally wiped her eyes. "I worry about what that concoction of pennyroyal and blue cohosh did. Sometimes now I have chest pain, at times an irregular heartbeat that scares me, and I have swelling in my feet and ankles. I wonder if I'll be able to bear Clay's child."

The kindly doctor asked for more details on the concoctions—the frequency, how many cups each time, and for how many days in a row she was given the mixture. Tally answered all her questions, holding back nothing.

"Would you be **willing** to lie back down for a moment and let me check some **things**?" the doctor asked.

"Sure." Tally did as she requested.

Dr. Mary listened to her heart, checked her feet and ankles, and held the lamp close while she pulled down Tally's lower eyelids, staring into them. Then she performed an internal examination.

"You can sit up now."

"What do you think, Doc?"

"You have some jaundice but I detect no heart damage from the blue cohosh. I'll make a milk thistle decoction for you to take three times a day and give you herbs for a nice tea. I think you'll be just fine. As far as internally, I see no problem. I suspect you suffer from anxiety attacks. Those can mimic heart pain and palpations."

No heart damage? "But I have trouble breathing and it hurts so much."

"I've run across people who have shooting pain whenever they're afraid or unsettled. After all you've been through, panic attacks make perfect sense, and the tea will help you relax."

Happiness hummed inside Tally. "Clay and I can have a child?"

"Only the good Lord knows about these things, Tally. Try not to worry too much."

They resumed with the tattoo removal, and a little while later, Tally emerged bandaged from the doctor's tent. She went straight to Clay, pulled him aside, and explained the tattoo removal and Mary's comments about the chance to have a child. But she left out the part about her anxiety attacks. No use adding more worry to his load. A few days of following the regimen and she'd be perfectly fine.

"I'm glad you asked her." Clay tugged her close and kissed her temple. "Does your cheek hurt?"

"A little. I'll be good as new soon. I hope you don't mind a scar." Tally slid her arms around his waist, counting herself fortunate.

"No scar will ruin the kind of beauty you have."

Life was full of ups and downs, and this wasn't the worst that they would face.

She'd heard the men talk about a bounty hunter Ridge had seen in Tascosa and the reward poster the man had been showing around.

Foreboding told her the worst still lay in front of them.

A surly visitor rode in the next afternoon, asking to water his horse, a pitiful-looking piebald. The minute the man dismounted, Clay knew he was trouble. Over the years, he'd seen hundreds like him, men eaten up with hate and looking for revenge. The hard face and long, angry scar running down his neck would give any seasoned outlaw pause. But it was the cold sneer and shifty, deep-set eyes that spoke of a killer.

"Name's Thompson." The man slapped his leg with his hat and dirt flew. "This used to be an outlaw hideout where a man could lay low for a while."

"Not anymore. We're building a respectable town here. If you're looking for something else, you'd best move on." Clay's gut told him to remove the thin leather strip holding his Remington secure in the holster.

Jack, Ridge, and Luke followed suit from their vantage points in the shadows. Montana rose from a seat in the sunshine he was soaking up.

"And if I'm not of a mind to?" Thompson growled.

"I think we can handle you. There's plenty of water at the windmill tank. Your piebald is about done in. You've been riding him awful hard."

"My business." Thompson yanked on the reins and led the horse toward the water tank.

"So it is." Clay had only taken two steps after the surly man when Belle January screamed, and Clay took off running.

Tobias had fallen from a ladder and lay on the ground, his face ghost white, gasping for air. Clay was the first to arrive. "Don't try to get up. Just lie there a minute and wait for the doctor."

"I'm here." Dr. Mary knelt down beside the old man. "Take it easy. You've had the wind knocked out of you, Tobias." She felt his legs and arms. "I don't feel anything broken."

"Praise be. I was so afraid." Belle twisted her gnarled hands.

Tobias finally got his lungs filled and quit gasping. "I'm just addled. Don't need no fuss." A few moments later, Clay and Jack helped him stand.

"How do you feel?" Clay asked.

Before Tobias could answer, Violet let out a bloodcurdling scream and a gunshot rang out. Clay whirled to see Thompson's blood soaking in the dirt, Montana standing over him, smoke curling from his gun.

Violet was shaking uncontrollably. "Daddy! Where are you?"

Clay ran and scooped her up. "It's okay, baby girl." He glared at Montana. "What happened?"

"Violet was finding her way toward me and her stick accidentally hit this piece of filth. He grabbed her arm and swung her around, cursing." Montana put away his gun. "I shot his ass. No one hurts this child. Or Miss Tally. No one."

Thompson lay frozen, his hand curled around his gun, Tally's wanted poster sticking from his pocket.

Thank goodness Violet couldn't see, but Clay hid the handbill from Tally. Anger raced through Clay. How many times in life would Violet and Tally have to confront danger? How many times would they narrowly miss death?

Clay laid a hand on Montana's wide shoulders. "Thanks. I'd have done the same and not wasted a second."

Ridge's long strides brought him over. He took one look at Thompson. "He's the bounty hunter I saw in Tascosa."

"He's no threat to Tally now."

Tally raced from the dugout in a panic. "What happened?"

"Ain't nothing that I couldn't take care of, Miz Tally." Montana gave Thompson a kick. "Reckon we'll have to bury the ugly bastard now."

Clay explained the situation and Tally took Violet's hand. "Let's wash your face with some cool water, honey."

Water had started the whole mess. The sad-looking piebald stood, his head drooping down, about to fall over. Clay lifted the reins and led the animal to the water tank. It appeared they had themselves another horse, assuming the gelding could recover.

And how many others like Thompson would come looking for his wife?

❧

Over the next two weeks, Tally often glanced at her reflection in a mirror and tried not to think about how scarred she might be when the bandage came off. If only she had smooth skin like Rebel's, and her beauty. She yearned to be pretty for Clay.

Sometimes the burning, horrible pain of the removal process brought tears to her eyes. The one thing she couldn't get out of her mind was the possibility that she couldn't have a child with Clay. Each day, she drank the teas and milk thistle, praying that her body would heal.

She'd begun rising before dawn and sitting in the cool breeze, clearing her mind and focusing on measured breaths, and it helped. She felt more settled inside.

Early one morning before the sun came up, Tally was enjoying the peace of milking the goats when she spied movement in some brush near the town's entrance. She yanked the Colt from the holster. Tarver had come back.

The figure stood. She noticed the woman's dress and relaxed, putting the Colt away.

The visitor kept to the brush and made her way to the side of the dugout where Josie slept. Tally hurried to catch her before she knocked on the door.

"Can I help you?"

The young woman turned. "Tally, I hope you'll forgive me but I had to bring news."

"Alice, what's wrong?"

"Hester went back to Creedmore and tried to get a little girl out. Shooting started and the girl was killed. I didn't even know her name." Alice put a trembling hand to her eyes.

"And Hester?"

"She got shot but made it back all right. The bullet went through her arm clean and we're doctoring her."

Tally put her arms around Alice. "Thank goodness. When you go back, tell Hester no more rescues. It's too dangerous. I'll be going to Creedmore soon. It's time to free the rest." But she couldn't ride until Josie got up and around.

A noise came from behind. Tally drew her gun and whirled, coming face-to-face with Rebel. From the look in Rebel's eyes and the heaving of her chest, she'd heard. "What are you doing here?"

"I was going into the dugout and heard voices. Who is your visitor?"

"It doesn't matter. Pretend you didn't see her." Tally pressed the gun to Rebel's chest and leaned close. "One word and I'll kill you."

"Tally, if I wanted to turn you in, I'd have done it by now." Rebel gave a short laugh. "That five hundred dollars would give me a good start at a new life. But even as much as I want Clay, I can't. I don't have to wonder anymore if you have what it takes to kill. My reason for keeping quiet wasn't that though." She paused a few seconds, then her eyes met Tally's. "We're living on the edge of civilization out here. Men outnumber us ten to one and most of them take what they want and ride on. Us women have to stick together to survive. We're all each other has. And…I kinda like you."

Shock rushed through Tally and she wondered if something was wrong with her hearing. Rebel had just confessed to liking her. Had she read the woman wrong all this time? She exchanged a glance with Alice.

"I'm relieved that you're not after the money."

Rebel gave a soft snort. "I tried to hate you. I really did. I was eaten up with jealousy and how I wanted Clay. But I see now that he only has eyes for you."

Tally smiled and touched Rebel's arm. "He's still your friend. That will never change. He owes you his life. I owe you too. Thank you for doctoring him."

"I just did what needed to be done." Rebel turned to leave.

Tally stopped her. "Do you think we could be friends?"

Rebel glanced down, then back up. "We already are, Tally."

"Do you think you can help me look prettier for Clay when I get this bandage off?"

"Shoot, you don't need my help. You're already pretty, and Clay thinks so too, but sure. I'll be happy to if you'll help me get the sort of clothes a normal woman should wear." Rebel returned her smile and stuck her arm through Tally's. "Let's get some breakfast. Alice looks like she can use some."

Twenty-five

Josie and the baby slowly improved. It was a joy for Tally, a week later, to see the little family finding sunshine in their lives again after such a close brush with darkness.

She found Josie sitting outside with the babe one warm afternoon, watching the men work. "It's really nice to see you regaining your strength." Tally pulled up a chair. "I confess there was a point when I wasn't sure if you'd live to see another dawn. Or the little one, either."

"That Dr. Mary is something, isn't she?" Josie grinned. "I think she has Dr. Jenkins at the Lone Star ranch beat, and that's saying a lot. Of course, I'd never tell him that."

"She's very smart." Tally reached for the baby, her tiny body swaddled in layers of blankets. "May I?"

"I would love it." Josie handed the child over.

"She's growing like a little dandelion." Tally cradled the babe next to her, enjoying the scent of the sweet girl.

"We're leaving tomorrow morning. Luke and I are returning to the Lone Star with our daughter." Josie's quiet words pierced Tally. She'd loved having them nearby, and Josie was like the sister she'd never had. "Do you have to go so soon?"

"Yes. We've been here far longer than we thought we'd be. The buildings are completed except for finishing the insides. Luke has to work his land and help Houston and Stoker with the fall branding. We also have to take care of all the letters that have piled up while we've been gone." Josie chuckled. "You'd never know this bride service was so demanding. And Stoker needs to see his new granddaughter."

"You've got to give her a name soon, Josie. We need something to call her."

"Well, actually we have. Here comes Luke now. We'll tell

you together." Josie watched her husband stride toward them, her face glowing with love.

Luke stopped next to them, removed his hat, and wiped the sweat from his forehead. "Don't overdo it, *querida*."

"I won't. We'll go inside and lie down in a minute." Josie took his hand. "I wanted you to be here when I tell Tally what we've named our daughter."

A teasing grin lit up his tanned face. "Oh, you mean Delilah May?"

"Hush now and do it right," Josie scolded with a pretty smile. She turned to Tally. "Her name is Elena Rose."

"That's lovely and very fitting." Tally lifted the blanket covering the little head full of dark hair. "Hello, Elena Rose. You have a real pretty name now."

The baby yawned and stretched. Thanks to the frequent feedings, she'd started to fill out.

Tally glanced up. "I take it the names are significant to you."

"Elena was my mother's name." Luke reached for Josie's hand, his dark gaze softening. Time ticked by with the married couple locked in a world of their own.

Finally, Josie broke the connection, turning to Tally. "And the Rose part came from two places. It was the name Luke gave me when I lost my memory, and it was also my mother Sable's middle name. I think it's perfect."

"Me too." Tally stared toward the working men, quickly singling Clay out by his broad shoulders and lean waist. No one had a figure like quite like his. Tingles danced up her spine.

"I'm glad this name business is settled." Luke bent to kiss his wife. When he straightened, he wore a mischievous smile. "Course, I'm still partial to Delilah May."

"You're just a big tease." Josie playfully slapped at him. "Go back to work."

Tally watched their exchange with a grin. It was great to see them so lighthearted and to see Luke's ready smile again. The conchos running down the legs of his black trousers flashed in the sun as he strode back to the men.

Josie stretched. "When will Dr. Mary remove the bandage, Tally? I want to see what it looks like."

"I peeked."

"And?"

"It's as black as a piece of coal. I think it's about ready to come off." Tally touched her bandage. "I just pray it doesn't look horrible forever. I want to look pretty for Clay. You know?"

"He'll be happy however it looks." Josie turned toward the men. "Clay thinks you're the most beautiful woman on earth and nothing will change that. I've seen the way he stares at you."

"We're two lucky women, aren't we, Josie?"

Her friend's words were soft. "That we are."

"Rebel has agreed to help me look better after we remove the bandage." Tally winked. "I think she knows a few tricks to hiding blemishes. She seems to think I'm pretty. Lord knows, that would take a miracle."

"You two are friends now?"

"We certainly are, and I'd say it's about time. She's not as bad as she pretends to be, and we need each other." Movement to their left drew Tally's attention.

Josie and the babe weren't the only ones on the mend. Montana was out and about, sunning on a bench outside the sod house he lived in, the shooting forgotten. It was no surprise to Tally to see Violet beside him. The girl and the outlaw had become attached at the hip. In fact, Violet had become the little town angel. Even Jack had made peace, of sorts, with Montana, because Violet had asked him to. Tally pitied anyone who tried to hurt that child. The men would deal with them before they could spit good.

Tally was grateful for the extra eyes and ears, because Violet kept them all on their toes. Her gaze moved across the rest of the town that she loved.

Rebel stood in the door of her barbering tent and waved. Tally hollered for her to join them and she started over.

The day had been a busy one. Tally closed her eyes and relaxed, soaking up the rays. She felt like a fat cat on a windowsill.

If it wasn't for the surety that Slade Tarver wouldn't give

up on finding her, she'd let this moment of tranquility wind around her heart and seep into her soul.

Would they be ready when he—and others—came?

Though Clay had tried to say that the dead man was just someone on the run, his guarded expression said he hid the man's real purpose for coming. Something in his voice didn't ring true. Was Thompson a bounty hunter?

A warning shot rang out and she jumped to her feet. Bullet, dozing beside her chair, leaped up and bounded toward the opening to the town, barking furiously.

Trouble seemed to have found them again. Despite all the men around with guns, her heart hammered. Had Slade and his cronies returned? She jerked her own gun from the holster around her waist, her gaze narrowing, searching for the source of danger.

Clay and the others ran toward the front opening with guns drawn. A lone woman wearing a man's Stetson rode into the compound and stopped in front of Clay. Tally relaxed and put away her Colt. Her skirt slapped her legs as she hurried to join the group.

"I need Clay Colby." The woman's striking voice carried to Tally. "I was told I could find him here."

Tally's breath caught. What did she want with Clay? Was this yet more trouble?

"Who sent you?" Clay slid his gun into his holster and stepped forward.

"A man named Brannick." The woman squinted into the sun. "Name's Susan Worth."

"What do you want?" Clay helped her dismount.

"Justice." The word shot out like a silver bullet.

The years had been kind to Susan. Her face was smooth except for a few lines around her mouth and eyes, but a smattering of gray in her dark hair spoke of the late-thirties range. Tally moved closer and saw the hardness in Susan Worth's eyes. Something bad had to have happened to send her to find Clay.

"What is it, Mama?" Violet slid her trembling hand into Tally's.

"Just a visitor—a woman. No cause for alarm, sweetheart." Tally took in Susan Worth's clothes. Her riding dress had cost some money, as well as the boots and dove-gray Stetson she wore.

"Is he here, or am I wasting my time?" Susan asked.

"Depends on what you want him for." Clay reached for her horse's reins.

"To hire. Three men rode onto our ranch, shot and killed my husband and sons, set fire to the house, stampeded our cattle." Susan pushed back a lock of hair with her trembling hand. "I survived by hiding in the hay loft. Luckily, our two ranch hands were out in the pasture."

"Did you try the local law?"

Tally respected Clay for being cautious. They had to be. But neither could they be cruel. To send her away might be tantamount to killing her. Her heart told her to trust.

Drawing in a deep breath, she pushed her way through the wall of men, gently taking Susan's arm. "Enough questions for now, Clay. Can't you see how exhausted she is? This woman needs some water and something to eat as well, if I'm guessing. She can tell you more in a bit."

"Thank you, ma'am. I'm obliged." A weary smile flitted across Susan's face.

"I'm Tally…Tally Colby." She met Clay's eyes and laid her hand on his leather vest. "Everything will be all right."

But would it? Or would Susan Worth lead Clay into a dangerous situation that he might not walk away from?

Twenty-six

THOUGH CLAY CHAFED AT THE DELAY, HE GAVE SUSAN WORTH time to eat and gather herself before he strode to where she sat with Tally and Violet. He didn't want to make things more difficult for the woman. Lord knew she'd been through hell. But he needed to find out why his old friend Brannick had sent her here. Why hadn't he helped her himself? Brannick was more than capable.

He sat down next to Tally. "How are you feeling, Mrs. Worth?"

"Better, thank you. I'm ready to answer the questions you have. The sooner I tell you, maybe the sooner you can ride after the killers. If you'll accept the challenge." Although Susan's chin quivered, she met his gaze and straightened her spine, clutching a lacy handkerchief with a trembling hand. "I apologize. My grief is still fresh."

"Before I answer your question, answer mine. Why didn't Brannick take out after them himself? He's more than capable."

Tally rose and took Violet's hand. "Excuse us. You need some privacy and we have to water the garden."

"Good idea, darlin'." Clay kissed Violet's cheek. "See you in a minute."

"Okay, Daddy."

Susan watched them go. "You have a beautiful family, Mr. Colby. Keep them close before trouble snatches them away." She gave a weary sigh. "To answer your question, Brannick was shot a week ago. He's bedridden for now. He told me not to tell anyone I was coming here and to make sure I wasn't followed."

Brannick shot? By who? Clay stared toward the corral, recalling the last time he'd seen him and the drink they'd had over talk of going straight. "He's a good man and a friend. What happened?"

Susan's voice was low. "Bank robbers shot him as they were fleeing Eagle Springs. They killed the sheriff as well, which is why I couldn't go to him about my problem. And the nearest U.S. Marshal is in Oklahoma Territory, tracking down a gang of murderers."

"I understand." Clay rubbed the back of his neck. Dammit, that left him to deal with things, and he didn't want the job. Having a wife and child to love and protect had changed things. "Did you recognize the man who killed your husband and sons?"

"Better than that, I have a name—Tarver. Slade Tarver. Two men were with him."

Clay's breath stilled. Dammit! The man kept popping up everywhere, like the devil he was.

"Do you know him?"

"He's got a bullet of one of my men in him, ma'am."

"That's why he shot my boys. He was dragging his leg and could barely walk. He wanted our wagon and was going to make my son drive him and the others to Stephenville. My Carl argued with Tarver, and when Carl pulled a gun, they shot him and Ben, then turned the gun on my youngest. I've never seen such rage. They started burning everything in sight—except for the barn. They would've burned it if sounds on the road hadn't spooked them." Susan's hand trembled. "I was sure they'd find me."

"Did they take the wagon when they rode out?"

"Yes. They hitched our horses to it because they'd run theirs into the ground."

"When did this take place?" Almost a month had passed since Clay ran the trio from the town. Of course, Eagle Springs was a week's ride from Devil's Crossing.

Susan drew her brows together in thought. "It took days burying my family, and another two, or maybe it was three, deciding what to do." She gave Clay a wan, apologetic smile. "In my grief, it's difficult to remember these details. I've been sleeping under the stars for five nights. The killings must've been about ten days or so, best I can recall."

That sounded about right. As shot up as Pete and Otis said they left them, the trio would've had to hole up for a while and doctor themselves before attempting to ride very far. Now, they were probably in a hurry to get back to Stephenville and Creedmore, where they could hide within the thick stone walls of the fortress. He stood, guilt rushing through him. The Worth men's blood was on *his* hands. They'd still be alive if he'd simply killed Tarver and his bunch when they'd ridden into Devil's Crossing. This was his mess to clean up.

"You've just hired yourself an avenger, Mrs. Worth. I'll ride out at dawn."

He was going hunting—and this time he'd relish killing the bastards. Clay would find justice for Tally and Susan Worth if it was the last thing he ever did.

❧

Later that afternoon, a little over two weeks from the day that Dr. Mary had begun the process of removing the Creedmore tattoo, Tally sat in the doctor's tent once more. All day, she'd felt the skin pulling at the place on her cheek. She dared not get her hopes of success too high. Bitter disappointment in the past had taught her that the world could play dirty tricks on a person.

"Well? Is it ready?"

Dr. Mary had removed the bandage but had yet to say anything. "The plug has come out. Does it hurt?"

"Not as bad as at the first. Can I see?"

Dr. Mary held out the gauze on which a blackened piece of skin lay. Tally touched it, amazed how much it resembled a piece of burnt leather. Her heart raced and panic swept through her. "Oh God! What does my face look like? Did it leave a hole?"

Would Clay want a wife with grotesque features? Had she done the right thing? Could Rebel help her looks at all? And if she couldn't?

The doctor handed her a small mirror. "See for yourself. It still has a great deal of healing to do, and the amount of scarring will depend on keeping aloe vera sap on it, so it doesn't become dry."

Holding her breath, Tally held up the mirror. The tattoo proclaiming her property of Creedmore was gone, and in its place was a very angry patch of skin. She went to the tent opening to get a better look, and calm filled her. It wasn't like the rest of her face, but it wasn't that bad. Maybe one day people wouldn't be able to tell what had been there.

"I expected far worse." Tally turned and sat back down. "I'm relieved to have the mark off." She plucked a tubular stalk from the aloe vera plant growing in a pot, broke it open, and smeared the sticky sap over the wound. It stung, bringing tears to her eyes, but then felt soothing.

"I'm pleased with the results." Dr. Mary's bullet necklace clinked with her movements. "Frankly, I didn't know how this would turn out."

"Thank you." Tally hugged her. "You've given me back my life. As soon as I can, I'll let the other women know that they have a chance to get rid of theirs, if they choose. I have to show Clay."

She found him talking to Jack and Ridge about plans to stock the mercantile and furnish the hotel. When he saw her, he broke away and strode to her.

"Notice anything?"

"Only a very beautiful woman who makes me weak in the knees." His eyes softened, his gaze taking in the raw patch of skin. "It's gone. I can't believe it. Does it hurt?"

"I won't lie. But it was worth every bit of pain."

He hugged her tightly, his mouth finding hers. The long, deep kiss settled in her soul like silt in a riverbed.

Tally slid her arms around him, inhaling the scent of the man she loved. Her world was almost perfect. Only one thing stood between her and complete and utter happiness—Slade Tarver.

When Clay broke the kiss, Tally stayed in his arms. She saw worry in his eyes. "You're leaving, aren't you?"

He relayed Susan's tale and that he had to go after Tarver

and the other two. "I can't turn a blind eye. I can't live with myself if I don't fix my mistake."

"I wouldn't want you if you didn't. Each man has to live by the rules he sets down for himself." She patted his vest. "You're a good, decent man, and the code of justice inside you calls you to make the world a safer place. You can no more stop being who you are than quit breathing."

"Thank you for understanding."

"You have to be you." She brushed her lips lightly across his, but worry gripped her. To lose Clay would be like losing her heart. "I'll never ask you to be someone else. When will you leave?"

"Morning. I have to make preparations. Even if I left last week, I couldn't catch them before they reached Creedmore anyway. Too much time has passed."

"I agree. I'm glad we have tonight." And she'd make it count.

"Excuse me while I speak to Luke and Houston." Clay gave her a quick kiss and went toward the two Legend brothers.

Tally went to find Rebel, and together they went to Tally's trunk, where Tally pulled out two plain dresses—one of muslin and one calico. "I didn't forget. These are yours if you still want them."

Rebel's smile was blinding. "Of course I do. Now let's see about hiding your scar. I'm glad you removed that awful tattoo."

For the next hour, Rebel taught her how to lightly dab cream from a jar onto her face and smooth it in. "What is this cream?" Tally asked.

"A concoction I make myself from almonds, butternut, and goldenrod. I'll teach you how." Rebel smoothed it around the edges of the wound until it hid a good portion. "Once this heals, it will be easier and take less time," Rebel explained.

"I'm happy with it now. Do you think Clay will notice?"

Rebel winked. "That man notices everything where you're concerned. He can hardly take his eyes from you." She opened up a small tin filled with a firm, rose-colored substance and put a tiny portion on her fingertip, then dabbed it on Tally's cheeks and lips, staining them a soft rose.

The results stunned Tally. Her skin was smooth except for the redness of the wound.

"The trick is to use very little where no one can tell. You simply want to enhance, not change totally. Remember that." Rebel put her jars away and went to change into one of the dresses Tally had given her.

Satisfied, Tally turned in search of Josie and found her in the dugout nursing the baby. "You wanted to know what my face would look like once this bandage came off."

Josie squealed, startling little Elena, who let out a cry. She put the babe on her shoulder and rose. "I've got to get a good look." She came closer to study the wound. "You know, when the red fades and the skin smooths over, no one will be able to see any difference in the left and the right. I'm so happy for you. Was it very bad?"

"The procedure was extremely painful but I have no regrets."

No one owned her. Not Creedmore, not Tarver. Not even Clay. She could determine her own fate. A headiness swept over her. The long nightmare was almost over. Clay was going to take down Tarver, and she was going with him. Only one task remained after that.

God help her, a reckoning was coming. One day, Lucinda Shannon would pay for her crimes.

The mood was somber around the fire that night. The looming fight weighed heavily on the men's minds as they passed a bottle of whiskey around the circle.

"I'm going with you." Jack delivered the statement in a voice that could've sliced through steel. "We'll teach the murdering, godforsaken bastards not to mess with us. They need killing for what they did to Tally and those women alone. And because of them, Mrs. Worth has lost everything and everyone."

"Count me in," Dallas Hawk growled, clenching his hands.

Skeet Malloy stood with his long-barreled six-shooter in hand. "I'm coming."

Everyone around the fire added their sentiments. All were ready to ride, to help Tally and Susan.

"Hold on." Clay held his hands out. "I appreciate you wanting to go along, but you can't. We're not going to leave these women and my daughter alone here and unprotected. I need you to stay behind and finish the interior of these buildings and start stocking them with supplies and furnishings. My Remington is the only help I need."

"Beg your pardon, but you're not an army." Skeet sat back down.

"No, but the element of surprise can put the odds in my favor. Number one, they won't expect me to appear in their domain. Number two, I can sneak in before they know I'm there." Clay hoped that would be the case. "If all of you ride up to the door with guns blazing, Tarver and his bunch will start killing the women. My way, I can get the women out before the shooting starts." And then, whatever fate had in store for him, no one else would suffer.

The fire crackled and popped. Somewhere in the night, an owl hooted.

Houston Legend spoke up. "I know I don't have a dog in this fight, but Clay's right. You can't leave the town unguarded. I've ridden beside him, seen his skill. No one fights better or smarter. Luke will tell you the same thing."

Montana hobbled from his living quarters and listened without saying a word. Clay cut his eyes to the man. What the hell was he up to?

"I know what Houston's saying to be true," Luke said. "Colby can whip any one of you, and he'll have no trouble with that bunch from Creedmore." Luke declined a swig from the bottle being passed. "On another subject, we're leaving at dawn, which will cut your numbers. Wish we could stay longer, but we need to get back to the Lone Star. We've given you a good start on this town. Don't let it go to waste."

"You can bet that won't happen." Clay signaled to Dallas to lift his fiddle, rose, and went to Violet. "Let's dance, baby girl."

A grin covered Violet's face from ear to ear. "How did you know I wanted to, Daddy?"

"Daddies know everything." He set her feet on his boots and held her tight.

Hopefully, his laughter covered the deep sadness inside him. He was smart enough to know that he might not make it back. This might be the last time he had to show his daughter the love he had for her.

"Yep, I think they do." She hummed softly as they swayed to the music. "And they know how to keep the people they love safe. Would you shoot someone if they hurt me?"

Clay glanced down into her sightless eyes. If anyone hurt his daughter, he'd kill them without blinking and feed them to the buzzards. He swallowed his anger and kept his voice even. "No one's going to hurt you, baby girl. Me and everyone else in this town will make sure of that."

"I'm glad."

He finished the dance, wondering why Violet feared for her life now. It had to be Mrs. Worth's coming that had triggered it, and he vowed to watch what he said. The last note of the waltz died, and he took her back to join the women.

Rebel took Travis's hand and they whirled off.

For a moment, Clay took in Tally's beautiful features, her face touched by the flickering light. He would use his last night to hold her. He held out his hand. "Dallas is playing our song."

She stood and smoothed her skirt. "I didn't know we had one."

Clay grinned and pulled her flush against him, hoping to banish the worry in her eyes. "Anything that I can move my feet to always gets my vote."

Tally laughed. "That's what I thought."

He held her tightly, the curves of her luscious body pressing against him. The ends of her hair brushing his hand were a little damp from her recent shower, and the smell of lavender drifted around him.

He could dance with her forever, this woman who held his heart.

"I wish I didn't have to leave at daybreak," he murmured in her ear, gliding, sweeping smoothly across the ground. He held her like the precious, rare china that she was, drawing her tightly to him, soaking up every inch of her.

Tonight he'd create a memory they both could keep—just in case this was all they had.

Couples moved around them. Luke and Josie waltzed slowly nearby, as did Rebel with Travis Lassiter. He was surprised to see Dr. Mary accept Ridge's hand.

"I'm coming with you, Clay." Tally leaned back to stare up at him.

"Not on your life."

"You don't think I can handle myself? Is that it?"

"You know it isn't. It's just too dangerous. As much as I'd like to have you with me, it's better if you stay here. Violet needs you."

Tally had a mulish tilt to her chin that he recognized. "Look, Clay. Like it or not, you'll need me to get Tarver and his bunch. I know every square inch of that place. I know where they sleep, and the places they'll set up an ambush. Without the things I know about that place, how to get in, how to move around, they'll slaughter you."

"No. It's asking them to capture and torture you again." He paused in the deep shadows where the firelight couldn't reach and slid his fingers across her jaw and down her throat. "I can do this better alone."

Where he could focus once and for all on killing the bastards and burning Creedmore to the ground.

As though she could read his thoughts, her voice rose. "I need to get the rest of those women out and you cannot do that alone. They trust me and will follow my instructions."

She did make a strong argument, but he'd find a way to succeed. He had to. He wouldn't have time to throw the women over his shoulder and carry each one out individually. And if one screamed...

But even that possibility didn't change Clay's mind. "No."

Damn her! Why couldn't she see this was foolish and that

she was no match for those Creedmore bastards? Hadn't she learned anything? Sweat formed on his palms just thinking about their level of violence as he tightened his hold around her and swept her away in the waltz once more. They glided effortlessly in large circles, Tally's pretty dress, a new one he'd bought her, swishing against the legs of his trousers.

Clay twirled her under his arm and pulled her close, his mouth next to her ear. "We'll talk about this later."

Tally tensed, her voice brittle. "No, we'll clear the air now. Why are you always so hell-bent on doing everything yourself, refusing to ask for help? Building this town, finding the right people to live here, making sure we have enough to eat, a place to sleep? Why are you determined to raid Creedmore alone, going in blind? Why, Clay?"

"Simple. Nothing works without someone pushing it. I have to make things happen. I'll take care of Creedmore. I have to rescue those women." He had to atone for those he let die in Vicksburg. He hit back with, "Why are you still unable to trust me? Admit that you're only marking time until spring. That you have one foot out the door waiting for a reason to leave."

Her eyes widened and she looked as if he'd slapped her. "I have no choice. The past delivered hard lessons."

"That's right and you're never going to let me forget it. Everyone among us here has suffered, bled, spent sleepless nights. All of us." The minute the words left Clay's mouth, he wanted to call them back, to apologize. But she jerked from his grasp.

"Leave." He lowered his voice to a whisper, his heart breaking. "It's what you do best."

Tally gave a cry and ran into the darkness, leaving him alone, angry words ringing in his ears like a funeral dirge.

Twenty-seven

TALLY READ A STORY TO VIOLET, THEN SLEPT ALONE IN THEIR unfinished house, her arms aching for Clay. She had no idea where he'd bedded down, or if he sought sleep. Wherever he was, he was sure to seek the company of a bottle to silence those demons in his head. She knew, come daybreak, they'd have more harsh words, because he wasn't going to stop her from riding along.

Not this time.

Tears ran down her face and she bit back sobs, not wanting to wake Violet, who would be sure to ask questions. Her fight with Clay had revealed deep cracks in their marriage. All the accusations he'd leveled at her were true. What she'd gone through wasn't much different from everyone else here. They all dealt with dark pasts. Rebel had her share. Clay had hinted at darkness he was unable to bear. Jack, Ridge, Dallas, Skeet, Susan Worth—they'd all endured the worst life could throw at them.

Who was she to say her pain was worse than theirs?

An inability to trust. That was really what lay underneath it all. How did she go about believing in Clay totally without doubt and having full confidence in him? Tally sighed and wiped away a tear. This loneliness was unbearable.

Why couldn't she relinquish this need to control?

Until Clay, it had always been just her. In Deliverance Canyon, she'd had to be the protector, and now it seemed turning loose of that and letting him assume that role was impossible.

The sudden stab of pain in her chest wasn't from heart damage. No, this was anxiety over the fight and the angry words. Tally clutched her chest, praying it would pass quickly. The squeezing tightness burned like pure fire, closing the narrow passage of her throat, cutting off air. She didn't know how long she lay there until she could relax and it passed.

At last, she let sleep take her and she dreamed of the musty halls and black stone rooms of Creedmore. Danger lurked in every corner and the success of their mission appeared uncertain. Shadows stalked the place of torture. Women's cries sprang from every crevice.

The sky was still dark when she stirred, determined to find Clay. She quickly dressed and found him standing at the base of the windmill, staring off into nothingness as though getting his mind focused on the task ahead.

Though he didn't turn, she knew he heard her as she stole quietly up behind. The need to touch him, to lay her face against his back, was more than she could bear. But would he welcome her touch? The angry words he'd thrown at her had stung to the quick. She reached out, fingertips away from his shirt, only to let her hand fall.

"Morning," Clay said low.

She put her arms around his waist and pressed her cheek to his back, breathing his scent. "I missed you."

His voice rumbled. "I missed you, too."

"I don't want this wall between us. Fighting is ugly, and I'm sorry for what I said."

"Then I hope you've come to see reason." He turned. "My way is best, and Violet needs you."

So nothing had changed. Tally stepped away, anger rising, and speared him with a glare. "Here's something for you to chew on. I started this job over two years ago and I mean to finish it. I'm going—either with you, or alone. Your choice."

His eyes blazed. "You're determined to get your way, aren't you?"

"It's not that. I have to go."

"Do you know why I try to do everything myself?"

She met Clay's anger and answered it with her own. "Enlighten me."

"Because there was no one around when I was left to make my own way. To find my own food, a bed, a way to silence the explosions of the cannons, the screams of the dying. I had to do that myself. And when I killed my first man, I had to handle that myself too. Just me."

The confession brought tears to her eyes and she saw the immense pain of the fourteen-year-old boy he'd been. She reached out, but not in time. He strode away with the wind-mill mimicking her crying heart.

It would be light soon. She should probably get the pack mule loaded. She saw Luke and Houston stoking the campfire. They, too, would ride out with the dawn.

Belle January stepped through the opening in their tent. Tally hurried to ask a favor.

"Yes, me and Tobias will watch after Violet. It's no bother. We love that little girl."

Tally kissed her cheek. "You're a godsend. Thank you."

She turned toward the hardest task—giving Violet a proper goodbye. It ripped her heart out to leave her daughter, but she had no choice. A light went on in Dr. Mary's tent—she must be an early riser too. When Tally turned, she noticed the slight, nightgowned figure carefully coming toward them, her walking stick out in front, the other hand clutching Bullet's fur.

Tally's heart melted. She pulled her shawl tight and went to greet the crying girl. This was going to be more difficult than she'd anticipated. She swallowed the lump in her throat.

"Mama, where are you?"

"Honey, I'm here." Tally knelt down and folded her arms around the girl. "Please don't be sad."

"I need you. I heard you and Daddy arguing. I don't want you to be mad. Are you both leaving me?"

Bullet whined and lay down next to Violet. The pet must sense the heavy heartache that surrounded them.

"Honey, big people say hurtful things they don't mean sometimes. We're going to be all right. And you will too with the Januarys." But would she and Clay return to what they'd had? That was the question in Tally's mind. She wiped Violet's eyes and smoothed back her tangled blond hair. "It won't be for long. I promise."

"My real mama said that too and she left me in that horrible place."

Pain and guilt pierced Tally's heart. "I promise I'm not going to do that. I will come back." *If at all possible*, she added silently. "We're a family and we love each other."

Sobs erupted from Violet. "I don't want you and Daddy to die."

"Honey, we're not going to die. What makes you think we will?"

"Mr. Tarver is a bad, bad man. He might kill you. He nearly did before. I hate him."

Clay came up beside them and laid a hand on Violet's head. "Don't waste time on hate. He's not worth it. Baby girl, he's no match for me and your mama, I guarantee that. Rotten-to-the-core men like him can't win. You know why?"

"No."

"Because they have no foundation, no soul, no heart. You have to have all three to be victorious. We have those."

His eyes raised to Tally's and acceptance there heartened her. She was able to take a deep breath for the first time that morning.

But what he'd said to Violet was right. People like Tarver would always fail in the end, because they had nothing to build on. She kissed Violet's cheek. "Remember the story I read to you last night—the 'King of the Golden River'? The good brother received riches beyond compare after he unselfishly gave every drop of his water to the old man, the sick child, and the poor little puppy."

"Yeah, and his mean ol' brothers got turned into black stones because they wouldn't share," Violet answered. "I was real glad."

Clay lifted her into his arms. "That's what we're going to do to Slade Tarver, so he can't hurt any more people."

"Good. Make their stones extra, extra hard."

More men were walking through what would soon be the main street of their town. The position of the sun said it was almost time to leave. Clay kissed Violet and set her down. "Tally, can I have a word?"

She told Violet to stay put and joined Clay.

"All right, we ride out together." His voice was low and curt at her ear, his breath teasing a curl at her temple. "At least promise to stay back when the firing starts. Can you do that?"

"I'll try my best." Their argument wasn't resolved by a long shot, but she'd make time to reason with him on the trail. She pasted on a smile as she went to collect Violet.

"Come, honey. Let's get you dressed and fix some breakfast." Tally took the walking stick and clutched her daughter's hand.

She didn't want to hold Clay up, and he was already itching to ride. Foreboding held her in its grip. All their lives were about to change.

❧

A pink blush swept across the sky as Tally stood with Clay and told the Lone Star visitors goodbye. It appeared everyone had turned out for the send-off—except for Montana Black. The outlaw was nowhere to be seen, and Tally wondered where he'd gone.

She put that out of her mind and swung her attention to their guests, relieved that Luke had made a comfortable bed in the back of the wagon for Josie and the baby. Hopefully, all the jostling wouldn't set the new mother back, although Dr. Mary had given them her blessing to travel.

Clay shook hands with Luke. "I can't thank you enough for the help. For you, Houston, and Josie to stop your lives and come here went above and beyond mere friendship."

"I wish I could go with you." Luke shot a glance toward his wife. "You understand."

"I certainly do. You're needed at the Lone Star. Get Miss Josie home, so she can get her strength back."

With Clay's strong arm to bolster her, Tally swallowed a lump and squeezed Josie's hand. "Take good care of little Elena Rose."

"I will. Good luck in ending the nightmare in Creedmore. Stay safe." Josie put her arm around Luke's neck as he lifted her into the wagon, babe and all.

Luke threw a light blanket over his pretty wife and patted his vest. "I have all the letters you men wrote. I'll deliver them to the ladies very soon."

His black trousers, shirt, and hat adding an ominous look, Jack Bowdre spread his legs in a wide stance and hooked his thumbs in his gun belt. "Don't add anything in about my cussing. Darcy Howard thinks I'm a Bible-toter."

"Fat chance of that," Dallas Hawk said.

"Hey, I'm a good guy."

"We'll just head on down the trail while you sort that out, *amigos.*" Luke shook the reins and the wagon wheels rolled.

Sensing the parting had come, Violet whimpered beside Tally and pressed against her, burying her face in the folds of Tally's leather riding skirt. Tally laid a hand on her shoulder, praying the child wouldn't become inconsolable. She couldn't leave her this way.

The other wagons fell in behind Luke, and Clay stirred. "We have to go too."

Panic filled Violet's face and she clutched Tally's skirt tightly. "No! I don't want you to leave. Please."

"Honey, it's only for a little while."

Belle came forward. "Sweet girl, I need your help. One of those baby goats has lost its mother. We gotta find her before the coyotes do. If she dies, her baby will, too."

"And I need someone to help me make cookies," Susan Worth said, winking at Tally and Clay. "We're going to have the best time, you and me, and your mama and daddy will be back before you can even miss them good."

Violet sighed and finally relinquished her hold on Tally. "Just don't forget about me."

"As if we ever could, honey." Tally gave her another hug and kiss. Fighting tears, she swung into the saddle.

The windmill that had always seemed so comforting now seemed to wail as though someone was dying. Would she ever see this place again? Would Violet have even more loss in her short life?

As they went through the opening of the town, Tally

turned for one last look at Devil's Crossing. It was here she had learned to be a wife, to open her heart just a little and find her way. To discover who she really was. To start to heal.

And it was here she learned to love and be loved.

The morning's thin light shone on the new buildings that would hopefully draw new settlers. Clay's dream was about to come true.

They rode in silence, Clay's face dark beneath the shadow of his hat. She cleared the lump from her throat. "Clay, I think we should rename our town."

"Devil's Crossing doesn't exactly speak of a bright future." The saddle creaked when he swiveled. "Any ideas?"

"Maybe something to do with hopes or dreams. How about Dreamer's Valley?"

"I like that. Or Hope's Crossing?"

She grinned. She liked his suggestion the best. "The others should also have a say. They have as much at stake as we do."

"Sounds like a vote is on the way." Clay maneuvered his mount closer until his leg brushed hers. "I wish you'd have listened and stayed behind. But I knew better than to insist. You'd have ridden after me anyway."

"You do know me." She'd adopted a pleasant tone, determined not to get upset.

"We'll stop tonight at a cave I know. I figure it'll take us four days to reach Deliverance Canyon, and you can check on the ladies. I know you've been worried about them."

"With Slade scouring the countryside, the risk of discovery is awfully high. But Alice assured me they continued to be very careful under Hester's guidance." Tally prayed they were all well. It had about killed her when two more of the women got sick last winter and passed because they had no access to a doctor or medicine. She'd always be grateful to Luke for providing basic necessities.

Even so, they were little more than rats huddling in a hole, and it was time to get them out of there and back among the living.

She turned her thoughts to Clay and his plans. They'd

have plenty of quiet time to talk through their problems. She wanted their marriage to work more than anything.

They rode single file through a mesquite thicket, staying close to each other, every nerve taut. A rider suddenly shot out in front of them from the side.

Her mare, Sugar, reared up, her legs flailing the air. Tally grabbed the reins and held on tight, keeping her seat.

Clay yanked his Remington from the holster and pointed it at the rider. "Who are you?"

The man's long, gray, shaggy hair looked oddly familiar.

Montana raised his empty hands. "Just me."

"What the hell? You know better than to ride out in front of me. I oughta shoot you where you stand." Clay reached for the mare's bridle and Sugar settled.

Though Clay tried to corral them, Tally heard the string of cusswords that spewed from his mouth. She didn't blame him for being mad. That was a foolish thing for anyone to have done in outlaw country.

Tally leaned forward to pat Sugar's muscular neck. "You missed the big send-off this morning."

"There'll be others. It's not the last time we'll see Luke Legend." Montana coolly picked his teeth with a long knife. "I'm coming with you," he announced.

"The hell you are! I don't want you within twenty miles of Creedmore." Clay angrily jammed his gun back in the holster. "My job will be difficult enough. If I had my druthers, Tally would stay behind as well."

Montana put his knife away. "I ain't gonna argue with you. I'm coming and that's that. I aim to make sure you both get back to sweet little Violet."

Tally narrowed her eyes. "Did she put you up to this?"

"Nope. Sure the hell didn't. Thought of it all by myself."

Tally watched the angry tic in Clay's jaw. She understood all the reasons why he'd be mad—the main one being that the old outlaw wasn't that trustworthy. Yet she sympathized with the man. Montana had a soft spot for their daughter, and that had put some good inside his rotten, black heart.

She moved her horse closer to Clay and leaned over so Montana wouldn't hear. "Let him come. Like it or not, we can use his help. Remember that he spent some time with Slade and his bunch after you shot him. They consider him a friend. And besides, there are a lot more men running Creedmore than just the three of them. They have about two dozen on the payroll to keep the women in line."

An irritated grunt rose from Clay's chest. He turned to the old outlaw. "Stay out of my way. I won't hesitate to shoot you. Again."

Montana grinned, showing his three missing teeth. "I always knew you liked me, Colby."

"You're a crazy old coot!" Clay spurred his gelding and took off at a fast trot.

Tally didn't spare Montana a glance as she hurried after Clay, but the horse's hooves striking the ground behind her said the old outlaw had wasted no time in taking Clay up on his invitation—such as it was.

They rode for two hours before stopping at a watering hole to rest and let the horses drink. Tally's thoughts were on the monumental job ahead.

She'd learned the hard way not to count on things in this desolate land.

Twenty-eight

THEY ARRIVED AT THE CAVE CLAY SPOKE OF FOR THE NIGHT. Montana took care of the horses while Clay hunted, and they dined on roasted prairie chicken and rabbit. Montana lost no time in going to sleep. Like a baby, get his stomach full and he started snoring.

Tally took Clay's hand. "Let's move to the opening and talk."

After moving away and getting settled, she glanced out at the stars. "Clay, what's happening to us? Why are we fighting?"

He shrugged. "Beats the hell out of me. I just want to keep you safe and for you to trust me to do so. I said a lot of hurtful things and I apologize."

"I'm sorry too." She rested her head on his shoulder and he put his arm around her. "You were right. I haven't gone through any more than the rest in our town. I've been wearing sackcloth and ashes, feeling sorry for myself. And maybe I have had one foot out the door, looking for an excuse to leave. It's easier than learning to trust, to put mine and Violet's welfare fully in your hands. I do want to. It's just so stinking hard. How do I do it, Clay? Tell me."

Clay kissed her temple. "I think you first have to believe deep down that I'm not going to let anything happen to you. Lady, you're the most precious thing to me. I would lay down my life to protect you and our daughter."

"I know you would. I really do believe that. The part I struggle with is turning over decisions to you. I can't relinquish that. I've done it far too long, as have you. We both want to be in charge." Now that she'd said the words aloud, she saw it clearly. "Two people can't handle the reins at the same time, not when I want to go one way and you the other."

"No, it doesn't work."

Tally raised her head and moved to face him. "So what do we do?"

"I don't know. I do want our marriage to succeed."

"Tell me what happened when you found you had no family left. Where did you go?" She ached to think about the scared boy with no one.

"I started walking west. I ran into an old woman and stayed a month or so with her, helping around the place. She gave me some clothes and burned my ragged uniform. Told me about the opportunities that waited and told me cattlemen were hiring young drovers to drive their herds to Kansas and other places. I worked for Charles Goodnight, Jesse Chisholm, and a few others, and bought a ranch outside of Cimarron with the money I earned." He ran a hand over his eyes. "Then trouble found me. I settled it with my six-gun. It put me on the run. I threw in with outlaws and found killing came natural." His voice lowered. "I had a talent for drawing fast, my aim sure, and developed a reputation that made any chance of a normal life impossible."

"But you want more now. I see it in your eyes, hear it in your voice."

"Yeah." He picked up a rock and threw it down below.

"You'll make it happen." She drew a small jar of aloe vera salve from her pocket.

Clay took it and gently rubbed a portion into the wound on her cheek. "So will you."

The night air whispered around them, and Tally took comfort in Clay's gentle fingers and thought about what he'd told her. He'd been a successful rancher. She could picture him in that life. He probably loved the peace it brought. Then someone had taken it all away. Like with her.

He gazed into her eyes. "Tally, I spoke to Luke and Houston about getting you a lawyer. We're going to take your stepmother to court and get back everything she stole from you. That is, if that's what you want to do."

"I'd like nothing better, but don't lawyers and court cost a lot of money?"

"I'll borrow, beg, or steal, but I'll get it." He nuzzled behind her ear. "Justice is worth any price, Mrs. Colby. I'm going to help you get it."

"I ask for nothing more. Thank you, Clay." She picked up his large hand and threaded her fingers through his. "Let's go to bed. I want to lie next to you and know I'm safe and loved."

❧

The sun sank below the horizon, and darkness was closing fast by the time they reached Deliverance Canyon. Clay gave the secret owl hoot that Tally told him to give to let the women know friends were coming. He'd passed close a number of times over the years, never knowing a canyon lay hidden below. But then, with the thick brush and overgrowth hiding the opening, a person had to know exactly where to find it. Very ingenious. Tally had chosen a good hiding place.

This wife of his was always full of surprises. He was relieved to have cleared up the friction between them. He didn't want to fight. Loving was more fun.

Tally seemed nervous. She spoke low. "I think we should leave Montana up here to guard in case we were followed. I won't bring these women harm."

Clay covered her hand with his and gave it a reassuring pat. "Don't worry." He turned to Montana. "You'll have to stay up top and guard. Think you can do that?"

"No one'll get past me. My word on that." Montana dismounted, scanning the area before untying his bedroll behind his saddle. "I'll camp right here. Are you taking the pack mule?"

"Nope. I'll leave it so you can cook some supper." Clay swung to Tally. "Ready?"

She gave him a blinding smile. "With you—always."

The steep descent was slow going, with drop-offs on both sides of the trail. Finally, they reached the bottom and women surrounded Tally's mare.

An older woman ratcheted a bullet into the chamber of her rifle and pointed it at Clay. "I don't know you, mister."

The hardness in her eyes gave Clay pause. He pointed to Tally. "I'm with her."

Tally laughed and dismounted. "Hester Mason, meet my husband, Clay Colby. He's harmless—for the most part."

"Had to make sure." Hester let the hammer down easy.

The woman appeared older than Clay by about twenty years. Her blond hair had faded, but there was a sharpness to Hester that belied her age. No doubt the woman was a good shot and had seen occasion to hone her skill. She looked like she'd happily kill anyone who messed with them and not feel one speck of guilt.

"How's your leg, Hester?" Tally asked.

"I'm hobbling around. It's getting better with every sunrise."

Clay watched the group of women around Tally. They obviously adored her. "And the bullet wound?"

"Healing. I'm a tough old bird."

"Yes, you are." Clay dismounted, taking in the pitiful dwellings made from scrap lumber and other things that perched among the boulders. This was no way for anyone to live. He was glad Tally was out—and soon maybe the rest would be too.

He put his arm around her trim waist and they strolled to the fire. A shy woman handed them two filled plates.

All the women wore the same Creedmore mark that Tally used to have. They ranged in age from around forty down to young women like Alice, who hadn't yet seen their eighteenth birthday. The sight fed his boiling anger. He couldn't wait to bring justice for these escapees, women who'd been thrown away by families they trusted.

The thin remaining light caught on three crosses, marking graves where they'd evidently buried the ones who would never make it out this canyon and find a better life. He had trouble swallowing.

"I have news for everyone." Tally set her plate down. "A doctor where I now live has the means to remove the tattoos. Come closer and look."

The women crowded around, oohing and aahing, gently touching the still-red patch of skin where the mark had been.

Tally's gaze moved over each one. "She can do the same for you."

"Did it hurt much?" one of the women asked.

"I won't lie. It did, but I'd do it again in a heartbeat." She raised her chin defiantly. "I belong to no one, not even Clay. No one will own me."

He nodded and met each measured glance. "That's right. You shouldn't let anyone own you either. You can claim yourselves back as well. We're going to Creedmore tomorrow and God only knows how this will go. But no matter what happens, Tally is already entirely free of them."

"I want to be free too." The speaker pulled a tattered shawl close around her. "Those bastards took a lot more than my pride, and I want it back."

"Me too."

"I don't care how much pain is involved. I want to look in the mirror again and not see their ugly mark."

"Amen to that!"

"What if I don't want to?" The woman who spoke next had burn marks up and down her arms. "I've seen more pain than I ever thought possible. I can't bear to think about facing more. I just can't."

"No one will ever force you to do anything you don't want, Ruth." Tally rose and went around the fire. Crying, she folded her arms around her friend and held her.

The love she had for these women brought a lump to Clay's throat. No matter where they'd all come from, they were family now. Their real ones had discarded them to be used and abused in ways that were inconceivable, and in the midst of horror, they'd formed a lasting bond.

He cleared his throat. "I'd like for you all to come live at Devil's Crossing. We'll take care of you and give you homes. No one will ever hurt you again. You have my word on that."

Hester Mason shifted the rifle she kept at her side. "If you make things safe for us, we'll consider it. If you can't, then we'll stay put. This canyon is pretty secure."

"That's fair. We'll talk about this further after I'm done at Creedmore."

A pretty, brown-haired woman scooted next to him. "I'm Darcy Howard. Do you know Jack Bowdre?"

"He's a good friend."

She nodded. "I met him when he came to treat Hester's leg. What kind of man is he really?"

"Honorable as the day is long and fearless to a fault. Jack will ride into hell with nothing except a burning need to put down evil. I've never known a better man." Clay chuckled. "Jack's also the most stubborn cuss I've ever seen. If he thinks he's right, he'll argue with a fence post until he's blue in the face."

"He sounds nice, but I'm not sure I want to marry him. Or anyone for that matter. I've been thinking about entering a nunnery." She paused, staring into the flames. "I have to find meaning to my life, you know."

Clay patted her hand. "I can understand that. After a tragedy, a person needs to do some soul-searching. Do whatever is right for you. Jack will understand."

"He seems real nice though." Darcy leaned forward to toss a twig into the fire. "I wouldn't want to hurt him."

"Don't worry about Jack. You figure out what you want to do with your life."

Jack would take the blow hard. The former lawman had pinned a lot of hopes on marrying Darcy. Without his dream of a home and family to keep him going, who knew what Jack would do? He might give up and return to a life of crime. None of that was Darcy's to deal with, mind.

Hope seemed a slender thread that was too easily broken.

Tally returned to her place next to him, snuggling against his side. He brushed a kiss on the top of her head and listened to the crackle and pop of the fire.

Ruth stared into the flames, her voice wistful. "I dream sometimes of walking down any street in any town and not having to worry." Her gaze swung to Clay. "I used to be scared of the shadows. Now I'm afraid of the monsters that hide in the dark and love to make me scream."

"We all are, Ruth." Tally squeezed Clay's arm. "I refuse to give in to that fear. Life can be so full of joy again if you let it."

"How's Violet?" Hester asked. "I hope she's doing okay."

Clay chuckled. "That girl has her own personal army of bodyguards surrounding her."

"She's learned to get about without help, using a long stick and walking trails that Clay and the men made for her." Tally rested her back against his chest. "She loves her new independence—and the fact that when she sneezes, every man in earshot runs with a handkerchief. I fear she's spoiled beyond hope."

Clay changed the subject and told them about Luke and Josie. "It sure didn't look good for her and the babe for a while, but they're both doing well now."

Hester clicked her tongue. "That poor woman. I'm glad everything turned out all right. Good luck to you both in this undertaking. Our thoughts go with you, and we'll pray for success in burning Creedmore down."

They talked a little more, then turned in for the night. Clay spread their bedrolls by the fire and pulled Tally down next to him. "I'm so glad you took a chance and came to marry me. This place, those lonely graves, break my heart."

"Mine, too."

Tally wiggled until she got comfortable and dozed off. Clay stared up at the starry sky and planned for his arrival at Creedmore.

He curled his hands into tight fists. Tally, Violet, these women, and Susan Worth had lost huge parts of their lives. He would make sure that they wouldn't lose anything else.

This time he would not fail. He would not lead those women in Creedmore to their death. He whispered that over and over until it was branded in his brain.

❧

The women gave them quite a send-off, echoes of "good luck" ringing out as they left the canyon early the next morning with Montana. Clay set a brisk pace at the start, energized by his desire to reach Stephenville and the asylum, but as the day wore on, they slowed considerably. He wouldn't put the horses in danger or have them exhausted when they really needed them.

On the second day after leaving Deliverance, they made camp, cooked some game he'd killed, and ate. Afterward, he stood silently by a low fire, lost in his own black thoughts. Montana lay down on his bedroll, placed his hat over his face, and was soon snoring.

Tally finished the dishes and slid her arms around Clay. "Those are some mighty serious thoughts."

Guilt rose and he sighed. "I'm not fit company."

"I ask for no apology." She kissed his back, running her hands across the width.

"No, but you deserve one." He glanced up at the early stars popping out in the evening sky. "I have this darkness in my head that sometimes takes over, no matter how hard I work and work to box it up and nail on the lid. This damnable blackness slithers out like a slimy salamander."

"Don't see it as some big fault." Tally moved around to face him. "It's what keeps you alive."

Leave it to her to see the positives of a flaw.

"Some might argue the point." He let his fingers drift across her face. When he encountered the rough skin where the tattoo had been, he sucked in a breath. That patch of skin represented what lay at stake.

"I know what that darkness is like because I have it in me, too," she said quietly.

Clay lifted a fiery strand of hair and worked the silk between his fingers. "You and me, we're like two wild horses that no man can ride. No matter how patient and gentle a person is, they simply won't let you ride them. They're too damn stubborn, with a wildness you can't ever get out. Maybe people like us can never make a marriage work." He closed his eyes and swore on his mother's grave that he'd somehow protect Tally, even if it put him six feet under. She would return to Violet.

The eerie silence of the land was loud in his ears. The enemy waited.

Tally trembled. "Hold me, Clay. The night is too dark."

"I have no idea how this mission here is going to go, but I swear that I'm going to stick my feet in the stirrups and hold on. This old wild horse is going to gallop to the bitter end." Clay pulled her closer and felt the beating of her heart. "If I get thrown off and stomped into the ground in the attempt, you can bury me."

"No! I haven't come this far to let Tarver kill you." Tally gripped his shirt, her eyes blazing. "We're going to win. We're going to return to Violet. We're going to get our happy life. *Both* of us. You got that?"

"Always." He covered her mouth with a savage intensity. His hunger for her was like a raging river roaring out of its banks, going wherever it wanted, often too difficult to contain.

And there were times like now when he had no desire to tamp it down.

They couldn't make love with Montana right there, but he could damn sure hold this woman who'd stormed into his life, hands on her hips, and filled every hollow place in his heart.

She wrapped her arms around him and held him flush against her. He trembled with need that refused to be quieted. For this woman, he'd do anything, be anything, go anywhere. All she had to do was ask.

But fear rode in his saddle. He'd never been so close to happiness before...

He released her and strode off to check the horses one more time, trying to escape the thick blackness crawling inside him like a thousand worms, twisting and turning, burrowing deeper into his soul.

Twenty-nine

ALTHOUGH THE MORNING WAS WARM AND INCHED TOWARD THE hot side, Tally couldn't get rid of the ice that coated her heart. The weary days of travel had brought them within a day's ride of their destination. She washed up the few tin dishes they'd used and returned them to a burlap sack on the pack mule.

Clay covered her hand. "I didn't get my kiss."

"That's because you were already up. Did you even come to bed?"

"No time for sleep. I had to think, to plan." He pressed a kiss to her lips.

Tally slid her arms around his neck and threaded her fingers in his hair. She could stay locked in his embrace forever. This man had so much honor and strength, always taking care of others. When would he see to *his* needs? When would it be time for *him*?

She murmured against his mouth, absorbing his jumpiness. "What is it, Clay?"

"I've never had so much to lose before." He took a step back, jerked his hat off, and ran his fingers through his hair. "In the past, the outcome of a fight affected only me. Now, it's you and Violet. If I fail...."

"You won't. We've been cheated out of enough and it's time for things to change." Bootheels struck the ground, telling her Montana was back from scouting the brush. She laid a palm on Clay's vest and spoke softly. "You don't have to do this. We can turn around right now. No one would fault you, least of all me."

He looked at her like she'd suggested he whack off his arm. His dark brown eyes snapped. "Like you, when I start something, I finish it." Then he turned to tie the bedrolls behind their saddles, giving the ropes vicious yanks.

She'd never meant to make him angry. But she suspected it wasn't her he was furious with—it was whole the situation. He probably yearned to be back in his town with his brothers-in-arms.

"What's got his goat?" Montana asked.

"Nerves, I guess."

Montana shook his head. "We all got 'em. Wouldn't be normal if we didn't."

With another glance at Clay, she finished breaking down the camp, then silently climbed onto her mare.

They rode for most of the day with little conversation, but Clay's gentle touches and quiet words told her he'd settled down. On the other hand, the closer they got to Creedmore, the colder she became inside. She must've been crazy for deciding to tag along.

Tarver, Finch, and the others were ahead. If they got her again…they'd kill her in whatever painful way their twisted minds could dream up.

A shiver raced through her. Her hands shook so badly she almost dropped the reins.

Montana moved closer and laid his palm over hers. "I got you, pretty lady. Ain't nothing gonna happen."

"Thanks." She noticed a gentleness in his eyes she'd never seen before. Although it seemed inconceivable that Montana Black was ever anything except a hard outlaw, maybe he'd once lived a life of substance. "Tell me your story, Montana. What led you to this hard life?"

The man rubbed his gray, grizzled chin. "You probably don't believe this, but I had a wife once. Oh Lord, she was a looker! Hair as soft as silk and smelled of honeysuckle." His eyes softened. "I thought we'd live out the rest of our lives together—just me an' her. We didn't have much, but we were happy."

"What happened?"

"While I was out huntin' game, some real bad hombres came along. She must've fought 'em. They tied her to a tree, doused her with kerosene, and set fire to her." He put his hand to his eyes, possibly in an attempt to wipe away the memories crowding close.

"I'm real sorry." Tally laid her hand on his arm. Violet had seen the good inside Montana—maybe because she was blind and hadn't judged by his looks.

"For a whole year I couldn't breathe. It was like someone had a fist around my throat." He gazed up the trail. "I went after 'em. Didn't take much to find the bastards. Took a mighty long time for 'em to die though." A strange smile formed on his lips. "Yes, it did. I never tried to go back to the good life after that. My soul was past saving."

He was silent a minute, watching Clay up ahead. "Until that little girl of your'n."

"Violet sees the good in everyone." Her voice was soft. "She loves you, you know."

"Don't know why in the hell she does." The outlaw barked a laugh. "I ain't no prize." Montana clicked to his horse and galloped ahead.

Something her father had said a long time ago drifted across her mind. *It's best to remember, girl—even the most saintly people have a past, things they've done wrong, regrets aplenty. And every sinner has a future.*

Except for her stepmother Lucinda and Tarver—their lives as they knew it were over.

While Tally rode, she thought about people like Montana and Rebel. When it all came down to brass tacks, everyone just needed to be loved and accepted—by someone.

Midafternoon, the landscape began to grow familiar. Groves of live oak trees dotted the plains, and little bluestem grass covered the hills. They skirted the small town of Stephenville around sunset. Her father's ranch—now the property of Lucinda—was less than five miles away. The hair on the back of her neck stood up. If she could take Lucinda to court and get her ranch back, maybe her father's spirit would be at peace.

They rounded a grove of live oak and rode up on top of a bluff. She gasped and shrank back in the saddle.

The black stone building of Creedmore lay poised down

below like a horrible, giant bird about to take flight. The asylum stood two stories high, the windows like hollow eyes, staring.

Tally sucked in a breath, releasing a little cry.

Clay stopped his gelding beside her and dismounted. He came around and lifted her from the mare, holding her with arms of steel. "It's only a building, darlin'. Just a building."

She inhaled the scent of the man she loved and buried her face in the hollow of his throat. She wasn't brave one bit. She was a coward through and through, letting horrors shake her to her bones. She could do this. She had to.

Paying Montana no heed, Clay held her for a while, murmuring against her ear, rubbing her back. Finally, she stepped from his arms. "I'm fine. We should make camp."

They silently went about the chore of readying for nightfall. Each had a routine and Tally did it by rote, feeling the magnitude of the storm about to engulf her.

She gathered wood to make a fire and made coffee while the men hunted. As darkness swept across the land, she swung around to find Clay staring at Creedmore, his jaw clenched tight, his eyes narrowed. The red glow from his cigarette illuminated a face of stone. The warrior in him was gearing up for the fight.

Tears stung her eyes, knowing he might not walk away from this one.

From his strange actions, he seemed to feel it too.

Oh God, she couldn't lose this man. He'd shown her what it was like to be loved.

He clenched his Remington and raised it, quarter-cocked the hammer, squinting the length of the long barrel. Then he twirled the cylinder and released the hammer, the metallic click echoing in the stillness.

The deadly sound sent a shiver down her spine.

Clay lowered the Remington to his side, then before she could blink, he jerked the weapon up again and put the hated stone building down below in his sights. All that pain and suffering, and they were only a half mile away.

Thirty

No one had much of an appetite that night, with the enemy so near. An impending fight always played havoc with Clay's stomach, knotting it like a hangman's rope. Only this was much worse.

He was suddenly back at fourteen in a ragged uniform. A war-torn captain took him aside and gave him and his friend the important mission of leading the group of women and children to nearby caves above the town to escape the shelling. The sound deafened him. Pure chaos was everywhere as people ran for their lives. One woman was swollen with child and clutched her stomach as though her hands would protect her unborn. Children sobbed and yelled. Buildings burned around the group. Dogs barked. Horses screamed. He'd take them to safety, Clay promised.

The next instant, it was all over and the world eerily quiet and his life forever and unalterably changed.

Clay emerged from the memories shaking, sweat rolling down his face. To fail again would destroy him. Of that much, he was positive.

Thin clouds drifted over the moon, giving it a ghostly appearance. Clay drank cup after cup of coffee and stood beyond the circle of light in the darkness, mulling over all the things that could go wrong. Sorting them out according to the level of danger.

Finally, he turned and sat down with Tally and Montana. "We've got to make a plan. We need a diversion to draw the men's attention while we get the women out."

Tally raised her gaze to him, worry and fear in her eyes saying so much more than words. "There's one other problem that we need to discuss."

"What's that, darlin'?" Clay added another stick to the fire.

"Some of these women in Creedmore really do have mental problems. What are we going to do with them? Who'll take them?"

Montana poured a liberal amount of whiskey into his coffee cup. "Now you tell me."

Clay snorted. "No one asked you to come. That was your idea, remember?"

Tally jumped to her feet. "Stop. We have to stand together or this isn't going to work. Clay, I think Montana may be the key to us getting inside undetected. Since Tarver and his cronies know him, they won't be suspicious when he rides up. We'll use that to our advantage."

Hell, she was right, but it irked him. Somehow, he had to put aside his personal feelings. Pushing to his feet, he took Tally's arm. "I don't know how far I can trust the man. Montana has betrayed us time and again."

Her winter gaze pierced him. "You either do or you don't. Personally, I think he's changed. He's not the same man you brought in to patch up. Violet changed him."

Clay pinched the bridge of his nose. "Okay. Our lives depend on you being right."

They returned to the fire. Tally told them about the horses and wagons on the property that they could use to haul the women to safety. Clay listened to each word. She figured there were around two dozen or more women who were actually insane, and probably close to thirty like her who had been put there to die. Over fifty women? Clay had never stopped to think how many there actually were imprisoned there. Or how much money Tarver and his goons made off the families who wanted people to disappear. It boggled his mind how rich they were getting.

And they said outlaws were animals.

Shaking his head, he drew his thoughts back to the situation. Their task was larger than he'd first thought.

Tally stared into the fire, her face carved from granite. "Some have been here since they were young girls and remember little of the outside world. Adjusting to freedom will be difficult."

Clay laid a hand on her tense shoulders, shaken by the reality she was describing. He'd never forget what she'd been through. This mission wasn't about him or Montana or even Susan Worth. They were here for Tally and her one goal, the one thing that haunted and kept her fighting.

The bigger picture, that was the important thing. Saving the rest of these women, not how Montana had tried to wreck Clay's dreams.

"Thank you for reminding me why we're here." He leaned to kiss her and let the fragrance of the night air and her gentle warmth cool his anger.

Montana drained his cup, but instead of pouring more whiskey and getting liquored up good, he set it down. "Just tell me what you need me to do and I'll get 'er done."

Clay nodded at the outlaw across the fire. "Create a diversion so we can slip inside." He turned to Tally. "Is there any other way out except through the front doors?"

"There's the kitchen, which will be dark this time of night." A little grin formed. "There's also a secret passage I found by accident. Someone had blocked it with rocks about ten years ago. Over many months of working at night, I unsealed it and escaped. If they haven't blocked it again, we can use that." She shivered and drew her shawl closer, recalling the darkness and scuttling sounds of nighttime creatures that had played on her nerves. "I have a friend on the inside. Edith works as a matron over the women, and although she pretends to side with Tarver, she is totally against everything he and the others do. She helped me get Violet out before she suffered too much abuse."

"Then she's my hero." Clay's words came out gruff. "As soon as we gain entrance, I want you to find her."

"She'll be a big help." Tally swung to him, excited. "Clay, I just thought of something. Edith once told me that there's a very good asylum at Austin and said that when she had done all she could at Creedmore, she was going to go to work there. I think she knew or was related to one of the higher-ups. She talked like it would be no problem getting hired. Edith had such a soft spot for these women here, and that's why she stayed. She's a saint if ever there was one."

"Perfect. We'll see if she's willing to take a wagon full of the worst cases." Clay glanced at Montana, who'd stayed quiet, brooding as he gazed into the fire. Whatever he was thinking, he kept it to himself. Clay hoped it wasn't a plan to stab them in the back.

He and Tally discussed the many little details they had to smooth out as they waited for midnight.

When they lapsed into silence, Montana leaped to his feet. "There's an orphanage over at Abilene. I lived there for a while. Never had any parents. Some of the women might go to work there. From what I saw, they're always shorthanded."

He grew pensive, as though he was peering back in time. "They had women to help with the kids. I remember this one who did nothing but rock the babies. She'd sit and rock for hours, humming a song. I used to hide behind her chair and pretend she was singing to me." He jerked off his hat and crushed it, drawing in a ragged breath. "Used to pretend she was my...mother. Maybe I was a fool even back then."

Tally rose and laid a gentle hand on his shoulder. "Mothers don't always have to be the ones that give birth to us. Some just give everything they have—their hearts."

"Hell!" Montana stalked away, wiping his eyes.

"Clay, he has a good idea. The women have options."

"If any want to come live at Devil's Crossing, they'll be mighty welcome." Except the ill ones who needed special care that they weren't equipped to provide. "I meant what I told Hester at the canyon. They can all find a home there."

Now that they had a plan in place for afterward, and Montana's distraction for the beginning, they only had to wait a bit longer. It was the middle part that was filled with nothing but danger. A million-to-one odds were stacked against them.

Clay sat in silence, smoking and staring at the black hulk of Creedmore, praying everything would go according to the strategy they'd laid out. He strode to his horse, took an extra gun from his saddlebag, loaded it, and stuck it into his waistband, then turned his attention to the one in his holster. Montana and Tally checked theirs too.

All were quiet.

It was time. They'd said all they needed to.

Finally, Clay tossed down his cigarette and stomped the fire out. "Let's ride."

He hugged Tally close. "If I don't make it, just know that you were the best thing to happen to me. I give you all the love that I have in me."

"Don't talk like that. You're not dead, so don't even say things like that."

"Yeah." He didn't believe in sugarcoating anything. He helped her onto her mare. Turning, he stuck a boot in his stirrup.

Montana took his bottle of whiskey and emptied it on himself, drenching his clothes. "A waste of good whiskey," Montana murmured. "Damn."

"Yeah, but it's for a good cause." The saddle leather creaked as Clay settled himself. "We'll celebrate when this is over. Now let's make these bastards regret they were born."

"Amen to that." Montana's horse shied away and turned in circles, but he calmed the animal at last and swung up.

Tally and Clay rode silently, side by side, through the thick blackness, and Montana brought up the rear. Once at the asylum, where lights burned in two of the front windows, he cut away and dismounted at the front doors.

Clutching the whiskey bottle, he pounded on the heavy wooden portal. "Slade Tarver, let me in. I've come to offer my services."

Clay waited long enough to see Tarver welcome the smelly outlaw. A group of men crowded around, slapping him on the back like a long-lost friend. He heard one of them holler they could always use one more without a conscience. Then Clay motioned to Tally to follow. They kept in the deep shadows of the trees and made their way around back to a barn and the wagons and horses. Clay swung to the ground and helped Tally from the mare. He saw no one, the low cries of human misery seeping through the cracks in the stone walls providing the only noise.

"Is it always like this?" he asked.

"You sort of get used to the sound after a while."

The wails of despair grew louder as they moved the wagons close to the kitchen door of the stone prison.

Sudden loud grunts reached his ears. Clay jerked his head around. "Hogs?"

"They keep around twenty or so. For food and to keep the women in line."

"What?" Had he heard right?

"They threaten to throw the women in there with the hogs when they give trouble." Her voice lowered. "I've actually seen them follow through."

"Unbelievable." Clay had come across a lot of things in his life but nothing ever like this.

Tally spoke low. "Prepare yourself for what you're about to see. Just remember, these women can't help their circumstances."

"Got it. When we get inside, keep moving but don't leave my sight. Montana can only buy us a short time. We go in and try to locate Edith, get the women out, and get them safely away. Montana and I will handle the men." He raised Tally's chin to stare into her shadowed eyes. "Understand? You're not to try to get Tarver and the others by yourself."

Her glare stripped off a layer of hide. "I have debts to pay and justice I promised to so many friends."

"Leave that to me, darlin'. That's why I'm here." Clay knew how it felt to burn with the need for satisfaction, but he also knew how quickly things could turn sour. "I'd never risk them getting their grimy hands on you again. Understand?"

Anger carved deep lines in her face. She jerked away but nodded once.

The kitchen door suddenly opened and a man stumbled out. He wore an apron. No visible weapon. Clay yanked Tally back into the deep shadows. The man stuck a cigarette into his mouth and rifled through his pockets for a match.

"Who is that?" Clay whispered at Tally's ear.

"Cook. Plays both sides of the fence."

He'd met plenty of those kind, who could turn on you in a split second, depending on which way the wind blew.

"Stay." Clay worked around behind the man, who puffed away on his cigarette.

The cook scratched himself, muttering, "Just wait 'til I catch Tarver alone. Do this. Do that. Empty the piss buckets. Mop up the blood. By God, I'm the cook. My only job is to fix their damn food. I oughta hack up a big glob of tobacco spit and cover their meat next time before they eat it and see how they like that. It ain't my job to take care of these crazies."

Clay carefully raised up, struck the back of Cook's head with his gun. He ground out the cigarette and dragged the limp form to a cellar door next to the kitchen.

The creak was far too loud when Tally opened it wide enough for Clay to toss Cook in. She dusted off her hands. "That should hold him awhile."

"Come on." Clay slid his Remington from the holster, took her hand, and pulled her along. "We don't have time to waste. They might've heard that cellar opening."

For a moment, Clay considered entering the house of torture through the tunnel Tally had mentioned, but it would take too long. And if it turned out to be blocked after all, they'd waste precious time. This mission called for swift work in order to succeed. He cracked the kitchen door and listened before stepping inside. After a quick check assured him the coast was clear, he motioned to Tally. On the way through, she grabbed a loaf of bread and stuck it inside her jacket.

He didn't ask what it was for but knew she had some purpose.

Without breaking stride, she led him down a dark, musty corridor, past locked rooms from which horrible sounds came, to one cubicle with an open door. A short, solitary candle burned on the floor, casting a dim light.

"Edith," she called in an echoing whisper. "Edith, it's me."

The small circle of light revealed no one, and to Clay, the

room appeared empty. Finally, he made out the dark figure of a woman slumped against the wall. A moan slipped past her lips.

Tally ran to her. "Edith? What's wrong?"

Clay grabbed the candle and held it to illuminate the woman's face. Both of her eyes were swollen almost shut, and blood trickled from the corners of her mouth.

"You shouldn't be here, Tally. Dangerous." Edith tried to rise but couldn't. She accepted their help and finally struggled to her feet. "Go. Get as far from here as you can, girl. I heard them talking, and they're gonna start slaughtering us one by one come daylight."

"Not while I'm standing." Clay set the candle down. "What happened?"

"Pollard Finch caught me loosening Crazy Cora's restraints. The straps had cut into her poor flesh and she was bleeding." Edith wiped the blood from her mouth. "Finch, Tarver, and Abram came back about ten days ago, all of 'em shot. Lordy, they were mad. After a few days' rest and getting patched up, they started in on the girls worse than ever." She clutched Tally's arm. "Not sure what all's broken on me yet."

Rage filled Clay. Tally had been here and borne every torture imaginable. He steadied Edith, cursing their luck. She wasn't going to be able to provide much assistance.

Tally gently wiped the blood from Edith's mouth. "Clay and I are going to get everyone out—tonight. We were counting on you to help, but you're hurt too badly."

Edith straightened with a groan. "Those bastards ain't got the best of me yet. I won't be able to tote much, but I can tell you where everyone is at."

"That's all we need." Clay went to the doorway and glanced up and down the hall. He could hear loud voices to the right. It sounded like Montana had managed to get in with them all right. After hearing the words *bet* and *raise* mixed in with the cursing, he assumed they were engaged in whiskey and cards.

"Go left," Edith said low, clasping a large ring of keys.

"Some of the girls are chained in the basement. Don't forget about them."

From one room to the next, they systematically released the prisoners. As they freed the chains of each, Edith silently led them out to the wagons. Some, like Tally, who were thinking clearly and not in too bad shape, helped Clay as he worked his way toward the basement.

Tally unlocked the door using Edith's keys. Holding a candle high, Clay descended into the pitch blackness. He was unprepared for the sight he found.

Bile rose as a foul odor struck him. He covered his mouth with a sleeve. Women subdued in heavy chains lined one wall. He took in their tattered clothes, long, stringy hair hanging in their faces, their bones barely covered with skin. As the light hit them, they snarled like animals. Who knew when they'd last eaten or had even a sip of water?

What the hell was he up against?

Greed led Tarver and his men to do this. They'd been paid to let the women die—however, whenever they chose.

How would he get such frail beings to Austin without killing them? Jolts in a wagon alone could break brittle bones.

Then, his gaze fell on a young girl, holding a rag, locked in her own world. She rocked back and forth, humming softly.

"Cora!" Tally pushed him aside and rushed to her.

Was this Crazy Cora that Edith had been beaten within an inch of her life for helping?

"Be careful, Tally," Clay warned.

As usual, she paid him little mind. She knelt on the wet stone floor, her fingers trembling as she hurried to unlock the chains, then put an arm around the girl.

"Oh, Cora. I've missed you so much and worried about you."

A mist came into the girl's eyes. "Mama?"

"Yes, dear. I've come to take you home." Tally tenderly brushed the hair from Cora's eyes. "And we're taking your baby too."

Cora clutched the piece of rag to her chest and whispered, "He doesn't like it here."

"I know. We're going to take him home."

"Okay, Mama."

Clay rushed to help Tally lift the girl to her feet. Cora could barely stand and would've collapsed if they hadn't had a firm grip on her.

"Can you carry her up the stairs, Clay? I don't think she can manage them."

"Of course." He easily lifted Cora and carried her into the dark hallway. After handing the girl off to Edith and two women helping her, he went back down.

Tally spoke calmly to each of the others, calling them by name. Then she offered them some bread, which they grabbed with greedy hands. Clay was amazed at his wife's deep compassion and skill in handling these poor, unfortunate souls. Anger washed over him at everything he saw around him. How she had survived this hell?

Slowly, she settled them down. As she unfastened their chains, Clay led the freed prisoners from the gruesome torture chamber. While some still had wild eyes, they made no move to attack, and for that, he was very grateful.

The stairs creaked as he made his way to the top. So far so good. He stepped out and began moving the women past him. The unmistakable click of a hammer cocking froze him.

"Hold it, mister."

Clay whirled, putting himself in front of the escapees. There was Jacob Abram, staring at him. "I'm taking these women out of here. You'll have to kill me to stop me." His hand inched toward his Remington.

"Then I reckon that's what I'll do," Jacob snarled. "You got no right to come in here."

"And you have no right to hold them in such deplorable conditions."

Abram's smile curled back over his teeth. Clay watched his eyes and knew the minute the man was going to pull the trigger. Faster than greased lightning, Clay drew and fired. A burst of orange left the barrel, the bullet knocking Abram backward. The close quarters and stone hall left no place for the sound to go except in Clay's ears. The shock wave swept inside him, creating a ringing in his head.

He turned to Edith. "That's going to bring Tarver. Hurry, get these women out of here. I hear you know of a properly run sanitarium in Austin. Take them there. You've been a great help. Thank you for all you've done."

"No more than you would've."

Tally hugged her friend. "Godspeed, Edith. I hope we meet again someday."

Clay grabbed Abram's shirt and pulled him down the basement stairs. If Tarver didn't find a body, he still wouldn't be certain that anyone had invaded his domain. And especially if Montana kept him good and drunk. With luck, he'd think his men were just jumping at shadows in the dark.

Clay was about to head back up when a scurrying sound came from those dark shadows. The hair rose on the back of his neck. Rats? Maybe. Then came a whimper that sounded almost human.

"Who's there?"

More scurrying and whispers. He held up the candle, but it had burned so low it barely provided any light.

"Is anyone there? I won't hurt you. I've come to take you out of this horrible place."

He strained to see as he moved the candle from side to side. "Hello?"

A drip of water somewhere in the cavernous space echoed like a cannon shot. He whirled, his gun drawn.

Chills crawled up his spine. Damn, he hated this place!

Maybe he was losing *his* mind and imagining people where there weren't any. The heavy stone walls and repugnant odors were enough to drive anyone berserk. He had to get the hell out of here and get these creepy-crawlies off him.

"This is your last chance. You can't stay here. I'm going to burn this place down. You have to get out."

Small, inky forms stole toward him out of the darkness. As they came closer, he could make out two children. A ragged boy of about seven was holding the hand of a much younger girl. Clay put her around three or four. They were extremely thin, their clothes falling off them. The silent little girl hid her head and pressed tightly to her companion's side.

The boy's eyes bulged with fear. "No."

Thirty-one

"HEY THERE." CLAY PUT HIS GUN AWAY AND KNELT ON THE stone floor in the dark basement of the asylum. "There's nothing to be afraid of, son. I won't hurt you. I've come to get everyone out and we have to hurry before they find us."

Anger spewed from the boy's mouth. "You lie!"

"I swear it's the truth. Why would I lie?"

The boy clutched the girl tighter. "To trick us. You just want to feed us to the hogs. You said so. But we got away where you couldn't find us."

Terror in the boy's face pierced Clay's chest. Whatever they'd gone through had probably been as bad as the rest he'd already seen. The loud grunts of the hogs outside suddenly swept through his memory and ice slid down his spine.

"No trick." He stretched out a hand. "I don't work here. I've ridden a long way to get here."

Just then, Tally appeared at the top of the stairs, holding a larger candle. "Clay? What's the holdup? I sent Edith on with her full wagon."

"I discovered these two." Clay stood. "And I'm going to need your help."

She hurried down, her worried eyes meeting his before shifting to the children. "Hi, I'm Tally. I used to live here a while ago. We've come to rescue you."

"Why?" the boy asked. "No one wants us."

"Oh, honey, that's not true." Tally inched closer. "I want you safe, and Clay does too."

"Our papa don't. He brung us here when mama died 'cause we were too much trouble an' this was closer than the orphanage." The boy glared. "Maybe you wanna take us someplace worse'n this." His voice dropped to a whisper. "Or kill us."

His words cut into Clay. "I promise, cross my heart and hope to die, that we're taking you home with me and Tally. We have a daughter who can't see and we didn't throw her away. You'll have plenty of food and a big place to play."

"You can grow up healthy and happy. Maybe you remember Violet. She once lived here too. Now, she's living with me." Tally gently pushed the hair from the little girl's face. "Let us love you. Please?"

"I guess we can give you a try." Tears rolled down the boy's cheeks as he reached for Clay's hand.

He led the boy from the wet tomb into the fresh air. Tally carried the girl and deposited her in the back of a wagon next to her brother.

One of the women put her arm around the children. "I'll look after these Carver kids."

Clay spoke to the driver. "Follow the other wagons and meet us at the Brazos River crossing. If we don't show by sundown tomorrow, you'll know we didn't make it. Head on to Austin and meet Edith there or catch up to her along the way." Clay swung to Tally. "Crawl in the wagon with them and get out of here."

She cupped his jaw. "As much as I love you, I can't. I'm not going to leave you here, and you're loco if you think I will. I have to see this to the bitter end."

Irritation rose. He couldn't have her anywhere near when the shooting started. "Tally, get in the damn wagon. We're running out of time."

"Sorry, but I can't." She spoke to the driver, then slapped the rump of one of the horses.

Clay clenched his teeth. She was going to make him as mad as a March hare.

Gunfire erupted just as the wagons rolled out of sight. Clay drew his Remington and pivoted to see the shooter in the kitchen door. He pushed Tally down and fired back.

The bullet hit the gunman's shoulder, spinning him around. He fell back, taking cover in the kitchen. Clay sprinted to the back door and pressed against the side of the stone wall.

A flurry of gunshots rang out from farther inside the building. Who was shooting?

With luck, Montana would keep some of the other men from joining the fight. Still, Clay knew there were more men on the property besides the few drinking with the old outlaw.

A shot burst from inside. Tally took aim from the ground where she lay and sent a bullet into the open door of the grisly stone fortress. At the same time, Clay moved from the wall and fired. A second later, he burst through the door and into the kitchen.

Surprise shone in the gunman's eyes. He jerked to his feet with gun blazing.

A bullet creased Clay's side, the sting sending fire through him. Damn it to hell! He took aim and orange flame spat from the end of the Remington. The shot sent the shooter reeling into a cabinet filled with dishes. The whole mess crashed to the floor, showering broken shards everywhere.

Clay sent a cursory glance at the man lying on his back. Blood poured from his chest wound, and Clay knew he was dead.

Tally raced through the door, relief on her face to see Clay standing.

"I'm all right." Clay quickly reloaded. "Since you're here, let's finish. But don't take on anything by yourself." He held her arm. "You got that?"

"Yeah." She emptied the spent cartridges and slid two fresh ones into the chamber of her Colt.

Her sharp answer did nothing to reassure Clay. Revenge and hatred burned in her eyes. She was determined to make Tarver and the others pay. The crazy thing was—he understood it. Though it would make him feel easier if she wasn't the woman he loved.

"I think the second floor is clear, but we need to make sure we didn't miss anyone."

Clay nodded. "Go ahead, but be careful." It had seemed clear while they were on that floor, releasing the women, but someone too afraid could've hidden.

Breathing a silent prayer that they'd live through this night, Clay stepped out into the long hall and inched quietly toward the front of the asylum. Tally climbed the stairs to the second floor. He prayed like hell he was right in thinking the men were gathering in the front, intent on making a stand.

Where was Montana? What had happened to him? Clay wanted to call out but didn't dare, so he just kept moving, trying not to make any noise.

Shadows leaped out at him and his nerves began to fray. Tension climbed up his back until his body screamed. He got closer and closer to the front and the echoes of loud voices. It sounded like an argument, but he couldn't make out the words.

He slid along the wall, taking one step at a time. How many men were there?

A sudden gunshot rang out from a few yards away. Clay cursed the darkness and took cover in an empty room as boots struck the floor, running toward him.

∽

Painful memories crowded around Tally as she stole along the upstairs hall.

The candle in her hand flickered and went out, plunging her into complete darkness, but she knew the familiar hell that she now walked through.

Panic sent a shudder running the length of her. She tightened her hand around the Colt. She passed the dark, empty rooms, her thoughts on Clay. Earlier, outside, she'd seen resignation in his eyes. He'd accepted whatever fate had in store for him. For some reason, maybe gut instinct, something seemed to tell him he might not get out of here. If he died in Creedmore, she alone would bear the blame.

Tally took a deep breath to calm her racing heart. They weren't dead yet. They had to rid this place of evil that left the spirit nothing but ash. Tarver and his bunch would soon rest in hell.

Convinced that no one appeared to be up here, she turned

toward the stairs. A large, dark form hurtled from the nearest room and pinned her against the wall. In the jarring contact, Tally's gun flew from her hand.

Her assailant pressed an arm across her throat. The moon came out from behind a cloud and shone light through the dirty window. She gave a cry and struggled to breathe while she kicked and twisted. The stranger's features became a mask of depravity and hate shot from his eyes.

"Get ready to die." The guard snarled like a rabid animal, tightened his arm, and cut off her air supply.

She clawed at his hands. Her vision blurred.

She couldn't see. Couldn't breathe. Couldn't swallow the fear building inside. Yet despite all that, determination rose.

I'm not going to die here. Not in this place of misery and greed and death.

In a sudden move before she lost consciousness, she brought her knee up hard into the soft flesh between his legs. Her last-ditch effort worked. The man gave a loud grunt and dropped his hold, bending double, clutching himself.

Tally groped on the floor for her gun. Where was it?

Hurry! Oh, for more light!

Her assailant began to get his breath and straighten, his gaze swinging to her.

Where was her Colt? *Oh God, oh God, oh God!* Feverishly, she felt along the boards.

"You're dead, girl," he rasped. "Dead."

As he stumbled toward her, Tally's hand closed around the barrel of her gun.

Closer he came, his meaty hands open to grab her. He lunged and caught the back of her collar. The fabric tore as she wrenched free and turned the gun around, getting hold of the butt.

He lunged at her again, his hand catching her skirt.

Tally squeezed the trigger at nearly point-blank range. He plunged on top of her, knocking her backward. Gasping, she sprawled on the floor, pinned by his weight. It took all her strength to roll from under him and free herself.

As she raced through the blackness toward the stairs, a

horrendous crash came from below, followed by shouts and loud yells.

"Clay!"

Only silence answered back.

❧

As the world crashed around him, Clay gripped his Remington and moved toward the sound. He was torn between rushing upstairs toward the gun blast and whatever was happening ahead of him in the dimly lit room at the far end of the long, gloomy hallway.

Tally's name was on his tongue before he bit it back. He couldn't give away his position.

If one of them had killed her, he'd gut the bastard like an animal.

A throbbing ache filled him, squeezing his chest until he could barely breathe. To hell with whatever was happening in front of him. He whirled toward the stairs, but as he reached them, he met Tally coming down. Trembling, Clay crushed her to him, burying his face in her hair. "Thank God you're all right. I was afraid for you."

She leaned back and brushed his cheek. "I shot a man. He tried to strangle me with his bare hands. What's happening down here?"

"I'm not sure. The voices are coming from the front, and I've not gotten there yet."

"A word of warning. Sound bounces around inside these stone walls and you can never know the location for sure." She kissed his cheek. "Please be careful."

"You wait here and catch any who get past me." Clay hurried toward the lit room, paying no heed to the sound of his footsteps. At this rate, no one could hear over the racket anyway.

"Sit your asses down! I ain't messing with you." The voice belonged to Montana. Why it made him happy to know the old outlaw was still breathing, Clay couldn't quite say.

What sounded like a scuffle reached him, then the loud explosion of a shot.

Montana's voice rose. "I'm going to blow your damn head off."

"Drop your weapon, Black."

Clay didn't recognize the voice, but he knew Montana was in trouble. Before he could take another step to help, a figure burst from a nearby room and fired at Clay. Then a second did the same, and a third! He ducked into the blackness of an open door and returned their fire. A hail of bullets shattered the walls around him.

"Don't you ever give up, Colby?" No mistaking Tarver's gravelly way of talking.

"Nope. Not when there's vermin like you running loose." Clay peeked around the corner. No one in sight, but movement flickered the candles in two sconces along the wall. He'd bet everything he owned that the rest were waiting to kill him after Tarver drew him out.

Montana had to be dead, or he'd be taking care of the problem from his end.

"You want me, come and get me!" Tarver yelled.

"Don't worry, I plan on it."

"You know better than to come into a man's domain with revenge in mind. I killed your drunk friend."

That laid to rest any question about Montana. Unexpected sorrow washed over Clay. At least the man who'd been an orphan and outcast had died for a worthy cause.

"You keep adding to the list of things I'll make you pay for." Clay closed his eyes and prayed his shot was straight and true. Then he leaned out and pulled the trigger, at the same time leaping across the hall.

Someone screamed in pain, confirming he'd hit one of them.

"I hope you brought Tally with you," Tarver hollered. "Me and her got some settling up to do. I'll make you watch while I cut out her tongue—first that, then other parts. She'll scream in agony and you won't be able to do one damn thing about it."

This was no idle threat. Tarver would and could do it—but only if he got the chance.

"You'll have to get by me first." And that might be a chore.
Clay darted down the narrow passage, getting closer to his
quarry. He needed to douse the two candles along the wall.
That would put them all on the same playing field. As it was,
they could see him coming and pick him off. He'd see how
they did blind. He'd have the advantage, having learned well
from Violet.

A closing door sent a chill through him. Someone had left.
One of Tarver's men could circle around and come in through
the kitchen behind him and Tally. Hell!

Knots twisted in his chest so tightly he could barely breathe.
She had no idea they were coming.

Thirty-two

TALLY PRESSED AGAINST THE WALL, MAKING HERSELF AS SMALL as possible. She knew this place and she knew Tarver. That gave her a big advantage.

She watched Clay run, zigzagging his way down the dim hallway. He was used to meeting trouble head-on, guns at twenty paces. In fact, he probably did his best work then. But Slade Tarver and the rest had a million tricks and the advantage of being on home ground. Still, they'd lost a few men. She allowed a tight smile. The best thing would be to hide and wait and protect Clay's back. She tightened her jaw. No one would get past her.

The darkness would be her friend this night, the same way it had shielded her when she'd escaped.

Memories tumbled end over end in her mind. The rank evil inside the stone walls stung her nose and tried to claw into her pores like a burrowing rodent. So much pain and misery, heartbreak and despair. She shook her head to clear the images. She'd survived, and now she'd helped give a lot of the other women a fresh start.

This was a fight she meant to win. It seemed she'd waited a lifetime for justice.

A door squeaked—the kitchen. Her breath caught in her throat and her heart pounded. She'd had ample time to memorize every creak, rattle, and clank when she lived here, and that door had always made a different sound from the others. Her hand tightened around the Colt.

The wait was agonizing.

Quiet footsteps moved behind her. She squatted down against the wall, barely breathing. They wouldn't expect her to be low.

The footsteps came closer, out into the hall. Slowly. One step at a time.

Her breathing slowed and calm washed over her. This night belonged to her and Clay. They would come out of this and soon be home with Violet.

A shadow moved, floating toward her in the thick gloom.

When the man's shape got even with her, she raised and pressed her gun to his head. "Drop your weapon."

The figure jerked in surprise, freezing. He made no move to obey.

"Drop it or die." She put her mouth close to his ear. "Having trouble believing a woman turned the tables on you? I'm itching for a little justice. Frankly, I hope I get to blow your brains all over these walls."

She recognized the guard named Jameson.

His smile irritated her. It was more of a smirk actually, which made her seethe. Just when she thought he was going to drop his pistol, he swung it around.

Tally squeezed the trigger. The blast deafened her and sent a shock wave through her.

Jameson slid down the wall. She felt for his gun and stuck it in her waistband. She never knew when she might need an extra.

"Tally? Tally? Answer me." Clay's urgent cry pierced her.

"I'm fine." Tally peered toward the light but couldn't make him out.

A dark figure suddenly rushed at her from the kitchen, his arm raised.

What had happened? Had someone else attacked Tally? Frayed nerves and worry jerked inside Clay. He started to turn back when a figure dashed across the hallway from one room to another, shooting as he went. The bullets barely missed Clay. He was a sitting duck. He raised his gun, took aim at the first candle, and squeezed the trigger.

Success! Another shot took out the second one, and total darkness enveloped him. Now they had a level playing field.

"Tally?"

No answer.

He called again. "Tally?"

An orange flash came from his right as someone fired at him in desperation. The bullet didn't come close.

"Don't worry, Clay," Tally said grimly.

Good. Clay waited until he could get a clear shot, then took it. The man yelled. Forward Clay went and rushed to the left of the doorway to the room where he thought Tarver had holed up. Unless he'd already gone out the front? Clay shook his head. No, he'd have heard the door. It had only opened once.

But maybe they'd all gone out. Sweat popped up on his forehead. Had he lost them?

Only…Tally had shot the one behind them.

He shook his head to clear it of doubts. He was positive he heard whispers coming from inside the room. Taking a deep breath, he rushed through the door and rolled across the floor.

A dark figure shot at him. In the brief muzzle flash, Clay made out the shapes of what he thought were four men.

Clay fired. A soft thud told him one had gone down.

"You ain't gonna get us all, Colby," Tarver drawled. "Are you ready to die?"

"Is this a Monday?" Clay tried to home in on where the voice was coming from. Keep him talking. Violet could determine a speaker's location by their voice and he could too.

"What difference does it make?"

"I hate Mondays. Never had anything good happen on one."

"Then I reckon this is Monday."

The lying sack of manure. Clay knew for a fact it was Tuesday, but he now had Tarver's location. The man was to his left.

"Tally dead yet?" Tarver asked conversationally.

"Nope."

"Good. I'm glad I still get the pleasure of ending her sorry life."

Clay fired two rapid shots. Had he gotten Tarver? Damn

this inky blackness. He heard a rustle of clothing as someone moved toward him.

He shifted and stretched out on the floor. His hand encountered warm flesh. But whose?

"That you, Colby?" Montana whispered close.

"Yeah."

"They got me."

"How bad?"

"Some." There was a pause. "I can shoot."

"Good." A plan took shape in Clay's head, but before he could move, a deafening explosion ripped through the building. Rock, mortar, and ceiling crashed down around him.

Panic twisted like a sword inside him. Something heavy pinned his leg.

Thirty-three

THE POWERFUL DETONATION SEEMED TO ECHO FOREVER. CLAY tried to breathe but found the dust from the blast going into his lungs, and a coughing fit struck him. When the last of the debris had fallen, he began pushing it off. From the feel of the wood, a support from above was on his leg. He tried to move it with his hands while pushing with his free foot, but it refused to budge. He groped around him for something to use as a lever and found what appeared to be a piece of steel. Placing it under the beam, he raised it enough to pull his leg out and lay gasping.

Nothing seemed to hurt, except where the bullet had grazed his side. That part stung like a red-hot ember pressed to his flesh.

He paid it no mind. Thoughts of Tally made him claw harder at the rubble. From her position by the kitchen, she'd probably borne the brunt of the explosion. She could lie mangled or, heaven help him, dead.

His desperation grew with each passing moment. When he felt able, he got to his feet, wishing he could hear. Men around him probably moaned and cried out, but he heard nothing.

Everything was eerily silent in his head.

With great care, he moved through the room until his hand brushed a lamp. The globe was broken but the rest seemed intact. He prayed it still held oil. Fumbling in his pocket, he located a match and struck it, using the faint glow to find the wick. The harsh light revealed the devastation around him.

Three paces to his right, he saw Montana's face barely visible under the gray debris. The outlaw's eyes were open, staring, his lips moving and pleading for help.

Although he wanted to rush to Tally, he couldn't abandon

Montana to die. He'd already been hurt bad before the blast. Clay knelt and hurriedly cleared the rubble away, carefully helping Montana to his feet. Blood poured from a head wound and his left arm was bent in an unnatural position. Strangely, he still clutched his gun in his right hand. Montana's mouth moved but no sound reached Clay's ears.

With an arm bracing him, Clay half carried him from the room out to the front door and into the night. He took him all the way out to the trees, about thirty yards from the doors, and set him down where danger couldn't find him in the shadows. Clay hurried back inside. He'd done his best for the outlaw. Now it was time to find Tally.

Men were slowly coming to life in the demolished room, but Clay didn't stop except to grab the oil lamp. He scrambled over the mound of debris as fast as he could. There was nothing much left of the hallway. The walls had been ripped away. He saw no movement or signs of life. Whoever had set off the blast had to be dead.

And Tally?

Clay swallowed the thickness in this throat. Anyone nearby would've also met their fate. Although he cried Tally's name out over and over, he knew she couldn't hear him even if by some miracle she'd survived.

Despair settled over him as he worked feverishly to clear a path to the stairs where he'd last seen her. Dear God, judging by the destruction, there'd be nothing left. Not one lock of her fiery-red hair or scrap of leather skirt to find.

Tally Shannon Colby had to lie in pieces under the bottom floor ruins of Creedmore.

Ignoring the agony of his bullet wound, he tossed the wreckage this way and that, his mind frantic. He wouldn't give up until he found some part of her, some proof that she'd been caught in the blast after all. Pausing to catch his breath, he noticed someone stumbling from the room where he'd been. The dazed man had no weapon and was bleeding heavily, so Clay turned back to his task. Each minute was crucial.

But when he cleared everything down to the floor with no sign of Tally, he collapsed with a sob.

Was this place going to keep her bound forever?

No, she had to be here. There had to be some sign of her.

Pieces of blackened paper lodged in the mess, catching his eye. On a closer look, he found three or four sections. Clay reached for them and held them to the light. He froze.

Dynamite.

From what he could tell, there had to have been at least five sticks. What had the damn fool been thinking? He'd blown up his own men in trying to kill him and Tally.

After resting a moment, he attacked another pile closer to the stairs. One piece at a time, he cleared jagged lumber and rock down within a foot of the floor.

Suddenly, his hand brushed soft flesh. Hope filled him. He grabbed hold and gently lifted up Tally's leg.

She was here, and the warm skin meant she was alive. But for how long?

He clawed at the pile on top of her with a fury. Little by little, he cleared enough to lift her out. She'd been tucked into a space next to the stairs that had shielded her from the worst of the blast. She opened her eyes and smiled, but the blood still worried him. She had wounds on her arms and face and God knew where else. He carried her outside and sat her next to Montana. The old outlaw smiled, laid his gun in his lap, and took her hand.

The two looked like pure hell, and Clay probably did too, but they were all alive—that was something to celebrate.

He knelt and felt along her bones but found nothing broken, just heavy bleeding on her arm and jagged shrapnel and wood embedded in her flesh. He removed his bandana and tied it around her arm, then gently pulled out the larger pieces of projectiles. He'd leave the small ones until he had light and something to get hold of them.

Tally tenderly touched his face, her winter-blue eyes meeting his brown. Clay pressed his lips to hers in a kiss, careful not to hurt her.

When he glanced up, Montana had pulled himself to his feet. The man hobbled a few steps, staring curiously at the building.

The odor of the blast hung in the air, stinging Clay's nose, and his ears began to ring faintly. Clay turned toward the hulking asylum to see a man with red hair and a trimmed beard standing outside the entrance.

Pollard Finch.

The man pointed a weapon at Clay. He had no time to react or to grab for his gun. As the bullet left the barrel, Montana fired back and threw himself in front of Clay.

The projectile tore into Montana's chest and sent him backward. Clay caught and lowered him to the ground, then drew and quickly swung to face Finch. But Montana's last-second shot had already blown a hole through the despicable bastard.

Horror lined Tally's face as she scooted to Montana and bent over him, placing her hands on his chest to try to staunch the flow of blood. Clay jerked off his shirt and knelt beside them, pressing the cloth tightly to the wound. Tally leaned back, her hands wet and red with Montana's blood.

Montana barely breathed, and Clay could only tell that by the slight rise and fall of his chest. The old outlaw's eyes were open, staring into his. Clay squeezed his hand and, although he knew Montana couldn't hear, thanked him for taking his bullet.

Montana fumbled in his pocket for a ribbon that Violet had worn in her hair. He smiled and mouthed, "For her."

Tears flowed down Tally's cheeks. She laid Montana's head in her lap and smoothed back his hair. Clay untied the outlaw's bandana and added it to the soaked shirt. The man wasn't going to last long. The hole was simply too large.

Something hit the ground beside him, spraying up dirt, and Clay realized it was a bullet. Then another hit near Tally. He swung around to see gunmen in the front windows. He stood and motioned to Tally to follow and dragged Montana behind some trees.

Through hand motions, he asked if she was hit, to which

she shook her head. Leaving Tally to guard Montana, he pulled his weapon and returned fire. One shooter tumbled from his perch. Good.

The gun battle didn't last long before the ones still inside decided the risk wasn't worth it. Clay had killed two of them. He knelt down beside Tally, the louder ringing in his ears suggesting that his hearing was slowly beginning to return.

Montana's breathing had grown shallower, yet by some miracle, he kept clinging to life. Maybe there was a reason. Clay had always heard that having something vital still undone was often enough to cling to life long after someone should've died.

The outlaw clutched his shirtfront and pulled him down. "Closer," he said weakly.

Clay put his ear near Montana's mouth.

"Not gonna make it. Take Tally home. Forget. Violet... needs you." Then death claimed the man Clay had once hated with all his soul.

Tally sobbed. She was still deaf from the explosion and didn't hear the words, but she saw life ebb from Montana's eyes.

Clay drew her close and held her while she cried. Over the days of riding here, she'd gotten to know the old outlaw, and his story had deeply touched her. And even though Clay had tried to cling to his old hatred, he'd found himself sympathizing as well. Sure, Montana had done lots of bad things, but Clay saw how Montana's early years alone and the murder of his wife had molded him into the killer he was.

If Clay had bothered to look beyond the outer shell, he'd have seen the man's heartache and need to find meaning to life. If he lived through this, he vowed to stop being quick to judge.

When Tally had cried herself out, Clay rose. All had become silent inside the ruins of the stone fortress, although he knew a handful had survived the explosion. Maybe they'd found the fight too much and had ridden off.

And if they were still huddled inside, they soon would

turn to ash. He had one last order of business. After relaying his intentions to Tally, he sneaked around back for the can of kerosene he'd hidden in the brush, stopping for an extra shirt in his saddlebags and putting it on. Listening through the ringing for voices or coughing, he pushed past the splintered kitchen door and splashed the flammable liquid around inside, then struck a match. Flames rose at once. Clay backed away from the heat and ran back out to the fresh air. Keeping a close eye out for trouble and avoiding broken glass, he slowly went around the asylum, igniting the kerosene.

"Come out while there's still time," he yelled. "You don't want to die this way."

By the time he worked his way to the front, flames engulfed the entire building. He headed for Tally and put his arm around her. She laid a palm on his chest and shuddered against him like a foal learning how to stand on its wobbly legs each time a timber crashed, sending a mass of sparks flying.

"Clay, it'll soon all be gone. We won."

"Has your hearing returned?"

"Some. I can barely hear what you're saying. It's like my head is inside a bell." She sucked in a breath and pointed to a second-story window. "Look."

Surrounded by searing flames, Slade Tarver stared down, barely trying to shield himself. The heat must be tremendous, and it boggled Clay's mind that he'd chosen such a gruesome way to die. A bullet would be a whole lot less painful. He pulled his gun to end his foe's suffering, but before he pulled the trigger, he stopped, transfixed.

An odd grin stretched across Tarver's face, like he was saying, "I beat you."

Maybe he was the insane one after all.

Thirty-four

TALLY STARED, TRANSFIXED, AT THE RAGING FIRE CLAY HAD SET in the structure that had harbored so much pain, misery, and death. The flames rose up high against the backdrop of the inky sky. The fierce crackle and roar was that of some kind of enraged monster, feeding on everything in its path, gobbling up every stick of wood, cleansing the place of evil.

Her soul finally seemed at peace. Almost entirely, anyway. She wouldn't find total quietness inside until she'd reckoned with dear stepmother Lucinda.

One last look at the second-floor window showed her that Slade Tarver was gone. He had to be dead, consumed by the horrific heat of the flames.

Well, she wouldn't waste one ounce of sympathy on the bastard. He deserved his fate.

Moments later, the remainder of the flaming timbers crashed down, and the whole structure collapsed, leaving only the thick stone walls, blackened by the fire as witnesses to the crimes that had occurred here.

Her heart ached for Montana. Though he'd done a lot of wrong, Violet had seen the good in him. And then when he'd spoken of his life and the things that he'd faced, Tally couldn't help but sympathize. He wasn't all bad, and she prayed the good Lord would take all of that, and the hell he'd been in while alive, into consideration.

She jumped at the sound of a galloping horse and Clay whirled, drawing his Remington, bending his knees and dropping low. Readying for another fight. A buggy raced from the darkness and pulled to a stop in front of them.

A woman leaned out to yell. "What happened here? Who did this?"

Clay's jaw clenched and his angled features revealed sharp

irritation. "Well, ma'am, I set fire to it, that's what happened. It had to be destroyed. Who are you?"

Pure rage climbed up Tally's spine at the sight of that familiar face. She slipped her hand around Clay's elbow. "Hello, Lucinda."

Tally watched surprise ripple across Clay's face. Finally seeing Lucinda in the flesh seemed to have a grim effect, judging by his stone features and hard eyes. The blackness inside that he'd admitted struggling with appeared to be rising. She didn't know what he had in mind, but killing the evil woman outright would be wrong.

No matter what she'd done, Lucinda wasn't worth getting hanged for.

"Who are you? Do you know me?" The woman leaned forward to peer at Tally, then recoiled and dropped the reins.

Tally didn't speak, but her glare said volumes. Now that she had the opportunity, face-to-face with her devil, she had too much to say for one short sitting. Where did one start to express the level of grief Lucinda had caused?

Yet, her stepmother wasn't one to take the low road. She recovered quickly and released her customary haughty venom, ice forming around her words. "I prayed you'd be dead by now, Tally. When Pollard sent word that you'd escaped, I rode over and gave him and everyone else a chewing out— then doubled the reward."

Even after the two years that had passed, Lucinda persisted in her single goal.

"All of that did nothing to change the fact that Tally was still free." Clay laid his hand on hers and Tally welcomed the warmth.

"How does it feel to know you couldn't destroy me? You gave it your best effort, and yet here I am. You failed. I've won." Tally leaned closer to deliver the part she'd waited so long to say. "I beat you."

"You just think you have. I have lots of other ways to kill you." Lucinda snapped her fingers. "Just like that."

"Don't you ever give up?" Tally wondered what else she'd have to guard against.

"Never, as long as you draw breath."

Clay straightened, the muscle in his jaw working. "Leave now before I lose control."

Lucinda bristled. "You can't tell me what to do. I have more right to be here than you."

"Your choice," Clay barked. "I won't warn you again." Clay swung the long barrel of his Remington up and pointed it at Lucinda, and Tally sucked in a breath.

"I've killed a lot of men over the years, but you'll be my first woman. Heed my words. If you don't turn that rig around and leave right now, I'll put a bullet in you so fast you won't have time to blink." He paused then thundered, "Decide and make it fast. You don't know how bad I itch to pull this trigger, lady."

An angry flush crept up Lucinda's face. She opened her mouth to protest, then appeared to think better of it. She backed the buggy up.

Tally circled around and grabbed the horse's bridle before Lucinda could speed away. "Expect a knock on your door. I'm taking you to court to get back all you stole from me. Once I tell them everything, they'll arrest you faster than you can swallow."

"I'll see you in hell first!"

"For two cents, I'd take *my* buggy and make you walk home. Unfortunately, it's too small for our needs. Our dead friend won't fit." Besides, Lucinda would have them arrested for theft. Tally moved to the side of the buggy to finger the hem of Lucinda's expensive dress. "After I get through with you, you'll have to wear rags. You'll be a pauper, a nobody. Too bad Clay burned this place. I'd like to stick you in here for a month, but I doubt you'd survive one day chained in the basement with the rats." She shrugged. "Mind you, I hear prison is just as bad. Murderers get no special favors or soft beds. You'll live out your days on a chain gang, toiling from sunup to sundown."

"This isn't over," Lucinda spat.

"No, ma'am." Clay patted the horse's rump. "It's just beginning and hell is awful hot."

Lucinda shook her reins at the horse. She left a trail of dust behind her, rising up like a buzzard taking flight from a rotted carcass.

Tally swung to Clay, shaking with hate and bitterness. "I wanted to claw her eyes out. But I kept thinking of Montana lying over there, and I knew he wouldn't want Violet's mother to get thrown in jail. I think we gave her something to chew on—I just wonder if it was wise to forewarn her."

Clay draped an arm around Tally's neck. "Probably not, but it sure felt good to watch her squirm. I really wanted to kill her—you don't know how bad—but a bullet would be too fast. She needs to suffer."

He looked at the hulk that was once Creedmore. "It's gone, Tally. I'll get a wagon, if one's left, and load up Montana. We're not burying him here. We'll take him to a peaceful, pretty spot. Maybe put him under a tall tree that has the breeze sighing through its branches."

Quick tears bubbled in her eyes, but she smiled. "He'd like that. One day we'll bring Violet to visit her old friend."

"We'll make that happen, darlin'." Clay strode to the back and returned with a shovel and a two-wheeled cart that Tally had seen used to remove the dead from the asylum. "This was all that remained."

"It'll do. I don't think Montana will mind." She shot a glance to the outlaw's still body, covered with her bedroll.

Clay hitched her mare to the cart and loaded Montana. "I hope you don't mind riding double."

"Not one bit." After all they'd been through, she didn't want to be separated from him for a minute.

A little while after they set out with Tally riding in front on Sundown, she found herself lulled by the horse's rocking and rested her head on Clay's chest. They'd been twenty-four hours without sleep and she couldn't hold her eyes open any longer. His arms were around her and she was safe, albeit a little worse for wear.

When she awoke, the sun was up and Clay had stopped at a cool stream to water the horses. "How far are we from Creedmore?"

"About thirty miles or so, I figure." He wiped his weary eyes and helped her down.

"Good."

The newly risen sun sparkled on the water, creating diamonds on the ripples. Clay's paint gelding and Tally's little mare eagerly drank their fill. After quenching their own thirst, Clay took out his knife and painstakingly removed the shrapnel from her that he'd been forced to leave earlier, then tended to her many cuts.

Finally, she pushed him away. "That's enough. Dr. Mary will finish when we get home. I want to get moving soon. I miss Violet. I'm needing to hug our daughter."

Clay returned his knife to his boot. "Me too."

She ran to the water and dunked her body in the stream. "I'm glad to get this filth off me."

"Let's take a bath. It won't take long and it'll feel mighty good." Clay waggled his eyebrows suggestively at her.

She knew if they got naked, they'd not get back on the road anytime soon. But they needed this time to regroup. She hurried from the water. "Our clothes can stand a good washing and we brought a change. You think of the best ideas."

"I can come up with one on occasion." Clay slid his arms around her waist, putting his forehead against hers.

Tally soaked up the feel of his body. "It's so beautiful here. The peace of this place erases the evil we survived back there."

"I couldn't agree more." Clay pointed to the grove of trees that dotted the rolling hills. "How about burying Montana on top of that next hill, darlin'?"

"That's perfect. And it's far enough away from the water source."

"Then that'll be the first order of business after we take that bath." He quickly shed his clothes and jumped in. He floated, whistling while he watched Tally undress.

Heat raced along her nerve endings. "See anything you like, cowboy?"

"Yes, ma'am. I believe I do. Hurry up, the water's nice and refreshing."

"You want me, you'll have to come and get me."

Hunger built in his eyes. As fast as he could draw his gun, he leaped from the water. Tally enjoyed a quick look at his sleek, naked body, then squealed and turned to run. Her heart beat wildly as he chased her before he finally hooked an arm around her waist.

Clay tenderly held her face between his hands and slid his lips across hers, her pulse racing as he settled them firmly into the kiss.

If it hadn't been for the small space she'd dropped into at the last second, she wouldn't be alive. Each time the thought crossed her mind at how close she'd come to losing him and Violet, her bones turned to a quivering mass of jelly.

She wanted to tell him how terrified she had been back there, but his eyes said he already knew it. Clay Colby didn't miss much, and maybe this extra time alone would help to settle their jagged nerves that little bit more.

He splayed his hand against her back to anchor her and deepened the kiss. Tally leaned against him, her knees giving way.

Breaking the kiss, she dropped to the soft grass and pulled him down. Just her and Clay and the gentle breeze that cleared the stench of Creedmore from their noses. While the rippling current serenaded them, she let his love renew and nourish her spirit.

≈≫

Fresh from her bath and dressed, Tally picked an armful of wildflowers while Clay dug a grave under a huge walnut tree. The large circumference of the trunk put it at several hundred years old. She smiled. It was perfect for an old, crusty outlaw. They could discuss the many things they'd seen.

She laid the flowers down and took Clay some water. He wiped the sweat pouring off him and guzzled from the canteen, then wiped his mouth on his shirtsleeve, his eyes locked on hers. "You always know when I need you."

Tally kissed his cheek. "Not yet, but I'm learning your ways. Rest. I can dig awhile."

"Nope. I've about got it." He winked. "Besides, I don't want to ruin that pretty skirt."

In no time, they were lowering Montana into his final resting place. Clay turned to her. "I doubt he ever darkened church doors, but we should say a few words over him."

"I agree, except we don't have a Bible."

"I don't reckon that makes a lot of difference. We'll just speak our minds."

"I don't think Montana is in any shape to protest."

Clay cleared his throat. "Dear Lord. I know this man smells worse than a gut wagon, and I'm still cussing a blue streak over him burning down the town I built, but a little girl sees the good in him and maybe you can too. Let him in and give him a good rocking chair. I figure he earned it. That's about all I have to say."

Tally laced her fingers through Clay's and fought back tears. "Please let Montana be with his wife and child. He's done good things and bad, mostly bad, but none of us are ever perfect. Without him, we couldn't have made it out of Creedmore alive. He sacrificed everything and paid the price for a little girl he loved with all his heart, so that has to count for something. Amen."

They stood in silence for a long moment and Tally stared out over the beautiful Texas landscape, reflecting on the man Montana was. She was going to miss him. How was she going to break the news of his death to Violet?

Without a word, Clay grabbed the shovel and filled in the hole and stacked rocks on top for extra measure.

Tally added the profusion of wildflowers and stood back, sniffling. "I think a lot of people will miss him. Do you think we get forgiveness for what we do?"

"Absolutely. Don't you?"

"I'm not sure but I hope so. I've done a lot of bad things."

He put his arm around her and kissed her temple. "I never killed anyone who didn't need it, and you haven't either. We have to stand up against evil. If we don't, where would we be? The bastards would overrun Texas, and we can't let that happen."

"I suppose." She glanced up at Clay, her heart—as always—racing double time. "Let's go home."

"Sounds good to me."

Around nightfall, they caught up with the wagons carrying the bedraggled escapees of Creedmore. Tally moved among them, checking on those who were injured. They reminded her of soldiers coming home from the war. Each had been through a horrible time and had difficulty believing they were free.

Thoughts turned to Edith and her group of the very ill. Tally prayed they would make it to help.

"I know an excellent doctor who'll fix you up in no time and remove that mark on your cheek," she told each one in these wagons. Indeed, Dr. Mary would be very busy for quite a while.

An overnight stop at Deliverance Canyon was met with happy tears. Finally, those women who'd stayed in hiding for so long could walk free without worry of being killed or arrested, regardless if they opted to remove their tattoos or not. The women loaded up their meager belongings and joined the caravan. First, they'd go to Devil's Crossing, where Dr. Mary would fix them up and remove the tattoos from those who wanted the procedure and, from there, decide where they wanted to go to build new lives. They were getting a new start.

Tally had kept her promise and her shoulders were much lighter.

She and Clay slowly led the caravan on its winding way toward the small, fledgling town.

At last, they reached their goal. The lookout sounded the call, and everyone came running. Bullet raced out ahead and danced around the wagon, barking his fool head off.

Belle and Tobias January each held one of Violet's hands. "Mama! Daddy!" the child hollered.

Tears filled Tally's eyes. She jumped from the wagon and ran, scooping their daughter into her arms. Clay arrived a second behind, encompassing them both in a big hug.

Violet beamed, patting Tally's face. "You came back—just like you said."

"Yes, and not a second too soon." Tally kissed her cheek. "I promised."

"Mama, I can't find Mr. Montana. I've looked everywhere. He's gone."

Clay picked her up. "That's because he came with us, baby girl."

"Where is he?" Violet stilled and cocked her head. "I don't hear him."

"Honey, we have something to tell you, but it can wait just a bit." Tally shifted her gaze to the milling crowd that was the men and women of Devil's Crossing welcoming the wagonloads of escapees. A mist filled her eyes. They were free to flourish and live normal lives.

Rebel hung back in one of the plain calico dresses Tally had given her, watching it all. Hesitation lined her face.

Tally gave her hug. "Is everything all right, Rebel?"

A smile curved the woman's mouth. "I'm glad you're back. You succeeded in freeing them."

"It wasn't easy, but yes, they are free."

Arm in arm, they moved to help the women climb from the wagons.

Tally finally turned to look at the town itself and gasped at the buildings. She couldn't see furnishings from there, but they had freshly painted signs above, each proclaiming the name of the establishment. The creak of the windmill blended with the joyful noise of the welcome-home party, filling Tally with contentment.

In the midst of all this, an older man wearing round spectacles and a frock coat like Ridge's pushed through the boisterous crowd to Tally. "Mrs. Colby? Phineas Hargrove, attorney-at-law. I have an urgent matter to discuss when you have the time."

Thirty-five

CLAY STOOD GAZING AT THE NEW ARRIVALS AND HIS THROAT closed up. He blinked to clear his vision. He'd done it. He hadn't failed this time. The women of Creedmore were safe. Maybe he could lay the demons that had haunted him for such a long time to rest.

Vicksburg, the war, and later, the men who'd tried to keep him from making a decent life were vanquished.

Tally strolled into his line of sight, her arm around Rebel. The sound of their laughter was a balm to his soul. Tally filled his heart with so much happiness. She was the only woman for him. He owed Rebel, though, for saving his life and not letting him give up.

A smile formed. He was glad the two were now friends. It made for a happier town.

That night, following a welcome-home supper, Clay sat with his baby girl. They hadn't had hardly a moment to themselves, what with finding the ladies a place to bed down, and Tally was still trying to get them all situated. She hadn't yet found time to talk with the attorney, who had been patiently waiting for their return. Houston Legend had sent him, and Clay was chomping at the bit to take Lucinda Shannon to court and let all the evidence come out. Bullet licked Clay's hand, chuffed, and dropped at his feet.

Violet moved closer and laid a hand on his arm as though to assure herself that he hadn't disappeared. "Daddy, I missed you real bad. I had scary dreams that you and Mama were dead."

Clay set down his plate of food and pulled her into his lap. "I thought of you every second. I'm sorry you didn't sleep well."

"Did that mean ol' Tarver turn to a black stone?"

"Yep." The image of Slade Tarver in that window with

flames licking around him crossed his mind. Clay let the fragrance of the night surround him, glad that Violet had been spared the scene. "Yep, he turned into a very hard black stone, just like the man in the story. He won't bother us ever again."

"Good. He shoulda been nice." Violet's voice dropped low. "Daddy, Mr. Montana ain't gonna come back, is he?"

The child was too smart by half. He and Tally were supposed to be doing this together, but it couldn't wait any longer.

"No, baby girl, he won't come back." Clay took a deep breath. "He got killed."

Violet gave a little cry and buried her face against him. He rubbed her small back. If only he could spare her every grief and sorrow, but that wasn't possible. Life held no promises and you had to accept the bad with the good.

Tears trembled on Violet's long lashes when she lifted her head. "I loved him, you know. Mr. Montana said I was the daughter he never had. And now he's in heaven. I miss him real bad."

In heaven? Clay silenced the snort. But who was to say? Montana Black had given his life for him and for Violet. He wiped her eyes, then kissed her cheek.

"I miss him too, sweetheart. Did you know his last words were about you? That's right. Montana worried that you needed us." Clay's gaze swept to Tally as she moved toward the campfire. God, that woman could open a heart he thought long dead! "Do you feel like dancing, baby girl?"

"I don't hear any music." Violet tilted her head, listening.

Clay signaled to Dallas Hawk to lift the fiddle, and the first strains of a waltz filled the air. "How about now?"

A huge smile covered Violet's face as Clay stood and set her on his boots. He moved across the ground, holding her tight, then closed his eyes and let the music soothe his ragged soul. Other couples joined them and soon the area was alive with moving bodies and laughter. Tally stood with an arm around the two children they'd rescued from Creedmore's basement. She'd bathed them and put them in clean clothes. Tally's eyes met Clay's, and he couldn't wait to get her next to him, but when the music ended, she brought the girl over. "Jenny wants to dance with you."

"Sounds good to me." Clay put his arms around Jenny Carver and anchored her on his boots. The child's eyes glowed with excitement. Judging by the rapture on her face, she'd never heard any musical instrument. "Do you like music, Jenny?"

"Yes."

"Does it make you happy?"

"Yes."

"That's good. Everyone should be happy tonight, don't you think?"

"Yes."

Boy, she was sure a talker. He grinned and told her all about Devil's Crossing, the goats, and Bullet, and that he was very happy she and her brother, Ely, had come to live with them. When he finished the dance, he took her back to Tally.

Violet took Jenny's hand. "You and me are gonna go exploring tomorrow. But you have to watch for snakes 'cause my friend ain't here anymore to save us. You'd have liked Mr. Montana."

Ely loosened his grip on Tally's dress. "I'm good at watching for snakes. Can I come?"

"Okay. We'll all explore together."

Tally chucked as the three moved toward a bench. "Those kids are going to be all right."

"Yep, they are." Clay offered his hand. "Care to dance, Mrs. Colby?"

"Always, my handsome cowboy."

She floated into the welcoming circle and slid an arm around his neck. Clay glided her around in wide, sweeping angles, avoiding the other waltzing couples. She moved against him, her soft curves brushing each line of his body. He groaned.

If she had been a match, the friction would have had them going up in flames.

"Man, I'm glad to be back home." He glanced up at the

moon. "We have much to celebrate." He held her hand against his chest. "Never again will I take anything for granted."

"I'm all for counting blessings." Her gaze wandered to some of the women of Creedmore and Deliverance Canyon who were waltzing with the lonely men. Her chin quivered and she bit her lip. "I never thought I'd live to see this moment."

"It just goes to show that life is full of surprises." He twirled her under his arm and lowered her in a dip before raising her up. "Darlin', what do you think about dropping the guard on the town? Tarver and his bunch are all dead. You really don't have anything to fear."

"You do, though. What about lawmen showing up, looking for you and the others?"

Clay sighed. "That's a risk we're all willing to take. But hiding in plain sight makes us awfully hard to find. We can't shut out the world and expect to thrive."

"I'm fine with dropping the guard for my sake. I just worry about you and the men. A posse could swoop in and get you."

"We've lived with this most of our lives. This is nothing new." He rested his mouth against her temple, breathing in the fragrance that was Tally Shannon Colby. "We should meet with that attorney fellow right after breakfast. And once you share everything you know about Lucinda with him, I want to see if he'll handle the matter of amnesty, at least for me and Jack."

"That's a wonderful idea, Clay. I pray he will. Every man longs to be free."

"I want to wipe the slate clean. I'm tired of looking over my shoulder and I know Jack is too. It's no way to live and you deserve better." He brought her hand to his lips and kissed it. "I am a lucky, lucky man. There's no doubt about it."

"And I'm the luckiest woman alive bar none." Tally looked over his shoulder and gave a soft cry.

"What is it?"

"Look over at the edge of the dancers."

Clay followed her glance to Rebel. The woman had the

children in a circle, holding their hands, dancing and laughing. "Well, I'll be."

"I'm so glad she's at peace. Everyone deserves a second chance."

He chuckled. "Three or four in this case, but who's counting?"

"Did I mention how handsome you look tonight?" Tally's eyes shimmered in the moonlight as she toyed with the hair at the back of his neck. "I can't wait to get you alone in our new house. You'll plead for mercy. That's all I'm saying, cowboy."

"Do tell." He brought them to a stop and lowered his mouth to hers. He nibbled his way across the seam of her mouth before finding he had no patience for teasing.

A familiar heat pooled inside Clay and swept the length of his body. Her nipples had hardened, and he could feel them through her bodice, pressing to his chest. She was his beginning…and end. His warrior angel. And he desired her more than anything he'd ever known.

His fingertips slid down the long column of her throat to the pulsing hollow where her heart beat wildly. A moan slipped from her mouth as her arms went around him and she melted into his arms.

If he lived to be a hundred, he'd never tire of holding, kissing, making love to her.

It took a moment for his addled brain to become aware that the music had stopped. He ended the kiss and glanced up. Everyone began clapping, hollering, and chanting his and Tally's name.

He took her hand and walked back to the fire, giving the audience a frown. "What was that for?"

Jack Bowdre stepped forward, hat in hand. "Surviving. We like seeing you two together. And we sort of like you around. Sometimes. Well, most times."

Clay gave a snort. "You love Tally, you mean. Me, you just tolerate."

Jack chuckled. "Yep. I reckon that's about the whole sum of it."

Someone gave a shrill whistle and the crowd parted. Ridge Steele, his gun hanging from his hip, his black boots coming to his knees, walked carefully toward them, balancing a tall cake.

When the ex-preacher reached Clay, he set the confection on a table. "For you and Miss Tally. A celebration for returning with all these beautiful ladies. Our town grew by leaps and bounds in a matter of minutes." Ridge paused. "And 'specially to celebrate you two making it back in one piece."

In the quiet that followed, a voice rose. "Give us a speech, Clay."

Clay raised his hand. "Now, you all know I'm not big on talking, but I want to say how proud I am of each of you. You put your shoulders to the grindstone to build this place, and never once let up."

He glanced at Tally. "My wife pointed out that we need a more suitable name—seems folks won't be very quick to bring their businesses to a place called Devil's Crossing. So be thinking. I'll set out a basket that you can drop the suggestions into. This is *your* town. What do you want it called? Also, we don't need to guard any longer. Unless I'm wrong, the men from Creedmore are all dead. We'll open up to settlers."

The crowd nodded, clapping and whistling.

"Now, let's get back to dancing. And I need some cake."

Tally slid her hand around his elbow. "Did anyone ever mention that you make a good politician?"

"Nope. Get that notion out of your head right now." He planted a kiss behind her ear. "Politicians talk more and say less than any people I know. Want some cake?"

"Absolutely. It looks good. I think it's fresh apple."

"Yum, my favorite." He spoke to several of the new women as they made their way to the dessert table, then turned to Tally. "The difference in these women after just one day is amazing. I saw Dr. Mary treating those who needed it. Did she look at your shrapnel wounds?"

"First thing. I'm all fixed up." Tally pressed closer, her auburn hair brushing his cheek, the warmth of her body teasing him. "You worry too much about me, Clay."

"Who will if I don't? Violet?" He grinned to hide the concern that his wife still suffered lingering effects of the explosion as well as the vile tea Tarver had made her drink and her anxiety attacks. "How are your chest pains? I'm sure getting the life choked out of you and then the explosion didn't help."

She played with the ends of his hair. "Stop it. I'm fine. Better than I've been in a long time. For your information, I haven't had any chest pains in a while."

"Good. You're all I've got and I'm just trying to make sure nothing happens to you."

"Pardon me, Mr. Colby." Susan Worth interrupted their conversation, patting her dark hair where a few strands of gray glinted. "I haven't thanked you yet for what you did in ridding us of Tarver and his bunch."

"Your smile is thanks enough, Mrs. Worth. What I did needed doing for a lot of people. And Tally deserves just as much credit—or more." He glanced down and got lost in Tally's winter blues. Shaking himself, he turned back to Susan. "What are your plans now?"

The firelight revealed the sparkle of tears in her eyes. "I have nothing left to go home to. If you'll have me, I plan to stay. This seems like an excellent place to start over. I'm a pretty fair baker. I'll open a small shop and provide pastries and breads."

"Susan, that's wonderful!" Tally gave her a hug. "I'll be a regular customer. Did you make this cake, by chance?" Tally cut a piece and handed it to Clay.

"Yes, apple cake was my husband's favorite." Susan glanced at the crowd and the Creedmore women.

The sorrow in Susan's face touched Clay. She was adrift without an anchor. Maybe they could provide that in time. "I'm glad you're staying, Mrs. Worth. We can use you."

Susan cut a large piece of cake and took it to one of the arrivals who sat alone, looking lost. Susan dropped down next to her and, in no time, had the woman smiling.

Clay warmed at Susan Worth's kind heart. The widow would fit right in and prove an asset, as would the others, and maybe, in time, she could find peace. His gaze swept the large gathering. Their new town was full of people who didn't fit anywhere else.

Maybe that's why he'd wanted to put a town here. All of them were misfits, but their common bond provided a place with opportunity to start over.

Sometimes when events shook a person's foundation, life stopped for a while, then started again, moving a body in a new, totally different direction.

His attention caught on Rebel in a plain cotton dress, sitting with both little Jenny and Ely on her lap. He couldn't stop the smile. This proved anything was possible.

Tally reached for his hand and threaded her fingers through his. "I still can't believe we made it, Clay. I keep thinking this is a dream. I want to cry because I'm so happy."

"Hey, I don't want my girl all weepy tonight. I have plans." He tilted her chin and gave her a tender kiss.

When the kiss ended, he noticed Jack standing apart, staring out into the black night, his shoulders slumped. A bottle of whiskey dangled at his side.

"Excuse me for a minute, Tally. I need to speak to Jack."

"I need to find Violet anyway."

Clay strode to his old friend. "There's nothing out there but a whole lot of darkness, Jack."

"Tell me about it. You should go back to Tally."

"Not until I find out what's wrong. I saw you speaking to pretty Darcy Howard. Did you two have words?"

"We're fine, and I want to marry her."

"So what's the problem?"

"Darcy's changed her mind. She's decided to enter a convent." Jack swung to him. The lines etched in the ex-lawman's face made him appear much older than his thirty-one years. "A convent." Jack barked a laugh. "She'd rather be a nun than marry me. A *nun*."

From Jack's position, it probably did seem laughable, but then, he hadn't seen Creedmore.

"Don't take this personal."

"How the hell am I supposed to take it, Clay? Huh?"

"You can't imagine what she's been through—what they've all endured." Bullet wandered up and Clay patted the faithful pooch's head. "Jack, you couldn't imagine that place. I've seen animals kept in better conditions, and I'll have nightmares for a long while. I imagine Darcy needs to find some inner peace and a way to forget."

"I reckon. I don't begrudge her that. Just disappointed is all. I'd counted the days until we could be married. We'd talked about tying the knot next month."

"There are other women. You'll find one. You just have to be patient."

"You don't think I have been?" Anger and hurt blazed in Jack's eyes. "I'm tired, Clay, and I'm not getting any younger. I want a family before I die. You know?"

"You can't give up." Clay laid a hand on his back. "No matter what, you have to keep reaching for what you want."

"Those are easy words for someone with a wife like Tally. You have *your* dream—a town, a wife, a daughter. You just about have everything you ever wanted."

"Except for amnesty. You're right. I have more than I ever thought I would."

"Yeah, well, don't preach to me." Jack pushed at him. "Go back to the party. I'll be all right tomorrow. But tonight, I'm going to get drunk."

Clay removed his hand. "Fine. But after breakfast, you'd best be here to talk to Phineas Hargrove. This lawyer is the best chance we've got to clear our names."

When Jack didn't answer, Clay turned away and went back to Tally. She'd found Violet, and his heart swelled to see the child holding hands with Jenny and Ely. The two Carver kids had climbed from Rebel's lap but stayed by her knee. The three children appeared to be fast friends.

"Care to waltz again?" He held out his palm to Tally.

"Yes, indeed, Mr. Colby. I saved this dance especially for you." Her voice held a breathless quality that whispered over his skin, arousing him.

He placed a hand on her waist and pulled her flush against him. "I could hold you like this all night. When you leave my arms, I feel so empty and cold. I'm never going to let you go."

But what about his promise to let her go come spring if she wanted to ride out?

The thought of the gaping hole she'd leave sent stabs of pain into his chest.

Her flushed face and shining eyes made her even more beautiful. She met his gaze, her fiery curls cascading over her shoulders and down to rest on the soft swell of her breasts. Her glorious smile blinded him, and she caught her bottom lip between her white teeth. "What if I want to do…*other* things?"

Here it comes. Clay steeled himself. Maybe what he offered wasn't enough. Maybe *he* wasn't enough for someone like her.

"Clay, you look so serious. Are you rusty at teasing banter?" Her soft words and coy glance released a thundering herd of wild horses inside him.

Clay brought her hand to his mouth and nipped at her fingers. "No. What *other* things do you suggest we do, darlin'?"

The tip of Tally's tongue left a wet trail down the column of his throat. "Like kissing and hugging and…making love."

This teasing, carefree side of his wife was one that he prayed never left. "Just wait until I get you alone." His heart thudded against his ribs as he murmured in her ear, *"My warrior angel."*

Thirty-six

THE PREDAWN HOURS FOUND CLAY ASTRIDE HIS HORSE ATOP the bluff overlooking the town. The place was just beginning to stir after the late-night homecoming celebration. He still carried the scent of Tally on him, and he smiled as he let the memory of their lovemaking wash over him. Each time with her was good, but last night's lovemaking had been deeper than ever.

Sundown danced, anxious to gallop, but Clay held the paint firmly in check. "Not yet, boy. Give me a minute."

A frown formed on his face as he gazed across the land. The town couldn't survive without food. That had been apparent from the start, but he'd pushed it aside to address later when they actually got Devil's Crossing on the upswing.

But now their numbers had almost doubled, and he had to think about growing crops. Except where?

Clay turned and rode to the long, narrow valley that butted up against his and Tally's new house. This section of ground held the most fertile soil. Everything higher up was too rocky.

Dismounting, he picked up a fistful of rich earth and let it fall through his fingers. This would grow everything they needed, but they had to get moving quickly for the crops to flourish. Once they plowed the land, the women could plant in nothing flat, and late-summer rains would soon have autumn crops reaching for the sky.

Memories of growing up on a farm, watching plants and animals grow, crossed his mind. He'd loved those special times—the fresh milk, helping his father pitch hay to the horses, walking barefoot across a meadow after a slow summer rain. The back of his eyes burned.

He blinked hard and turned at the sound of hoofbeats. Jack and Ridge pulled to a halt and swung from their saddles.

"I thought we might find you here." Ridge stooped for a

handful of dirt. "We've had the same thought. We have to start becoming self-sufficient or the town will die out."

Jack agreed. "This section is the only good land nearby that will grow anything."

"A question for you both first." Clay studied his old friends. "I need to know if you're in this for the long haul."

Ridge wasted not a second. "You can count on me."

"Jack?" Clay asked. "You've had a setback in your plans. Will you pack up and leave?"

The former lawman's eyes met his, and while they still bore bitter disappointment, they reflected a bit of hope. "I'm staying. Maybe things will change for me one day, but even so, this is my home. You need too much help here for me to leave now."

"Tobias and Belle brought a lot of seeds with them," Ridge said. "I'll see what they have in addition to what I bought when I went into Springer for Dr. Mary's medicines."

"Good. Then I think we need to set about plowing today and get something in the ground soon." Clay reached for Sundown's reins. "Let's go fill our bellies. I'm hungry."

Maybe they could have community farms, where everyone worked with no one person lording over the others. He wouldn't stand for greed. If that took root, it would destroy everything he'd built.

His dreams had been crushed for too long.

Following breakfast, Tally and Clay sat in their old dugout across from Phineas Hargrove, while Belle and Susan Worth rode herd on Violet.

Tally gripped Clay's hand, studying the lawyer. Would he be the man to get justice for her? His kind brown eyes behind his round spectacles seemed to reflect a gentle heart. The black bowler he wore had a small, jaunty feather stuck in the band on one side. Phineas Hargrove had long, elegant fingers and appeared young—somewhere near Clay's age.

Phineas opened his case and removed paper and pencil.

"First, give me the facts that you have concerning your stepmother, Lucinda."

"This will be hard to believe, but it's the truth, sir." Tally told him about Lucinda's instant dislike of her and her brother upon her marriage to their father. "She used to terrorize my brother and myself. Dumping pepper and spices into our food to make it impossible to eat and ripping up our clothes and leaving them in strips in our room.

"We tried to tell Father, but he was smitten with her. She had him wrapped around her finger until he couldn't see the truth that was in front of him. He died six months after they married, under suspicious circumstances, and I know in my heart she killed him."

Phineas glanced up from his notes. "Tell me how he died."

"He became violently ill—couldn't hold anything down, couldn't swallow, couldn't speak. A paralysis set in and I knew he wouldn't recover. We called the doctor, but he couldn't save him." Tally paused, remembering the horror and Lucinda's cleaning frenzy following the funeral.

Clay reached for her hand and she welcomed his comfort. "Take your time, darlin'."

"A few days after the burial, I found a hurried letter to me and Brady in my father's handwriting, warning us to watch out. Father said there was evil and danger afoot on the ranch. He said that if anything happened to him, we should go to the sheriff." Tally took a deep breath. "The sheriff left town very suddenly before Brady and I got to."

"Regardless of what your father's will said, by Texas law, Lucinda would get half plus one third and the right to live on the ranch until her death. You and Brady each were entitled to a third." The man of law took off his spectacles and chewed on the earpieces.

Tally nodded. "Only that wasn't enough for dear, greedy stepmother. She wanted it all."

"To do that, she *had* to get rid of you and your brother." Phineas put his spectacles back on and feverishly wrote something else.

"And that's what she did. Brady's death came a short time after my father's. She made it appear like an accidental horse trampling, but I know it wasn't. About that time, a stranger arrived, and he and Lucinda spent many hours locked in my father's office."

Phineas got excited. "Do you have a name for this stranger? He could provide the proof we need."

"I'll never forget it. The man was slimy and dirty. Always staring. Jude Dominick."

Clay jerked in surprise. "I know him. Had dealings with him about two years ago."

"Do you know where we might find him?" Phineas Hargrove asked.

"If he's not dead, he'll be at the Crystal Palace in Waco most nights. He's the owner. Better take a loaded gun when you talk to him. No…make that two." By the way Clay's face hardened, Tally knew whatever had happened between him and Dominick had been bad.

For several long moments, the only sound was Phineas Hargrove's pencil against paper. "Thanks. You've been very helpful. Continue, Mrs. Colby."

"After Brady was out of the picture, Lucinda turned her attention to me. She cornered me, snarling that she could make me disappear unless I toed the line. That night I tried to escape but Dominick caught me." Tally rubbed her eyes to erase the images of all that had followed. "She saved the worst for me." Her voice dropped to a whisper. "The living hell of the Creedmore Lunatic Asylum."

Tally told him about the days and nights of horror, about death pressing close, about her escape, and ended with Clay burning the place.

A moment's silence followed. Clay rubbed her back, and Phineas's furious scribbling filled the dugout. Finally, he glanced up. "Thank you, Mrs. Colby. You've given me more than enough to get my investigator on this."

"An investigator?" Tally scowled. "I thought you did that yourself."

"No, ma'am." Phineas removed his spectacles. "I have no talent for that. My expertise lies in the courtroom, and when I finish with Lucinda Shannon, you'll get your father's estate— the land, money, and everything else he owned. If things go right, this will lock the woman up for a very long time."

"Mr. Hargrove, we should discuss your fee." Tally worried that the cost would be too rich for their blood. "Clay and I are just starting our life together and don't have much."

The lawyer patted her hand. "We'll talk about that later."

"No, sir," Clay objected. "We'll know now. I want no surprises."

"Fine. Give me ten dollars to start and fifty when it's done. Agreed?"

Clay stuck out his hand. "Agreed. How soon can you start?"

"Immediately." The lawyer shook their hands and started to rise.

"Wait. Before you leave, I have another matter to discuss." Clay went to the door and got Jack. "Will you help us get amnesty?"

Phineas smiled. "I'd wondered when you would ask. Of course. I'll write the governor, pleading your case. Sit down and list your crimes and include—in your own words—why you're confessing and asking for amnesty."

An hour later, Clay handed over the money for both Tally's and his cases. Jack's shoulders lifted when he paid for his own.

Tally shook Mr. Hargrove's hand. "Thank you for handling these. You don't know how much I…how much *we* appreciate the help."

Phineas placed his spectacles inside his vest pocket. "Your cases intrigue me. I'm especially looking forward to getting justice for you, Mrs. Colby. That woman should be hanged for what she did. And she might end up that way, by the time it's all said and done." He turned and left the dugout.

Justice. She was finally getting justice. Tally inhaled a cleansing breath. One day, she'd look back and remember this as the instant hope bloomed fully in her heart.

Clay threaded his fingers through hers. "I'm very proud of

you. It takes courage to confront evil and slay dragons. What are your plans for the rest of the day?"

"I have to sit down with these women and find out their ambitions, see how many are leaving. Will you help arrange transportation for them to get where they want to go?"

"Of course." He moved her hair aside and kissed her neck.

"Stop this. I have to get started. I'll see you in a little while, cowboy."

❧

While Ridge took a group of men to plow, Clay worked inside his and Tally's new house. He wanted to get the interior finished and have their little family moved in before dark. Jack led a group to help, and it went fast.

Each time Clay went for water or food, he saw Tally huddled with the new arrivals. More than just food and shelter, she was giving them fresh hope and bandages for the scars deep in their hearts. His chest burst with pride. He couldn't have chosen a fiercer fighter for a wife.

Violet found him. "What'cha doin', Daddy?"

"Working." Clay wiped the sweat from his face with an arm. "I'm getting our new house ready to move into."

"Will Jenny and Ely live with us?"

"I don't know. Would you like if they did?"

Violet nodded. "They could be my brother and sister." The child's face darkened. "I used to have some sisters, but they didn't like me. My brother used to be very mean to me. He tripped me all the time and laughed." Violet never talked much about her other life. That she was doing so now, well, it probably meant she was worried that maybe this would turn out like before.

Clay sat down and pulled her onto his lap. She snuggled against him. "Don't you worry about Jenny and Ely. They're not like those people from your past. I'll make sure."

"I know." Violet pulled out a small cloth bag from her pocket. "Wanna see what Mr. Montana gave me? He said it's a secret but I know you won't tell."

Clay opened the sack and removed two yellow rocks, turned them in the light, and stilled. What the hell? "Violet, did Montana say what these were?"

"Yep. Rocks. He said I could sell 'em."

Clay held them up to examine. How did that kind of gold wind up in Montana's possession? "Did he say where he got them?"

"Nope. Will you tell?"

"No, baby girl. This is our secret." He returned them to the bag and stuck it back in her pocket. "Put them in a safe place, and one day I'll take you to sell them."

Violet stayed close on his shirttail, and he welcomed her company. She talked a lot about Montana and he learned much more about the man now than he ever had when Montana was alive. It was odd how he kept revealing more and more about himself through a little blind girl.

Midafternoon, a wagon arrived full of large crates. Clay hurried to meet the shipment of furniture that, unbeknownst to Tally, he'd ordered a month ago. Though she glanced up with curiosity, she didn't come over to see what the fuss was about and kept on making a log of each rescued woman's name and her plans.

He swore the men to secrecy and asked their help in setting everything in the house. Waiting until nightfall would be difficult, but he wanted to have the beds made, curtains up, furniture in place, and flowers in the vases. This was what he'd wished for the day Tally arrived to marry him sight unseen, just a mail order bride. So much had happened since then— good things and bad.

By the time he'd finished and had everything perfect, the sun had started its trek toward twilight. Clay gave his and Tally's bedroom a final glance before closing the door. Anticipation hummed beneath his skin.

The fact it was a Monday caused no alarm. Maybe they weren't so bad after all.

❧

Tally closed her log book and stretched, satisfied with the day's work. So far, fifteen of the women wanted to move on and get as far from Texas as they could. Savannah Lyle had broken off her original plans to marry Ridge and was going to live with relatives back East. Others like her had definite destinations in mind, where they knew they could work and support themselves.

Darcy Howard had chosen to live in a convent instead of marrying Jack. Darcy simply needed a chance for contemplation, faith, and peace, and Tally could certainly understand that. Of the women, Darcy could have been the most scarred. Even now, she couldn't bring herself to tell Tally all of her story.

Tally gazed at the outdoor fire where Belle and Susan were cooking, putting Jack and another of the men to work helping. Some fresh onions and tomatoes would be wonderful with the meal. She hurried to the garden to pick them. From the corner of her eye, she saw Rebel striding up the slight incline, her face set in determined lines.

She waited until the woman drew close. "Hi, Rebel. Something bothering you?"

"What are your intentions for Jenny and Ely Carver?"

"Clay and I haven't really discussed the matter. Why?"

"If it's all right…" Rebel bit her lip and started over. "If it's all the same, I want them."

"That's wonderful!" Tally laid her hand on Rebel's arm and spoke softly. "This can help fill the hole left when your son died."

"I want to be a mother again. And who knows? Maybe a wife. Travis and I get along well. Maybe he'll ask me to marry him one of these days."

"I'm very happy for you." A horse's angry snort reached Tally's ears. Where was it coming from? A slight ripple in the breeze whispered that trouble was coming. The hair on her arms rose as though lightning had hit close. Something was wrong, but she couldn't pinpoint the source.

A strange foreboding filled the air, and even though she

stood with her friends a stone's throw away in the bustling town, that feeling in her gut wouldn't subside. She scanned each new building, the windmill, the row of tents they'd stretched for the new arrivals. Nothing seemed out of the ordinary. It was a normal summer day. Everyone was happy. All their troubles were behind them.

Animals smelled trouble, and her time at Creedmore had broken her down to where she was little more than an animal, surviving on instinct alone. Maybe her senses were so sharpened by going back there that she could taste danger where it wasn't. She had to hurry back to her friends at the fire.

Rebel screamed, "Watch out, Tally!"

A sudden, deep growl made her skin crawl with fear. Then a hand closed around her arms from behind, holding her immobile.

Her blood turned to ice and she steeled herself, already looking for a way to freedom.

A gravelly voice spoke at her ear. "Did you think you were safe?"

Chills raced up her spine. "Run, Rebel! Get to safety."

The children. Violet, where was she? She'd be unable to see the danger. Tally prayed Violet would somehow sense her panic and hide. She had to see his face. She twisted against the iron grip far enough to see the shiny gold tooth and went stone cold.

Slade Tarver.

Thirty-seven

TALLY SHOOK HER HEAD TO CLEAR IT. TARVER WAS DEAD. Wasn't he? He'd burned up in the fire. She'd seen him standing in the window with flames all around him. Large blisters on his face oozed puss. He should've died. How could he come into their town with no one paying him any mind?

He turned her to face him. "Say your prayers, Tally Shannon." Her old adversary's chilling grin sent a shock cartwheeling the length of her body. She stared into his gun barrel. "You forgot about the tunnel underneath Creedmore. Now, I'm gonna kill you. Slow. One bloody scream at a time."

His crazed eyes told her that this time it would be to the death. One of them would not live beyond this encounter, and right now, the odds were not in her favor.

Rebel moved into her line of vision, terror freezing her features. She should run, not stand there.

Tarver leveled his pistol and squeezed the trigger. Tally kept her eyes open. She'd meet her death like she'd lived her life—head-on with no apologizes.

"No you don't!" Rebel yelled and raised the hoe she held that they used to chop weeds in the garden. She brought it down across Tarver's shoulders.

"You worthless bitch!" Enraged, Tarver swung around. Two bullets struck the saloon girl in quick succession, ripping into her chest. Amid the spray of blood, Rebel crumpled to the dirt. Blood also splattered Tally's face where she stood rooted in horror and disbelief.

Run! her mind screamed. But before she could move, Tarver grabbed her arm, reached for the reins of a horse he'd hidden in the deep evening shadows next to the dugout, and threw her over the animal's back on her belly. She screamed Clay's name as Tarver swung up into the saddle. She hung upside down across the horse, a panicked, ragged breath burning in her lungs. She squirmed, trying her best to get free.

She couldn't let him take her—not again. Even if she fell to the ground and the horse trampled her, it would be preferable to Tarver's torture.

The man she hated with all her being quickly kicked his mount into motion. They flew across the rocky, uneven ground, and he sent shots toward the men on foot racing behind.

If only she could get to the gun she wore strapped around her waist. But that was impossible in her present position. The running gallop jarred her with each impact, driving her teeth into her bottom lip. Agony and despair raced through her.

Ahead, men hurried to roll wagons across the entrance of the canyon, rifles aimed to block Tarver's escape. They released a flurry of shots and one bullet tore into Tarver. At the moment, she couldn't tell where, just heard his scream and felt his body tense.

Tally readied to slide off, but he didn't slow down. Not until, with a yank of the reins, he swung around and reined up at the foot of the same bluff where a guard had kept watch—until yesterday.

The moment the horse stopped and Tarver dismounted, she slid off and ran, making it two steps before he grabbed the back of her dress. He jerked her against him, dragging her up against the rock wall of the bluff as though she weighed no more than a child. She struggled with all her might, trying to tear away, but his cruel hand dug into her arm.

He backed her against the rock wall, holding her with his body while he seized her gun and tossed it half a dozen paces away. Then, Tarver yanked her in front of him and released a volley of gunfire.

Clay raced forward, his Remington drawn. Fear gripped her and everything screamed for him to stop. After everything they'd survived, she couldn't bear to watch him die at Tarver's hand.

"Stay back or she dies!" Tarver yelled. "So help me God, I *will* kill her."

"Do that and you'll never draw another breath." Clay's bark carried a razor-sharp edge. "I can promise you that."

The men formed a half circle around Clay, blocking off all escape. Tally's heart ached for Rebel. She said a silent prayer that Rebel had survived the blast. But there had been so much blood. Thank God Violet didn't seem to be anywhere nearby.

Bullet broke free of someone's hold and darted through the circle of men. The dog bit down on Tarver's leg but even that didn't break his hold on her. Cursing and yelling, the killer shook the dog loose and kicked him hard over into some low brush. The dog let out three loud yelps as he tumbled, then lay silent.

Tally struggled against her captor, trying to breathe against the stench of him, to think, to devise a plan.

Tarver sucked in a loud breath and groaned, his body rigid, his face a mask of pain, his shiny gold tooth a symbol of heinous acts. He pulled her into a crevice in the wall that offered more protection, should anyone shoot.

In the small space, she was pressed even tighter to him. So much she could feel his thundering heartbeat.

"Release me and we'll get the doctor to treat you." A slight turn of her head let her see blood oozing from the hole in his shoulder. His shirt was soaked. Soon he'd be weak and then Clay would get him.

But could she survive until then?

"You and me—we got unfinished business, girl." His words sent ice tumbling through her veins. "You'll never be free."

"Can't you see I already am? You have no hold over me anymore. I'm not afraid of you. You did your best to break me, but you failed." Her racing heart calmed. She realized the truth of what she'd said. Even though he held her in a grip of steel, she *was* free.

"Let her go!" Clay ordered.

Jack inched forward, his gun drawn. "You're some man to hide behind a woman. Give yourself up."

Looking at the former lawman, Tally could see why he'd been so good at his job. His face had turned to stone, and his determined black eyes snapped with the kind of hate that would make any man have second thoughts.

"Don't even try it." Tarver waved him back with his gun.

Tally spoke. "If you shoot me, you'll instantly get a dozen more bullets in you."

"Let's bargain. What do you want?" Clay shouted. "Name your price. Anything—except Tally." Clay took a step, then two. Tally prayed he wouldn't do anything foolish. "Let her go and I'll give you whatever you want."

A trickle of sweat inched down Tarver's forehead and into his eye. He pressed his gun to Tally's temple. "Get the hell back or the next bullet goes in her brain."

Everyone retreated, but the yells and cursing from the crowd grew louder. Tally stomped down on Tarver's foot and jabbed him in the ribs with her elbow. If only she could reach his wounded shoulder, where she could do more damage.

He grunted hard, but his arm tightened even more across her chest until she could barely breathe. Her gaze sharpened on her gun, lying in the dirt a few paces away.

If only she could distract him.

Tarver placed his mouth next to her ear. "I wanted to take my time with you, make your death slow. But I don't mind killing you now."

"Then do it," Tally spat, tired of his threats. "Just get it over with, you bastard."

Clay took a wide stance and removed a sack of Bull Durham and rolling papers from his vest pocket with his free hand. His loose body signaled a ploy of some kind. Maybe he was trying to ratchet down the tension, and there were plenty of other guns aimed at Tarver. "I'm waiting. What is it you want?"

"Money," Tarver snapped. "You took everything from me. I want a stake so I can start fresh somewhere."

Sliding his gun into his holster almost casually, Clay rolled his cigarette and lit it. "Money?" Smoke circled his head. That and the low brim of his trail-worn Stetson hid his eyes, but from the sound of his voice, Tally knew they would be narrowed on his prey. "What makes you think we have any?"

"You're outlaws. Outlaws have loot, so don't give me any cock-and-bull story."

"I'll have to consult my *compadre*." Clay and Jack put their heads together.

Tally spoke. "Are you sure you want to end your life this way? Clay's killed a lot of men, and he'll enjoy adding your name to the list." She gagged from the smell of Tarver's putrid breath but kept talking. "You can't have more than one bullet left. What will you do after you kill me?"

An angry grunt at her ear told her she'd made him think. Maybe reasoning would get through to him. She couldn't beat him by force, but maybe she could mess with his mind.

She dropped her voice low. "Outlaws know a million painful ways to make a man suffer before they kill him." She moved a hand behind her to lightly pat his crotch. She gave a crazy cackle like she'd heard so often in the asylum. "I know how much you enjoy your manhood. Will you chance them cutting it off?"

"Shut up."

"I shared some of your favorite games with Clay, so I can guarantee that you'll be on the receiving end of a lot of pain before you die."

Tarver shifted uncomfortably and yelled, "You're taking too long, Colby. I reckon you'll hurry it along if I make Tally Shannon bleed! First the legs, then arms. Maybe the sight of blood thrills you."

Clay drew his Colt as quick as lightning and aimed it, his face a dark, fierce mask. Tarver jammed the barrel the gun under Tally's chin, pushing her head back. She sucked in a breath. She wouldn't give in to fear or she'd be done for.

"I'll give you one hour to bring me five hundred dollars." Tarver dug for his watch and flipped it open. "One hour."

He'd dropped his grip on her. Could she take a chance and run? But the gun lodged painfully into the soft tissue under her chin told her it would be too risky. If she moved an inch, he'd pull the trigger. Best to watch and wait for a better opening.

Clay raised his hands. "All right, you no-account bastard. One hour. If you harm one hair on her head, all bets are off."

"You'd best hurry, Colby!" Tarver slid his watch back in his pocket and lowered the barrel of his gun.

Tally watched the men flanking Clay. They were ready, if only she could do her part and stay calm. The ransom request worried her—they had no money to hand over. How were they going to trick him?

Tarver licked his dry, cracked lips and pus oozed from one of the blisters on his cheek. Infection had already set in and he had to be in enormous agony.

"Slade, I can see you're in a lot of pain," Tally said softly. "Let our doctor treat you."

"Not until you pay for destroying my life." He snarled and shoved the gun into the soft flesh of a breast. She bit back a cry. "You took everything I'd worked for. Everything."

"What about my life? What do you think you did to me?" She tamped down her rising rage, the wild beast within her baring its teeth. She'd wait and bide her time, letting anger keep her alive.

"You?" Tarver snorted, his gold tooth an inch from her face. "You're just a woman."

And that sums it all up in his small mind.

She tried another approach. "The blame is all Lucinda's. If she hadn't put me in there, Clay wouldn't have burned it down and taken everything. Lucinda has money, land, cattle. She needs to pay up and you're just the man to make her."

"I'll deal with her later." His rough hand moved down her body to her breast. He squeezed so hard it brought tears to her eyes and she bit back a cry. Like all those dark days and nights in Creedmore, she took the pain inward, refusing to give him the satisfaction.

"You can deny it all you want but I know you liked it." He licked her cheek. "You all did."

She shivered with disgust, loathing, and anger. Desperate to get her mind off her situation, she turned her attention to

Bullet, who lay in the brush, waiting for help. Her heart went out to the dog. Please let his injuries be treatable. Violet had lost too many friends already.

Clay and three others hurried toward the new town's buildings. She didn't know what they had in mind, but they had to have a plan. The ones remaining resumed watch with guns drawn, their faces grim. To a man, they must have been itching to put a bullet in Slade Tarver.

Time dragged and Clay didn't return. Sweat and pus rolled down Tarver's face. A fly buzzed around his head and he kept trying to shoo it away. It came back and landed on his nose.

"What's keeping him? Where's that money?" Tarver hollered. "Half an hour or she dies!"

Someone yelled, "It's coming! Hold on to your shirt! We have to dig it up. It's in a deep hole."

"Make it fast."

Tally still wondered what their plan was. This waiting was unbearable, and she had so many unanswered questions. The biggest in her mind, of course: Who was to say that Tarver wouldn't kill her once he got what he asked for? Maybe Clay could trick him somehow, but Tarver wasn't stupid.

Minutes ticked away. The coming night was darkening the sky and soon they would be unable to see. But maybe that's what Clay was waiting for. That's probably what she'd do. One thing she knew—he'd never abandon her. He was a good man and he loved her as much or more than she did him. That surety untangled a few of the knots in her stomach.

Susan and Belle lit lanterns, the light reflecting on their grim faces. Tally scanned the deepening shadows for movement but saw nothing.

A tall figure emerged from the darkness. Ridge Steele held up a bottle of whiskey. "Bet you could use some of this."

Tarver ran his tongue across his lips, his eyes riveted on that bottle. Tally could've hugged the tall ex-preacher for this diversion. It had to be the start of whatever rescue Clay and the men had planned. Now, she had to be ready to act and get to her Colt before Tarver shot her.

"Drop your guns and bring it to me," Tarver ordered Ridge. "No tricks."

Hope grew. She had one shot. One chance to get this right.

Ridge stopped two feet away. Every nerve taut, Tally closely watched the outlaw preacher's face. When Tarver swung his gaze to some movement, Ridge mouthed the words, *They're coming. Be ready.* She gave him a slight nod.

Tarver snatched the bottle. "Get back."

"Mind if I take the dog? He needs attention," Ridge said.

"Make it quick."

Tarver waited until after Ridge had picked up Bullet and moved away before he turned the bottle up to guzzle the fiery liquid. Intent on slaking his thirst, he lowered his gun for a moment.

Tally tore herself from his grasp and scrambled to get away, but her feet didn't want to work. They hadn't worked right since Tarver had beaten the bottoms of them.

The women watching from a distance screamed, the men yelled encouragement. She closed her hand around the grip but couldn't find the trigger.

Hurry. Hurry.

Movement from above drew her gaze for a split second. Clay and the three who'd left with him threw ropes over the side of the bluff from above and descended like silent spiders on slender threads of silk.

Tarver didn't see them. He was too busy coming for her.

She made a diving lunge for the gun, found the trigger and pulled. Fire and smoke spat from the barrel.

At the same moment, hanging a foot above Tarver's head, Clay fired his weapon into the cold-blooded killer. "Here's your money. Shake hands with the devil, you ugly piece of shit."

Thirty-eight

THE OTHER MEN FIRED SIMULTANEOUSLY, RIDDLING THE KILLER'S body with bullets as Tally lay on the ground away from the line of fire, her heart pounding in a struggle to regain control. Tarver had to be dead this time.

Her breath came in harsh gasps, and she stood on wobbly legs. Clay picked her up and raced toward Dr. Mary's brightly lit tent.

"Put me down, Clay. I'm all right."

"Let the doctor decide that."

Dr. Mary was bending over Rebel and only glanced up when they entered. "Put her on the other cot. Are you badly hurt, Tally?"

"I'm fine." Tally shot Clay a scowl. "My husband thinks different. How is Rebel?"

"The bullets went in underneath her left bottom rib. If I can get them out, control the bleeding, and infection doesn't set in, she'll probably survive."

"Tally?" Rebel weakly called her name.

Tally could barely hear it. She rose and went to take Rebel's hand. "I'm here."

Rebel licked her gray lips, her breathing shallow. "I loved Clay too."

"I know. Don't talk. Save your strength."

"He always loved you. Never me. Even before..." A coughing fit stopped her. Blood trickled from her mouth.

"Shhh. It's all right. All of that is behind us." Tally squeezed her hand. "We're all going to have a bright future now, and all you need to do is get well so you can raise those children. They need a mother and you're more than up to the job."

"That's enough for now." Dr. Mary put an arm about her. "Let her rest."

With a nod, Tally turned to Clay. "What about Bullet? Did anyone see to him?"

"Ridge is." He ran a fingertip down her cheek, across the scar where her tattoo had once been. "If you'll lay back down for a bit, I'll go check on the dog. And Violet."

Travis came through the opening and, without a word, went straight to Rebel.

Tally dragged her gaze from the tender way the man held Rebel's hand. "I'm coming with you. There's nothing wrong with me, and I'll not waste the doctor's time."

He pressed his lips to hers. "Very well. I know better than to argue."

She lightly traced his sensual mouth and counted her blessings. She'd survived the final blow in Tarver's reign of terror, and Clay was the reason she was alive.

❧

Outside the tent, Clay removed his hat and ran his fingers through his hair. He gulped in huge draughts of air, trying to calm his stampeding heart.

He'd almost lost her, lost the person who held his world together.

"Are you all right?" Tally asked, rubbing his back.

"I'm good." When his knees no longer threatened to buckle, he put an arm around her and strode toward the commotion and lanterns at the campfire. As he drew closer, he noticed the men were working on Bullet.

"How bad is he?" Clay found relief when the dog raised his head and whined at him.

Jack glanced up. "He has a broken leg and probably some busted-up ribs, but he's not bleeding."

"That's a miracle." Tally moved closer to pet the dog's thick fur. "He was only trying to save me."

"Save all of us. He didn't want that scum in our town." Clay blinked hard.

"Got a minute, Clay?" Jack asked.

"Sure."

They moved apart from the others. Jack spoke low. "I took Tarver's body out about a mile. He'll feed the animals tonight. Didn't want you to have to deal with that. You have your hands full with Tally and the kids."

"Thanks. Tarver got his just deserts." Clay scanned the area. "Have you seen Violet?"

Jack pointed toward two figures coming toward them. "Mrs. Worth has her."

Clay hurried Tally to them and lifted the child in his arms. "Hey, baby girl."

Violet wiped her tears. "I was scared, Daddy."

Tally took her hand and kissed it. "You were a brave, brave little girl."

"I thought the bad man killed you, Mama. I was so scared and…and I couldn't find Bullet."

"Bullet's hurt, but he'll get better and be up guiding you places in no time." Clay noticed Jenny and Ely standing alone, apart from the others, holding hands just like when he'd first seen them in the basement of Creedmore.

He set Violet on her feet and went to put his arms around them. Jenny was crying, too. "There now, sweet girl. Don't cry."

"Did that awful man kill Miss Rebel?" Ely's voice was hard. "She was gonna be our mama."

Clay's eyes met Tally's. He didn't know what to say, how to give them back the faith Tarver's newest assault had left damaged.

Tally sat down in one of the chairs that someone had brought over from the saloon and pulled Jenny into her lap. The girl stuck her thumb in her mouth. "No, that man Tarver did not kill Miss Rebel but she's kinda sick. Mark my words, she'll get better in a few days. You're going to be a family."

Clay prayed she hadn't given them false hope, but they desperately needed something to cling to. Everything else had been stripped from them.

Ely frowned and kicked the dirt with the toe of his worn shoe. "Folks always say that when someone is about to die. Or maybe she don't want us anymore."

"Honey, we wouldn't lie to you. Miss Rebel will get better and does want you more than anything or anyone," Tally said softly, brushing a lock of hair away from the boy's hard eyes.

Clay sat down next to Tally with Violet on his lap and pulled Ely to him. "Given what you've been through, you don't have much reason to trust anyone. I wouldn't either. I know Miss Rebel getting shot is a big disappointment and makes you afraid, but no matter what happens, we're never going to send you away. You belong to us now. We're all family here."

"I guess so."

"No, there's no guessing, son. We speak in facts. You're going to go home with Mrs. Colby and me until Miss Rebel gets well, and tomorrow, I'm taking you fishing." Even if he had to do it in the windmill tank. Somehow or another, he'd give Ely a reason to smile.

"Okay." The boy took Jenny's hand and pulled her from Tally's lap. "We need to wash up now."

Clay watched the brother and sister slowly head for the tank. "Let's feed them, Tally, and put them to bed. They appear to have had all they can take for one day."

Violet yawned. "Me, too, Daddy. I'm tired. But my belly's hungry."

In no time, they had the children fed, then he and Tally took their hands and led them to the new house.

Clay set Violet down on the porch. "Wait here and let me light the lamps. I have a surprise."

Barely inside the door, Tally waited with the children. She let out a soft gasp as he touched a match to the wicks. "Clay, this is amazing. Everything is so pretty it takes my breath. When did you get all this furniture?"

He followed her gaze to the simple green-and-white floral sofa and the settee that matched. He'd gotten a great deal on the round table on which the lamp sat. The rich wood shone in the light and reflected the colors in the room. Tally moved to the needlepoint side chair and ran her hand across the back before a large landscape of the plains hanging on the wall caught her eye. He didn't blame her for staring. It was quite a departure from the dugout.

"When did you get all this?" she repeated, her expressive eyes full of tears.

"I ordered it shortly after we married. It arrived earlier today. In fact, I was in here working when I heard the gun blast that felled Rebel." He moved to her and brushed back her wild, flaming curls. Aware of little ears listening, he couldn't say exactly what he wanted. "Do you know how much I'm looking forward to us being together in our own completed house?"

"I'm all dirty, my hair needs combing, and my dress is torn."

"Doesn't matter. That's not what I'm looking at." Clay glanced down, remembering they needed to put the children to bed. He guessed any other discussion would keep.

About an hour later, with the kids tucked in and two stories told, Clay stood in the doorway with Tally. He put his arm around her waist. "What do you see?"

"Home." She turned, and he noticed the tremble of her chin as she tried to hold back tears. "This is home, and earlier today I didn't think I'd live to see it." She laid her hand on the side of his face, her eyes searching his. "I love you, Clay."

"The feeling is mutual." He kissed her palm. "Want to see our bedroom?"

"Wild horses couldn't keep me from it."

He opened the door to their sanctuary and let her take it all in—from the patchwork quilt on the bed to the soft lamps and the hasty curtains Susan and Belle had hung, the flowers, and the rugs on the floor. She covered her mouth in surprise, her pretty eyes glowing.

She cleared her throat but the words came out raspy. "I don't have words enough to say what this means or how much I love it. How did you do manage all this?"

"I had help and swore everyone to secrecy."

"No, I mean where did you get the money for the furniture and special touches? I thought we were broke."

"We are." He laced his fingers through hers. "I sold some things. Leather goods that were quick to make."

She glanced up, and he fell into her blue eyes. "When? You haven't had time to make anything."

"You forget how long Josie was sick. All those days and nights you were at her side? I kept busy every spare minute when I wasn't working on the buildings. Jack and Ridge took them to Tascosa and sold them." He moved in front of her and took her face between his hands. "I love you so much, and I want to give you everything that makes your life easier."

Lowering his head, he pressed his lips to hers in a long, searing kiss. She melted into him, putting her arms around his waist, her breasts molding to his chest.

He broke the kiss, sweeping her into his arms. He carried her to the bed, setting her on the edge of the feather mattress. "I have one more surprise."

Tally glanced around the room. "No, Clay. This is enough. It's more than enough—I don't need anything else."

"I beg to differ. Besides, I love giving my beautiful wife gifts." He grinned. "Don't steal my pleasure."

"All right, I won't. Where are you hiding this mysterious surprise?"

He reached underneath the bed and brought out a box wrapped in brown paper. A perfect red rose lay on top.

"Oh, Clay." She held the flower to her nose and breathed in the scent.

"The man who delivered all these furnishings brought the rose from his garden. That plus the fact that I almost lost you today made this the perfect time." He sat next to her and jostled her arm. "Aren't you going to open it?"

"Did you know the last time I received a gift wrapped in pretty paper?" Her lip trembled. "It was right before my father died. He gave me a beautiful amethyst necklace. I'm sure Lucinda's sold it by now."

"It doesn't matter. Nothing matters except your happiness and safety."

"You're right of course. I think I'm fine and then another memory pops into my head."

"Getting rid of ghosts takes time." He was an authority on the subject.

Tally unwrapped the box and removed the lid. She froze. Clay waited for her to say something. Did she not like them? Were they all wrong?

She raised her eyes, which were bubbling over with tears. "Oh, Clay. You know exactly what I need."

Without wasting a moment, she lifted out the boots he'd crafted with his own hands and ran her fingers down inside to touch the layer of soft lamb's wool.

He knelt and slipped them on her feet. "How do they feel?"

"Heavenly." She stood, beaming. "It's like I'm walking on a cloud."

"They fit okay?"

"They're perfect in every way. Nothing hurts. You couldn't have given me anything I needed more."

"I got the idea when you told me about your sore feet." Warmth spread through him that she had no pain in the shoes. If he had his way, she'd never have any more. But he knew trouble and sorrow were a part of life. He just prayed the happiness came in greater measure.

Tally threw her arms around him, her fingers tangling in his hair. "You're amazing, and I don't know what I did to deserve someone like you. Thank you for rescuing me today."

"No, lady. You got that wrong. You saved yourself. I was just there to help out."

"I couldn't believe my eyes when I saw you dropping by rope from that bluff like a spider. If Tarver had glanced up, he'd have killed you."

"Only he didn't." He worked at the buttons of her dress and pulled it over her head. One piece of clothing at time found a place on top of the dress in a puddle on the floor until she was naked and barefoot.

He seated her in a chair and collected the bowl of water he'd left sitting on the dresser. Fighting her for the washcloth, he tenderly began washing every bit of dirt and blood from her.

"I can do this, Clay." She reached again for the wet cloth, and he jerked it away.

"Nope. Stop trying to take this from me. Let me wash away every bit of Tarver and make you feel clean again. This is bringing me such pleasure."

"But I'm not an invalid."

"I know. This isn't about that." He finished up. "Now go get in bed, darlin'." He tucked her between the sheets. "Don't go away."

"As if I could. You've probably got the place rigged with steel traps." Her gaze followed him as he undressed and turned down the wick in the lamp. When he finally slid in next to her, she murmured, "It's about time, cowboy. Thank you for my bath."

"It was too late and too dark to go to the outdoor bathing room, so that had to do." Clay gathered her against him. "Tonight, I'm just going to hold you and say thanks for surviving yet another close call. Besides, I don't think you're up for more."

"How did you know?"

"Tiredness in your face gave you away." He rested his chin on top of her head. "Do you really like the boots?"

"I've never had a better gift. I'll shoot anyone who tries to take them." She snuggled into the curve of his body. "I hope Rebel makes it through the night. You should've seen her with that hoe. Tarver almost went to his knees. If I'd gotten my feet to work, I would've run, except I wouldn't have left her there with him."

"All I know is that I'm glad we've seen the last of Slade Tarver."

"Me too. I just feel so sorry for Rebel though. All she wants is another chance and she may have used them all up."

"Something tells me she's going to be all right. We have the best doctor this side of the Mississippi looking after her."

"Yes, we do." Tally glanced up at him. "Clay, I'm sorry

we had cross words before we rode out for Creedmore. You were right."

He was? With her looking at him, the big smile on her face playing havoc with his brain, he couldn't remember what they'd even fought about. "About what, darlin'?"

"I see now that a marriage is give and take, not about who can be boss. I do trust you—with everything." She let out a sigh.

Ahhh. Yes, he remembered now. He lifted her hand to his lips. "My darling wife, I'm happy that you don't see a marriage as an either/or proposition. We'll always be a team, discussing problems, finding solutions together. You're awfully wise and I never want you to keep silent. Say what's on your mind. I may not agree, but I'll always listen." He tightened his arm around her. "I deeply respect you. There are times when you should be the boss."

"Not sure I want that pressure again. I'm glad we sorted that out." She wiggled closer and kissed him.

He breathed in Tally's scent. A man didn't know how long he had left on this earth, but Clay could spend an eternity with his warrior angel and it wouldn't be near long enough.

He kissed the woman who held the keys to his heart and a mist filled his eyes. She was his needle on the compass that would always lead him home, no matter how dark or how stormy the way.

Thirty-nine

TALLY HURRIED TO DR. MARY'S TENT AT FIRST LIGHT TO FIND the doctor scrubbing blood off her hands. "How is Rebel?"

"She lapsed into unconsciousness shortly after you left last evening. The poor thing had a rough night, hovering between this world and the next. A time or two worried me and I don't worry easy. I have a feeling she forced herself to stay awake until she spoke with you." The woman dried her hands.

Tally shook herself from her thoughts. "You don't look like you had a wink of sleep. What can I do?"

"I don't know of anything at the moment. This is a waiting game for now—waiting to see how hard Rebel fights. Waiting for the good Lord to touch her. Waiting for something else to try that I haven't thought of. Just like with Luke's Josie, we have to leave Rebel to God's will."

"Let me sit with her for a while." Tally laid her hand on the doctor's arm. "Get some coffee. Take a walk. You've been so busy with the new ladies you haven't had a moment to yourself."

"I think I might just do that if you're sure you don't mind."

"I insist." Tally gave her a gentle push toward the tent flap. "I'll call if there's any change."

"I'll bring you back a nice cup of tea."

"Thanks, Dr. Mary." Tally sat down next to the cot and took Rebel's hand. She started talking, telling Rebel about Ely and Jenny and how hard they'd taken the news. "You'd better live. You'd better not disappoint those kids."

She listened to the low murmur of voices outside the tent. The day was starting.

"Rebel, I need you. That's right. I need you, and you know why? You showed me what it means to keep pushing forward." Tally smoothed Rebel's hair back from her face.

"Thank you for saving me, but next time, don't fight someone who's holding a gun."

Clay stepped through the tent opening. "The children are still asleep. I brought coffee. Dr. Mary said you're spelling her."

Their hands touched as she took the cup, and she marveled at how strong their connection was. She'd never thought loving someone could be such a powerful force. Her parents had had that kind of marriage, but her father hadn't loved Lucinda. Tally wasn't exactly sure why he'd fallen under Lucinda's spell. Maybe he'd been lonely and thought the woman would be what he needed.

Sometimes people made mistakes they regretted. Not her.

Tally knew her marriage to Clay was the forever kind that was ruled by love and respect.

Clay pulled a chair next to her and took Rebel's limp hand. "How is she?"

"Not good."

"It's early, you know. A wound like hers…it'll take time. I just saw Travis taking Ely to wash. He sure seems to care for those kids." He draped his arm across the back of Tally's chair. She smiled into her cup. It seemed no matter what they were doing, he needed to touch her.

"I'm wearing the new boots and they're every bit as comfortable as they were last night," she murmured. "I never had a pair this good in my life, not even when Father was alive."

"I want my wife to have only the finest."

She'd learned early on there was a lot of difference between *want* and *get*. Sometimes you had to settle for what you could manage. And the fact was, they had very little money. Even if she met with success in taking Lucinda to court, who knew what remained of her father's estate? There could be nothing.

"How soon do you think before we'll hear from Phineas Hargrove?"

"Sweetheart, he just left yesterday morning. I'm sure it'll be at least a month. They have to find a judge to hear the case and schedule a time in his court. Then they have to locate all the witnesses."

"How do you think our luck will be at finding Jude Dominick?"

"Frankly, I think he'll disappear. I hope not, but that tends to be his way." Clay scowled. "I may have to hunt him down, and if I do, he won't look so pretty in court. I don't want you worrying about that. Lucinda is going to get justice. I'll see to it personally."

Tally released a troubled sigh. "I just wish it were all over and done with."

Clay leaned to brush a kiss behind her ear. "It will be soon."

"What if she wins? I don't think I can take that."

"Sweetheart, she won't so put that fear out of your head."

"Have you ever had to stand trial?"

"Yep. Believe me, when it's a hanging offense at stake, things move fast. Outlaws are pretty much judged and convicted before they ever make it to a courtroom. A good friend of mine was caught and hanged in the same day."

"I'm sorry."

"He was a good, decent man who just got mixed up with the wrong people. A husband and father." He lapsed into silence, his features dark and angry.

She wondered how many of his friends had met a similar fate and prayed that Hargrove would be able to get Clay amnesty.

If they didn't, how soon before lawmen caught him? A shudder swept through her. She wouldn't be able to watch him swing from a rope. The terror of the previous few days seemed to turn into that image, watching the man she loved with every piece of her heart, his lean form dangling in the wind—choking, gurgling, struggling to breathe.

❧

The next three weeks passed in a flurry of activity. Clay, Jack, and Ridge escorted the women who wanted to leave Devil's Crossing to the destinations they chose. They'd traded for supplies to stock the mercantile, and the hotel finally opened to visitors.

Rebel steadily improved, much to Tally's delight, and Ely and little Jenny spent many hours with their new prospective mother. Travis took Ely fishing and taught Jenny how to milk the goats. It did Clay's heart good to see his involvement with the orphans. Maybe a wedding was somewhere in the cards.

Clay tried to calm Tally's nerves as best he could, but each day that brought no news from Hargrove, the more tightly wound she became.

A chill filled the air on a late September evening when Clay called everyone to a meeting. They all gathered around the campfire. He raised his hand to silence them. "Just a moment of your time. We have reason to celebrate."

"Yeah, it's cooler weather," Dallas Hawk said to chuckles and amens.

"Well, that too, my brother." Clay turned to Tally. "My wife has an announcement."

"You need a bigger house?" someone asked.

"Not yet." Clay yelled, "Look, I'm going to shoot the next person who interrupts! I don't like it when you won't let Tally speak. Show her some respect." Clay put his hands on her waist and lifted her onto a chair.

"Hi, everyone. As you know, we need a new name for our town." Tally held up a paper with a long list on it. "You've all had your say and some were quite creative. Whoever put in Gunbarrel City and Hanging Hollow, the answer is no. We're proud of what we've accomplished and we want to attract more people instead of drive them away." She reached for Clay's hand. "So, the new name is…Hope's Crossing."

Everyone clapped as Clay lifted her down and he took her place. "Hope's Crossing says we're optimistic and looking forward to a bright, shiny future. It's going to take all of us to make this work. We need every hand, every sharp mind, every able body. Soon we'll have to elect a mayor—"

"I vote for you!" Tobias January hollered.

"Thank you, but no." Clay scanned the faces. "There are a lot of good people in this town who are better at this than I am, and I'll gladly hand over the reins. But be thinking of who you want to lead us. We'll also need a sheriff. I can think of no one better suited than Jack, if he'll take it, but you might have other ideas. Speak up and be heard. That's all for now. Dallas, pull out your fiddle."

Clay put his arms around Tally and Violet, scanning the sea of happy faces as couples paired off. What a difference from when he'd first dreamed of a town where folks could settle and thrive. He didn't regret one minute of the hardship.

Pretty soon, the music seeped into his soul and his leg started twitching. He never had been much of a watcher.

As he set Violet on his boots, he noticed Travis doing the same with little Jenny. The man would make a mighty good father. He looked to be a fast learner and he seemed to adore Rebel, sitting for hours by her side, getting her anything she needed, whispering in her ear.

Maybe life was just learning how to roll with the punches and trying not to get knocked down or step in something.

"Are you happy, baby girl?"

"I'm all full of sunshine, Daddy—except for missing Mr. Montana." She lifted her face to him. "Sometimes I can hear him talking. Do you think he's lonely?"

"Nope. He's too busy trying to tell the angels what to do." Montana Black was going to run the show no matter where he was. But Clay owed him for saving his life and that was a fact.

༄

A young stranger rode in the next morning with a message for Clay and Tally from Phineas Hargrove. Clay laid the leather piece he was working with aside and greeted the lawyer's assistant. He took the young man's horse and led the animal to the water trough, then propped his foot on a rail. "Give me the news. What's the holdup with the trial?"

The man, who still looked to be wet behind the ears, peered at him through a pair of round lenses. "Well, sir, we can't find Jude Dominick. And unless we do, we won't ever have one."

"Figured this would happen. What's your name, son?"

"William."

"Tell me, William, what does Hargrove want me to do?"

"Find him, sir. Mr. Hargrove said you won't fail like others have." William glanced around the town, and to his eyes, there probably wasn't much to look at. He stumbled over his own feet and lowered his voice. "You're an outlaw and I'm guessing all these others are too."

"That's right."

William moved closer. "Outlaws can do things we can't."

Clay threw back his head in laughter. "That's true, as long as we don't get caught." He winked. "Go back and tell Hargrove he'll have his witness, and there's no need to thank me."

"He'll be pleased, sir. And hurry. The trial starts in two weeks."

Not a lot of time, seeing as he'd have to cover half of Texas.

"Then I'd best ride. Help yourself to a meal or whatever else we have. I need to find my wife and get ready to leave." Clay hurried to find Tally.

She was sitting with Rebel. The two women had discovered a great friendship, always doing something together. Still recovering from her bullet wounds, Rebel was able to do very little. Right now, she was brushing little Jenny's hair.

Tally glanced up. "Who was the man who rode in?"

"Works for Hargrove in his practice. Can I speak to you?" Clay took her arm and moved away for privacy, where he told her the news.

Frustration built in her eyes. "I knew something like this was bound to happen."

"Don't worry. I'll find Jude Dominick." And he didn't much care how or what the man would look like after, but he'd haul him in. One way or another.

"What can I do?"

He tucked a strand of loose hair behind her ear. "If you can put together a bit of food, I'll speak to Ridge and saddle up. He'll have to bring you to Fort Worth for the trial. I'm sorry I won't have time to come back and get you."

"Hush with your apologies." She brushed her face against

his hand cupping her jaw. "We'll see each other soon enough, and Ridge is a good choice. He'll be the least likely to draw attention. They'd spot Jack and Dallas right off, and the Januarys are too old."

"I agree." He lowered his head to kiss her waiting mouth.

Hunger swept over him. Damn, he hated to leave her. One taste of Tally had ruined him for spending nights alone. Once this was over, he'd never leave her side.

Someone tugged on his sleeve. He broke the kiss and looked down to find Violet.

"Hey, baby girl. I'm glad you're here." He lifted her up. "I'm going to have to go away for a few days, but it won't be for long. I need you to take care of your mama. Can you do that?"

"I won't let anything happen. If anyone comes, I'll whack him with my stick real good."

Clay lifted an eyebrow at Tally only to get an innocent shrug. "That's my girl. I think your mama's been teaching you some things."

Violet nodded. "Not to cuss, not to be mean, and not to let bad people win."

"That's the spirit." Laughing, he put her down and hurried to Ridge, filling him in. "I'd take it as a favor if you'll bring Tally and meet me in Fort Worth."

"I'll get her there." Ridge met his gaze. "Watch your back. They'll come at you."

"I will."

An hour later, wearing a long black duster, Clay paused at the entrance and waved to Tally. He tucked the image of her pretty face and that glorious smile deep inside his heart.

He needed her like he needed air and sunlight. Unbearable loneliness so thick it strangled him already rode in his saddle.

Forty

CLAY TROTTED INTO ABILENE SIX DAYS LATER AS THE LAST RAYS
of the orange sun slid below the horizon. His black duster was
covered with dirt from the trail and he was worn out and starving. Except for two- or three-hour stretches of sleep a night,
he'd ridden straight through. Sundown was as exhausted as he
was. He patted the paint's thick neck. "We'll rest some here,
boy. You've earned a bucket of oats."

He recalled Jack saying that Jude Dominick once lived in
Abilene and probably still had family. He'd ask around. The
young stable hand at the livery promised to brush the horse
down and feed him, but he didn't know Dominick.

"Mind if I sleep in the loft?" Clay asked.

"Sure, if you don't mind sharing with a couple of snorers."
The boy grinned, showing a large gap in his front teeth. "They's
awful loud." He handed Clay some cotton.

"Great." Clay pinched the bridge of his nose and sighed.
He'd have to make do. As tired as he was, he probably
wouldn't hear an explosion. "How about a place to eat?"

"Two streets over and three doors down. Best food in
town. My grandma runs it."

"Thanks, kid." Clay pitched him two bits. "Do a good job
and there'll be more."

He followed the directions and strolled into Maxine's Café,
his duster slapping against his legs. The place was packed, but
he found a table against the wall and sat down. He soon placed
his order and enjoyed the best steak he'd possibly ever had.

The pretty waitress stopped by and collected his empty
plate. "Any dessert, mister? Granny makes peach cobbler that
will make a grown man weep."

"Sounds good." He gave her a smile. "I'm looking for a
fellow—Jude Dominick. Name sound familiar?"

"He used to come in once in a while, but I haven't seen him since he bought the saloon over at Waco. His kin here all died so he doesn't have a reason to come anymore."

"Thanks. I just wondered is all." Clay ate his peach cobbler and it was every bit as delicious as the waitress had said. Still, it didn't compare to Tally's cooking. He paid his bill and left.

Light, music, and laughter spilled from each saloon he walked past, but he didn't stop. If he didn't keep going, he'd curl up on the sidewalk and sleep. To run into Dominick in his current state of exhaustion would be a foolish move.

Back at the livery, he climbed the ladder to the loft and was out like a light. He dreamed of Tally and dancing with her in the moonlight, her fiery curls spilling onto her creamy shoulders.

A while later, he was aware of others moving about him in the loft and then the god-awful snoring commenced. Clay stuck the cotton in his ears but that helped very little. He finally rose and went to sleep with his horse. Sundown didn't snore—too much.

Clay missed home, his wife, and his daughter. Hope's Crossing seemed a million miles away.

❧

The clock was ticking in Clay's head as he donned his long duster and rode out of Abilene, racing toward Waco. Breakfast filled his belly, and a canteen of water hanging from the saddle horn would have to last until he reached a water hole.

With the brim of his hat providing the only shade, the fall Texas sun drained him of energy and sweat soaked his shirt. He kept a wary eye out for lawmen—he'd have to until, hopefully, Hargrove obtained amnesty for him. Not having to look over his shoulder… Well, he rightly wouldn't know what freedom of that nature would be like, but he couldn't wait to see.

Each time he rode out, he knew his chances of coming back got a little slimmer.

Tally was far too young to be a widow.

Clay kept off the beaten path and used caution through the

narrow places. Soon he arrived at a small stream and stopped to let Sundown drink. Clay stretched out on his belly and scooped cool, fresh water into his mouth. He rose and sat down under a spindly tree to think.

Logic told him that since Lucinda knew what was in the air, Dominick would be staying far away from the Crystal Palace and from Waco in general. Where would he have gone until everything died down?

He wasn't too familiar with the man or his habits and had just had the one run-in at the saloon a while back. But he knew how men like him thought. Outlaws didn't go near family or people they didn't trust, but according to the waitress, Dominick's kin had passed on.

No, the man would hole up in a hideaway, someplace he'd set up long before. And who better to know where that might be than some of Dominick's cronies?

The decision made and his horse rested, he left the water hole at a gallop. He had no time to waste. Only one week remained to find the man and get to the trial in Fort Worth. A knot grew in his stomach. That would cut it too close.

If he failed, if this long shot didn't pay off, if everyone refused to talk…

A million ifs. He ran a hand over his weary eyes and blew out a worried breath.

The evening was late when he trotted into Waco four days after leaving Abilene. Dirt and sweat covered Sundown, and the horse needed hay and water, so Clay left him at a livery and walked to the nearby saloon.

The Crystal Palace was doing a booming business, judging from the noise. His duster slapped his legs like claps of distant thunder as he pushed through the doors and strode to the long oak bar.

"Beer," he told the barkeep. He'd get the lay of the land before asking about the man's boss.

While the barkeep filled a mug, Clay took his measure. Probably late forties, with beady eyes under a shock of graying hair that he'd parted in the middle and combed to each side.

He slid the mug in front of him. Clay took it and turned to scan the crowded room. Spying one small table in a corner, he headed that way and sat with his back against the wall.

"Hey, sugar, you look mighty lonely." The saloon girl with her reddish-blond hair had a honeyed voice that could draw a whole swarm of bees. "Care for some company?"

"Don't mind if I do." Clay put an arm around her and pulled out a chair at the table. "What would you like to drink? I'll get it."

"Whiskey."

In a few minutes, he was back and sat down. He raised his beer. "Here's to you, miss."

"You can call me Marta, sugar."

Clay leaned closer. "Marta, that's a right pretty name."

"My grandmother's." She patted her hair. "You passing through?"

"Yep. Looking for Dominick. Have a business proposition. Know where I can find him?"

"No." She stood, her face darkening. "If that's the only reason you're being nice, I have paying customers who need me."

Clay watched her make the rounds at the tables. Soon, another saloon girl approached him. She claimed not to know any more than Marta. It was getting late and he was about to leave when he got his first nibble. A plump working girl sat down next to him. After making small talk, he got to the question.

"I haven't seen him in a week or so. Why are you looking for him?" she asked.

He told her Dominick had offered him a job.

The woman leaned closer. "I keep my nose to myself. Healthier that way. Your best bet is to find Amanda. She sometimes hears things. I hope you get what you're after, cowboy."

After sitting there another hour, Clay was ready to leave when a young woman appeared at his elbow. He started to send her away but saw sadness in her scared eyes. She was a child, only about fifteen if she was a day, and sure as hell didn't belong in a place like this.

He rose. "Care to sit a spell?"

"I'm Amanda." She sat in the chair he pulled out for her. "I haven't seen you around before."

"Just passing through."

"What brings you to Waco?"

"Looking for someone." He sipped his beer and propped an elbow on the table. "You're awful young to work in a place like this."

"Well, you know what they say—everybody has a story. You don't want to hear mine." Desperation and misery on her face made him think she was yearning for a bit of kindness.

"Actually, I would. How about something to drink?"

"Sure." Her dress had fallen off her shoulders and she tugged it up, as though embarrassed to be wearing it.

Clay motioned to the barkeep to bring two more beers, then turned back to her. "Maybe you can help me. I'm looking for Jude Dominick."

Amanda scooted back, her eyes filled with terror. "I don't know where he is. I'm paid not to know."

"Hey, I understand. But if he's here, I'd like to ask for a job."

The barkeep brought two more mugs and plopped them down, sloshing beer all over the table and giving the pair of them an evil eye. Then he turned around and stomped back to the bar.

She lowered her voice. "You don't want to work here. This is a bad place and Dominick has a mean temper. A few weeks ago, I watched him kill a man, out in the alley."

Nothing surprised Clay. "You should've told the sheriff."

"The law can't touch him. He's too smart and always keeps an alibi handy—someone who'll lie for him." Amanda shook her head. "It's better for my health if I don't see nothing, hear nothing, or say nothing."

"My wife would like you." Clay leaned forward and touched her arm. "Her stepmother put her in Creedmore to get rid of her."

"I heard the place burned down."

"I made sure it did." He rested his elbows on the table and leaned closer. "She suffered a great deal of pain in there. Now, we're taking the stepmother to court. We really need your help. If I don't find Dominick soon, the judge will throw out the case. Lucinda Shannon will get off scot-free, and who knows what she'll try next."

"So, you're not really here looking for a job?"

"No. Dominick has information we need." Clay finished his beer. "But that's all right. I'll find another way. I won't put you in danger." He reached for his hat.

"Wait." She clutched his arm. "He has a hideout and he took me there once. I'll tell you where it is if you take me with you. Please don't leave me here."

Everything stilled inside Clay. "Are you being held against your will?"

She nodded. "His lackeys kidnapped me and he says I have to work off my father's debt."

That was the Jude Dominick he knew—the lying, cheating, murdering bastard. Fury rushed through him.

"The big bear of a man at the end of the bar is watching us," Clay said low. "Pretend we're just having a good time. When I get up, slip your arm around me. I'll put on a good show of lusting after you and say I'm taking you to my hotel room."

"I hope this works or I'm dead."

"Relax and trust me." Clay rose and pulled her close. He nuzzled behind her ear and slid a hand down her body. "I'm paying for you the entire night, sweetheart," he said loudly, slapping her on the rear.

"The whole night, handsome? That'll cost you a lot of money," she purred, running a fingernail down the front of his shirt. She slid her other arm around his waist and held tight.

"I got plenty for a wildcat like you, sweetheart." He lowered his voice. "Okay, here we go, Amanda. Don't stop for anything and keep laughing."

Clay weaved between the tables, anchoring her to his side. She clung, laughing her head off along with him. They almost made it to the batwing doors before the big bartender yelled for Clay to stop. He kept striding forward until the man planted himself in front of him, blocking the exit.

The brute's arms were almost as big around as tree trunks. Clay sized up his opponent and decided he'd opt for a bullet instead of a fistfight. "Hey, me and this sweet little Amanda are going to my hotel room right down the street. She's going to show me a good time. Aren't you, sweetheart?"

"I shore am, handsome." She plastered herself against him.

"She's not allowed to leave. If you want her, you use the rooms upstairs." The man tried to wrench Amanda away and told her to get back to work.

Clay yanked back his duster, drew his Remington, and jammed it into the man's stomach. "Step aside or take a bullet," he barked.

The bodyguard slowly moved aside, his dark, glittering eyes promising death. "Better watch your back, mister."

"I always do." Clay moved past the huge mountain of muscle and guided Amanda onto the boardwalk. "Keep walking fast." He kept his gun trained on Dominick's hired man until they reached the café next door. He shoved his revolver into his holster, hurried her inside, navigating the tables to the kitchen, and went out the back door.

They weaved through the town until he knew he'd lost anyone following. He turned to Amanda. "Where can I take you?"

"I don't dare go to my family or the few friends I have. That's where they'll look first."

"Then you'll stay with me. I'll find us a place to sleep." If only Sundown wasn't in such dire need of rest. But he wouldn't kill the animal by riding him out again so soon. "How far can you walk in those shoes?"

She glanced up and he saw strength and determination in her eyes. "As far as you need me to."

"All right. We'll walk out to the edge of town and try to find shelter." He explained about his horse's exhaustion. "In the morning, I'll come in before dawn, get Sundown and whatever else we need. How far away is Dominick's location?"

She wiped rouge off her face. "About ten miles due north. The cabin is well hidden."

North was good. That would put him closer to Fort Worth and with a mere four days left before the trial...

Doubt turned his blood cold. What if he didn't make it? What if Tally didn't get justice because of him? Ice crawled up his spine. Clay rubbed the back of his neck. He could not, would not let down the woman he loved.

He moved Amanda off the road into the brush. By the time they made it beyond the lights of town, she had started limping and slowing down. He'd had to stop and wait a few times and finally gave in and carried her. He scanned the area, thankful for the moon's light. A rocky formation ahead should offer some type of cover. A few minutes later, he lowered her underneath a small outcropping hidden by brush. Not ideal, but it would have to do.

The thin dress she wore offered little in the way of warmth. He shrugged out of his duster and draped it around her.

Amanda smiled up at him. "Thanks."

"We might as well get comfortable." He sat with his back against the rock wall and put an arm around her trembling shoulders. "Try to get some sleep."

"When you strolled into the saloon tonight, I knew I could trust you. You have kind eyes, not hard like most men I see there." She leaned back to look up at him. "I tried once before to ask for help, only the bastard told Dominick and it went real, real bad for me."

"I'm sorry." Clay could just imagine. He'd protect her with his life.

She snuggled into the duster. "I heard some things that might interest you."

Clay's ears perked up. "What things?"

"Lucinda Shannon, only her name back then was Kirkpatrick. She used to work at the Crystal Palace, and from what I hear, she and Dominick have been lovers for a long while. A friend of mine there said she overheard them plotting to get her married to Mr. Shannon and take everything he had. She also said Cormick Shannon frequented the saloon and that's where Lucinda met him."

"Very interesting indeed. Does this friend have a name? Where can I find her?" If they could get her to testify, that would give them a rock-solid case.

"I don't know if she'll talk. She's really scared."

"It doesn't hurt to ask. If she says no, I'll disappear and she'll never see me again."

"Okay. Her name is Kate Marshall. She works at the Crystal Palace, but now you'll never be able to get inside to even talk to her. They'll kill you if you show your face back in there."

"I'll manage something." The muscle in Clay's jaw tightened. He'd face a firing squad to talk to Kate Marshall. Early tomorrow would be the best time. After that, he'd ride to Dominick's hideout. He pulled his hat over his eyes. "Get some sleep. We'll need it."

"Your wife is a lucky woman," Amanda murmured, laying her head on Clay's shoulder.

"No, you're wrong. I'm the lucky one."

There was a time when he'd have been tempted to offer Amanda more than a shoulder, but Tally was the only woman who interested him now.

Clay listened to the night creatures pawing around for food and thought of his warrior angel. He couldn't wait to see her, to feel her sweet lips, her body moving against him.

He'd crawl through a mile of cactus to get to her.

But would he survive to make it to Fort Worth?

Forty-one

THE CRYSTAL PALACE APPEARED LIKE A SILENT TOMB IN THE early morning light. Clay climbed up a back trellis to an upstairs window that Amanda had said opened into a hallway. He carefully maneuvered himself inside without too much noise.

The carpet runner down the center of the hall muffled his footsteps. He paused in front of the second room on the right. As he raised his hand to knock, a man hollered from below. "Who's up there?" He froze, his heart racing. When no one answered, someone, probably the guard, began to climb the stairs.

Clay quickly glanced for a place to hide but found nothing. The heavy steps approached the top. Dammit to hell! He slid his gun from the holster, ready to use it if he had to. Holding his breath, he turned the knob of Kate's door, praying it wasn't locked. It swung open on rusty hinges. He slid inside and eased it shut just as the man stomped onto the landing.

"I said who's sneaking around up here? Martha? Kate? Jolene? Answer me, dammit."

His breath suspended in his chest, Clay moved into the deeper shadows. He hunkered down low against the wall just in case the guard looked inside. The man went the length of the upstairs, opening each door. When he got to Kate's, Clay held the knob so it wouldn't turn and would appear locked. After a moment, the guard grunted, then left.

The breath Clay had been holding rushed out. He stood, glancing around the room. The lowered window shades blocked the light of the rising sun. The sleeping form had to be Kate Marshall. She hadn't stirred. He tiptoed toward the bed, hating to wake her but knowing he must. He put his hand over her mouth as a precaution.

She came instantly awake, struggling against him.

"Shhh, I'm not here to harm you. Amanda sent me. I'm Clay and I'll remove my hand if you promise not to scream."

Kate nodded and Clay released her. "What do you want? Where's Amanda?"

"She's safe. I just want to talk, hopefully appeal to your sense of justice."

"There ain't any of that left." She rose and slipped a filmy wrap over her equally thin nightgown. "Amanda did a foolish thing, leaving here last night with you. It's going to get her killed."

"Staying will get her—and you—killed. Nowhere in Waco guarantees living." Clay relayed everything that Amanda had shared, as well the details of the upcoming trial. He ended with, "My wife and I need you to testify to what you know."

"Colby, if I go within ten miles of that courtroom, I'm dead." Kate paced back and forth in front of him. The guard would return any second—the noise she was making assured it.

"Please, can you sit? I'd rather not draw the guard back up here."

She pulled a key from her pocket. "Better lock the door."

While Clay obliged, she went to a decanter on a table and poured herself a jigger of whiskey, tossing it back. Then she came back to the bed and sat down. The lines of her once-beautiful face were set, a dark bruise covering one cheek.

Clay knelt in front of her. "I'll protect you. I'm going to drag Dominick before that judge, no matter how I have to do it. You and Amanda can come by a separate way."

Kate glanced around the sparse room in which only a few personal belongings were in view. "I didn't choose this life. I hate selling my body, men taking piece after piece of me until I have nothing left." Her voice lowered to a whisper. "Everything is gone."

"How did you wind up here?"

"My folks died, leaving me with a sickly brother. I had to provide for him somehow, and no one else would give me the time of day. He passed on several years ago, but by then, Dominick refused to let me go."

Clay thought of Rebel. "It's never too late for change."

"And what would I do?" She snorted quietly. "Who would hire someone like me? This is all I've ever known."

"You need to talk to my wife." Clay rose and sat down beside her. "Doing the right thing can set you free of these chains and help you reclaim yourself."

The door suddenly rattled. Both of them jumped. Clay was glad he'd locked it. He'd been so intent on what Kate was saying, he hadn't paid attention to noises outside the room. He slid his gun from the holster and moved to one side of the door.

"Kate, what are you doing in there? Why is this door locked?" the guard yelled.

"I'm sick, you bastard," she moaned. "Don't come in. I'm throwing up. You'll step in it."

"Is anyone in there with you? I heard voices."

"No, George. Oh God, I'm sick. I think I'm dying. Get the doctor." She let out several moans and the footsteps faded. Clay assumed he went downstairs.

"Please, we don't have much time. Get dressed and come with me, Kate. Take this chance that I'm offering. You *can* have a better life. What do you really have worth staying for?"

"All right, you've convinced me."

He listened at the door while she quickly pulled on some clothes, then dragged a worn carpetbag from beneath the bed and began stuffing various and sundry items into it.

Once she was done, Clay grabbed the bag and eased out into hallway, listening to the voices below. "Come on, we have to hurry."

The words no sooner left his mouth than she moved past him. Clay hurried her to the window, tossing out the carpetbag. In no time, they were on the ground and running to the horses. Kate mounted the one he'd gotten for Amanda. He had barely swung into the saddle of the other before George leaned from the open window, firing shots.

Bullets peppered the ground around them. The horses took off at a gallop, their long strides eating up the ground. Within a short time, Clay and Kate reined up where he'd left Amanda. The two women embraced.

"I hoped you'd come," Amanda said. "They really need your help."

"Wasn't easy. I had to do some persuading." Clay reached into his saddlebags for the breakfast he'd bought, handing biscuits and slab bacon to the women. "Eat up. We should get far away from here. Amanda, draw me a map to Dominick's cabin. I'll go there while you both head for Fort Worth. When you arrive, find Phineas Hargrove and he'll take care of your needs."

He scribbled on a piece of paper and handed it to Kate. "Give this to him." Clay took a bite of bacon. "Amanda, when this is over, I'll get you and your family safe. I won't forget what you've done for us."

"Sometimes you just have to take a chance. I'm glad I did." Amanda's smile conveyed deep gratitude.

Kate tugged her hair down around her face to hide her bruised cheek. "I'm not a bit sorry for coming. I'll tell that judge all about Jude Dominick and anything else he wants to know."

"I appreciate it more than I can say." Clay washed his food down with water, wishing for a hot cup of coffee. He fished three silver dollars from his pocket and handed the money to Kate. "This should get you by until you reach Fort Worth."

Amanda set her food aside and drew a map, handing it to Clay. "Follow this and you'll find him."

"Thanks." He nodded, sticking it inside his shirt. In no time, he slipped into his duster and helped them onto the extra horse. "Head straight north and keep a sharp eye out for trouble. Ride steady and you should get there in a day and a half easy. Be careful."

"You too." Kate leaned down to shake Clay's hand. "I have no regrets."

With parting waves, they left. Clay watched until the two women vanished from sight, then turned down his own trail in the direction Amanda's map indicated. Since the guard from the saloon would certainly have hightailed it out to inform Dominick of the two escapees, Clay avoided the well-traveled path, opting instead to navigate through tangled vines, briar patches, and thick saplings.

The sun was high in the sky by the time the run-down cabin came into view. He tied Sundown a short distance back and moved closer on foot, taking cover in the brush.

The door opened and a shirtless Jude Dominick stepped out. The man's hair hung to his shoulders and he had a gun strapped low around his hips. Thick arm and chest muscles said he did more than push paper and order supplies for a saloon. That didn't concern Clay though—getting him to Fort Worth did.

He drew his weapon and was about to order Dominick to raise his hands when a rider galloped up in a cloud of dust. Clay faded back into the trees, recognizing the guard he'd tangled with.

"What are you doing here, George?" Dominick growled. "Someone could've followed you."

"I was careful. Trouble in town, boss. Kate and Amanda are both gone."

"What do you mean 'gone'?"

"Some tough fellow came in last night and Amanda must've spilled everything. All I know is he drew his gun and forced his way past me." George mopped his forehead. "I didn't recognize him, but I could tell he was a desperado and had experience with weapons. Had this hardness in his eyes."

"So, you just stood there twiddling your thumbs while he waltzed right past you with our merchandise."

Clay grinned. Dominick was ready to swallow a horned toad backward. Angry men grew careless.

"Boss, he had this long-barreled gun out and stuck in my belly before I could draw a breath. I ain't gonna die for those whores. So I moved aside." George rested his considerable weight on a porch support with one hand. Dominick knocked it away, making the man jump back.

"By God, George, you'd better get to talking. What

happened to Kate? Did she just pack up and march out? Or did this desperado you're so afraid of come back?"

"He came back this morning—alone. Climbed the flower thingamajig out back and slipped in upstairs." George told about Kate pretending to be sick and then described her crawling out the window with the same stranger. "I did all I could. Woke up the whole blamed town, shootin' at 'em."

"Hell and be damned! While you're here bellyaching to me about it, this desperado is probably getting the rest of my girls out."

"No, he's not. I locked 'em in the cellar where we keep the beer kegs."

"At least you did one thing right."

"You know, I don't have to take this." George marched to his horse. "I quit. Find yourself another poor bastard to take your abuse. You never paid nothing to start with." He stuck one foot in the stirrup and turned. "You might just have to find another hidin' place after I tell that lawyer who's looking for you where you're at."

Dominick drew his pistol and fired three shots into George. The large bodyguard plunged to the dirt and breathed his last. Clay could dredge up little sympathy for the man.

Smoke still curled from the end of Dominick's pistol when Clay stepped out with gun drawn. "Toss the weapon!"

The killer jerked, his eyes glittering stones. "I knew George was followed."

Clay moved forward. "I said throw the gun aside or you'll join your friend."

The surly saloon owner finally dropped his Colt. "Who are you? Have we met?"

"Once. Recall Clay Colby?"

"Hell! I should've killed you that day."

"I reckon so. I'm here to take you to Fort Worth for Lucinda Shannon's trial. You're going to tell them about the plot you and she cooked up, and the killings that went with it."

"That's a lie," Dominick spat. "You don't have any witnesses. No one will believe Tally. She's gone crazy."

"That's where you're wrong. She has an excellent memory, she's sane as any of us, and she's now my wife." With his pistol trained on his quarry, Clay took some piggin' strings from the pommel of George's horse.

"You'll never get me there," Dominick spewed. "I'll kill you the first mile."

"Way I see it, you're in no position to make claims. Or threats." Clay poked him with his gun. "Get on the horse."

Dark, sullen eyes glared, revealing the depth of the saloon owner's hate. He stuck one foot in the stirrup and whirled, delivering a jarring strike to Clay's cheek, jerking his head back. Into the saddle he vaulted, spurring the animal into a gallop.

Clay swung his gun up and fired at the fleeing witness, attempting only to wound. They needed him alive. His bullet struck the saloon owner's arm, but Dominick didn't slow. Clay raced toward the spot where he'd left Sundown, untied the gelding, and took out after his quarry. As he rode, he wrapped the extra piggin' rope around his pommel, praying he'd get a chance to use it. He'd tie Dominick's hands so tight he'd have trouble picking up a bottle of whiskey.

They rode through heavily vegetated land with mountain cedar and oak trees scattered across the rolling hills. The time Clay wasted in getting to Sundown was made up in having the better animal. The dun cob horse of George's was beginning to slow. No use in wasting lead and risk killing Dominick— Sundown was reeling him in like a fish on a hook.

Dominick turned around at one point to check how close Clay was...and missed seeing the low-hanging branch. He flew from the saddle and lay gasping in the dirt, unable to draw air into his lungs. Clay leaped from the paint, piggin' string clutched tight. He rolled the saloon owner over and tied his hands.

"All right, take it easy," Dominick protested. "Watch my arm."

Clay slowed his stampeding heart and yanked him up. "I've bled more shaving myself. Quit whining or I'll shoot you again."

He threw the man back on the dun and tied his hands to the pommel.

"You're a sonofabitch, Colby, you know that?"

"It's men like you who taught me to be. Do us both a favor and shut up." Clay grabbed the dun's reins and swung onto his paint.

They rode until twilight, stopping only to rest the horses and relieve themselves. Dominick bellyached the whole way about this, that, and the other. Clay pulled up next to a stream, keeping one eye on his prisoner. He didn't trust the man and knew one slip would be all it took for him to get away. Those dark, sullen eyes followed his every move.

Waiting.

Studying.

Watching.

He untied Dominick's hands and yanked him from the horse. He took his rope and made a loop on the ground. "Step into it."

"Make me."

"I reckon you come from Missouri." Clay adopted a calm tone to hide the anger boiling inside.

"What do you mean by that?"

"They raise nothing but corn, Cain, and cockleburs. And their mules have to be shown how to behave." In a lightning flash, Clay stuck his gun between Dominick's mutinous eyes. "I won't tell you again."

Biting back the angry words he obviously itched to say, the man stepped into the loop. Clay pulled the rope tight around his legs, then flipped him onto his stomach and pulled the end up, tying his hands. Trussed up like a fat sow, Dominick couldn't sit up or roll over.

Satisfied with his handiwork, Clay pulled his rifle from the paint's scabbard and went hunting for game. Dominick's angry glare followed Clay to the edge of the clearing and then again an hour later when he returned with a mess of quail. He could imagine how it irked the man to be hog-tied and helpless. Ignoring his prisoner, he made a fire and cleaned the birds.

"I'm hungry, Colby." Dominick wiggled around for a better view.

"Open your mouth and a bug might crawl in. Several might fill you. Or at least shut you up." Clay slid the quail onto some hastily made skewers and propped them over the fire.

"My arm hurts too. Ain't you even gonna wash it? I could die from lead poisoning and there would go your trial. Lucinda would get off and poor, sweet Tally would be up a creek." Jude Dominick eyed him. "Look, I'll dicker with you."

"Why should I? I'm holding all the cards. What can you offer that I don't have?"

"How about me spilling my guts to the judge? Untie me and I'll swear to tell everything."

"I like my chances." Clay leaned against a tree stump and pulled his hat over his eyes.

"Go to hell, sonofabitch."

Now there were the true colors shining through. The man might as well get ready to spend the night in his predicament. By this time tomorrow, they'd be in Fort Worth. Clay couldn't wait to kiss Tally. It seemed like they'd been apart a year, and he was anxious for her smile and to see those pretty winter-blue eyes he loved.

After they put Lucinda and Dominick away, she'd have lots more reasons for real smiles. Come hell or high water, he *would* put them behind bars—either in Fort Worth or Hope's Crossing. Make no mistake about that.

Even if he had to build his own damn jail. Better yet, drop them in a deep hole and place a piece of weighted wood over the top.

Forty-two

Jude Dominick was gone.

Clay forced his eyes open wide and reached for his gun. His Remington was gone too. His heart sank. Dawn's thin light revealed the rope laying on the ground, but no prisoner. He jumped to his feet and hurried to the horses. Both mounts had vanished as well.

Damn Mondays!

From the jumble of boot- and hoofprints, Dominick had ridden west. Maybe if Clay hurried, he could catch the man. He went back to look at the ropes. They'd been cut—sawed through with a sharp rock that lay inches away. It would've taken him all night.

But when could he have picked up the rock?

Clay thought back. It had to be when he'd untied Dominick to let him eat. He'd washed the gunshot wound then and let him relieve himself. This is what he got for caring even a little about that low-down bastard.

Hell and be damned!

Clay struck out after his quarry. Sundown would balk—at least he was counting on it. The paint didn't like other men to ride him. Once Clay had a horse under him, it would be a matter of time before he caught up to the man.

A clock ticked in his head. He had to get Dominick to Fort Worth before court let out.

But two hours later, he was sweating under the scorching sun, his feet aching, his mouth as dry as a shriveled turnip. He couldn't go on like this. He had to find water.

A little farther, down in a draw, he spotted a narrow creek. Clay stumbled down to it, fell on his belly, and gulped his fill. A noise that was completely out of place reached him. He rose and followed the nickering to find Sundown, calmly nibbling on some rye grass.

This changed things. Maybe the horse had given Dominick trouble, or maybe he'd broken free. Clay wasn't about to spend time wondering. Three long strides took him to the horse. He stepped into the saddle and took off, following Dominick's tracks. He yanked his rifle from the scabbard, thankful to have an equalizer.

The gelding raced up a hill and the scene that met Clay's eyes gave him a jolt. *Dominick.* He spurred Sundown and they flew across the ground. His quarry saw him and tried to get his nag to go faster, but the plow horse was already moving at top speed.

Coming alongside, Clay leaped onto the man and they tumbled to the ground. Clay knocked the gun from his hands and delivered a punishing blow to his jaw, then another to his stomach.

Dominick kicked him backward into a cactus bed. Hundreds of needles pricked him, drawing blood. Clay ignored the stinging pain and rose, ramming his head into the man, knocking him away from the gun on the ground that glinted in the sun.

Both men breathed hard, trading blows. Clay jabbed him in the ribs with an elbow and brought an arm down on the back of Dominick's neck. Then, he pummeled his fists into the man's gut and face until finally the saloon owner collapsed in the dirt.

"Get up!" Clay grabbed Dominick's shirt, only to have it tear apart in his hands.

The bastard scrambled away and took off running. Clay tackled him, sat on his back, and put an arm around his neck.

Yanking his head backward, Clay yelled, "Stop or I'll kill you right here. Then you won't have to worry about a judge or a trial."

Finally, Dominick went limp. "You win."

His breath coming in harsh gasps, Clay wiped blood from his mouth and shoved Dominick toward the dun. "Get on."

Clay was a bloody mess, one sleeve hung by a thread, and he was sorely out of patience. The clock in his head ticked as he tied Dominick's hands extra tight to the pommel. They couldn't make it in time. Fort Worth was too far.

Still, he'd get the man there and pray that somehow, someway, he wasn't too late.

∽✦∾

Tally took Ridge's arm and hurried toward court. Thoughts tumbled this way and that, and she was worried that Clay hadn't made it. If she should lose him... But she wouldn't. She thrust her shoulders back. They'd win this suit and go home to Hope's Crossing.

A woman stepped into her path. *Lucinda.* She should've expected a confrontation.

"I'm going to expose you for a liar," Lucinda snarled. "After I get through with you, you'll be lucky to have one friend." Lucinda gave Ridge a once-over, curling her lip. "You always have to have a man, and it doesn't matter much to you which one it is."

Tally shook with anger, but she would rise above her dear stepmother's level. "Step aside, please."

"Or what? Will you draw a gun and shoot me like you killed the others?"

Ridge grabbed her arm. "Move or else you might find yourself facedown in the dirt."

"Get your hands off me!"

A crowd was gathering and the last thing Tally wanted was a public airing of their differences. She leaned closer, putting her nose next to Lucinda's. "I asked you politely to move. I'll not say it again. I'm going to win and take every single thing you own. I have justice on my side. What do you have except killers?"

"You're the one who killed your poor father!" Lucinda screamed. "You gave him that poison. You were livid because he married me. So you made sure he paid."

Rage swept through Tally. She drew back her hand and struck Lucinda's cheek as hard as she could. The slap sounded like a rifle shot and the crowd rushed for her. Ridge grabbed her elbow and half carried her inside the doors.

Tally sagged against Ridge. "What have I done?" Had she just given Lucinda the ammunition she'd searched for?

Tally swiveled in her seat next to Phineas Hargrove and glanced toward the door, hoping Clay would stride though any minute. What if Jude Dominick had killed him? She couldn't bear to live without Clay's light. She'd sink into darkness.

Ridge sat at the back, his hat lowered to avoid recognition. She knew the danger she'd thrust him into but was grateful he was there. He gave her a slight nod of encouragement.

Clinging to the strength she found in the former preacher's gaze, she turned back to face the imposing judge. He was a tall, distinguished man, and she imagined that she could see fairness in his kind eyes. That was more than she'd hoped for. She inhaled a calming breath and readied for whatever the trial might bring. Right now, she feared the presiding judge would throw the case out unless Dominick arrived. Where was Clay?

How could they proceed without Dominick's testimony?

Called to order for a mere five minutes, and already her case was in jeopardy.

Lucinda smirked at her from her seat at the defense table, quite satisfied with what had occurred outside, sure she'd won.

Hargrove's chair screeched on the floor as he slid it back and stood. "Your honor, I'd like to request a short delay. One of our witnesses isn't here yet."

"Sorry, counselor. Either present your case or we leave." The judge banged his gavel.

"Very well. I'd like to call Kate Marshall."

A woman that Tally had only met briefly before the trial got to her feet, and Lucinda let out a sharp curse. Tally really had no clue as to what Kate might say but only knew from Hargrove that the woman had damaging information. She prayed it would be enough.

Kate sat in the witness box, stated her name, and swore to tell the truth.

"Now, Miss Marshall, do you work at the Crystal Palace?"

She glanced at Lucinda and raised her chin in defiance. "Used to, sir, until two days ago when Clay Colby helped me escape."

A lump rose in Tally's chest. Clay was that kind of man. Maybe Kate knew what happened to him. She'd ask when the judge dismissed them.

"Clarify that, please."

"I, along with other women, was held against my will by Jude Dominick."

Tally gasped. Kate's story was so like her own. Maybe Jude was a friend of Slade Tarver. They almost had to have known each other, and it explained how Dominick knew to take her there.

"Miss Marshall, do you know Lucinda Shannon… I believe her former name was Kirkpatrick?"

"We worked together for about a year."

Tally shifted her focus to Lucinda. Her stepmother was slumped in her chair, her face ashen, picking at her nails. From Lucinda's reaction, whatever was about to come out seemed to be something she didn't want known.

Hargrove paced back and forth. "What was her association with Jude Dominick?"

"They were lovers. Lucinda spent a great deal of time in his bed."

Shock raced through Tally. No wonder Dominick had showed up at her father's house and helped her with her evil plan. It all made sense now. The many hours together, Lucinda's locked bedroom, Dominick wearing her father's suits.

Lucinda jumped to her feet. "That's a bald-faced lie!"

The judge banged his gavel. "Sit down, madam!"

Clenching her hands, Lucinda dropped into her seat and whispered something to her attorney.

Phineas Hargrove removed his frock coat and draped it over a chair, then mopped his forehead. "It's a hot day. Now,

Miss Marshall, I believe you overheard many conversations between Lucinda Kirkpatrick and Jude Dominick. Tell us about those."

"Shortly after Mr. Cormick Shannon became a regular at the Palace, I heard Lucinda and Dominick talk about ways to get her married to the man. Other conversations were about what they'd do once she became Cormick's wife, how they'd take everything he had—his money, his land, and his life."

"Lies!" Lucinda shouted. "All lies. I never said any such thing. I loved Cormick Shannon. I slept by his side, nursed him when he was sick. I buried him and tried my best to care for his daughter."

Tally gripped the table edge so hard it left an imprint on her palm. It took everything she had to remain silent and in her chair.

"Sit down!" the judge ordered Lucinda. "Take your seat or I'll order you to jail."

With arms folded across her chest, Lucinda sank down next to her lawyer, who was scribbling furiously. Worry slid along Tally's spine. The truth was coming out but so were the lies.

Which would the judge believe?

After several more questions, Lucinda's lawyer got his turn. "Miss Marshall, isn't it true that you didn't like my client and were jealous of her—that you wanted Jude Dominick for yourself? That you'd be willing to say anything to hurt her, even tell vicious lies?"

Tally prayed that Kate stayed strong and wouldn't be intimidated by the lawyer's dark demeanor and loud accusations.

"It's true I never liked Lucinda, but I abhor Jude Dominick with every fiber of my being. Many times he tried to force me into his bed, putting his hands on me, kissing me against my will." Kate's hand visibly shook as she pushed back her hair. "Everything I've said is the truth about my boss and I have witnesses."

The courtroom was silent. Lucinda's face was stone cold, her eyes glittering with hate.

Lucinda's lawyer badgered Kate for what seemed like hours,

but the woman didn't veer from her story. Tally liked her for standing up and being heard. It had to be terrifying. Kate had to be scared of being silenced—permanently—just as Tally's father and brother and so many others had been.

But unless Clay showed up with Dominick, and Dominick testified, they didn't have any rock-solid proof. Just Kate's word against Lucinda's.

Each time the door opened, Tally swung around, hoping and praying to see Clay.

Maybe he'd been unable to find Dominick. Maybe he was lying somewhere, injured and bleeding. She stilled.

Or maybe Jude Dominick had killed him.

After Kate Marshall left the witness box, the judge turned to Phineas. "Do you have other witnesses?"

He called Tally next. "Mrs. Colby, please tell the court what you saw your stepmother do with your own eyes."

"The threats started immediately after marrying my father." Tally told about Lucinda's ruining her and Brady's food, ripping up their clothes, and taking whatever she wanted from their rooms. "She wrenched my arm and said she could make life extremely miserable for me." Tally smiled at the judge. "I'm not very biddable. I meticulously recorded everything she did in a journal, but I'm sure she long destroyed that account. About two weeks following my father's marriage to Lucinda, he became very ill. He was a robust rancher who'd never been sick a day in his life. In a week's time, he had become a frail ghost of a man." Her voice lowered. "He died a week later."

"And then what?"

"Jude Dominick appeared. He and Lucinda would hole up in my father's office for hours. I saw them kissing several times."

Hargrove glanced at his notes. "What did you think about that?"

"Objection!" the defense attorney shouted.

"Withdrawn." Hargrove smiled. "What else did you observe?"

"Dominick spending the night in Lucinda's bedroom, for

one. They were as thick as thieves and I warned Brady to watch out. But a few days later, workers also found him dead. The doctor said he'd fallen and been trampled by horses. He had broken his spine in several places."

"But you didn't believe that, Mrs. Colby?"

"No. I knew Dominick had somehow arranged his death. Brady was an excellent rider."

"Do you have any proof that he killed your brother?"

Tally stared at Lucinda, who gloated back, her smile smug. She wanted to slap the woman again. "No. But I can say with certainty what happened to me." She told her story, all of it. "My stepmother put my obituary in the newspaper to cover her tracks in case anyone got curious."

To have someone finally listen to her brought huge relief. Tears hovered behind her eyes, but she refused to let them fall.

Lucinda jumped to her feet, pointing her finger. "Lies, all lies! She's the real murderer. She killed Cormick out of anger for him marrying me."

Tally gasped. The gold-digging woman was determined to ruin her any way she could. *Please don't let anyone believe her.*

"Why would she do that, Mrs. Shannon?" Hargrove calmly asked. "Why not kill you? By all accounts, you brought discord and anger into the house."

"She probably tried that too, but I kept vigilant."

"Sit down, Mrs. Shannon." The judge leaned forward to speak to Tally. "You're a brave woman, Mrs. Colby, and I find your testimony most compelling. But what proof do you actually have? This is all hearsay."

"I have no proof beyond what I've stated. The man who can back up my claims is absent."

"You can step down, Mrs. Colby. Counselor Hargrove, do have anyone else to call?"

Hargrove turned to Tally with an apologetic gaze. They'd lost. "No, Your Honor. As Mrs. Colby stated, my other witness hasn't made it."

"Are you going to believe two lying, conniving, scrawny whores against me, Your Honor?" Lucinda yelled. "I'm a pillar of society, with land and money. I can make and break people."

Tally's heart sank. All their hard work and hoping to make Lucinda pay was for naught.

"Then I have no choice but to—"

The door flung open. "Not so fast, Judge." Clay stood with Dominick locked in his grip. "This man has something to say that may change things."

Lucinda released a sharp curse. Tally wanted to run into Clay's arms. It was all she could do to keep seated. A million questions filled her mind as she took in his bloody, torn clothes. Whatever he'd been through getting Jude Dominick here had been bad.

"Who are you?" the judge asked.

"Clay Colby, sir. Tally is my wife. And this is Jude Dominick." He pushed Dominick forward. "He has a confession to make." Clay squeezed what appeared to be a gunshot wound in Dominick's upper arm. "Don't you?"

"Yes," Dominick answered. "I'll tell you what you want to hear. Then for God's sake, can I have a doctor?"

"Take the witness box and place your hand on the Bible," the judge growled.

Clay slid into the seat next to Tally and reached for her hand. Her world righted.

For the next hour, Jude Dominick spilled his guts, with Lucinda elbowing her lawyer to object every few minutes. At one point, Dominick pierced her with his gaze. "You can lie all you want, Lucinda, but it's over. I'm not going down with you. You were always full of greed, never satisfied with what you already had." He turned to the judge. "She killed her husband with rat poison, forced me to arrange an accident for her stepson and find a place to put Tally away to die. She did it for the money and land."

Lucinda jumped to her feet. "You're a bald-faced liar! You're just trying to save your own stupid neck. I never trusted you. You're the one who did it all. Not me. You framed me!"

"It's over, Lucinda. Just stop," Dominick growled.

Hargrove rested his arms on the wooden witness box. "Thank you, Mr. Dominick. I think justice was served here today."

"Now can I have a doctor? And keep Colby away from me. That's one crazy bastard." Dominick's gaze darkened when he spared Clay a glance. "You might want to arrest *him*. He has a price on his head, Judge."

Tally tensed. He couldn't get arrested now, not after all they'd been through. She yearned to cry out, tell him to run and hide—only it was too late.

"Is this correct?" the judge asked.

Hargrove fished a document from his case. "No, sir. Amnesty just arrived from the governor. I've got his papers here to attest to the fact. Clay Colby is a free man."

"Well, what do you know?" Clay appeared stunned. "It really happened. I'm free, Tally. I don't have to look over my shoulder any longer."

"I'm so happy." Tally squeezed his hand. "You're not wanted by anyone but me and Violet."

"I'm glad."

The judge read the amnesty paper Hargrove gave him and straightened. "It appears this is all in order." He turned to the sheriff who stood beside the door. "Arrest Lucinda Shannon and take her to jail to await trial for murder, theft, lying, fraud, and anything else you can find. If she even spits on the sidewalk, add that to the list."

"Get your hands off me!" Lucinda yelled at the sheriff. "I'm innocent."

"I'd worry, Mrs. Shannon." The judge's stern voice filled the room. "If your trial lands in my court, I'll hang you. I've never seen a more callous, cruel woman in my life. Mrs. Tally Colby, your father's estate and all it entails is hereby returned to you, and I'm declaring the spousal entitlement of your stepmother null and void." He addressed Dominick. "Don't leave town. Until we can sort out the truth, I don't trust you as far as I can sling a snake. But I can assure that you won't get off without some jail time."

He banged the gavel with a sharp rap. "Court's adjourned."

Tally flew into Clay's arms. "We won. I can't believe it. We beat her."

"We sure did." He lowered his head, his lips meeting hers in a kiss that seared down to her soul. They were together and all was right—at least for the moment.

Forty-three

THE CELEBRATION THAT FOLLOWED THAT AFTERNOON IN THE hotel dining room probably set a record for being the noisiest ever. There were lots of whooping and hollering with Ridge, Kate, Amanda, and Phineas Hargrove. During a slight lull, Clay took Phineas aside to personally thank him.

"When you came to visit us in Hope's Crossing, I didn't give a nickel for our chances." Clay met the lawyer's eyes. "You sure earned your money and then some."

"I'd like to hear your story. How did you get Jude Dominick here?"

"I just told him how it was going to be. He'd come or I'd shoot both legs off."

Hargrove chuckled. "From the looks of you both, I figured it was something like that."

"If you'll give me Jack Bowdre's amnesty papers, I'll be happy to take them to him."

"Sorry, Clay. Jack didn't get his."

Sadness and surprise crawled up Clay's spine. "Can I ask why?"

"The governor said he'd betrayed the code of lawmen and he couldn't allow that. I know this is going to hurt Mr. Bowdre."

A slight understatement. It would shake Jack to the marrow of his bones. His friend had lost the woman he was going to marry and now his freedom as well. Dammit to hell! Clay swung away, trying to hide bitter disappointment.

Attuned to his every mood as she was, Tally seemed to sense a problem. She moved quickly to his side. "What's wrong, Clay?"

Her sweet fragrance drifted over him. He should forget this momentary setback, sweep her into his arms, and carry her up to bed. But he couldn't yet.

He faced her squarely. "Jack didn't get his amnesty. Only me."

Instant caring flashed into her wintery-blue gaze. "Oh no, I'm so sorry. I know how much he wanted freedom. This breaks my heart."

"Yeah. Mine as well." He caressed her shoulders and nuzzled her neck. "Hargrove said the papers have been signed to return your father's estate to you. The land itself should be worth a lot of money, though he wasn't sure how much cash or personal items remain. Any thought what you'll do with all of it?"

She traced the scar, made whiter against his tanned cheek, and laid a palm tenderly against his jaw. "Sell the lot. I will never live there again—too many bad memories. So I'll instruct Hargrove to find a buyer. My place is in Hope's Crossing."

"I was hoping you'd say that." He'd been prepared to support whatever decision she made but had feared she'd want to live on her father's land. One thing for sure, he'd go wherever she went. Home wasn't a place—it was being with the person you loved. And Tally was his. "After we take care of a few things in the morning, we'll start back. I can't wait to see Violet."

"I can't either. She threw a fit to come, but she'd have been bored without Jenny and Ely to play with." Tally brushed her lips across his, a wispy, featherlight touch that added fuel to the hunger already exploding inside him.

"Clay, do you know what I'm going to do with my windfall?"

"I'm sure you'll make a wise decision." He lifted her palm and kissed the sensitive flesh of her wrist.

"I'm donating some to the town, and the rest will be for Violet. In a few years, when she's older, I want to send her to a school for the blind. I've heard they have a special way of teaching how to read with their fingers. It's called braille. I want—we both want—to open up her world to all kinds of exciting possibilities. She needs the kind of education that we can't give her."

It would kill him to send their daughter away, to see her only on certain occasions, but Tally was right. They couldn't hold Violet back. She was a bird that already yearned to fly.

Clay blinked away the sudden mist in his eyes. "I'll make sure she gets whatever will help her thrive in this crazy, dangerous world."

"Good. I'm glad you agree. It's important for everyone to be able to live as best they can, and the odds have been stacked against her from the start."

Tally's nearness, the glistening light in her blue eyes, her curves pressed against him proved too much. He'd always heard that timing had a lot to do with a rain dance. Despite the celebration, the onlookers, and the fact that it was still daylight, Clay swept her up into his arms and proceeded to the staircase.

Their bed was waiting, but he wasn't any longer.

After a long, arduous trip, Clay rode through the entrance and into Hope's Crossing with Tally by his side. Ridge had decided to make a side trip to visit his old homestead and would come later. Everyone ran to greet them, all asking questions, but he only had eyes for one.

"Daddy! Mama!" Violet jerked away from Belle's hand.

Laughing, he slid from the saddle to snatch Violet into his arms, holding her close. "I've missed you, baby girl."

"I'm glad." She patted his face. "I thought you might find another little kid."

"Oh goodness, no." Tally pressed kisses to her daughter's cheeks after Clay lowered her. "But maybe you found another mama you liked better."

Violet giggled. "No. I just want you and Daddy. That's all."

Jack pushed through the throng of welcomers. "Give us the news. Did Tally win?"

Clay met the eyes of his friend, wishing he didn't have to tell him the disappointing part. "The trial went great and we won. The judge returned everything Tally's stepmother had stolen from her. And the woman is in jail awaiting trial for the murders she committed."

A hip hip hurrah went up from the crowd.

Tally raised her hands to silence them. "That means you all have greatly benefitted. Other than what Violet will need, I'm donating every cent to the town. We'll be able to get all the supplies we've had to scrounge and wait for. We're all rich."

"That's mighty generous!" Tobias January shouted with lots of people seconding that.

"We have news too," Hester Mason said. "Five weddings. My ladies are marrying these men here. They're going to tame the wildness out of them and start families."

Tally beamed. "That's excellent."

"How about that?" Clay could barely recognize the women they'd saved—both from Creedmore and Deliverance Canyon. Many wore a bandage on their cheek from Dr. Mary's treatment, and all but a few had started to lose the haunting pain in their eyes. This was what freedom did. He filled his lungs with the fresh night air, where hope and dreams rode on the wind.

He set Violet down, telling Tally he needed to speak to Jack. He might as well deliver the bad verdict now. The two men moved a short distance away.

"What, Clay? Is it the amnesty? Just spit it out."

"Yes, it is concerning that." He met the eyes of his best friend. "I got it but you—"

"I didn't," Jack finished for him. His voice was flat. "Did the governor say why?"

"It's because you were a lawman and held to a higher standard than me." Clay glanced at their fledgling town. Jack had worked so hard—far more than anyone in town—and yet he could still be arrested by a posse at any time. Nothing about this was fair.

"Don't give up. I'll help you refile next year."

Jack started to walk away but stopped. "Thanks for trying, Clay, but we both know it's wasted effort."

Clay watched the hard, whipcord form as Jack strode toward the corral. Jack would saddle up and ride—his way of dealing with crushing disappointment. He just prayed his friend and trail partner wouldn't do anything of a permanent nature.

After a long moment, he turned toward the woman he loved and addressed the fire building inside him.

Tonight was theirs. They were home.

&

That night, Tally slipped through the flap of their outdoor bathing room while Clay held it open. He already had buckets of water lined on the shelf overhead, ready to drench them. The moon provided plenty of light, and the windmill made beautiful music that wound through her soul.

The good thing about wearing nothing but a wrap was that it only took untying the bow to strip down. The night air brushed against her bare skin like soft feathers.

With his gun belt and vest behind at the house, Clay undressed in nothing flat.

A naughty smile stretched across her face. She laced her fingers together around his neck, her breasts cozying up to the hard wall of his naked chest. Her kiss let him know exactly what she wanted in no uncertain terms.

She remembered making Clay promise to release her come spring. So foolish. "Clay, about spring—you can stop wondering. As long as I breathe, I'll never leave your side. We're bound by a bond that is stronger than rawhide."

Clay seemed so still. Wasn't he happy? At last, he put his hand under her jaw and she realized it was trembling. "You don't know how happy I am. I didn't know how on God's earth I was going to keep my end of the bargain. I never want to lose what we've found. I never knew what happiness really was until you waltzed into my life on a sunshiny day."

Love for him surged from the depth of her being as his large body seemed to steal every inch of the space and then some. His hands splayed against her back and drew her ever closer to him, then slid down her spine to her buttocks.

She released a soft whimper and met his tongue in a mating

dance. Her breath came in harsh gasps against his mouth. She was barely able to think, to feel, to speak anything other than the language of the heart. Her palm moved between their bodies, searching for and finding his jutting need.

"Watch it, lady"—his breath whispered across her cheek—"or this will end before it starts."

"I'm not afraid. I know your secret."

He nuzzled behind her ear. "What's that?"

"You have staying power—both in lovemaking and in life. You don't quit, only get tougher and more determined, no matter what comes."

And maybe she did too. She felt as though she'd crossed a stormy sea in nothing but a dinghy, the waves pummeling and threatening to drown her every inch of the way. But that was just life and other people had similar problems. She was no fool. More trials lay ahead, some that would block out the sun for a bit. Still, with him, she could get through anything.

They made a tough team to beat.

"We're going to make it, Clay."

"Yes, ma'am, we are." He nibbled her neck. "Do you know what caught my attention the first moment I saw you?"

"What?"

"I was struck by the strength carved on your face. You, with your wild, fiery hair flying around you like some avenging angel. I knew right then you were perfect."

"Oh, you did?"

"Absolutely. We're those wild horses that can never be tamed. This land needs people like us who won't tuck tail and run at the first sign of trouble."

Tally curled a finger in his hair and dropped feathery kisses along the seam of his mouth. "Do you know what I saw?"

"A broken-down outlaw who'd outlived his time, most likely."

"Not even close." Her touch slid across the hard wall of his chest and down his lean, scarred frame. The caresses made his breath hitch. "I saw on your face the toughest man I knew. And I noticed the yearning in your sensitive brown eyes for

someone to share your dream with. You were afraid to hope
that you'd found one."

"You see too much, lady," he growled and pulled a rope
that sent a bucket of water cascading down on them. Then he
reached for the soap again and lathered her good, his hands
sliding down her curves.

The sensations dancing along her body made Tally's breath
ragged. Hot, aching desire curled inside, demanding attention.

She kissed her way down his throat, nibbled across his
collarbone, caressed the muscles rippling in his deeply tanned
chest. She kissed each scar that proclaimed he'd fought and
won many battles.

Soon, this teasing would end and she'd feel him pulsing
inside her. She was ready.

The nearby windmill played her favorite tune in harmony
with the night creatures. Her body hummed under Clay's
fingers like the strings of Dallas Hawk's fiddle.

Unable to bear another minute, she stole the soap and went
to work on every inch of his rock-hard body. After rinsing
him, she maneuvered herself into place, taking him deep into
her core, where pleasure burst and spread through her. Clay's
groan told her he too was riding waves of delicious, fiery heat.

He assisted with the thrusts, nipping at her bare shoulder
before dropping his head lower to take a breast into his mouth.
She rose on towering waves and, amid low cries, plunged
down the other side to blessed pleasure so intense she could
barely breathe.

His mouth found hers at the exact moment she was swept
into a sea of froth and plumes of glorious, sparkling light.

At the peak of her release, she raised her arms, fumbled for
the ropes on two more buckets of water, and gave them a jerk.
The cool deluge broke over them like a waterfall, washing
away every bit of pain and bad memory. Only love remained.

"Tally Colby, it's a good thing you don't know what you
do to me," he mumbled against her wet mouth, their breath
mingling, hot and steamy.

"Why is that?" Her voice was teasing and light.

"There'd be no living with you. I wouldn't get one lick of rest."

"That sounds downright pitiful. Are you registering a complaint, my dear?"

Clay's white teeth showed in his wide grin. "Hell no."

"Then hush, my darling. I have something to tell you." She placed two fingers over his mouth. "You're going to be father again."

He stilled, studying her through squinted eyes. "For real?"

"I'm happy to say so. Dr. Mary confirmed what I'd suspected. We're going to have a baby." She laughed, raising her arms high to the heavens. Every nerve ending pulsed. It was great to be alive and to have this wonderful life with the man she loved.

Clay let out a war whoop and crushed her to him. "Imagine that. You're my life, my world, my whole reason for being, my warrior angel. We're going to have one heck of a life, you and me." He lifted a lock of wet hair from her eyes and pressed a reverent kiss to each eyelid. "Is this Monday?"

"Last time I looked."

"Great, I love Mondays. It's my favorite day of the week."

About the Author

Linda Broday resides in the Texas Panhandle on land the early cowboys and Comanche once roamed. Their voices often float in the stillness and tell stories of the days when the land was raw and unsettled. She grew up loving museums, libraries, and old trading posts and credits those and TV Westerns for fueling a love of the Old West. There's something about Stetsons, boots, and tall, rugged cowboys that fan a burning flame. A *New York Times* and *USA Today* bestselling author, Linda has won many awards, including the prestigious National Readers' Choice. Visit her at lindabroday.com.

Also by Linda Broday

Bachelors of Battle Creek
Texas Mail Order Bride
Twice a Texas Bride
Forever His Texas Bride

Men of Legend
To Love a Texas Ranger
The Heart of a Texas Cowboy
To Marry a Texas Outlaw

Texas Heroes
Knight on the Texas Plains
The Cowboy Who Came Calling
To Catch a Texas Star

Outlaw Mail Order Brides
The Outlaw's Mail Order Bride

Texas Redemption
Christmas in a Cowboy's Arms anthology

Can't get enough cowboys? Keep reading
for a sneak peek at Amy Sandas's

RUNAWAY BRIDES
THE GUNSLINGER'S VOW

Boston, Massachusetts

August 2, 1881

"Miss Brighton? Miss Brighton, did you hear me?"

Alexandra blinked away her shock to meet the concerned gaze of her unexpected suitor. "I...yes," she said finally, though her voice felt off—not quite her own. "That is, I believe so."

Mr. Shaw's worried expression smoothed into a handsome smile. "I have just declared that I would like to make you my bride, Miss Brighton."

His words were no less a surprise the second time around. Peter Shaw was the quintessential Eastern gentleman of distinction. Though only twenty-six, he was already gaining momentum in political circles. He was charming, attractive, full of confidence, and met every one of Aunt Judith's criteria for an advantageous match.

And for some inexplicable reason, he had just asked *her*, Alexandra Brighton, to be his bride.

She couldn't have heard him right.

Alexandra gave a tiny shake of her head to free up some

words. "I am sorry, Mr. Shaw. I am a bit stunned. I had not expected such an offer." Nor had she expected the creeping sense of anxiety that came with it, making her throat tight and her palms clammy. Had he been falling in love with her all this time, and she had never even noticed?

Despite her awkwardness, he was all grace and charm. "See, that is what I like about you, Miss Brighton—your innate modesty and lack of pretense. You are unlike other young ladies in town. Their perspectives are so narrow, so limited. Most of them have never experienced anything beyond our tight little social niche, let alone life outside of Boston."

His eyes were a soft brown in the light that extended from the ballroom just visible beyond the balcony doors. "I admire your story, Miss Brighton. It is my opinion that your…unusual childhood afforded you a more valuable view of life." He took a slow breath as he clasped his hands behind his back and lowered his chin, as if confessing some great secret. "I have ambitions, Miss Brighton, plans for my future—for the future of Boston and this great state of Massachusetts. In order to secure that future, it is imperative that I appeal to a broad audience." He smiled again, his eyes crinkling gently. "You can help me do that."

Alexandra released her breath in a slow decompression of tension.

Now it made sense. Mr. Shaw hadn't inexplicably fallen in *love*. He was proposing a business arrangement.

She should have known.

Shaw was a member of the elite Boston social group known as the Brahmins, and marriages amongst his exclusive set were not made out of such an inconstant, imprudent thing as affection. The acknowledgment cleared away some of her confusion, but had no effect on her growing sense of dread.

"You leave me in a state of suspense for your response, Miss Brighton," he teased. Despite his words, he was as self-assured as ever.

Alexandra smiled, but the act felt tight and forced. She

would accept. *Of course* she would accept. Not a single person of Alexandra's acquaintance would understand if she refused. An offer from a gentleman such as Peter Shaw was everything her aunt had been grooming her for.

He was waiting.

"I would be honored," she finally replied. But as the words left her mouth, she felt a moment of panic and wished she could call them back.

What was wrong with her?

Now that he had her agreement, Peter gave no sign of joy beyond a shallow nod. He did not appear the slightest bit aware of her growing discomfort. She had no idea she had gotten so good at *maintaining a social face*, as her aunt called it.

"I have already spoken privately with your aunt and obtained her blessing," he said, "but I will come by tomorrow to finalize the details. I have no doubt this marriage will be a tremendous success."

Then he stepped forward and very deliberately propped his fingertips beneath her chin, tilting her face upward as he bent down to press a quick kiss to her lips. It was Alexandra's very first kiss, and was over just as soon as it began. The impact of it faded away almost faster than she could acknowledge its occurrence.

Peter offered his arm and flashed another one of his charming almost-smiles. "We had better return to the ball before people start to talk." He led her, unresisting, back through the crowd to where Aunt Judith stood with her group of friends.

Alexandra's stomach churned the entire way. The ballroom felt too cloying, too hot. She was assailed by a fierce desire to return to the fresh air on the balcony. Alone.

Stop, she thought, even as she fought to remember how to breathe. *Aunt Judith will never forgive you if you make a scene.*

It was becoming increasingly difficult to care about that—to care about any of the fine Eastern manners she had so carefully been taught.

Mr. Shaw offered a few complimentary words to the matrons gathered with Aunt Judith before he bade his farewell to Alexandra with another comment about calling the next day. Then he walked away. Alexandra barely caught sight of the triumphant gleam in her aunt's eyes before she was set upon by her two best friends.

Courtney Adams was a flurry of pink silk and lace, vivid red curls, and sparkling green eyes set within pert features that also boasted elegantly arched brows and impishly curved lips. She was beautiful, but it was her bright personality that most people were drawn to. Courtney stepped in close to Alexandra to murmur dramatically, "You and Mr. Shaw were out of sight for quite a while. I wonder what the two of you were up to."

"Hush, Courtney." This was from Alexandra's cousin Evelyn, or Evie, as she and Courtney called her.

At twenty-one, Evie was a year older than both Alexandra and Courtney, but in many ways, she was far more naive. Protected and guided by Aunt Judith her entire life, she had had few opportunities to experience anything beyond the small world she had been born into. Evie's older brother, Warren, had betrayed the family's dreams of becoming a prominent Boston social figure by becoming a doctor instead. With Warren off saving lives across the country, Aunt Judith was left to pin all her hopes for climbing Boston's social ladder on her daughter...and Alexandra.

"Shall we all go for some refreshment?" Evie suggested. Her motivation was clearly to distance them from her mother so they could talk more freely.

After making their excuses to Aunt Judith, the three young ladies strolled across the ballroom at a sedate pace, despite the energy bristling among them. Alexandra found she could breathe more easily now that she was away from both Mr. Shaw and her aunt, but that cloying dread was still there, hovering about her shoulders in a heavy cloak.

Once settled in a corner of a connecting sitting room, lemonades in hand, Courtney urged in tones of whispered excitement, "So? What did the renowned Mr. Shaw have to say?"

Alexandra hesitated over her response. The conversation

on the balcony still did not feel quite real. "He proposed marriage," she answered quietly.

"I knew it!"

Alexandra looked to Courtney in surprise. "You did? How could you? He gave no indication whatsoever that he had such an inclination. We have spoken less than half a dozen times."

"Yes, but that is still twice as much as he deigned to speak with any other girl," Evie noted reasonably. "He was obviously showing an interest in you."

"I wish someone had told me. Maybe I wouldn't have made a fool of myself by being so surprised."

Evie's eyes grew wide. "I thought you knew."

"You said yes, of course," Courtney said. "Tell me you said yes."

"I did."

Her friend clapped her hands and gave a bright smile. "Excellent. Now we are both engaged. We just need to find someone for Evie, and we can all become brides together."

Courtney's excitement only accented the churning discordance that had taken up residence inside Alexandra. She should be thrilled by the prospect of becoming Mrs. Peter Shaw. Ecstatic, even.

Instead, she felt…dishonest.

And on the verge of serious panic.

"Alexandra," Evie said softly, leaning forward to place her slim hand on Alexandra's wrist. "What is the matter?"

Meeting her cousin's compassionate gaze, Alexandra sighed. "I do not know. Something just feels…wrong."

"How do you mean?" Courtney asked, a flicker of concern crossing her features.

"I do not know," Alexandra repeated. "I am not sure I made the right choice in accepting. What if I am not the person Mr. Shaw believes me to be? He barely knows me."

"You will get to know each other better during the engagement and after, once you are married," Courtney assured.

Alexandra looked between her two closest friends. One

red-haired and vivacious, the other slender and elegant with pale-blonde hair and soulful eyes. They knew her as no one else on the earth knew her, and loved her anyway. She could be nothing but fully honest with them.

"The truth is," Alexandra admitted, "I barely know myself anymore. Evie, you remember what I was like when I first arrived from Montana."

"Yes, and you have come such a very long way since then."

"That is my point," Alexandra said. "I barely recognize that girl in comparison to who I am now. But it *was* me. She might *still* be me somewhere deep down."

Her friends exchanged a quick glance, but did not interrupt.

"How do I know all this is not just a false facade? How can I commit to a future as someone's wife when I do not even know who I truly am?"

"What will you do?" Evie asked in a low whisper.

Alexandra took a bracing inhale. "I must tell Mr. Shaw that I need more time before committing to my answer."

"It will shock him to his toes," Courtney declared.

"It might be too late to withdraw your response." Evie directed her pointed gaze across the room.

Peter Shaw stood nearby, looking dapper and fine in a group with some of the most prominent gentlemen of Boston society. His smile was modest as he accepted toasts and congratulatory handshakes. The way the gentlemen kept sliding surreptitious glances toward Alexandra suggested that he had already announced their engagement.

Panic expanded through her, tightening her chest.

She was trapped.

But a small, defiant part of her whispered: *Or maybe not.*

They were not married yet. Some engagements lasted months or even years. She had time.

A fierce little flame of rebellion sparked in the midst of her panic. The more she focused on that flame, the greater it grew, spreading out like a slow-burning wildfire. She had become the perfect Boston lady, but after five years of learning to curb her impulses, Alexandra pushed all that careful training aside and embraced the reckless urging inside her. "I am going back to Montana."

Her words slipped free before she completely thought them through, but the moment they were uttered, she knew the rightness of them.

She was suddenly flooded with memories of her childhood: how the Rockies rose majestically beyond the plains, how wildflowers spread across the ground in spring, and how the land made one feel unbelievably small and infinitely powerful at the same time.

The compulsion to see it all again—to go home—was overwhelming. And perfect.

Evie and Courtney stared at her, wide-eyed and in shock.

Her cousin recovered first. "Mother will never allow it." Her voice was low and almost sad.

"Your new fiancé will never allow it," Courtney added with conviction.

Alexandra leaned toward her friends and lowered her voice. "That is why they cannot know."

"But how will you manage it?" Courtney asked, awed excitement creeping into her words.

"I have money tucked away. Father gave it to me before I left home. I never had cause to use it. Now I do."

"But why?" Evie asked. "Why go back now?"

Alexandra had to think of her reply. It mostly felt like an instinctive certainty. Before she could consider going forward, she had to go back.

"I must discover unequivocally who I am. My life has been split into two very different halves: my childhood in Montana and the five years I have been here in Boston. I need to know how much of my past is still a part of me... or if it is time to put it to rest for good." She lowered her gaze as another realization hit deep in her heart. "I need to see my father again."

Her friends were silent for a moment. Then Courtney said, "How can we help?"

Ideas and plans tripped over themselves in Alexandra's mind

as she considered everything she had to do to make good on her escape.

"I will leave tonight. All I need is time to get away. I must rely mostly on you, Evie. You will have to tell your mother I was not feeling well—the excitement and all—and I decided to head home early. Then tomorrow, when she asks after me, you can say I developed an illness—I don't care what, just something to keep me abed. She won't come to check on me. We know how she detests being around anyone who is sick."

Evie's delicate features were tense with concern. Alexandra knew it went against her cousin's nature to be deceptive in any way, especially toward her mother, but she nodded in agreement, and Alexandra felt a rush of gratitude for her dear cousin's loyalty.

Looking to Courtney, she said, "Will you lend me your carriage? I must return to the house to gather some belongings, then I will need a ride to the train station."

"Of course," Courtney agreed readily. "I will go with you to help you pack."

"No, you mustn't. If things go bad, you can deny that you knew anything of my plans. At least Evie's perfidy will be kept within the family. Can I trust your driver to keep my activities secret?"

"Absolutely. Edward is as discreet and steadfast as they come."

"Once it is discovered where I have gone and it is too late to stop me, Aunt Judith and Mr. Shaw will have no choice but to await my return. Surely, they will eventually come to understand my desire to visit the land of my childhood one last time."

The other women's expressions seemed dubious, but Alexandra ignored their uncertainty. Her confidence was more than enough to sustain her. It all made such perfect sense. Surely she wouldn't be able to breathe so easily if this were *wrong*.

She should have realized long ago that she would never truly be happy until she knew where she belonged.

With a swift round of hugs, Alexandra bade heartfelt goodbyes to her best friends. Then she rose and made her way toward a discreet exit while Courtney and Evie loitered with their lemonade to give her as much time as possible before going to inform Aunt Judith of her departure.

As she slipped from the grand Boston mansion into the fresh night air, Alexandra breathed deep and wide. Catching sight of Courtney's family carriage, she glanced around to make sure no one else was about, then she lifted the skirts of her ball gown in both hands and sprinted off into the darkness.

Montana was waiting.